NEW BEGINNINGS

"Your food'll be here *short*ly," Annie Mae announced as she set his teapot in front of him. "Naomi's cookin' it up just the way ya like it, Short Stack."

As she flitted away from the table—and that was the only way to describe how Annie Mae swiveled to grab a carafe and refresh Tom and Gabe's coffee—Adam heard muffled chuckles around him.

"Short Stack, is it?" Matthias teased from across the table.

"Better watch out," Bram warned. "She and Luke Hooley have been quite the pair—"

"Not to mention that Mennonite guy—Yonnie Stoltzfus—before Luke came to town," Seth Brenneman pointed out. "I suspect a cartload of fellas'll be eyeballin' her now that her *dat*'s out of the picture."

Short Stack, is it? While Adam had always been the shortest guy in his class—and plenty of folks still teased him about his height—something about Annie Mae's nickname made him chuckle. Why would a looker like Hiram Knepp's daughter flirt with *him*?

**More Seasons of the Heart Books
by Charlotte Hubbard**

Summer of Secrets

Autumn Winds

Winter of Wishes

An Amish Country Christmas

Published by Kensington Publishing Corporation

BREATH
Of SPRING

Seasons *of the* Heart

Charlotte Hubbard

ZEBRA BOOKS
KENSINGTON PUBLISHING CORP.
http://www.kensingtonbooks.com

ZEBRA BOOKS are published by

Kensington Publishing Corp.
119 West 40th Street
New York, NY 10018

All Kensington titles, imprints and distributed lines are available at special quantity discounts for bulk purchases for sales promotion, premiums, fund-raising, educational or institutional use.

Special book excerpts or customized printings can also be created to fit specific needs. For details, write or phone the office of the Kensington Special Sales Manager. Attn.: Special Sales Department. Kensington Publishing Corp., 119 West 40th Street, New York, NY 10018. Phone: 1-800-221-2647.

Zebra and the Z logo Reg. U.S. Pat. & TM Off.

First Mass-Market Paperback Printing: May 2014
ISBN-13: 978-1-4201-3307-3
ISBN-10: 1-4201-3307-1

First Electronic Edition: May 2014
eISBN-13: 978-1-4201-3308-0
eISBN-10: 1-4201-3308-X

10 9 8 7 6 5 4 3 2 1

Printed in the United States of America

ACKNOWLEDGMENTS

Thank You, Lord, for bringing me these words as I sat down to write each day. It continues to amaze me how scenes, conflicts, and characters I'm not expecting appear exactly when I need them.

Continued gratitude to you for your enthusiasm, Alicia Condon and Evan Marshall, as we continue this series. Your enthusiasm and belief in my work mean so much, and I'm honored to be working with such respected veterans in the publishing industry.

Many thanks to Jim Smith of Step Back in Time Tours in Jamesport, Missouri—the largest Old Order Amish settlement west of the Mississippi River—for your continued assistance with every little question I have about the Amish and their ways. It's a pleasure and a privilege to work with you, and I value our friendship more with each passing day!

Much love to you, Neal, for being the Breath of Spring that makes all things new in our lives, even as we celebrate more than thirty-eight years together.

1 Corinthians 13: 12

For now we see through a glass darkly; but then face to face: now I know in part; but then I shall know even as also I am known.

Revelation 21: 4–7

4 And God shall wipe away all tears from their eyes; and there shall be no more death, neither sorrow, nor crying, neither shall there be any more pain: for the former things are passed away.

5 And he that sat upon the throne said, Behold, I make all things new. And he said unto me, Write: for these words are true and faithful.

6 And he said unto me, It is done. I am Alpha and Omega, the beginning and the end. I will give unto him that is athirst of the fountain of the water of life freely.

7 He that overcometh shall inherit all things; and I will be his God, and he shall be my son.

Chapter One

"You'll do just fine, Annie Mae. This bein' January—the first Monday after we've been closed so Ben and I could get hitched—most of our crowd'll be fellas from around Willow Ridge," Miriam Hooley assured her. "And if the younger ones give ya any sass about workin' here, they'll be dealin' with *me*. We're mighty glad to have ya helpin' us out."

As Annie Mae Knepp gazed at the tables set up for breakfast in the Sweet Seasons Café, her heart thudded. Never in a million years had she figured on waiting tables to support her family—but then, she'd never believed her *dat*, the town's former bishop, would scheme up a new Plain settlement under such dubious circumstances and get himself excommunicated, either. And for sure, she'd never dreamed she'd have the nerve to announce that she wouldn't be going to Higher Ground with him. Defying their father was the scariest thing she and her sister Nellie had ever, *ever* done . . . and now they were looking over their shoulders, waiting for Dat to get back at them.

"It's you who's been helping, Miriam," Annie Mae

murmured. "I sure hope Dat won't cause you and Ben any trouble because you've taken Nellie and me in."

"Puh! We've handled your *dat* before, child," Miriam replied. "We're real sorry Hiram's lost his way and his place in our church district, knowin' how it tore your family apart. But God loves us still, and He's countin' on us all to love one another as we deal with life's trials and tribulations. Let's look at this cash register, before anybody comes in."

Ever so patiently, Miriam showed Annie Mae how to enter numbers . . . how to cancel an incorrect entry . . . how to change the paper roll when a pink line appeared down the side. "Shall we try a practice round?" Miriam asked. "Let's say Bishop Tom gets the breakfast buffet."

Annie Mae squinted at the menu on the counter and then tapped in $5.95.

"And let's say Tom also picks up the tab for Preacher Gabe, who ordered a number two breakfast—"

She jabbed the keys for $3.75.

"—along with a side of cheesy hash browns and two sticky buns from the bakery counter to take home."

Annie Mae willed her fingers to find the right keys for those items. "Twelve dollars and seventy cents?"

"You're a natural, Annie Mae!" Miriam sang out. "Don't forget to put all your receipts on the spindle so the money matches up, come the end of the day. You'll have Rhoda workin' with ya in the mornings and Rebecca will be here, too," she added with a warm smile. "And with Naomi and me in the kitchen—and Naomi's Hannah helpin' us cook—why, you'll be servin' up your orders with a big smile before ya know it. Where there's a woman, there's a way!"

Miriam beamed at her with eyes as warm as a mug

of cocoa. "We're all in this together," she said softly. "Every one of us started workin' here so's we could keep our families fed, Annie Mae. And now there's no stoppin' us."

We're all in this together . . . there's no stoppin' us. Such a comforting thought couldn't have come at a better time, considering how Annie Mae's heart was beating so fast. Working at the Sweet Seasons would be a far cry from running the house for her *dat,* tending her little brothers and sister all day until Nellie got home from school. When their precious faces flashed through her mind, she had to blink back tears. What were Joey, Josh, Sara, and Timmy doing these days? Who was caring for them while Dat started up his new colony?

Miriam gently rubbed Annie Mae's shoulders. "I know this is a big change for ya," she murmured. "But you're stronger—and smarter—than ya know, Annie Mae. God'll see that the right things come out of this situation for you and Nellie, and for all of your family, as well."

Annie Mae swallowed hard. "*Jah,* that's what we have to believe."

"You're a *gut* girl. And I hear our other cooks comin' in the back door."

As Miriam strode into the kitchen to greet her partner, Naomi Brenneman, and Naomi's teenage daughter Hannah—who had worked in the café only a few weeks—Annie Mae decided to quit sniffling and get busy. She pushed the button on the big coffeemaker and set napkin-wrapped silverware bundles on each of the tables the way Miriam had showed her. Soon the aromas of sausage, sweet rolls, and fried apples filled the café, and when Rhoda and Rebecca came in to begin their day, Annie Mae felt a lot better about the new job she was taking on. After all, these sisters had each caused her own stir in Willow Ridge: Rhoda had fallen in love with a divorced Englishman, and Rebecca had returned to the Lantz family after being raised by an English couple who'd rescued her from floodwater when she'd been a toddler. If these girls could win the acceptance of everyone in Willow Ridge, then surely folks would come to understand how she and Nellie still needed to fit in here, as well.

"Annie Mae, we're really glad you're here," Rebecca said as she tucked an order pad into the back pocket of her jeans. "Mamma's been getting lots of new customers who've seen the Sweet Seasons website, and what with Rachel staying home to start her family—"

"And me lookin' after Andy's *mamm* and kids in the afternoons," Rhoda chimed in, "we were mighty shorthanded in December. But it's a new year, and we've all got a whole new outlook. Especially Mamma, now that she's hitched to Ben," she added in a conspiratorial whisper.

"She's like a first-time bride again," Rebecca agreed as they all glanced at Miriam through the serving window of the kitchen. "Don't tell her I said so, but I'm betting those two lovebirds'll be feathering their nest soon, just like Rachel and Micah are."

As Rhoda and Rebecca giggled at this thought, Annie Mae was once again amazed at how similar these sisters were even though they'd been raised apart . . . even though Rhoda had long ago joined the church and Rebecca, with her collar-length hair and plaid shirt, had no intention of giving up her computer business to become Amish.

"Don't say that too loud," Rhoda murmured. "Mamma has told us she can't have any more babies—"

The jingling of the bell above the door ended their conversation. As though the café's regulars had all agreed to arrive at the stroke of six, here came Seth and Aaron Brenneman—Naomi's boys—and Miriam's nephews, Nate and Bram Kanagy. Tom Hostetler and Miriam's Ben were holding the door for Preacher Gabe, who seemed more hunched over than usual this morning.

"*Gut* mornin' to ya, fellas!" Miriam called out as she bustled toward the steam table with a big pan of sausage gravy. Hannah was behind her, bearing a basket of biscuits, and Naomi followed with fried apples that swam in buttery sauce and cinnamon. "We'll be gettin' the rest of the buffet out in two shakes of a tail. The girls'll take *gut* care of ya—and Bishop Tom, your meal's on me today, in honor of your new callin' amongst us."

"Hear, hear!" Ben called out and everyone applauded. Chairs scraped against the floor as the men draped their winter coats over the backs of them.

Tom Hostetler looked flustered as he pulled out a chair for Preacher Gabe. "You've got no call to treat me special, Miriam," he protested. "I planned to spring for Ben's meal this morning, on account of you two bein' the new mister and missus amongst us."

"*Jah*, it's a busy new year in Willow Ridge," Ben replied as he sat down with the two church elders. "And if January's already been this eventful, just think what the comin' months might bring."

Annie Mae approached their table, praying she didn't pour scalding coffee on Preacher Gabe's hand as he scooted his mug toward her. "And looky who's here this morning," he said as a smile deepened his wrinkles. "It's *gut* to see you've landed in a safe haven, Annie Mae, after all the fuss your *dat* has kicked up."

"And I was pleased to see you and Nellie sittin' tight when he interrupted Ben and Miriam's wedding," Bishop Tom joined in. "I suspect your *dat*'s not finished with us, though. Count on me if ya need any sort of help—"

"Oh, Preacher Tom—I mean, *Bishop*—" Annie Mae's face burned with embarrassment. It was all she could do to hang on to the coffee carafe as gratitude welled up inside her.

"Don't fret over it. It'll take *me* some time to get used to that new name, too," Tom assured her gently. "Let's remember that we're all God's children—even your *dat,* despite the shenanigans he's pulled. But Jesus stood up for the weak and the oppressed while He chastised those who took undue advantage of them."

"Hiram Knepp will always be your *dat*," Ben added quietly. "But we'll all look out for you and Nellie if he retaliates for your not goin' to Higher Ground with him, like obedient daughters."

"Amen to that," Naomi stated.

"Ya said a mouthful, fellas," Miriam affirmed. "The Knepp kids are our special blessing now. We look after our own."

Annie Mae swallowed so hard she wondered if everyone heard the click of her dry, tight throat. The dining room rang with a silence that somehow felt sacred, and as Rhoda and Rebecca and the rest of them gazed at her with such love in their eyes, how could she not feel lifted up? *The Knepp kids are our special blessing . . .*

"*Denki* ever so much," she murmured. "Nellie and I will do our best to deserve your—"

Once again the bell above the door jangled, and the Wagler brothers stepped in out of the cold. "Well, your day can officially start now, ladies," Matthias teased as he shrugged out of his coat.

"And a Happy New Year to all of you, as well," Adam, the younger one, chimed in. "Here's hoping everyone gets the year off to a fine fresh start."

"And speakin' of fresh starts, this seems like a *gut* time to let you all know about mine." Bishop Tom looked around the dining room like a kid about to burst with a big secret. "Now that my ex-wife, Lettie, has passed on, I'm courtin' Nazareth Hooley with the intention of marryin' her real soon."

"Oh my stars, Tom! That's wonderful-*gut* news," Miriam gushed. "I've always thought you and Naz were made for each other."

"Congratulations to both of ya!" Ben crowed as he headed toward the buffet table. "That's cause for celebration—although I'm not surprised. Aunt Naz has been twinklin' like a star lately."

"Glad to hear it, Tom. Life's a lot better with a *gut* woman by your side," Preacher Gabe remarked. Then he glanced up at Annie Mae. "How about you bring me one of Naomi's omelets with lots of ham and cheese and onions? Side of hash browns. And a couple of Miriam's sticky buns in a go box."

"We'll get right on it," Annie Mae murmured as she scribbled the items on her pad. This was her very first order, and writing it down tickled her more than she'd anticipated.

"I'm in no hurry. No place else to go today," the old preacher remarked as he nodded toward someone behind her. "But those Wagler boys, I bet they've got jobs lined up. Adam looks ready to order off the menu rather than go to the buffet."

When she turned, Adam was indeed seated at his table rather than joining the other fellows, who were ladling sausage gravy over biscuits while Rhoda and Rebecca filled more pans at the steam table. The Wagler place was just down the hill from where she lived—or *had* lived—so she'd known those fellows all her life. Their parents had passed on, their two older sisters had married and moved away, and Matthias had been widowed a couple years ago, so the two brothers lived there as bachelors. Matthias ran a harness shop in front of their house, while Adam's home remodeling business kept him busy in all the nearby towns.

"Annie Mae! Wow, but it's *gut* to see you!" Adam stood up, a smile lighting his face as she approached his table. "I was hoping you hadn't gotten sucked into going along with—I mean—"

Annie Mae gripped her order pad, not sure what to think. Adam was a few years older and a few inches shorter than she was, and he'd always been the more outgoing of the two Wagler brothers. Was he really so glad to see her, or was he just eager for a hot breakfast like he wouldn't get at home?

"I think I've just stepped in it and then put my foot in my mouth," Adam lamented. "I'm sorry about all that business with your *dat,* and I'm glad to see you here, still amongst us. I was worried about you—and Nellie, too, of course," he added quickly.

Could this morning get any more surprising? Never had she anticipated such an outpouring of support from everyone who entered the Sweet Seasons. "I got real lucky," she murmured. "At least Nellie and I have a place to stay while we figure out what comes next. Can I bring ya something off the menu? Pour ya some coffee?"

Adam kept gazing at her. "How about a number four, with a pot of *gut* strong tea—two bags in it, please."

Annie grabbed the menu on the table behind her so she wouldn't have to reach around Adam. The laminated page looked smudged and she wished the print were a whole lot bigger. "Sorry," she mumbled as she stared at it. "Might take me a day or two to learn what-all food goes with which numbers—"

She sucked in her breath. Adam had taken something out of his shirt pocket . . . was slipping a lightweight pair of glasses onto her nose. He positioned the sides over her ears carefully, so he wouldn't mess up the hair that was pulled into a snug bun beneath her *kapp*.

"I carry several pairs of these in my wagon for my remodeling jobs," he explained quietly. "They bring the details into focus."

Annie Mae felt even taller and skinnier and uglier than usual. Her cheeks surely must be cherry red and her heart felt as though it was trying to pound its way out of her chest. But when she looked at the menu again, the words jumped right out at her. "Short stack of pancakes," she rasped.

"Eggs over easy and ham with that, please," Adam added. "Keep the specs, okay? I've got more."

"*Jah,* I—I'll be right back with your tea." Annie Mae scurried into the kitchen, scribbling Adam's order on her pad. What in the world had just happened? Of all the nerve, for Adam to put *glasses* on her, as though he could tell she was as blind as a bat—and wanted the rest of the world to know it, too.

Is that such a bad thing? Teacher Alberta told Dat *years ago that your eyes needed to be checked but he thought ya could keep house and tend the kids without readin' much . . .*

"So Adam wants a short stack with over-easy eggs and ham, does he?"

Naomi's words brought Annie Mae out of her befuddled state. "*Jah,* and he also ordered—"

"Hannah, the teapots are on that bottom shelf and the bags are beside them," the cook instructed her daughter. "Adam always wants two bags in his. And if he doesn't go to the steam table, he generally gets the number four."

Annie Mae inhaled, hoping to pull herself together before she had to face Adam again. "Ya make this look so simple. I don't *mean* to mess everything up while I'm figuring out—"

Naomi set down her spatula to grasp Annie Mae's hand. Miriam's partner looked calm and motherly, and after these past few years of having to act as her younger siblings' *mamm,* it felt good to be looked after. Cared about.

"In a couple days you'll know what these fellas usually eat, and you'll feel like you've been workin' here forever, dearie," Naomi said warmly. "Always take your time. Folks appreciate it when ya get things right, even if it means they wait a few moments longer."

"Those are awesome specs, too," Hannah piped up. She handed over a little silver pot with two tags dangling out the side, which she'd put on a plate. "They're like *jewelry,* but for your face!"

Annie Mae blinked. She had no idea what Adam's glasses looked like—and wouldn't she seem even more clueless if she took them off to find out? "I need all the help I can get, ain't so?" A nervous laugh escaped her and she flipped back a page of her order pad. "And Preacher Gabe wants an omelet with lots of ham and cheese and onions, and a side of hash browns. And I'll put two sticky buns in a go box for him."

"I'll get that omelet goin'. You're doin' just fine, Annie Mae." Naomi nodded as though she'd just stated the most obvious of facts—as though she truly believed the morning was off to a perfect start.

So maybe you should believe it, too. After all, she'd kept her father and her five younger siblings fed and dressed after her stepmother had passed. She'd done what she had to do. And she could do it again, now that another crisis had changed her life.

Putting on a resolute smile, Annie Mae took the plate the teapot was on and glanced out the pass-through window. She knew every man in the dining room—not to mention Miriam, Rhoda, and Rebecca. She could *do* this. And she could do it right.

Look out, Short Stack. Ready or not, here I come.

Chapter Two

As his brother and the two Kanagy boys returned from the steam table, Adam tried to pretend he hadn't just humiliated Annie Mae. What had *that* been about? He hadn't stopped to consider how jangled *his* nerves would feel if someone—say, Annie Mae—had perched a pair of reading glasses on his nose. It would serve him right if she left his breakfast sitting on the serving counter to get cold.

"Sure you don't want some of those fried apples from the buffet?" Matthias asked as he cut into a biscuit he'd smothered with sausage gravy. Seth and Aaron Brenneman took the other chairs on that side of the table, their plates heaped high.

"Looks like Hannah's bringin' out more food," Nate remarked as he took the chair to Adam's left. "Cheesy hash brown casserole, and a bunch of bacon."

"I'm *gut,* thanks. My cakes'll be here in a few," Adam said.

Bram dropped into the chair to Adam's right, and then he murmured, "If Hannah starts givin' me the eye, don't egg her on. I got engaged over New Year's, to a cute little redhead from Cedar Creek. Hannah's not gonna like that much."

Adam's eyes widened. "How'd *that* happen? Seems mighty fast—"

"Oh, and it was contagious," Nate confided as he leaned toward Adam's other ear, "on account of how *I'm* engaged to that redhead's twin sister. And we bought a place between here and Cedar Creek, where Bram and I can set up barns for our businesses. The girls're gonna run a B and B, soon as their *dat*—who would be none other than Amos Coblentz—builds the four of us a big house with extra guest rooms."

Adam's mouth dropped open. "I thought you were swearing off girls, Nate. So—"

"*Jah*, well, *these* girls hit us broadside." Nate shook his head, grinning like a lovestruck puppy.

"We didn't see it comin'," Bram confirmed with a happy-go-lucky shrug. "And we didn't stand a chance once Mary and Martha set their minds on us. Just something in the air after Christmas, I guess."

Something in the air . . . Adam glanced up to catch Annie Mae watching him through the serving window. The chatter and the clang of silverware around him faded away.

He was in for it. Annie Mae wore that same determined expression whenever she corralled her ornery five-year-old twin brothers.

As she strode toward the table with his tea, Adam noticed how the reading glasses accentuated her face. He'd known Annie Mae all his life, yet he'd never realized her eyes were so blue . . . and while the specs gave her a sophisticated, rather scholarly look, Adam sensed she didn't want to hear that. She had a set to her jaw, a purpose to her gaze rather than the flummoxed, fearful look he'd seen when she'd fled to the kitchen.

"Your food'll be here *short*ly," Annie Mae announced as she set his teapot in front of him. "Naomi's cookin' it up just the way ya like it, Short Stack."

As she flitted away from the table—and that was the only way to describe how Annie Mae swiveled to grab a carafe and refresh Tom's and Gabe's coffee—Adam heard muffled chuckles around him.

"Short Stack, is it?" Matthias teased from across the table.

"Better watch out," Bram warned. "She and Luke Hooley have been quite the pair—"

"Not to mention that Mennonite guy—Yonnie Stoltzfus—before Luke came to town," Seth Brenneman pointed out. "I suspect a cartload of fellas'll be eyeballin' her now that Hiram's out of the picture."

Short Stack, is it? While Adam had always been the shortest guy in his class—and plenty of folks still teased him about his height—something about Annie Mae's nickname made him chuckle. Why would a looker like Hiram Knepp's daughter flirt with *him*? She could see right over the top of his head. . . .

Might as well let this train of thought roll on down the track. No sense in getting interested—flirting back—because being somebody's husband isn't part of your plan.

For a moment, a cloud settled over him. Adam didn't often dwell on that fateful day anymore, but he dared not forget how—had he not been joyriding when he was supposed to be fetching his sister Ruth—Mamm wouldn't have hitched up a rig . . . wouldn't have been thrown into the road when her horse spooked . . . wouldn't have died because he'd been so irresponsible.

Adam blinked. Then he got his heartbeat slowed down again. Checked to see if any of his buddies had noticed his momentary trip down memory lane . . . but they were speculating about which fellow they could convince to distract Hannah from the fact that Bram was now courting a Cedar Creek girl.

"Well, Hannah's only sixteen, and plenty cute enough," Matthias stated philosophically. "It's not like she's doomed to be a *maidel* because you've found another gal to hitch up with, Bram."

And who will Annie Mae hitch up with? Adam poured more syrup over his pancakes as he furtively watched her greet an English couple who'd just come in. *Let Luke or Stoltzfus keep her company,* he told himself. He had no business taking up with a girl whose *dat* would probably come back to Willow Ridge to stir up big trouble—a girl who might be taking care of Joey, Josh, Sara, and Timmy for years to come. *Waaay more responsibility than you can handle. And what man wants an instant family to feed and clothe and—*

"So, Adam, do ya figure to finish your cakes and eggs anytime today? We can wrap up that kitchen job over past New Haven if we get a move on." Seth Brenneman chortled at him from across the table, where he, Aaron, and Matthias sat with their empty plates in front of them.

"*Jah, jah,*" Adam muttered as he split his egg yolks with his fork. "Let me sop up these eggs with my last pancake and I'm *gut* to go. Head on over there, if you want. You can fit the countertops before I second-coat the walls."

With a decisive nod, Aaron stood up to fish out his money. "This being a new year, I've decided we can start payin' for our food, Brother. So I'll cover yours this morning if you'll get the tip."

Seth, too, rose from his chair—a sturdy piece he and his brothers had built in their cabinetry shop, along with the other chairs and the tables, when Miriam and their *mamm* had opened the café. "That's one of your better ideas," he teased. "No reason the Sweet Seasons has to keep feedin' us, when Mamm could be takin' home wages instead."

"And what with Hannah and Annie Mae wantin' to earn some money now," Nate Kanagy chimed in, "it wouldn't hurt us to pay, either—even if Aunt Miriam did say we'd get our breakfast in exchange for the veggies Mamm grows in her truck garden. So you can go first, Bram! Fork it over."

Bram laughed. "I can do that—and I'll be leavin' Annie Mae a nice tip, too," he said as he tossed three dollar bills on the table. "So where's *your* tip, Nate?"

His older brother tucked four dollars under his empty coffee mug. "Never let it be said that I shorted a friend in need," he murmured as he glanced toward the checkout counter. "She's holdin' her own today. Pullin' her weight—and we all know she's not nearly over the hump."

Across the table, Matthias stood up and slipped his money clip from his jacket pocket. "I'll match Nate's tip and raise it," he murmured. "See ya when ya get home tonight, Adam."

"I've got a quick fix-it job for Lydia Zook after I finish up with the Brennemans," he replied.

"Bring us home something easy for supper, then, since you'll be at the market."

Adam sighed as he stood up. He and his brother muddled by on mac and cheese, lunch meat, and whatever else required little cooking, now that it was just the two of them. With Matthias's wife dying from an asthma attack while she was carrying their first child, they led a quiet life. . . .

When Annie Mae laughed, Adam saw her grin as Ben Hooley and Preacher Gabe chatted with her at the front counter. With her black hair and blue eyes, she was a striking girl—even with his cheap reading glasses perched on her nose. And despite her penchant for more brazen, free-spirited fellows, she was a hardworking young woman who could keep a household together. Her desserts and bread had occasionally graced the Wagler table after Mamm and Sadie had passed.

Keep on rolling, he reminded himself. Now that the house on Bishop's Ridge sat empty, he and Matthias wouldn't be finding any more goodies on their porch swing.

He toted up the tips the other five fellows had left her, somewhat surprised that Matthias's had come to nearly as much as his meal had. But it was for a good cause, wasn't it? And didn't the Amish help their own?

Adam pulled out a ten-spot. He wouldn't be this generous every morning, but on Annie Mae's first day she deserved a boost. He stacked all the other money in the center of the table and then slipped his beneath it, however, so she wouldn't know how much any one of them had given her.

When Annie Mae returned to the table where the two English couples were eating, Adam headed to the front counter to pay. The Sweet Seasons was filling up now that it was nearly seven o'clock, and he nodded to a couple of farmers he'd done some remodeling for. Friendly chatter and the clatter of silverware filled the dining room, along with the aroma of coffee and the cinnamon sweetness of the warm sticky buns Miriam was placing inside the glass counter.

"You might as well box me up half a dozen of those," Adam said as he pulled out more cash. "Maybe there'll be one or two left for Matthias by the time I get home tonight. And maybe not!"

Miriam laughed as she made his change. "You fellas have a *gut* day—and a Happy New Year, too. Seems to me Willow Ridge is off to a fine fresh start even though God's brought some mighty big changes our way," she remarked. "And I have a feelin' He's not finished surprisin' us."

As she reached beneath the counter for a pastry box, Adam couldn't help smiling. Just being around Miriam and her girls in this cozy down-home café made everybody feel brighter—even in January, when snow was piled high along the roadsides and the gray clouds suggested that more might be on the way.

As he took the box of warm rolls, Adam glanced toward the table where he'd eaten. Annie Mae was picking up her tip. Her jaw dropped and her eyes widened like saucers as she quickly riffled through the stack of bills—and then got to his.

Adam ducked out the door. Was it his imagination, or did the jingle of the bell sound merrier than usual? As he climbed into his wagon, he sincerely hoped Annie Mae was off to one of those fresh starts Miriam had talked about.

That's as far as it goes, though, he reminded himself. *She deserves a* gut *life . . . better than I can give her.*

Chapter Three

Annie Mae rushed up the stairs inside the smithy, glad Ben Hooley wasn't working at his forge and that Nellie wasn't yet home from school. What a day she'd had! And she'd come home with enough leftovers for supper, too. Only after she entered the upstairs apartment that she and her sister now shared with Rhoda did she lay out the tips she'd collected. She separated the tens and fives and ones into piles .·. . counted them as she held her breath.

My stars! There's more than a hundred dollars here!

Unable to believe that friends and complete strangers would be so generous—giddy with the first wages she had ever earned—Annie Mae counted her money again. Miriam had said this first day after the holidays would probably be slow, but if she'd collected this much during Monday's breakfast and lunch, and would also get a wage from Miriam, it didn't take advanced math to predict what she might earn in a week . . . a month.

I've got to sock this away and keep a record. Nellie and

I will need to buy shampoo and fabric and such, and we can't live on the generosity of friends forever.

As she boiled water for tea, Annie Mae noticed an empty plastic coffee canister in the wastebasket—the perfect piggy bank. She would ride into New Haven next time Miriam deposited the café's income, to open her own account . . . a positive, responsible step toward looking after herself and Nellie. For now, Annie Mae tucked the red canister in the back of the closet she shared with her sister. Here in this four-room apartment, where the interior walls rolled on tracks to allow more flexibility and space, storage—and privacy—were hard to come by. She arranged her oldest pair of shoes in front of her secret bank, hoping nobody cleaned out the closet when she wasn't around.

As Annie Mae sank into the small wooden rocker to rub her aching feet and sip her tea, footsteps on the stairs announced someone's arrival. Rhoda had gone to stay with Andy Leitner's family until later this evening, so this surely had to be Nellie. *Should I tell her how much I made?* Dat *never let on about what he earned selling his Belgians. . . .*

"You home, Sister?" Nellie called out as she opened the apartment door. "Ah! And how'd your first day go? I thought about ya a lot—so much that Teacher Alberta caught me with a question I wasn't ready for."

"And did ya give her a *gut* answer?" Annie Mae took in her younger sister's snug brown cape dress, which barely reached beneath her knees. "As I recall, Teacher Alberta could be led astray with details that sounded logical but that ya made up on the spur of the moment."

"Annie Mae!" Nellie laid her books on the small kitchen table. "I've never had the inclination to fib that way—or, truth be told, could never come up with quick answers like you could. I told her I was thinkin' about ya waitin' tables at the Sweet Seasons." Nellie went to the cupboard for a cup. "Teacher Alberta sends ya her best. She told all the scholars to keep us in their prayers."

Annie Mae's throat went tight. While Alberta Zook—storekeeper Henry's cousin, who'd come from Jamesport when Willow Ridge needed a teacher—had never impressed her as the sharpest pencil in the pack, she appreciated the young woman's thoughtfulness. "Tell her those prayers are bein' answered," she murmured. "The folks in the café were mighty *gut* to me today. I think we'll get by just fine, Nellie."

Her sister dipped a tea bag by its string. "Do . . . do ya think we'll ever see the twins and Sara and little Timmy again? I miss them something fierce now that they're in Higher Ground, without Naz and Jerusalem lookin' after them."

Annie Mae gripped her cup, struggling for an answer. At fifteen, Nellie was more sheltered and less adventurous than she herself had been at that age—and more upset by their *dat*'s unthinkable behavior over the past month. "I wish we knew they were bein' looked after, too," she agreed. "But what with Nazareth and Bishop Tom lookin' to get hitched someday soon—and Tom says Jerusalem's visitin' that nice bishop from Cedar Creek—"

"Jerusalem's *seein*' a fella? At *her* age?" Nellie blurted. "My stars! You heard *all* the *gut* gossip today!"

"—and me workin' at the café," Annie Mae went on,

"we'd have to find somebody to look after the kids. They couldn't stay here by themselves—even if this apartment was big enough for us and the four of them."

Nellie sighed. "*Jah*, there's that. But *someday* I want all of us to be together again, Annie Mae," she murmured wistfully. "I want us all to be *home* . . . even though I for *sure* don't want to go to Higher Ground with Dat. And I feel like such a disobedient daughter for sayin' that."

Annie Mae sipped her tea rather than responding. *Home* . . . Where exactly was that now? While these pastel walls and simple furnishings made for a nice temporary place to stay, this apartment would always belong to Rhoda Lantz and her *mamm*. Annie Mae and her sister had marched out of the house on Bishop's Ridge of their own free will, and they were facing the consequences. She didn't have the heart to tell Nellie that they might never live with their siblings again . . . might never feel Timmy's chubby arms wrapped around their necks or hear Sara singing or—

Don't dwell on such sad, lonely thoughts. Get Nellie thinkin' on something else.

Annie Mae raised her eyebrows. "Heard another tidbit today, too. Millie's stayin' at Preacher Gabe's now, helpin' with Wilma."

"*No!* I can't see *that* lastin'." Nellie squeezed the liquid from her tea bag and tossed it in the trash. "Boy-crazy as she is, she'll be sneakin' out as soon as both her grandparents are nappin'."

Boy-crazy. Folks used to say that about me as well as my best friend, Annie Mae thought. "I'm thinkin' Preacher Gabe can't afford to pay anybody—and Millie's the only one of Atlee and Lizzie's kids that's old enough, so she's takin' care of her grandmother whether she wants to or not."

"*Gut* thing Miriam wanted ya at the café. Lots more fun to be a waitress than a caretaker."

"So true." Annie Mae gestured toward the boxes on the counter. "And Miriam sent me home with sticky buns, green beans, and some sausage and rice casserole. Rhoda said she'd be at Andy's until he got home later tonight, so we can eat our supper any time we care to."

"Supper? It's only three o'clock!" Nellie teased.

Annie Mae had to laugh. "The breakfast shift ran right into the lunch hour," she recalled, "and by the time I realized I was hungry, it was two o'clock and we were closin' up. I've only eaten a few spoonfuls of fried apples all day."

"And whose fault is that?" Nellie challenged as she peered inside the carry-out containers on the counter. "Ya can't tell me Miriam won't give ya time to eat, while . . . Oh my, but that big, gooey sticky bun *is* callin' my name."

"I'm hungry for some of that casserole. After watching Naomi stir up the fried sausage and rice with cans of mushroom soup, I could make that without a recipe." Annie Mae rose to join her sister, who had always been more inclined to eat than she was. And her ploy had worked: Nellie was fetching plates from the cabinet, distracted from her forlorn thoughts about their younger siblings. When they sat down, their mealtime prayer was very brief as the aromas of their food wafted around them.

"Mmm." Nellie closed her eyes over her first bite of pastry. "This is so wonderful-*gut*, Sister. Soft and fresh, with just the right amount of nuts and gooey glaze. You can bring home Miriam's leftovers anytime."

"You've gotta taste this casserole while it's still warm," Annie Mae replied with her mouth half full. "Naomi cooks the main courses while Miriam bakes the pies and rolls and desserts. Hannah's workin' in the kitchen now, too."

"Really?" Nellie tore off another inch of the coiled cinnamon roll. "Didn't think her *dat* wanted her workin' so soon after she got out of school—especially where she'd be around English folks."

Annie Mae shrugged. "She got tired of hangin' around home, I think, what with Ezra workin' at the hospital and her brothers runnin' their carpentry shop and her *mamm* cookin' with Miriam. She um, wasn't real happy to hear that Bram's engaged to a girl from Cedar Creek, either."

"*Really?*" Nellie's eyes widened. She didn't say as much, but she longed for the day when she turned sixteen and could begin dating, as most of her friends were. "I think you learned more today than I did, Sister. How was Hannah takin' that bit of information?"

"She spent a lot of time pretendin' to look for stuff in the storage room," Annie Mae replied. "I guess Bram—*and* his brother—fell head over heels with twin sisters when they went to fetch their new sleigh and courtin' buggy. Not much Hannah can say about it."

And wasn't that the way of it, with guys? One minute they were eager to please the girl they were seeing, and just that fast another gal could turn their heads. It was one more reason Annie Mae planned never to marry. She figured to have her fun while it lasted, but not to get caught and trapped—the way Mamm and a lot of her friends had—by marrying men who made pretty promises.

As she absently wiped her hand on her apron, she felt Adam's reading glasses in her pocket. Now *there* was something she wouldn't show her sister. The specs had come in handy while she was learning the items on the menu, but there would be no end to Nellie's insinuations about Adam Wagler if her sister found out what he'd done this morning.

But wasn't it thoughtful of him to see her problem and fix it, without making a fuss? She'd heard several compliments about those glasses today . . . allowed herself to recall that startling moment of awareness when Adam had gently positioned them on her nose.

Enough of thinking about Adam. Nothing will come of it.

Annie Mae reached for the remaining sticky bun while Nellie spooned green beans and sausage noodles onto her plate. They were fed and sheltered. Prayed for. That was enough for now.

As Adam's Belgian gelding clip-clopped along the county blacktop toward home, he took in the last rose-colored streaks of the sunset on the horizon. What with helping the Brenneman boys finish that kitchen on the other side of New Haven, and then returning to Willow Ridge to repair and repaint some of the shelving units in Zook's Market, he'd put in a lot of time and miles for one day.

He was grateful for the steady work, though. It got him out among folks who appreciated his skills and trusted his judgment, far as what species of wood they should use for cabinets, or what colors of paint and wallpaper were popular. Tomorrow he'd be sanding an oak parquet floor for a lady who lived in Warrensburg, and the refinishing would take him a couple of days by the time he made the trip there and back.

"*Gut* boy, Jerry," he murmured when his horse turned left at the crossroads. "Take us on home now, fella."

The sturdy horse's ears perked up, along with his pace. It was Jerry's way to head quickly toward the barn once Adam guided him onto Bishop's Ridge Road. As they passed the stately white house where Hiram Knepp and his family had lived, it seemed to Adam that the windows watched him like eyes . . . empty and soulless now that the place was unoccupied. Just beyond the house sat the huge custom-built barn where Hiram had raised and sold his prize-winning horses. A white plank fence stretched as far as the eye could see around the property.

Quite a chunk of change, sitting there empty, Adam mused as his wagon rumbled past the arched entry sign for Bishop's Ridge Belgians. No doubt Hiram Knepp had a plan for these structures and the acreage they sat on—certainly the most impressive property in Willow Ridge. But who could guess what their excommunicated bishop would do next?

Jerry trotted up the Wagler lane with an eager whicker. Adam unhitched his big enclosed wagon before leading the horse into the barn to brush him down and feed him. It was a soothing routine at the end of each day, yet this evening Adam's gaze wandered to the back stall they used for storage. Beneath an old blue tarp, his motorcycle sat as a reminder of the trouble it had gotten him into . . . how a yen for forbidden English transportation had turned his *rumspringa* from a time of youthful adventure into a nightmare.

"Really should sell that thing," he muttered as he poured Omolene into Jerry's trough. He stroked the Belgian's massive shoulder, inhaling the molasses scent of the feed. "Should've stuck with you and the other horses, ain't so?"

Jerry blew air from his nostrils and kept chewing, contented now that his workday was behind him.

Even though Adam resisted the urge to lift the blue tarp, memories of his mother engulfed him. He retrieved the Zook's Market sack and his bakery box from the wagon before he strode toward the back door of the house. Why was he thinking about Mamm, anyway? Because he'd seen Annie Mae at the Sweet Seasons? The two women weren't much alike—

Unless you consider how they both kept their families looking clean and healthy and . . . happy.

Adam entered the kitchen and sighed. Matthias stood at the old black cookstove, arranging slices of bacon in a cast-iron skillet that was already smoking— probably because it needed a good washing. The countertop was piled with their dirty dishes, and the heavy odor of grease hung in the air. "Time for Ruth or Etta to come and clean this place again," he remarked as he set his parcels on the cluttered table.

Matthias let out a humorless laugh. "You really want to hear our sisters howl when they walk in here? They're probably glad they married guys from Clark and Carrollton, so they can't come clean up after us very often."

Adam didn't press his point. Talking about their

messy house invariably started Matthias reminiscing about how his Sadie had rescued the two of them and Dat from their own grime after Mamm's passing—which led to recalling how his wife had suffocated during an asthma attack before he could call the doctor.

Depressing. This place reeks of sorrow and unrealized dreams. Adam pulled out the cans and boxes he'd picked up at Zook's Market. "How about some pork and beans to go with that bacon?"

"Nothing I love better than a one-skillet meal," Matthias replied. "What-all did ya bring home?"

With a shrug, Adam stuck the paper sack with the others that were crammed between the counter and the pantry cabinet. "Same ole same ole. Cold cereal, mac and cheese—and I saved you a couple of sticky buns Miriam was putting out when I was leaving the Sweet Seasons," he added as he held up the flat white box.

"Thank the *gut* Lord for Miriam's café—and maybe for the added attraction of Annie Mae workin' there now," Matthias teased. "I saw ya watchin' every move she made this morning."

"Your imagination's working overtime," Adam retorted. "Didn't you have enough harness business to keep you busy today?"

"Matter of fact, I got a big order from an English fella who's wantin' tack for his six-horse hitch of Percherons," his brother said smugly. "He wants all the shiny silver hardware on it, too, on account of how he competes at a lot of big shows."

"Glad to hear it. What with Hiram moving away, I wondered how you'd make up for the business he gave you." Adam was glad their topic of conversation had changed, and he wasn't giving his brother another chance to come at him about Annie Mae. "So—what'd you think of the way Bram and Nate *and* Bishop Tom are all of a sudden connected to women? We single guys are a vanishing breed."

Matthias dumped a can of beans into the skillet of crackling bacon and then doused the concoction with salt, pepper, and ketchup. "The Kanagy boys fell into a real sweet deal," he replied. "Amos Coblentz'll build them a fine home and the best barns for Bram's auction business and Nate's horse trainin', too. Sounds like they're set for the rest of their lives."

Adam couldn't miss the hint of envy . . . his brother's assumption that nothing wonderful would ever happen to him again. It seemed that no matter what subject he brought up, their talk circled around to the misfortunes and tragedies of their past. And Adam was suddenly tired of it.

"I'm really happy for Tom," Adam asserted as he pulled the last two clean plates from the cabinet. "I mean, who could've guessed that he'd become our new bishop *and* that Lettie would pass on *and* that Nazareth Hooley would be waiting for him, ready to be his wife?" he asked in a rising voice. "Maybe God's trying to tell us that if Tom can start a whole new life—"

"Don't let me stand in your way, Brother. You *go*, guy."

When Matthias set the skillet on a towel in the center of the table, Adam bit back his immediate reaction to their main course. Strips of partially blackened bacon stuck out of the soupy beans, with little pockets of grease forming around them.

But what could he say? His brother had made

supper and he had done the shopping . . . each of them filling in the blanks of their lives as best they could. They sat down across the table from each other and bowed their heads.

Lord . . . Lord . . . help me to be more grateful for what I have. And help me to move beyond it.

Chapter Four

As Miriam took in the seventeen people gathered around her kitchen table, her heart filled to bursting. This being a Sunday when they didn't have church, she'd invited all of Ben's family and hers for a day of visiting, along with the Knepp girls. Even though it was snowing outside, laughter and sunshine filled her cheerful yellow kitchen, along with the aromas of the food everyone had brought to share.

As Ben passed her the platter of ham loaf, he leaned toward her with a glimmer in his eyes. "Honey-girl, if you'd've told me last year at this time that I'd be sittin' at this table amongst all our family and friends, I couldn't have believed it," he whispered. "And I thank ya, Miriam, for bringin' me into this fine life."

Miriam tingled all over as Ben's kiss teased at the rim of her ear. She set down the platter to grasp his hand. "No, Ben, it's *me* who's thankful," she insisted. "Had ya not blown into my life during that storm— and then loved me, and then had this wonderful-*gut* home built for us—I couldn't have *so* enjoyed every moment of these three weeks we've been married. You're a gift from God, ya know it?"

As always happened when they focused on each other, the chatter around them—the whole rest of the world—faded away and it was just the two of them, lost in love. While her first marriage to Jesse Lantz had been a good, solid relationship, this union with Ben Hooley was taking Miriam beyond anything she'd ever anticipated, bringing her affection and tender devotion that made her as giddy as a girl again.

"A gift from God, eh?" Ben teased. "I'll remind ya of that, come the first squabble we have."

"Maybe we won't have one."

Ben's laughter rang out in the crowded room. "Oh, Miriam, one of these days I *will* do somethin' that sets ya off. I'm not nearly as perfect as you're settin' me up to be."

"Truer words were never spoken!" Ben's aunt Jerusalem crowed from farther down the table. "I could tell plenty of tales about how our Bennie tried my patience—and tormented his brothers and sisters whilst they were growin' up."

"But that was my job, as the firstborn," Ben protested as he gestured toward Ira and Luke. "And look at these fellas *now*, gearin' up to open their new gristmill on their own parcel of land. Where would they be without my wise counsel and guidance?"

"Runnin' the roads of Lancaster County, doin' as we please," Ira piped up.

Miriam laughed. At twenty-eight, Ira was still unmarried and full of himself, but he had a talent for coaxing the locals to raise the trendy grains, cage-free chickens, and eggs that city dwellers demanded these days. "When do ya figure to open for business?" she asked.

"Lots of folks in the café have been askin' how you'll get through the winter and the summer before your first harvest is brought in."

Luke raised a serving spoon, indicating that she'd made a good point. Then he scooped up a huge second serving of Jerusalem's macaroni and goat cheese. "We've received a big shipment of grains and dried corn from back East," he replied, "and once we get them ground and bagged, we'll be runnin' ads. I figure, come warmer weather, folks hereabouts will be ready to discover us—and we'll be ready for them."

Rebecca, who was seated beside Miriam, joined in. "When you've got those grains bagged, Luke, I'll post photos of them on your website," she said. Then her face brightened. "And speaking of websites, I can't wait to finish Andy's! After his clinic on wheels arrives, I'll post a picture of it, alongside a listing of the house call services he'll offer."

"Oh, but I'm ready for that!" Rachel declared as her hand fluttered to her abdomen. "Havin' this first baby won't be nearly so scary, now that we've got a nurse in Willow Ridge."

Miriam smiled at her newlywed daughter, seated across the table beside her burly blond husband, Micah Brenneman. "You're doin' just fine, honey-bug. A little mornin' sickness is part of the package, and you'll soon be past it." She leaned forward to look down the table then, to where Andy Leitner sat with his two kids, Taylor and Brett—with her daughter Rhoda smack in the middle of them. "Your new wagon's arrivin' soon, then?" she asked. "From the looks of things, your clinic building's comin' along, as well."

Andy nodded, clearly excited about the skills and the new facilities he would bring to their little town.

"The carriage maker in Cedar Creek is so excited about making his first rolling medical center, he bumped me up on his schedule," Andy replied. "But the *best* news? I think I've sold my house in New Haven!"

Exclamations and applause filled the kitchen, and once again Miriam's heart fluttered. Such a kind, warmhearted man, Andy Leitner was, with enough determination—and love for her daughter Rhoda— that he was letting go of his English life and possessions to become Amish. *Lord, once again I thank Ya that all things are workin' to the good of those who love Ya . . . that my Rhoda has found a wonderful man and that my Rebecca's computer trainin' is helpin' so many of us Plain folks attract the English customers who'll help us prosper.*

"My brothers and I will concentrate on your new place now—and just in time, it sounds like," Micah remarked as he reached for the green beans. "I'm hopin' Adam Wagler can put in some time with us, on account of how he's best at all that finishin' work— and he lives right down the road. We'll fix up your livin' quarters first, before we do your clinic and office."

"We've . . . already started our . . . packing," Andy's mother said in her halting voice. Betty Leitner was recovering from a stroke, but wearing a Plain-style dress covered with bright red poppies, she radiated a courage and determination that inspired everyone around her. "Your Rhoda . . . is a godsend, when it comes to . . . tucking things into boxes and . . . convincing the kids to get rid of . . . *stuff!*"

Laughter filled the room again, as seven-year-old Brett grinned at his grandmother's remark. "Yeah,

Rhoda the Raccoon is pawing through all our toys and computer games," he said. "I bet we've donated a hundred boxes to the homeless shelter in Warrensburg—"

"Maybe a dozen," his older sister, Taylor, corrected quickly. "And Rhoda's sewing us new Amish clothes for when we start at the one-room school, too. It'll be a big change from the classes we've got now, but . . . but we really want to do this so she can be our new *mamm*."

Miriam's heart swelled again, and her eyes got wet. The two Leitner kids really had no idea how major the changes would be once they began living the Plain life, yet she knew Taylor and Brett would do *anything* for Rhoda. And Miriam was more than ready to welcome these two grandchildren, even before Andy completed what might be a lengthy transition period before he was baptized into the Amish church. *Yet another gift I'm so very grateful for, Lord . . .*

Across the table from Miriam, Nellie Knepp laughed and elbowed Annie Mae. "It would *almost* be worth my stayin' in school to watch Teacher Alberta when Taylor and Brett start comin'," she said playfully. "But at the end of this term, I'm outta there."

"You know," Andy responded in a pensive tone, "I've been thinking the kids might adjust to their new Amish school more easily if we had them tutored or homeschooled after we move here. With Rhoda already so busy getting us settled, what would you think of becoming our teacher, Nellie?" he asked as the excitement rose in his voice. "We might be coming here sooner than we anticipated—"

"And havin' an Amish gal teach ya *Deitsch* and other Plain ways would be a big help to all of ya," Bishop Tom remarked. He was seated at the other end of the table, very interested—and invested—in the Leitners' transformation of faith and lifestyle.

Nellie set down her fork. "I—I've never thought about bein' a schoolmarm—"

"But you'd be so *gut* at that!" Annie Mae declared. "You've already been teachin' our little brothers and sister Sara—"

"And ya have a steady head and a lovin' heart," Jerusalem chimed in. "After all the years Nazareth and I spent in the classroom, I can tell ya that kids need love and patience more than anything else in this world. The way I hear it, kids in English schools aren't gettin' nearly enough of that these days."

"You are *so* right about that," Andy said emphatically. "In my years as a teacher, before my nurse's training, I became very concerned at the way parental support for teachers was disappearing—and about the level of commitment of some newer teachers." Once again he focused on Nellie. "I know this is a spur-of-the-moment idea I've thrown at you, but if you're interested, we'll get the kids started with you as soon as we can on whatever schedule works for you."

Miriam fell back against her chair, somewhat amazed at this development. *But then, why am I surprised, Lord? You're here amongst us, workin' out Your will.*

Nellie was fiddling with her napkin, yet smiling shyly. "I'd *like* workin' with your kids," she murmured. "It might lead to becomin' a teacher at the school someday. Can we talk about it soon?"

"Any time you're ready," Andy confirmed. "You folks here in Willow Ridge—the way you share so much of yourselves to help my family—are truly an inspiration."

The group quieted for a moment. Forks scraped across plates and satisfied sighs confirmed that everyone had enjoyed the meal. Glancing at the desserts on the back counter, Nazareth cleared her throat. "You'll want to try the hot fudge cake I pulled out of the oven before we came," she hinted. "And Tom made ice cream to go with it."

"The kids helped me bake the lime bars, too," Rhoda said as she stood up to scrape their dirty plates. "When I told them we'd all bring food we made ahead of time, so we didn't work on the Sabbath, cookies were the first thing they thought of."

"You all're lucky we had any left to bring," Brett piped up.

Laughter and pleasant chatter filled the kitchen again, and as Miriam rose to clear the table she feasted her eyes, her soul, on the dear folks who surrounded her today. What a blessing, to have so many new connections and new developments as they moved out of January into February. As Ben had said, last winter she couldn't have imagined the changes she would be witnessing in this new year—and best of all, she was watching her three daughters grow into fine young women.

Rachel, Rhoda, and Rebecca possessed different abilities, yet they were triplets in every sense of the word . . . even if Rebecca sported short hair, jeans, and a tie-dye hoodie today. How wonderful it was, that everyone in Willow Ridge accepted her girls even though two of them had chosen uncommon paths. Miriam felt especially indebted to Tom Hostetler for his open attitude—his willingness to consider nontraditional options for her family and for their community.

And it was Tom who struck up a new topic as they passed around Nazareth's gooey cocoa cake along with a bucket of ice cream and a big plate of lime bars. "Along with all of these new situations we've been discussin', our district needs to select a new preacher real soon," he said. He looked at Andy as he went on to explain this. "Because I've become the bishop, that leaves only Gabe Glick as a preacher, and a district this size needs two. Truth be told, with his health deterioratin' and with his Wilma needin' more assistance, Gabe's asked me to replace him as soon as we can."

Everyone considered this as they took their first bites of dark chocolate cake and homemade ice cream. It occurred to Miriam that, except for Tom, she had been a member of the Willow Ridge district longer than anyone else in the room. "Gabe was a preacher when Jesse brought me here as a bride, more than twenty years ago," she murmured. "While he's supposed to have that job for life, we can't argue about why he wants to let somebody younger and healthier take his place."

"That'll involve a process we call the fallin' of the lot," Tom continued—partly for the Leitner family's benefit, and also because it had been so long since they'd chosen a new preacher. "At one of our afterchurch meetings, members will whisper the name of the fella they feel should be the new preacher—a married man, he has to be. Then the men who get mentioned the most will sit up front at a table. Out of their sight, I will have slipped a Bible verse into an *Ausbund*—our hymnal—and mixed that hymnal into a stack with the same number of books as we have men. Nobody—not even me—knows which book the verse is hidden in."

As Andy, his kids, and his mother listened closely, Miriam ran the names of potential preachers through her mind. There weren't but a handful eligible for the position.

"So if a preacher has to be married," Andy said, his brow furrowed in thought, "how is it that you've been selected as the new bishop, Tom? I'm not meaning any disrespect, understand, but you've told me your wife left you, and then divorced you . . . and that she's recently died."

"I'm not takin' it as disrespectful in the least. You've asked a pertinent question," Tom replied quickly. "A lot of Amish leadership decisions depend on the other bishops in the area—and our situation's more troublesome than usual, what with our previous bishop bein' excommunicated. Jeremiah Shetler, Vernon Gingerich, and Enos Mullet all said right off that Willow Ridge needed a local preacher to fill the bishop's position immediately, to keep our members united and strong in the faith after losin' their leader under such . . . unfortunate circumstances."

Andy nodded, as did most of the adults around the table. "I can see the wisdom of that. And the folks here couldn't ask for a more levelheaded, compassionate leader than you, Tom."

Their new bishop smiled, but then quickly resumed a more serious expression. "We see it as the will of God, this whole episode in our district's story. If I'm the right man for the job, that's the Lord's doin'—just as we believe that the fella who picks the book with the verse in it has been chosen by God to be our new preacher." Bishop Tom continued his previous explanation. "He comes to the service that mornin' as an ordinary man, but when he leaves he's a servant of the church. That means he'll tend to our members' needs—which includes tellin' them when they've

sinned and need to confess. He'll start preachin'
sermons, and he'll sacrifice time he would've been
spendin' on whatever work he normally does, and
time with his family. He'll serve us for the rest of his
life. Without pay."

"Oh my," Rebecca murmured. "That's a huge commitment. What if the guy says no?"

"That's not an option," the bishop replied somberly.
"When a man marries, he also vows to serve the
church if he's selected. When God calls ya, there's no
duckin' out. No excuses."

"And this fellow will serve and preach sermons without going to a seminary?" Andy asked. "How will he
know the right things to say—and be able to speak for
an hour or more without any notes, the way you and
Bishop Gingerich did at Miriam and Ben's wedding?"

Tom squeezed Andy's shoulder. "I like the questions
you're askin'. You're figurin' out that for Amish, our
faith is *everything*—our devotion to God comes even
before our love for our families," he replied. "We'll
give this new preacher a few months to study the Scriptures, and I'll be spendin' a lot of preparation time
with him, too. But once he gets up in front of that
roomful of people, he preaches on the day's Bible pas-
sage accordin' to how the *gut* Lord leads him."

The bishop paused to spoon up some of the ice
cream that was being passed around the table. "And
when he hears of folks who might be veerin' off the
path—maybe usin' their teenagers' cell phones or
drivin' around like Hiram was doin'," Tom clarified,
"he and the deacon'll have to go tell them, straight-
out, that they've gone astray. If they don't put away the
gadget or stop whatever they're doin' wrong, they'll

get a visit from the bishop and will most likely be instructed to kneel in church and confess."

Andy's expression got very serious. "I've read about that in my online explorations, but I can't imagine most folks would like having their shortcomings pointed out that way. Even in private."

"You've got that right!" Ben replied with a chuckle. "But our families have been teachin' us right from wrong since they rocked our cradles. It's not like a preacher or the bishop is tellin' us what we don't already know."

"And that's why, when outsiders say they want to become Amish, we require such a long period of transition." Tom gazed steadily at Andy, and then glanced at the younger folks seated around the table. "Even our own kids must take instruction, once they've decided to be baptized into the church, because it's a vow they take for life."

Tom stroked his steely-gray beard then, considering what he'd say next. "I'd be remiss not to tell ya, Andy, that for every ten English who start down the path to become Old Order Amish, maybe *one* is accepted into the membership. It's very rare, because either the *Englischer* can't make all the necessary changes, or the district won't vote him in. Even when he's left his former life behind to follow our simpler ways, the life-long members feel he's still too different. Not fully immersed in the faith."

"It's the biggest challenge I've undertaken in my entire life," Andy agreed.

"I should also say that while it was a fine thing for Rebecca's English *dat* to buy your building for ya," Bishop Tom went on, "there'll be folks who suspect you're usin' the existin' electricity for more than

Rebecca's computer business. I'll be checkin' on that personally, so I can assure them—"

"But we're gonna have solar panels!" Brett blurted. "Won't that be *cool?*"

"*Jah,* we removed the electrical wiring from the living quarters and even from Andy's main office," Micah spoke up. "Once we showed him how we charge our shop tools with solar panels—like Ben and Adam Wagler do—he decided that was the better route to go."

"I'll have a solar panel on top of my clinic wagon, too," Andy chimed in. "When the Brennemans showed me how to adapt my medical equipment, solar power seemed the ideal way to keep my practice Plain yet up-to-date."

"Pleased to hear that," Tom remarked with a nod. "But understand, there's still room for abusin' solar power. I've had to get after a couple fellas for runnin' TV's their *rumspringa* teenagers had. And Rhoda knows she's not to have modern kitchen appliances plugged into your panels, either."

"No more microwave popcorn," Taylor acknowledged matter-of-factly.

Andy smiled at his kids. "I appreciate your honesty, Bishop Tom," he murmured. "I believe we're all working together on this, though. And I believe Rhoda's the woman God intends for me to marry . . . the mother my children so badly need after my first wife divorced me and left us all behind. That's the best incentive a man can have."

Once again, Miriam felt as though her kitchen was filled with love and the presence of God Himself. Rhoda's face turned a pretty shade of pink as she slipped her arms around Taylor's and Brett's shoulders.

The way those kids gazed up at her tugged at Miriam's heartstrings, too.

"So who-all might be eligible to preach?" Jerusalem asked as she cut into her chocolate cake. "What with comin' to Willow Ridge just last fall, I might not know all the men we're talkin' about—except, of course, that our Bennie is now up for consideration."

"*Jah*, he is," Tom confirmed. "Henry Zook comes to mind, and Ezra Brenneman—"

"And my sister Leah's husband, Dan Kanagy . . . and Preacher Gabe's son, Atlee Glick," Miriam added as she, too, made a mental trip along the roads that crisscrossed their rural district. Her gaze lingered on the row of sturdy young men seated across the table from her. "And now you're eligible, as well, Micah," she said, smiling at Rachel's new husband. "Yet it seems we have nearly as many single fellas in town as we do married ones."

"From what I've seen of how the preachers here and back in Lancaster have to deal with family disputes and issues with the local government," Luke said as he took two lime bars, "it makes sense to me not to get hitched. Why would I want to take on such a load of other people's business while sacrificin' my own?"

Ben stiffened in his chair. He had spoken to his two younger brothers often since they'd arrived, about how they were twenty-eight and thirty and still not members of the Amish church. Bishop Tom seemed taken aback by Luke's tone, as well, while Nazareth and Jerusalem frowned at each other and then at their two younger nephews.

Miriam cleared her throat. "You make a point, Luke," she said, striving to speak with patience. "My Jesse served as the deacon of this district for most of his married life, and my brother Moses is a preacher, so I can tell ya firsthand about the hours of discussion and intervention and prayer that go into livin' your life on behalf of others. It's no small burden for a man's family to bear, either. But I believe that preachers, deacons, and bishops who've sacrificed wages here on Earth go on to reap greater rewards in Heaven."

"Hear, hear," Jerusalem murmured.

"Ya said a mouthful, Miriam," Nazareth agreed as she patted Tom's arm. "There comes a time when we all have to take responsibility and be accountable for the gifts and talents the *gut* Lord has given us."

Ira rolled his eyes and his spoon clattered into his empty bowl. "From what I can see of Bishop's Ridge, Hiram Knepp didn't sacrifice much in the way of wages," he retorted. "He was surely makin' money hand over fist—"

"And that'll be enough of such talk at this table." Ben stood up slowly, glaring at his brothers. "I'm ashamed of ya, speculatin' about Annie Mae and Nellie's *dat* while they're sittin' right here amongst us. You were raised better than that."

The sudden silence squeezed every person in the room, like a shoe laced up too tight. Miriam sat up straighter, believing Ben was absolutely right to chastise his brothers' careless chatter. Andy's eyebrows rose and his two kids knew better than to make a peep. Tom looked as close to delivering a lecture as Miriam had ever seen him, while her three daughters wore stricken expressions. Poor Nellie was blushing, staring down at her lap.

But Annie Mae leaned forward to look down her side of the table at the two Hooley brothers. "*Jah,* it's true that our *dat* kept some mighty big secrets and that he's done things folks are shakin' their heads over," she said in a low voice. "But he's human, like we all are. And though he doesn't seem inclined to confess or to ask our forgiveness—and though I don't like it one bit that he's run off to start another town, or that he took our innocent brothers and little sister with him—in the end, he'll answer to God, ain't so? Just like every one of us will."

Once again the kitchen seemed to hold its breath. Ben placed his hand on Annie Mae's shoulders. "Ya said that just right, young lady," he murmured. "Bless ya for remindin' us to look to our own issues before we judge anybody else's."

As Ben sat down, everyone relaxed and finished dessert. Miriam hoped this terse discussion wouldn't shorten the afternoon's visiting—although it wouldn't be unusual for the young people to go their own ways to socialize after the dishes were cleaned up. Bowls were being scraped and satisfied sighs escaped a few folks— and then a little voice broke the silence.

"Can I have another one of those lime bars?" Brett asked Rhoda in a loud whisper. "They're wonderful-*gut,* ain't so?"

Rhoda rumpled Brett's hair as she reached for the cookie platter. "We'll be bakin' those again, I can see."

"That hot fudge cake was *awesome,*" Taylor chimed in. "You've warned us about eating two desserts, Mamma, but if I could have just one more spoonful—"

"Honey-lamb, ya cleaned up your plate, so you can have whatever your dear little heart desires," Jerusalem replied quickly. As she extended the warm cake pan across the table, her face lit up. "That was our *mamm*'s recipe from a long time ago, and it's still one of my favorites."

Taylor grinned, grabbing her spoon. "The macaroni and goat cheese was really *gut,* too," she said. "Even though I wondered about it when I heard the *goat* part."

Everyone laughed then, and the Hooley sisters clasped each other's hands in delight. "Oh, if you'd meet our little goats, you'd love them just as we do," Nazareth said. "And the three girl goats are gonna have their kids any day now."

"Can we go see them?" Brett asked eagerly. He looked from his *dat* to Rhoda with expressive brown eyes. "Can *we* have goats, too, after we move here?"

Andy gazed at Rhoda with such love that Miriam could feel the strong current running between them. "One thing at a time, son," he replied. "But if your new *mamm* says it's all right, we'll figure out where to put them."

"If ya want a little practice at tendin' goats, to see if ya really like them, we'd welcome your help," Nazareth replied with an encouraging smile. "We keep our four in Bishop Tom's barn, ya know. Right there amongst his horses and dairy cows."

As the two children and the aunts talked about their animals, the harmony and goodwill Miriam craved was restored. After the desserts made it around the table again, she and the other women began scraping plates while the fellows made their way to the front room to visit by the fireplace.

The next couple of hours passed in pleasant chatter as Miriam and her girls washed dishes and put away the leftovers with the help of the Hooley sisters, Nellie, and Annie Mae. It had been a long while since she'd cleaned up after a meal for seventeen, but she was happy to have her three daughters—and young Taylor and Betty—talking together as their many hands made light work of so many pots, pans, and dishes.

As they were wiping the countertops, Miriam noted that it was nearly dark outside, and not yet five o'clock. Soon Bishop Tom would be leaving to milk his cows and the others would start home, as well. Such a blessing it was that everyone she loved lived within sight of her and Ben's new home. . . .

A movement at the kitchen door caught her eye. There stood Luke, beckoning Annie Mae with a crook of his finger. After the way Annie Mae had stood up to the younger Hooleys during dinner, Miriam wondered how long she would continue to come every time Luke called.

It might still be winter, but things are heating up all over Willow Ridge. . . .

Chapter Five

"Would ya get a load of this?" Matthias slowed his horse's pace as he and Adam peered out the buggy's windows. They'd spent the day in Clark visiting their sister Ruth and her family and had gotten a late start home. "I *thought* Higher Ground had to be in this area."

"Can't miss it, either, what with that big sign at the road," Adam remarked as he leaned forward for a better look. The stone marker with HIGHER GROUND carved in large letters seemed awfully grandiose, to his way of thinking. "And electrical poles. Now *that's* interesting."

As Adam scanned the rolling, snow-covered landscape, he took in the homes under construction on the hillside. One structure had to be a schoolhouse . . . a row of brick buildings sat close to the road. Stores, perhaps? Considering how Amish folks almost always had their businesses on their home property, Higher Ground had a very unusual layout. "We're on the back side of Morning Star, ain't so?"

"*Jah.* A lot of different Mennonite groups live out

this way," Matthias replied. "So Hiram's no doubt sayin' that God found him this big plot of land where he could set up amongst other Plain families—"

"Surely he won't be the bishop," Adam interrupted as his mind kept spinning. "Folks around these parts all know how he was kicked out of Willow Ridge for not confessing about that car in his barn."

"Who knows what stories Hiram's been tellin' them?" Matthias countered with a sigh. "I can't imagine anybody would come to his new town—except folks from other states who don't know what he's been up to."

Adam pointed to a large house on the highest rise, which appeared to be nearly completed. "What do you want to bet that's his place? And the other building will probably be the new barn for his Belgians."

"How do ya suppose the foundations of these buildings will hold up, what with the concrete bein' poured in the snow and cold weather? It's a puzzle all the way around—especially with his house in Willow Ridge sittin' empty," his brother speculated. "I figured the underhanded real estate fella that found him this land would've put up a FOR SALE sign at Hiram's other place by now."

"*Jah,* it's not *gut* for a house to be left untended," Adam remarked. "Even if two-legged vandals aren't involved, there might be all manner of coons or rats gettin' inside to do their damage, once they figure out nobody'll shoo them off."

As the dusk settled around their buggy, Adam continued to gaze at the new settlement—and then he let out a gasp. "Streetlights just blinked on! Now *that's* different!"

"Seen enough?" Matthias asked.

"*Jah*," Adam replied, although he was still very curious about this settlement. "We don't want to seem like we're checking the place out. Hiram's likely to come down and ask if we're prospective new residents."

"Puh! He'd know better when he saw who we are." Matthias clapped the reins lightly across Herbert's broad back.

That doesn't mean he wouldn't give us a pitch . . . or an earful, Adam thought as the buggy rolled on down the road. The truth was that he didn't trust Hiram Knepp anymore, and that was the saddest thing a man could say about the bishop who'd led their church district for so many years.

As they left the cluster of stores in the English section of Morning Star and then passed into open countryside again, Adam let go of his troublesome thoughts concerning Hiram. God was in charge of this situation, so they should allow it to play out—and he had a workweek ahead of him. Even though their older sister Ruth had crammed their cooler with leftovers, that didn't take care of the dirty shirts and pants piling up in the mudroom. . . .

"So you'll be working on that English fella's tack tomorrow?" Adam asked. "I've got a floor to refinish, but I could probably start the laundry on Tuesday—"

"And I'll let ya do that, too!" Matthias replied as he turned on the buggy's lights. "So I suppose it's only fair that I wash that mountain of dirty dishes piled in the sink—but it's Sunday," he added with a laugh. "So they'll all have to wait until tomorrow."

Adam sighed inwardly. The two of them were good at letting the household chores slide, even if they

realized that living in such a messy house only added
to their sense of despair.

But as he and Matthias pulled off the county blacktop onto Bishop's Ridge Road, his mood improved.
They had horses to feed and water troughs to fill, jobs
that gave them a sense of purpose because even on the
Sabbath their animals needed tending. When his
brother pulled Herbert to a halt beside their barn,
Adam hopped out of the buggy. Their visit to Ruth's
house, where nieces and nephews and good food had
lifted his spirits, had been a welcome respite from his
day-to-day life with Matthias in this very quiet house.
Yet he was feeling an inner itch lately . . . a frustrating
need for his life to change.

When he saw the blinking red message light on the
barn's wall phone, Adam quickly lit the lantern and
then tapped the PLAY button.

"*Jah*, Adam, it's Micah. Just got back from visitin'
at Miriam and Ben's place, and it seems Rhoda's Andy
will need the livin' quarters of his building finished
sooner than he thought. We could sure use your help
with that, hopefully this week. Gimme a call. Bye."

Andy's pulse thrummed. Inside work, close to
home, was the best kind this time of year. He was
reaching for the receiver to return Micah's call, but
another message began playing.

"Adam, it's Tom, and I hope you fellas had a *gut* visit
with your sister today." The bishop's voice filled the
barn with a sense of calm and peace . . . an authority
Adam respected. Here was a man who'd endured all
manner of trials and tribulations with his ex-wife and
Hiram, yet he resonated with an unshakable faith.
"What with Nazareth and me gettin' hitched in the
near future, I'm hopin' you can freshen my place up

with some paint—say, within the next month or so.
We can talk about it over breakfast sometime this
week—my treat. *Denki*, Adam."

Adam was tickled to hear that Bishop Tom and
Nazareth Hooley would soon tie the knot—*maybe
there's hope for you and Matthias after all.* He laughed at
that thought as he again reached up to punch in
Micah Brenneman's number.

But another message began to play. "Adam, I recall
your attention to detail and your reasonable rates
when you did the finishing work inside the Sweet
Seasons Café, so you're the man I hope to hire as we
complete our first buildings in Higher Ground. I'm
willing to pay double—even triple—what you usually
charge because it's imperative that these homes and
stores look attractive to our incoming residents.
They'll begin arriving in a couple of weeks, so please
call me *now*."

Hiram Knepp. Adam swallowed hard, staring at the
receiver as though their former bishop might suddenly pop out of it. Was it coincidence that Hiram had
called on the same afternoon he and Matthias had
passed through Higher Ground?

We Amish don't believe in coincidence or chance, he
reminded himself. *It's God at work again, fulfilling His
purpose. . . .*

Annie Mae said her good-byes at Miriam and Ben's
place and slipped into her heavy black coat and
bonnet. As she stepped outside into the dusk, her
thoughts were spinning like the dry leaves caught in a
little whirlwind in the corner of the front porch. Not
once in these past four weeks had Luke come by to see

her, nor had he paid her any particular attention the few times he'd eaten in the Sweet Seasons. While she'd been tired after her busy days of waiting tables, she would have welcomed Luke's company . . . long moonlight rides and warm, eager kisses like they'd shared before.

But if Luke thought he could pull her strings any time it suited him, after ignoring her for so long, well—*two* could play that game. She'd considered turning him down this evening. But maybe this ride would give her a chance to fetch a few things from the house . . . if Dat hadn't already cleared everything out.

She clambered into the enclosed buggy while Luke finished hitching up his horse. It seemed like a good idea to let Luke speak first . . . to see if he apologized or explained, or continued in the same arrogant tone he'd used during dinner.

Luke hopped inside and slid the buggy door shut. His breath escaped in wisps of vapor as he instructed his horse to back up . . . then told the gelding to turn left when they reached the county blacktop. He looked over at her, his eyebrows rising. "You're mighty quiet, Annie Mae. Had enough talk about preachers and church for one day?"

She shrugged, remaining on the far side of the seat as she glanced out the window. The snow-covered countryside appeared silvery as darkness fell around them.

After a few moments of her silence, Luke let out an exasperated sigh. "Look, things got sticky at dinner, sure. But Saint Bennie was conveniently forgettin' that he didn't marry until he was thirty-five—and that he only joined the church when he thought he was gonna hitch up with a gal back in Lancaster, years ago."

Annie Mae considered this information, which sounded as though Luke was making excuses for himself.

"And ya surely realize that Ira didn't mean anything by it when he got to talkin' about your *dat* and the money he was makin' with his Belgians."

So if he didn't mean anything, why'd he say it? Dat's money went back into his business, so it's not like we lived any better than anyone else.

It was too soon to shut Luke down, however—especially before they got to the topic she was most interested in. "Everybody around here talks about Dat," she murmured. "And why wouldn't they, after finding out about his car and then hearing how God told him to start up a new town?"

Luke guided the horse down the snow-packed gravel road that ran past Bishop Tom's dairy farm. After a few more moments of silence, he gazed at her more intently. "So what's the bee in your bonnet, missy? I thought you'd be glad to get away from Miriam's and all the boring chitchat about—"

"Ya haven't exactly been bangin' down the door to take me out lately," Annie Mae pointed out. "I keep lookin' out the apartment window of an evening, but—"

"Miriam would be watchin' us like a hawk."

"You're afraid of *her?*" Oh, but she wasn't buying into this horse hockey. Not when Luke was a grown man, running his own business.

"Of course I'm not afraid of her," Luke snapped. "We just don't need her pokin' into our relationship—speakin' of which, why'd you start workin' for *her,* when we'd talked about you runnin' the salesroom in my mill?"

"You won't be open for weeks yet!" Annie Mae blurted. "I can't sit around twiddlin' my thumbs—I have a sister to look after. I don't expect anybody to pay my way just because Dat up and left, ya know."

This conversation was getting on her nerves—not so much what Luke was saying, but what he *wasn't* saying, and his tone. He'd expected her to come running to the mill, pleading for a job that didn't exist. *That* would cause talk, her working for two unmarried fellows! She was trying to stay out of the gossip now, while so many tongues were wagging about Higher Ground and what the excommunicated bishop of Willow Ridge might try next.

"Let's go by the house," Annie Mae suggested, hoping this sounded like a favor rather than an order. Luke and Ira noticed right off when women nagged . . . or maybe they didn't care about anyone's opinions and needs, other than their own.

Luke frowned. "Why would you want to poke around there? We could go to—"

"That was my *home,* Luke—until Christmas," she retorted. "I haven't even been past it since Nellie and I walked out. Has Dat moved all the furniture?"

"I have no idea. It's none of my beeswax."

Annie Mae bit back a smart remark. Wasn't it funny how Luke was interested in his own business, but didn't show an inkling of curiosity or compassion about *her* life since her apple cart had been overturned? "If he hasn't cleared everything out, I—I want the sewing machine. Would ya help me get it?"

Luke stared at her in the deepening shadows. "You'd really *take* stuff?"

"Puh! I don't see my *dat* sewing up clothes anytime soon. Nellie needs new dresses." Was Luke being exceptionally dense, or was she losing her sense of perspective?

On the other hand, it did seem a little nervy to help herself to whatever Dat had left behind . . . and what if her father had rigged up one of his security cameras from the Belgian barn, to catch whoever might slip inside the unoccupied house? If Dat got wind of her going there, no matter how practical her reason, Annie Mae knew he would punish her for it.

But why was it wrong to want *one useful piece,* which had belonged to her and Nellie's *mamm* rather than to Linda, Dat's second wife? It wasn't as if she wanted to take things and sell them for the money. . . .

"Wouldn't you rather go to Higher Ground?" Luke asked. "You could check on the kids."

Just that fast, at the mention of Joey and Josh, Timmy and Sara, Annie Mae had to blink away tears. It wouldn't do to cry, because Luke would think she was manipulating him. "I want to see those wee ones more than anything on this Earth," she rasped. "But I can't suddenly show up and then upset them when I have to leave. And where would we look for them?"

She paused to get better control of her quivering voice. "It's not a *gut* idea to go snoopin' around in Higher Ground," she insisted softly. "Who knows if Dat's built a house, or—if ya don't want to take me to Bishop's Ridge, I'll ask Ben or—"

"Hey, it's no big deal. We'll head up this next road and be there in a few," Luke replied tersely. Then he cleared his throat, and his face took on the playful slyness Annie Mae remembered from when they used to run the roads late at night. "So . . . what'll I get in return for doin' ya this favor, missy?"

Oh, but his low tone brought to mind long, slow

kisses . . . lessons only an older man could teach . . . sweet whispered words that had made her feel special. *Beautiful.* Good enough to become Luke Hooley's wife—or had she been fooling herself all along? His thoughts on staying single, to escape responsibility and commitment, had come out loud and clear when Bishop Tom had talked about picking a new preacher.

But Annie Mae didn't want to miss this chance to fetch the sewing machine. She didn't have a buggy at her disposal—couldn't possibly lift the awkward treadle machine by herself. She didn't really want to bother Ben for help, either, although he'd told her he'd do anything she needed.

"What'll you get in return?" she echoed, hoping to maintain Luke's playful interest. "I guess we'll find out, ain't so?"

Luke chuckled low in his throat. "Now *there*'s the Annie Mae I know," he murmured. "I'm glad she hasn't disappeared. I've missed her."

Why did figuring out what guys really meant have to be so complicated? Once again Annie Mae felt silence might serve her best . . . and it would keep Luke guessing, at least long enough to go inside the house. As they rode along the rising road, past the Wagler place, her *dat*'s big barn and the familiar white house came into view.

The moonlight and the snow created an ethereal glow around the place—or did it seem ghostly? Part of her was spooked about going inside, yet her heart longed to be in those rooms again, among the comfortable furnishings and the mementos her *mamm* and step*mamm* had left behind when they'd died. *Or am I settin' myself up for a big heartache? What if those rooms are empty now, and they echo with our footsteps?*

But it was too late to back out. Luke was urging his horse under the arched Bishop's Ridge sign, into the driveway that circled in front of the tall white house where her heart still belonged. The horse had to slow down, as the pavement hadn't been cleared—and the untouched snow told her no one had been here within the last few weeks.

We're making tracks. Will folks wonder who's been here and why? Maybe you should've thought this through before you—

"Do you suppose your *dat* locked up?" Luke's voice broke the silence. "If he figured he wasn't going to live here anymore—"

"We can try the back way, into the kitchen," she murmured. "And if the doors are locked, that's just the way of it. I'm not breakin' any windows, or—"

Luke pulled the horse to a halt and then gently laid a finger upon her lips. "No reason to sweat this, Annie Mae. We're gonna fetch your sewing machine. It's a simple in and out."

Was anything simple anymore? Annie Mae nodded, eager to go in yet just as eager to get this over with before someone caught her—even though she didn't believe she was doing anything wrong. It was so confusing, when her emotions kicked in from all directions on top of the conflicting remarks Luke had made that day.

When she got to the back door and turned the knob, she was surprised it opened. Steeling herself to handle whatever she might—or might not—find inside, Annie Mae reached for the lantern and matches on the little shelf beside the door. She shivered with the cold and her fingers trembled so badly she could barely light the wick.

"Let me take that," Luke murmured as he reached around from behind her. "Don't want you dropping the lamp and setting fire to—"

Annie Mae sucked in her breath and then wished she hadn't. The house felt chilly but the propane heaters had been left on a low setting . . . so the stench of rotting chicken and vegetables made her recent meal rise up into her throat. Their Second Christmas dinner still covered the table, along with their dirty dishes. Nothing had been moved since she and Nellie and the rest of them had walked out on Dat when he'd expected them to join him in Higher Ground. The gravy, stuffing, and mashed potatoes were fuzzy with white and green mold. The cobbler and cookies on the side counter showed signs that mice—or *something*— had been in here eating the pastry and berries . . . tracking fruit filling along the countertop.

"Ohhhhh," she moaned as she clutched herself. How she hated the sight of such a mess in her kitchen, yet she couldn't look away. She didn't want to think about why the creamed corn seemed to be moving in the bowl. . . .

"I can't believe somebody didn't clean this up," Luke muttered.

"That would be women's work, and all of us left Dat to clean up the mess he'd made," Annie Mae reminded him as she fought back tears. "We need to get a garbage can and throw away this rotten food, and wash the dishes and—"

"No way," Luke stated. "Show me where the sewing machine is, and then we're outta here."

With a shuddery sigh, Annie Mae pointed toward the front room. Much as she hated to leave the spoiled food on the table—knowing she would see it in her mind forever—she couldn't ignore Luke's order. "It's in the spare bedroom at the back of the house," she said, walking ahead of him.

Even in the glow of the lantern's light, even though she'd crossed the front room hundreds of times— and Luke was right behind her—Annie Mae wrapped her arms around herself and didn't look at anything too closely. She was sick at heart and sick to her stomach. All she could focus on was fetching the treadle machine . . . the fabric and thread and pins she would need from the shelves. . . .

Chapter Six

Adam left a message on Micah's shop phone, saying he could start working at Andy Leitner's building on Wednesday. Meanwhile, Matthias had unhitched Herbert and filled the troughs with water. "You can put out the hay while I take our cooler in," his brother said. Then he laughed. "And how will ya answer Hiram, about hirin' on at Higher Ground—for triple your usual wage?"

"Like I'd really do that," Adam retorted. "Might as well sell my soul to the Devil."

Matthias slapped him playfully on the shoulder. "At least ya can tell him you've got jobs lined up for the next several weeks. Can't get to his finishin' work as soon as he needs it done."

"*Jah*, I'll get back to him soon. I sure don't want him to keep calling." Adam yanked the twine from around a couple of square hay bales and divided the fresh-smelling feed among the stalls where their horses stood waiting for it.

As he closed up the barn for the night, Adam looked over toward the Knepp place, once again wondering what was going on with their former bishop. Then he frowned. Why would a light be bobbing in that downstairs window at the back of the house?

His first thought was that Hiram had returned to fetch some things—*at this time of the evening? And does that mean he's coming here next, expecting you to sign on with him?*

An uneasy feeling twitched inside him. What if it *wasn't* Hiram, or any of the Knepps, for that matter? What if an intruder was helping himself to whatever was left in the house?

When the light came to rest in the window, Adam jogged down the lane toward the road. Maybe it wasn't smart to go to an abandoned house alone, but he felt compelled to let this visitor know that the neighbors here watched out for each other. He would never forgive himself if someone stole the Knepps' belongings— or worse yet, accidentally set fire to the place—while he'd been aware of their presence. Adam ran faster, noting that the lantern remained at the window. As he sprinted under the arched Bishop's Ridge sign and into the snow-covered driveway, he prayed for God to watch over him, just in case this after-dark visitor was up to no good.

Instinct told him to go around back. He was relieved to see a horse and buggy there even if he didn't know who owned it. Adam paused outside the back door to catch his breath, planning how he would handle this situation.

He slipped inside, entering the kitchen where he'd visited occasionally throughout his life. His hand flew to his mouth and nose, and as his eyes adjusted to the dimness, he gaped at the long table covered with dishes of moldering, spoiled food. But there was no time to deal with that mess. He heard voices—

"Are ya tellin' me ya don't know where you're gonna put this?" an impatient male demanded. "How do ya think I'll heft this up the stairs to your apartment?"

"Never mind about where I'll put it. I'll ask Miriam—"

That's Annie Mae—and Luke Hooley's with her, Adam realized as he strained to hear her faltering voice. *What's she want that's got him so bent out of shape?*

"Ya mean to tell me ya haven't told her you're bringin' this—*really?*" Luke demanded. "I don't want any part of goin' back to Miriam and Ben's today. Maybe—"

"All right, *forget* it!" Annie Mae retorted, but she sounded really upset. "Maybe this wasn't my best idea, but I thought I could sew up some clothes for Nellie—"

Adam snapped. He had no desire to get caught in the middle of this argument, but he should reveal his presence. Rapid-fire footsteps were coming through the dark front room, without benefit of that lantern he'd seen earlier. "Is everything all right?" he called out. "I saw the light in the—"

Annie Mae screamed and something—several things—hit the hardwood floor just outside the kitchen.

"Who's that? Who's in here?" Luke demanded from farther behind her. Something else landed heavily on the front room floor as Adam stepped cautiously toward the doorway.

"It's Adam Wagler," he explained quickly. "Didn't think it looked right that somebody was in the house—"

"And why would that be any of *your* business?" Luke

challenged as he steered Annie Mae into the shadowy kitchen ahead of him.

Adam stopped, wishing he hadn't gotten involved—yet Hooley's attitude was rubbing him the wrong way. "If this were *my* house sitting empty, I'd appreciate my neighbors checking it out if they saw somebody inside," he replied firmly. Then he softened. "I didn't mean to scare you, Annie Mae. Can I help you with something?"

"Yeah," Luke retorted. "You can help me haul that stupid, awkward sewing machine out to—"

"Forget it, I told ya!" Annie Mae rasped. "If you're gonna be so testy about—"

"I've carried it this far," Luke argued as he turned to face her. "I didn't come all the way out here to—"

"Then leave. *Now.*" Annie Mae's voice and stance toughened up as she crossed her arms at her chest. "Whatever ya saw in me has obviously worn off. Don't let the doorknob hit ya in the butt, *got* it?"

"Loud and clear." Hooley strode out of the kitchen and slammed the door so hard, its glass rattled.

Releasing the breath he'd been holding, Adam searched for the right thing to say. Annie Mae's shoulders slumped and she covered her face with her hands. "Oh, but I've made such a—a mess of things," she said in a voice that finally surrendered to tears.

Adam stood still for a moment. Crying women baffled him, but Annie Mae clearly didn't deserve to be treated so harshly. Cautiously he stepped forward. She was tall enough that putting his arms around her shoulders seemed awkward, so he placed his hands lightly at the sides of her waist. "From what I overheard, you came after your sewing machine?"

"*Jah.* I thought—oh, never mind what I thought,"

she muttered as she swiped at her eyes. "I'm out here without a ride back, and I've gotten ya mixed up in—"

"I came to check on things," Adam reminded her quietly. "Seems like a small favor, asking Luke to fetch your sewing machine so you and Nellie can—"

"And when I saw that—that awful *mess* still on the table—"

When Annie Mae crumpled and lurched forward, there was nothing for Adam to do but catch her . . . wrap his arms around her, even as he sensed he was getting in deeper than he wanted to. She felt slender and firm, and she was more distraught than he'd ever seen her. As he lightly rubbed her shaking back, her tears wet his neck. What could he say to help this situation without getting himself too entangled? "That moldy food's a magnet for animals," he murmured. "So how about if we get it out of here and wash those nasty dishes?"

Annie Mae raised her head, blinking at him. "You'd help me with that?"

"Sure I would. I don't know what your *dat* was thinking, leaving that food to rot—but it doesn't matter now," he added quickly when he saw her lips quivering again. "Won't take us long to clean it up. Then I'll get my wagon, and load your sewing machine into it, and take you back to your apartment. Okay?"

A smile flitted across Annie Mae's face even though she wasn't yet finished crying. "That would be ever so nice of ya."

Adam eased away from her. "You'd help me if *I* was in a bind, I'm pretty sure."

"*Jah. Jah,* I would." With a loud sniffle, Annie Mae straightened to her full height. "I'll fetch the lantern. There's a trash barrel in the mudroom—"

"I'll go get it. Don't you worry about a thing."

Adam went into the small room off to the side of the door he'd come in. Why had he assured Annie Mae that this crisis was resolved? Instinct told him that cleaning up the messy table and then taking her home with her sewing machine wasn't nearly as simple as he'd made it out to be . . . not the way his heart was thumping, and the way he noticed her clean scent lingering on his jacket. He hadn't held a girl in years—hadn't dated much after his *mamm* died—and all manner of red flags were flapping in his mind.

Oh, get real. What else were you supposed to do after Hooley gave her such a hard time? She's the girl next door. More like a sister than . . .

When he returned to the kitchen with the trash barrel, Annie Mae was setting the lantern on the counter alongside the sink, where its glow illuminated the table as well. "I'm wonderin' how long the propane'll hold out so the pipes won't freeze," she murmured as she began running dishwater.

"I'll check your outside tank gauge tomorrow, in the daylight," Adam replied. "And I'll set some mousetraps. No sense in letting the critters overrun this place until—"

"*Denki* so much, Adam."

He set the trash barrel beside the table and looked over at her. *Big mistake.* With the lantern glow surrounding her like a halo and the steam rising in the sink behind her, Annie Mae could well be somebody's wife—*his* wife—gazing at him with those big blue eyes and that grateful expression on her face. She looked ready to hug him again, so Adam picked up the platter with the disgustingly moldy chicken on it.

"You're welcome," he murmured as he dumped it

in the barrel. Then he gagged and coughed. "Maybe you'd better stay there at the sink until I get this food off the plates, because it's kicking up a real stink now that I'm messing with it."

"I'll pick up the fabric and thread I dropped when ya scared me half to death. But I really was glad to see ya, Adam," she added quickly as she headed for the front room. "I have no idea what's makin' Luke so snippy—not that you'd care about that."

But he did care. He'd gotten more riled about Hooley's tone than he wanted to admit, so it was just as well that Annie Mae was leaving the kitchen . . . just as well that he was dealing with bowls of putrid food covered in fuzzy green and white mold. Holding his breath, Adam dumped mashed potatoes, creamed corn, stuffing, cranberry sauce . . . what a feast they'd had here, and what a shame that the situation with Hiram had blown up in their faces while they'd been eating it. Ira and Luke had mentioned the scene their former bishop had made, and how every last person around the table had refused to join him in Higher Ground—

And what'll Hiram do if he finds out you've been in his house, helping his daughter take that sewing machine?

Adam decided he couldn't be concerned about that right now. He slid the empty serving dishes into the hot, soapy water to soak, and then scraped the plates . . . keeping himself too busy to consider the consequences of this unexpected evening alone with Annie Mae. He was relieved when she set a box filled with fabric near the back door and then went right to the sink to wash the dishes. No chitchat to get him further involved with her . . . no eye contact to distract him as he dumped the desserts into the barrel and gradually stacked the rest of the dishes and glasses beside her. It seemed like a pretty good system as they worked together in a companionable silence—until Annie Mae flashed him a tremulous smile.

"This is a big load off my mind, gettin' rid of this mess," she said softly. "I'd be havin' nightmares about mice and maybe even rats gettin' in here to eat this stuff. You're a *gut* man, Adam. A real *gut* friend . . . Short Stack."

As she turned back toward the sink, her giggle made his heart skip like a stone across a pond—*jah, and it'll sink right to the bottom, too,* he warned himself. Her nickname should have galled him, yet he fought a smile as he carried the last double handful of silverware to the sink. "Nice of you to remind me of my *short*comings, Annie Mae. Sets me straight about where I stand."

The gurgle of draining water accompanied her look of utter dismay as she gazed down at him. "Oh, Adam, I never meant to make ya feel bad about—"

"Not a chance," he insisted as he took up a dish towel. "I *am* short, compared to you—and most every girl I know. We Amish are to strive for humility, so my height's a built-in reminder that I'll always be a lesser man than—"

"I did *not* mean it that way!" Annie Mae placed her wet hands on his shoulders and shook him firmly. "You can stop puttin' yourself down right this minute, too. There's a difference between humility and whinin'— and I won't tolerate your whinin'. Get over yourself."

As she gazed directly into his eyes, Adam knew it was time to be quiet—not that he could think of a single comeback. He hadn't meant to whine. He was just stating the obvious—most girls looked right over his head and never really saw him.

But though there was no escaping Annie Mae's meaning, he didn't intend to let her have the last word, either. Matthias's wife had ruled the roost with her opinions and emotional outbursts, and Adam wasn't going to fall into that same trap. "While I'm getting over myself, you can get over me, too, Annie Mae," he said quietly. "If you think you can pick up with me where you left off with Hooley, think again."

Her mouth formed a perfect little *O*, and she looked like she might cry again. But then she took her hands off him and began to run fresh dishwater. "Fair enough. Guess I got my licks in and so did you. Not that I'm keepin' score."

Adam chortled at the way Annie Mae kept coming at him without missing a beat. His chuckle escalated into full-scale laughter when Annie Mae began laughing, too. "Makes us even-up, then. But you women *do* keep score—"

"*Jah,* and Luke Hooley's a loser, no matter how ya look at it," she said in a more serious tone. "Time for me to move on . . . to concentrate on takin' care of Nellie and me instead of fallin' for his come-ons. The way I used to."

Adam considered this as he stood beside her, drying plates. Instead of bemoaning her responsibilities, Annie Mae was facing them—and for a girl who wasn't yet eighteen, she'd acquired more than her share. It was the only decent thing to do, helping her tonight. He was just being a friend when she needed one.

As she put away the dishes, Adam set around a few mousetraps he'd found in the mudroom. "Will you be okay here while I get my wagon?" he asked. "Between the two of us, we can load your sewing machine and then set it in Ben's smithy until you figure out where ya want it, *jah*?"

"*Denki* for makin' this a whole lot easier," she murmured gratefully. "You *are* a *gut* man, Adam. And that's the long and the *short* of it."

Chapter Seven

It was pitch-black, only four o'clock, when Annie Mae slipped into the back door of the Sweet Seasons kitchen the next morning. For a moment she lingered in the comfort of the dim lights, soaking up the homey warmth and the heavenly aroma of Miriam's daily baking—the perfect antidote to the troubling dreams she'd had during her fitful night's sleep. Just breathing deeply . . . just the sight of Miriam rolling out dough for piecrusts set Annie Mae to rights again.

Miriam turned and smiled. "You're up way before the chickens, Annie Mae," she said cheerfully. "I'm guessin' you've figured out that early morning's the best time to think your best thoughts while ya work, ain't so?"

Annie Mae hung her coat on a peg beside the door and then washed her hands. "That's when I could get a few things done at home, too—before the kids were up," she replied. "And it's better than wakin' Nellie and Rhoda with my tossin' and turnin'."

"Ah. There's that—although I think my Ben could sleep through a tornado." Miriam turned back to her dough, rolling out circles of the pastry with quick precision . . . waiting for Annie Mae to explain why she hadn't slept well. It was a strategy Annie Mae recognized, and she felt compelled to confide in Miriam, knowing her thoughts and secrets would go no farther than these sunny yellow walls.

"What can I help ya with?" Annie Mae asked as she glanced at the pans along the back counter. "My word, you've already baked all these Danish and breads and cupcakes?"

"It's my therapy." Miriam met her gaze then, with deep brown eyes that glimmered with patience and wisdom. "The squabblin' between Ben and his brothers yesterday got me wound up. I suspect we've not heard the last of it."

Had Miriam read her mind? Spotting the big bowl of apples in the sink, Annie Mae picked up a paring knife. "Well, ya won't be seein' me with Luke anymore, because I told him to hit the road. When we left your place, I asked him to run me by the house to see if the sewing machine was still there—"

Miriam's eyes widened. "And how did *that* go? How did the house look?"

"—and you'd've thought I asked him to move every stick of furniture there," Annie Mae fumed. "Honestly, I wonder what I ever saw in him. *Pigheaded* doesn't begin to describe that man!"

As Miriam arranged crusts in pie pans, she chuckled. "Now don't take this wrong, honey-bug," she murmured, "but I always figured that you and Luke dated mostly to get your *dat*'s goat. And now that your *dat*'s not around, maybe the goat's not so much fun to chase after, either."

Annie Mae's knife stopped halfway around a large,

red apple. This woman certainly had a way of nailing a situation. "I . . . hadn't thought about it that way."

"Of course not. We seldom see ourselves the way other folks do—and we girls refuse to believe that a fella we're sweet on is all wrong for us, even when folks we trust tell us so."

Annie Mae let this observation soak in as she sliced the apple into the bowl and began to peel another one. How many times had her *dat* and plenty of other people told her that Luke was too old for her? Yet she'd grabbed at every chance to sneak out with him. . . .

"I'm glad ya broke it off with him," Miriam murmured. "While he's Ben's brother and a smart fella when it comes to his business, I can't admire a man who talked the way he did about our preachers yesterday. He's either in or he's out, far as the church goes— and Luke's pretty much announced where he stands by bein' unbaptized at thirty."

Annie Mae nodded, but breaking up with Luke still felt like a freshly scraped knee. It was a good time to discuss something less personal. "Um, the sewing machine is sittin' in the corner of Ben's smithy, because I didn't know where else to put it. What with Nellie's dresses lookin' so short and snug—"

"*Gut* for you, takin' care of your sister." Miriam gazed at her then, obviously curious about the sewing machine story. "Not a lot of room in that loft apartment, what with you two girls and Rhoda bunkin' up there. I could have Ben set it up in our spare room downstairs. You could come over and use it anytime, honey-bug."

"But I never meant to take up space at your—"

"Ah, but if we put your machine at my place, I could

sew on it, too," Miriam pointed out. "I left mine at the house where Rachel and Micah are livin', ya see. Seems like a practical answer for both of us, ain't so?"

How did this woman arrive at the best solutions so easily? Annie Mae released the tension in her shoulders. "That's more than fair—and mighty generous of ya," she murmured. "It was Mamm's machine. . . ."

Before she knew it, Annie Mae was pouring out the story of going to the house, and how Luke had gotten so testy, and how Adam had helped her clear away the mess on the table before he'd driven her back to the apartment. Miriam listened attentively as she trimmed the bottom crusts for ten pies. It felt so good to talk with an older woman—one who understood the complications of dating and raising a family and . . . a *mother,* much like the one Annie Mae had lost when she was only eleven. And because Miriam had been at the house for that fateful Second Christmas dinner, she knew why everyone had left before the meal was over.

As they stirred brown sugar, grated lemon rind, cinnamon, and lemon juice into the bowl of apple slices, Annie Mae got a sudden inspiration. "Do ya think I could give one of these pies to Adam? I'd pay ya for—"

"Oh no, you won't!" A little grin overtook Miriam's face. "If any fella has earned a pie, it's Adam. And nobody would appreciate it more, what with him and Matthias scrapin' by as bachelors. Let's make his with a lattice top, so it looks extra-special."

By the time they got the pies into the oven, Rhoda and Rebecca came in to set up the dining room. Soon Naomi and Hannah arrived, as well, and the Sweet Seasons was filled with the aromas of sizzling bacon, simmering chicken, and the hamburger and onions they were frying for the soup and the beef-and-bean stew on the lunch menu. The café's morning routine had become second nature to Annie Mae, and when Bishop Tom arrived just ahead of the Brenneman and Kanagy brothers, she took their orders and poured their coffee as though she'd been doing it all her life.

The Waglers came in, as well, and while Matthias went straight to the buffet behind Seth and Aaron, Adam remained at his table. Annie Mae knew the menu well enough now that she seldom wore Adam's glasses, but she kept them in her apron . . . ran her hand over the ridge they made in her pocket as she greeted him. "Havin' the *short* stack, ham, and eggs over easy?" she teased. "I'll get your tea right out."

When Adam smiled at her, she noticed that he'd washed his dark brown hair and combed it a little differently, back over his ears—not that he'd done it for *her,* of course. "Got any baked oatmeal this morning? Maybe with some fruit?"

"*Jah.* We've got warm peaches, or bananas, or—"

"Perfect, both of those. And so you won't think I'm eating too healthy, I'll want syrup to drizzle all over that, please."

Well, this was a switch. As Annie Mae strode to the kitchen to place his order, she reminded herself that folks tried something different every now and again. And the baked oatmeal really was tasty—a lot like a moist, fruity coffeecake. Did Adam seem extremely cheerful this morning, or was she reading more into his mood than she should? She filled a teapot with boiling water, dropped in two tea bags, and then headed back to his table to tell him how she and Miriam had worked out her sewing machine dilemma.

When the bell above the door jingled, the man entering the café riveted Annie Mae with a gaze that stopped her in her tracks. As he removed his black coat and broad-brimmed hat, he looked familiar, and yet—

Oh my stars, it's Dat . . . but he's trimmed his beard close to his face and—and he's cut his hair English-style and colored it black!

The whole place suddenly got quiet.

Rhoda and Rebecca, who'd been waiting on a few tables of English guests, exchanged a glance and then looked at Annie Mae. Rebecca put on a smile and breezed over to greet their unexpected guest. "Good morning, Hiram. Sit wherever—"

"*Is* it?" he challenged, his gaze never wavering from Annie Mae. "I prefer to give my order to your new waitress."

Unruffled, Rebecca gestured around the dining room. "Sit anywhere you like then. I'll be right there with your coffee."

Annie Mae's knees turned to jelly and her mind went blank. She tried to tell herself this was no different from when she'd put her father's breakfast on the table at home—but she didn't believe that and neither would her *dat*. And he *would* have to sit at the same table as the Waglers. She set Adam's teapot on the front counter so she wouldn't drop it on somebody and scald them.

"*Gut* morning, Hiram," Adam said as he scooted his chair over to make more room. "You've saved me a phone call by coming—"

"You'll get your turn after I order my breakfast—if

the waitress will ever come to the table," her father replied tersely.

Somehow Annie Mae got her feet to move. She gripped her order pad as though she were hanging on to her last thread of rational thought. Dat sounded testy, and she could think of several reasons why. "*Gut* morning, Dat. What can I get ya?" she asked in the strongest voice she could muster.

He looked her over as though he was trying to find fault with her dress or her *kapp*. "A ham and cheese omelet with hash browns—and then an explanation for why you've been to the house when I told you not to return until you'd begged my forgiveness."

He did *have one of his security cameras set up in the kitchen and*—

Annie Mae swallowed hard, willing her body not to shake. "I'll be right back with that," she rasped. She fled toward the kitchen, wishing she could keep right on going through the back door, never to return. But that wasn't the answer. She would have to face her *dat*—have to take her licks rather than leaving Miriam to deal with him.

"What's the matter, child? Ya look like you've seen a ghost," Naomi said when Annie Mae got to the cookstove.

"Dat's here," she rasped.

As one, Miriam, Naomi, and Hannah stared out into the dining room. "Are my eyes goin' bad, or are we talkin' about the fella sittin' beside Adam?" Naomi whispered.

"What's Hiram up to, cuttin' his beard and hair and dyin' them black?" Miriam muttered. "He was the first to say how *evil* it was when my Rebecca first showed up here with her colored hair."

Annie Mae exhaled loudly. "He—he wants a ham and cheese omelet with hash browns. Not to mention my explanation for goin' over to the house last night."

Miriam removed her oven mitts and smoothed her apron. "Looks like a *gut* time for me to chat with our breakfast guests," she said matter-of-factly. "I don't know what's keepin' Ben, but we'll handle it. What with Tom and the younger fellas—and God—bein' here with us, we'll help ya settle this right off, honey-bug."

Annie Mae sighed. Though it was a wonderful thing to have Miriam and everyone else in the Sweet Seasons pulling for her, her *dat* would make a point of humiliating her even more, saying she couldn't face him by herself. And then he would light into the rest of them for supporting her.

But she couldn't worry about that right now. She picked up the teapot with the two tags dangling from it and focused on Adam as she followed Miriam from the kitchen.

Please, God, Ya gotta help me, she prayed. *Ya gotta help us all.*

Her father was gazing sternly at Adam. "I called you yesterday with an offer of work and you didn't respond," he said archly. "That's very rude. Very unprofessional."

"Matthias and I were visiting our sister's family in Clark all day," Adam replied with a shrug. "Didn't get your message until last night, and since it was *Sunday* I figured to call you first thing after breakfast today.

I'm sorry, but I can't help you, Hiram. I've got jobs lined up—"

"*Jah,* Adam's workin' with us on the new clinic for the next few weeks," Seth Brenneman chimed in as he set his loaded plate on the table beside Adam's.

"And after that he's makin' repairs and paintin' the whole inside of my place," Bishop Tom spoke up from his table in the corner. "I'm gettin' the house freshened up before Nazareth and I get hitched next month, ya see."

As Annie Mae set Adam's teapot next to him, she managed to return his smile even as her father glared at the men who'd spoken to him.

"I can't think you'll pass up what *I'll* pay you, when your work in Willow Ridge could wait a few weeks," Hiram insisted as he looked purposefully into Adam's eyes. "As I told you, we have new residents coming from Indiana and Ohio, expecting the finished homes I promised them."

Adam took his time pouring a cup of his tea. "And I've told *you,*" he said quietly, "that I'm already committed to—"

"Thicker than thieves, the lot of you," her father snapped. Then he looked up at Annie Mae. "And you've lowered yourself to waiting tables now? That, and breaking into the house to *steal* things?"

"She's doin' honest work, supportin' herself and her sister, Hiram," Miriam said as she topped off his coffee. "She wants to sew Nellie some dresses on her *mamm's* machine—"

"And we cleaned up that spoiled food you left on the table, before rats and coons overran the place," Adam said in a voice that resonated with disdain.

"You've got about two days' worth of propane left before your heat goes off. Why you're ranting at Annie Mae instead of looking after your property is beyond me, Hiram."

"Quite frankly, it's none of your business," her father retorted as he smacked the table with his hand. "Did you think I wouldn't see those footprints in the dust—the wagon tracks in the driveway? If I find other things missing, I'll know who to report to the police."

Miriam set her coffee carafe on the table with a loud *thunk*. "That's the most outlandish—well, I can see ya haven't picked up any pointers in the parenting department, Hiram. If ya think I'm gonna let ya rail at Annie Mae in front of my other customers—"

Her father rose to his feet so fast, his chair fell backward. "You, woman, have *no* place telling *me* what to—"

The bell above the door jangled just as Bishop Tom and Matthias were coming toward the table, ready to defend Miriam in this escalating confrontation. Annie Mae wanted to find a hole to hide in. Why did Dat always have to cause a scene and suck everyone else into it? To make matters worse, a uniformed police officer was walking in, looking around the dining room as though someone here was in big trouble. Had her *dat* arranged for this fellow to show up and scare them all? Or to arrest her and Adam for being inside the house?

"Excuse me, folks," the officer said loudly, "but I'm looking for the owner of that black Cadillac parked by the door."

Once again the dining room got quiet. Her father stopped pointing his finger at Miriam and turned toward the policeman. "Officer McClatchey," he said in a congenial voice. "I hope you've not come to report that someone has hit my car or—"

"No, sir, Mr. Knepp. I couldn't help but notice that you're parked in the space designated for handicapped drivers," the policeman replied in a businesslike voice. "And I didn't see the appropriate blue and white placard in your car."

Her *dat* straightened to his full height. "All the parking slots are filled—mostly with buggies," he added under his breath, "so I had no choice but to—"

"No, sir, I parked on the other side of the quilting shop, where there are several spots," Officer McClatchey stated. "According to the law—and clearly stated on the sign—there's a fine ranging from fifty to two hundred dollars for parking in that space if you're not handicapped. I'll have to write you a ticket."

Somehow Annie Mae kept from gaping. She wasn't surprised her father was driving the car that had gotten him excommunicated from the Willow Ridge district, but why had he ignored the blue and white sign by the door? Miriam, Tom, and the other fellows were sharing looks that suggested they, too, were curious about the situation—and pleased to see this officer enforcing the law.

When Adam winked at her, Annie Mae sensed her luck might take a turn for the better. Yet Adam couldn't possibly have called the policeman. . . .

"A ticket won't be necessary," her father insisted. "I'll simply move my car—"

"Sorry," Officer McClatchey said as he pulled a notepad from his back pocket. "I must assess the fine whenever I see a violation of—"

"Let's you and I step outside and settle this," her father said as he took the policeman's arm. "I'm sure we can come to terms about—"

The policeman stepped back, removing his arm from her *dat*'s grasp. "If you refuse to comply, Mr. Knepp, I'll have to arrest you—and from the way you were harassing Miriam when I came in, I can add 'disturbing the peace' to the charges. Need I go on?" he asked impatiently. "You'll pay the fine, as anyone would be expected to. You're not above the law, *sir.*"

Her *dat*'s intake of breath nearly sucked all the air from the dining room. Annie Mae could see it on everyone's faces: Hiram Knepp indeed believed that he could sidestep the rules, or pay his way out of them, and folks were glad to see this man in the blue uniform holding him accountable.

Oh, but her father despised losing, or being made a fool of. His mouth was a tight line as he reached into the back pocket of his pants—

Since when do Plain fellas wear Lee jeans? Annie Mae wondered when she noticed the label.

"Fine," her *dat* spat as he dug into his wallet. "Here's the fifty dollars—"

"Your ticket's for a hundred," Officer McClatchey replied as he continued writing on his pad. "Had you not given me so much backlash, we could've settled this matter for less, but—"

"*A hundred dollars?* That's highway robbery!" her father blurted. "You have no right to—"

"Ah, but I do—and I could make it two hundred. Or we could go to the station, where you'd have the *right* to call your attorney and then wait for him in a jail cell." The officer stood firm, returning her father's angry sneer with an unruffled expression. "I'm sorry all these other folks have had to witness this situation as their breakfasts get cold, sir. But I'm fully aware of the wheeling and dealing you and Conrad Hammond have engaged in since I assisted with your sons' sleighing accident. Don't think you can bribe me to look away and pretend none of these things ever happened."

The Sweet Seasons rang with silence as everyone in the dining room watched the two men with a sense of fascinated expectation on their faces. Muttering, with anger stiffening his every move, her father reached into his wallet again and then threw some money on the table.

"I'm leaving—but I'm not finished with *any* of you," he said as he glared at Miriam, Bishop Tom, Adam— and then at Annie Mae. "The wages of sin is death. Not even Jesus can save you if you're burning in eternal damnation." Out the door he stalked, slamming it so hard, the windowpanes rattled.

Officer McClatchey picked up the money, smiling grimly at Miriam. "I'm sorry we caused such a commotion during your breakfast rush, but—"

"No, no," Miriam insisted as she gestured toward the place Hiram had just vacated. "We're mighty grateful ya showed up when ya did. Your breakfast is on me this mornin', sir. Maybe ya don't know it, but Hiram's no longer our bishop—"

"We're not usually so confrontational," Bishop Tom joined in, "but we believe he's gonna cause trouble whenever he can. We've got to watch out for Annie Mae here, and her sister Nellie—Hiram's two older girls—on account of how they walked out on him rather than goin' to that new colony he's started over past Morning Star."

Outside, they heard a revved-up engine and the loud screech of tires on the blacktop. The policeman's eyebrows rose as he sat down at the Waglers' table. "I'd heard a new Amish group was starting out there—"

"Oh, don't go callin' him Amish," the bishop insisted. "This is the first we've seen Hiram with his hair all cut off, drivin' his car right to our doors. The Old Order has excommunicated him, so he's not welcome in Willow Ridge unless he asks our forgiveness and changes his ways back to ours."

"Well, I don't see *that* happening." Officer McClatchey sighed, looking up at Annie Mae then, an expression of great compassion on his face. "I'm sorry all this is happening, dear. And how are your twin brothers doing now?"

How was it that when folks were being their nicest, it was hardest to accept their support? Annie Mae closed her eyes, willing herself not to cry. "I . . . I wish I knew," she murmured. "We don't know who's lookin' after them or—and I don't dare go over to Higher Ground to see for myself."

"I'd stay away from there, yes," the policeman confirmed. A pensive expression settled over his face then. "I'll give Clyde Banks—the sheriff in that district—a heads-up about what's going on, because I have no jurisdiction there."

The back door to the kitchen closed with a *whump* and everyone looked up to see Ben Hooley striding toward the dining room with an odd smile on his face. "By the way Hiram took out of here just now, I take it he was none too happy to see ya, Officer McClatchey," he remarked as he slipped out of his coat.

"You called me at just the right time," the policeman said as he stood to shake Ben's hand. "As you suspected, Hiram was in here stirring up trouble."

"*You* called him, Ben?" Miriam chirped as she threw her arms around him. "I was wonderin' why ya hadn't come in for your breakfast—"

"That black Cadillac could only belong to one fella." Ben noisily bussed Miriam's cheek and then looked at Annie Mae. "You all right? Sorry to say, I figured your *dat* might've come to spit some of his vinegar at you."

Annie Mae nodded, once again fearing she might burst into tears. "*Jah,* I'll make it. Tell ya what, though, I'm gonna take a little break. Be back in a few."

"Take as long as ya need, honey-bunch," Miriam called after her as she hurried past Naomi and Hannah, through the kitchen.

Grabbing her coat from the back wall, Annie Mae wondered what to do with all the emotions welling up inside her. When she'd seen her *dat* looking so—so *English*—she'd sensed she was in big trouble. And now that he knew she'd been inside the house, he'd keep closer track of her. Where would she be without Miriam and Ben and Bishop Tom and Adam taking her side?

Annie Mae stepped outside into the brisk winter air, where tiny snowflakes swirled in the breeze. It was so blessedly quiet out here . . . so peaceful. She looked out over the parking lot full of buggies and cars to Ben's smithy, and then on down the long lane to the Lantz home, where Rachel and Micah Brenneman lived now that they were married. She closed her eyes, seeing a different white house. How she missed stepping out of her home on Bishop's Ridge to hang out the laundry or to get an idea where the kids might be . . .

But I'll never live there again. Everything's changed, and I've got to change, too . . . got to be strong, because Dat*'s not nearly finished with me.*

Annie Mae inhaled deeply to settle her racing pulse. When she opened her eyes, it was Adam's remodeling wagon she saw, with Jerry hitched to the post in front of it. Big and boxy-looking, the vehicle was painted royal blue with dark yellow lettering that said WAGLER REMODELING, with PAINTING, PAPERING & REPAIRS and Adam's phone number on the next lines.

She slipped back into the kitchen then, to tuck his lattice-crust apple pie into a bakery box. Everyone in the dining room was chatting happily, so no one noticed what she was doing.

As Annie Mae returned to the parking lot and stepped onto the running board of Adam's wagon, she was glad she'd set aside one of these fragrant apple pies for him. It was still slightly warm and radiated the rich scents of cinnamon with a hint of lemon. Adam had come to her defense today—had put himself in her *dat*'s line of fire when he could've stayed out of it.

Denki for that, Short Stack, she thought as she set the box in the center of the driver's seat. He was still only a friend—but he was a mighty fine one.

Chapter Eight

Adam stepped up into his wagon and stared at the flat, white box on his seat. Without opening it, he knew it contained something wonderfully delicious because the inside of his vehicle smelled like Miriam's kitchen.

So this is why Annie Mae took a break . . . .

But he dared not assume the poor girl had really had *him* in mind when she'd left the dining room, nearly in tears. Adam was impressed that she had returned to work this morning. By the time he and Matthias had scooted their chairs under the table, she was at the checkout counter ringing up Bishop Tom's bill and boxing some fresh pastries out of the display case for an English couple. Annie Mae was a tough cookie on the outside, even if he suspected she was more like a cream puff inside—especially after what her *dat* had dished up today.

Adam clapped the reins on Jerry's back and headed toward the day's job of refinishing an oak floor. If things worked out the way he hoped, he could sand it and stain it today, return tomorrow to seal it, and then work on Andy Leitner's clinic. *And I thank You, Lord, that these Willow Ridge jobs will keep me busy with folks I respect, who'll pay me an honest day's wage.*

Adam blinked. While he attended church regularly, he didn't pray a lot on his own . . . hadn't had anyone to remind him or persuade him to pray, after Mamm died. So thanking God out of the blue caught him by surprise and would give him one more thing to think about—in addition to Hiram Knepp's appearance and ulterior motives—as he worked on that hardwood floor. . . .

As Jerry clip-clopped past Hiram's abandoned home that evening, Adam glanced at the Knepp place but kept on going. He'd done the decent thing, helping Annie Mae and checking the propane tank's level, but he was staying out of that family's affairs now. After a strenuous day of sanding and staining, all he wanted was a quiet night at home . . . and another slice of that fabulous apple pie that tasted like nothing he'd ever put in his mouth.

Adam chuckled as he pulled his horse to a halt outside the barn. Matthias was going to rub him good for eating half of that pie already, but he didn't care— Annie Mae had given it to *him,* after all. As he fed and watered the horses, Adam allowed his mind to wander to the tall, slender girl he'd known all his life but had only recently *seen.* If he asked Annie Mae, would she go out with him? Especially now that she'd given Luke Hooley the boot?

And why would you want to get that started? Sooner or later, you'll be a major disappointment to a girl like Annie

*Mae, because she likes wild excitement . . . running the roads
and looking for trouble. She said so herself—even though she
also said she was finished with that sort of thing.*

Adam turned. Like a magnet, the motorcycle in the
back stall drew him . . . coaxed him to remove the tarp
and take a good hard look at *temptation.* The shiny
black fenders, red accents, silver studs, and the sleek
black helmet on the seat seemed like something the
Devil himself had designed—which was exactly why
Adam had gotten a cycle license and acquired this
sleek machine when he'd been sixteen. For a very
brief time during his *rumspringa,* he'd known all about
running the roads, looking for trouble.

And he'd found it. And his mother had died because
of it.

Just as Mamm hadn't had any idea about this motorcycle he'd hidden away at a friend's house, nobody
else knew the awful, exact details of how her buggy
had raced into the intersection where the county
blacktop crossed the highway . . . the heavy secret he
couldn't bear to confess because he'd been young and
scared—

"Ya really ought to sell that thing," Matthias said
from behind him. "Not doin' it any *gut* to sit there and
get rusty as time goes by."

Adam nearly jumped out of his skin. He'd been so
absorbed in his memories that he hadn't heard his
brother enter the barn—and he didn't want to let on
about how those memories still haunted him, either.
"*Jah,* you're right. What with Hiram hiding that
Cadillac in his garage—and now driving it around in
front of God and everybody—I'm not much better
than he is if I've still got this cycle tucked away," he

agreed. "But I don't have the first clue about where to sell it, or—"

"Ask Rebecca. She could probably get on her computer and find all sorts of fellas lookin' for a wicked-*gut* ride like this one." Matthias ran his hand over the cycle's black leather seat, which was outlined with red leather piping and steel studs. "And ya traded a *horse* for this mean machine?"

Adam shrugged. "It wasn't the smartest deal I've ever made, but you *knew* I'd swapped Jake for something else. And since I'd bought him with my own money, and I was getting into *rumspringa* then, Dat didn't fuss about my gelding being gone."

"Somebody must've been desperate."

"Remember Allen Stoltzfus, Yonnie's cousin?"

Matthias frowned, thinking back. "The one who got two girls in trouble but could only marry one of them?"

"He suddenly needed a *gut* horse a lot more than he needed this motorcycle—which he told me had driven him straight to the Devil." Adam sighed a little louder than he intended to. "And Allen was willing to stash it away for me at his place . . . so Mamm and Dat wouldn't find out."

And that's all you're going to say about that.

Matthias cleared his throat to cover a laugh. "*Jah*, well, we all had our little secrets," he teased. "That's what our runnin'-around time is about. And because you were the little brother with the big mouth, I never let on about the smokin' and drinkin' I did with a couple of English friends who thought it was pretty hilarious to lead a backward, backwoods Amish kid astray."

Adam raised his eyebrows. "So that explains the

times you slipped out of church to puke around back of the house?"

"Uh-huh. Dat knew what was goin' on, but he also knew better than to say anything to Mamm. He figured I'd get sick enough—or smart enough—to stop such foolishness eventually."

"So what brought you around?" Adam decided to enjoy these moments of confession while Matthias was in the mood to share them; these recollections of his brother's *rumspringa* were putting him in a much better frame of mind.

"Sadie." Matthias sighed, yet he didn't plunge into the black pit his late wife's name usually opened up. "She was a sweet girl, lookin' for a fella to take her away from a heavy-handed *dat*. So I gave up the English sins and brought her home with me."

Adam recalled their whirlwind courtship—although it wasn't all that unusual for Amish young people to get engaged before either of them had met the other's family. It *was* the more normal thing for newlyweds to live with the girl's parents for a year or so, but now Adam understood why Sadie and Matthias had stayed here with them. "Truth be told, the folks would've been in a bind if you'd moved to Windsor, what with Dat having his heart attack not long after that."

Matthias again ran his hand over the motorcycle's seat and then stepped back to openly admire the vehicle. "I'm no expert, but somethin' tells me this cycle's old enough to be *worth* somethin'. Anything *vintage* is a big deal these days, and this ride's got some fine style to it," he said emphatically. "Any man would understand why ya wanted to go joyridin' down the country roads on it. The question is, why'd ya stop?"

Adam looked his brother squarely in the eye. "I joined the church."

"That could've waited a while. You were barely seventeen—"

"It felt like the right thing to do after Mamm's buggy wreck, all right?" Adam quickly draped the tarp over the motorcycle and then grabbed the lantern handle. "So what'd ya throw together for our dinner? I brought home a real tasty dessert from the Sweet Seasons. Actually saved some for you."

Matthias got a startled look on his face. "Rats! I left it cookin' on the stove!"

As his brother sprinted out the barn door, Adam wished again that Mamm hadn't raced out to fetch Ruth on that fateful day . . . wished his *dat* had let Matthias call the ambulance when he'd felt the first chest pains . . . wished that Sadie and her unborn child hadn't died during her asthma attack.

But what good were wishes, when they never seemed to come true?

Chapter Nine

"Well, here it is the first Friday night of February and I haven't read *The Budget* from the end of January yet." Ben chuckled as he settled beside Miriam on the sofa. "Sounds like quite a hot date for us, ain't so?"

Miriam leaned against him and kissed his cheek. His new beard was getting long enough to be soft instead of bristly, and she loved nuzzling it. "It's the perfect night to stay in by the fire," she replied. "And isn't it a treat, hearin' Rebecca and the Knepp sisters chatterin' like magpies, havin' a little sewin' frolic in the spare room?"

Ben glanced toward the doorway where the girls were as he picked up the newspaper. "Annie Mae surely must miss goin' out with fellas on the weekends."

"She's learnin' that workin' on her feet all day, all week long, can take some of that run-around out of ya," Miriam replied. "Could be she feels safer stayin' tucked away with us, too, instead of bein' out where Hiram might meet up with her. His visit to the Sweet Seasons spooked her."

For a few moments they read in comfortable silence

as Miriam rested her head on Ben's shoulder, holding one side of the paper while he held the other. *The Budget* was made up of page after page of letters from the Amish and Mennonite settlements all around the country. She and Ben first read the reports from towns where they had family and friends, before glancing at the scribes' letters from other areas. Ben had just turned a page to read about his home district in Lancaster County when he let out a gasp.

"And what do we have here? A report from Higher Ground, Missouri!" he said, jabbing the page with his finger.

Miriam sat straight up, scanning to the bottom of the column. "Written by a scribe named Delilah Knepp," she murmured. "Ohhh, Ben, are ya thinkin' what I'm thinkin'? There's nobody but Hiram livin' there yet, ain't so?"

"We don't know that for a fact," he pointed out. "But obviously some gal named Delilah is there, too. Truth be told, when I saw what Hiram had done to his hair, I figured he was fishin' for his next wife."

"Well, he's gotta have somebody to watch those four little kids," she remarked sadly. "Who knows what he might've told this Delilah gal to get her to marry him?"

"Who says he's married to her? Lots of Knepps live over past Morning Star, and he might've convinced one of his cousins or aunts to keep the kids while he latches on to a wife," Ben speculated. "And he's havin' her write up a weekly letter so it looks like the town's all set up. Nothin' about that man surprises me anymore."

They both read the column for a moment before Ben spoke again. "Hmmm . . . says here they've got fifteen new homes and the school completed, plus a dry goods store and other shops. Quite a pitch here, for more folks to come to his new colony. Still time for us to sign on, honey-girl."

"Puh! I'm guessin' Higher Ground's gonna be a cesspool of surprises and all manner of deceptions in the fine print, which unsuspectin' new residents will learn about the hard way." Miriam shook her head. "You'll notice the letter's heading doesn't say it's an Amish or a Mennonite settlement—so who knows what sort of *religion* he intends to preach? We need to keep Josh, Joey, Sara, and Timmy in our prayers."

"I see no need to show this to Annie Mae and Nellie." Ben glanced toward the open door of the spare room as a burst of girlish laughter erupted. "They'll find out soon enough what-all's goin' on with their *dat.*"

"No point in spoilin' the fun they're havin' with Rebecca," Miriam agreed. "It's real special to me that my English daughter's gettin' to be such *gut* friends with the Knepp girls, since Rhoda's so busy helpin' the Leitners pack up and Rachel's gettin' ready for a baby. Now that Millie Glick's livin' with her grandparents, she's not gettin' out with Annie Mae like she used to, either."

"*Jah,* it all works out. God's bein' *gut* to each of us—most especially to me." Ben leaned into her, kissing her firmly on the lips. "The girls can entertain themselves, so any time ya feel like goin' upstairs—"

A burst of jazzy music signaled that Rebecca's cell phone was ringing, and then she stepped out of the spare room to take the call. Rebecca waved at them and remained at the far end of the front room so she wouldn't disturb them. "Well, hello there, Adam," she said in a low voice. "I wondered when you'd call—let me get my laptop and see what we can find."

Miriam chuckled. It was different, having a girl who carried a cell phone and did her work from a flip-top computer, but she respected this daughter for her skills. It wouldn't be long before Rebecca was situated as Andy Leitner's receptionist and had her website designing office in the upstairs of the building he was renovating, so Miriam was enjoying this time while her third daughter lived in their *dawdi haus*.

A few moments later Rebecca had her computer up and running on the kitchen table. "And you say it's an Indian . . . a Chief?" she murmured.

It looked awkward to Miriam, the way Rebecca held her phone between her shoulder and her ear while she typed on her computer, but young people didn't seem to notice any discomfort when it came to being connected to their electronics.

"Got any more information on it?" she asked in a businesslike tone. "Like a date, or a model? Okay, so it's . . . black with a red edging around the seat . . . and Matthias says it's *vintage?*" For a few moments Rebecca focused on her screen as her fingers tapped the keyboard. Then her eyes got wide. "I just brought up a photograph of a motorcycle like you've described—a really hot-looking Indian Chief Roadmaster, fully restored, black all over, with silver stud decorations," she said in a rising voice. "Dates back to 1946—"

Miriam glanced at Ben. "What would the Waglers be doin' with a motorcycle?" she whispered.

Ben shrugged, gesturing for her to be quiet.

"Holy cow, Adam! If this is even close to what your cycle looks like, it's worth—well, before we get all excited, I need to come over and see it, to be sure we're on the same page," Rebecca suggested. "I'll need to take a picture of it anyway, if you want me to post an ad . . . yeah, if it needs to be cleaned up, you should do that first. But I would really like to *see* this motorcycle!"

About that time, Annie Mae and Nellie came out of the spare room, carrying their mugs. Miriam could tell by their expressions that they'd overheard Rebecca, and that curiosity as much as the desire for more cocoa was luring them into the kitchen. Without a word, Annie Mae slipped behind Rebecca to look at her computer screen. Her hand flew to her mouth and her eyes got wide.

"Yeah, I could be there in about ten minutes," Rebecca said. "Great. I'm on my way."

When she clicked off her phone, Annie Mae pointed toward the screen. "Did I hear ya right, that Adam's got a motorcycle? And it looks like *that*?"

Rebecca chuckled. "I'm going over there to see exactly what it looks like so I can help him sell it. Want to come along?"

"But—but Adam joined the church a long while back, after his *mamm* got killed," Nellie protested. "What would he be doin' with a—"

"And why didn't we know he had it?" Annie Mae asked incredulously. "Surely we would've seen him ridin' it, or—"

Rebecca shrugged as she folded the top of her computer down. "Come along and ask him yourself," she said. "I'm leaving as soon as I grab my coat and keys."

From where she sat on the couch, Miriam watched amazement, confusion, and doubt play over Annie Mae's face as she shook her head. "Well, this puts a whole new spin to the bottle, ain't so?" she murmured to Ben. "All these years we've thought Adam was tamer than most fellas—joinin' the church without havin' a girlfriend, even."

Ben glanced around his side of the newspaper to observe the scene in the kitchen. "Solid fella, though. And he did a fine job of finishin' out your new kitchen and paintin' our walls here."

"*Jah,* and Annie Mae's more interested in him than she wants to let on," Miriam murmured. "But she's heatin' more water for cocoa, it seems, instead of goin' along with Rebecca."

"Bye, Mamma. Good night, Ben," Rebecca called to them as she slipped into her bright yellow parka. "I won't be long."

"You're an adult, honey-girl," Ben replied as he waved to her. "Your comin' and goin' is your business."

"But I like it that ya keep us posted," Miriam chimed in. "We'll see ya in the morning."

"Bright and early to open the café," Rebecca replied. "Bye, girls."

"*Jah,* see ya tomorrow," Annie Mae called after her.

"*Gut* talkin' to ya while we sewed our dresses," said Nellie.

When Ben looked at Miriam, his eyes as warm and dark as hot fudge, her heart danced. It was easy to see what he had in mind now—and it had nothing to do with Higher Ground or motorcycles or the news from Lancaster. And wasn't it a fine way to end a winter's day, snuggling beneath the quilts with her handsome younger husband?

Ben folded the newspaper and they rose from the sofa together, clasping hands.

"Won't take us but fifteen minutes to finish the two dresses we've been workin' on," Annie Mae said as she and her sister emerged from the kitchen with their steaming mugs. "But we'll come back another time, if you'd rather—"

"Stay as long as ya want, girls," Miriam assured her. "Sounds like ya made some *gut* progress tonight."

"Leave the kitchen lamp burnin' for Rebecca," Ben suggested as he lit a lantern to take upstairs. "And give our best to Rhoda when she gets back to your apartment."

As the tattoo of Ben's boots on the wooden staircase quickened her heartbeat, Miriam felt a rush of desire. Her husband's affection was giving her a whole new outlook on life—the kind of love she hoped Rebecca and the Knepp girls would find for themselves someday. But as she and Ben entered their room, their faces lit by the lantern's glow, Miriam promptly forgot about everyone else.

If the lot fell to Ben on Sunday morning, would they sacrifice these delightful private times because he was learning how to serve the church as a new preacher? Miriam reached up to kiss him, determined to fully enjoy every moment of every day—and night—she shared with this wonderful man.

Chapter Ten

"As we begin our Members' Meeting, I'm especially blessed that my longtime friend, Bishop Vernon Gingerich, has come from Cedar Creek to be with us today," Bishop Tom announced to the folks who sat crowded on the pew benches. "What with needin' to select two new preachers, we welcome all the help and wise counsel God sends our way."

Ben's heart skittered. Not many men in Willow Ridge were eligible to become a preacher, so the odds that the lot would fall to him seemed high. He gazed across the Brennemans' expanded front room to catch Miriam's eye . . . to settle himself as she focused on him with her gentle, encouraging smile. What a blessing that such a stalwart, faithful woman was now his wife and helpmate.

"Before we proceed with the selection process," Bishop Gingerich said as he rose from the preachers' bench, "I'm delighted to announce that Jerusalem Hooley has agreed to become my wife. We'll be wed later in the spring—as soon as I can prepare my home to welcome her."

An excited "oh!" was followed by a buzz of voices as the men craned their necks and the women beamed at Ben's middle-aged aunt, who sat in their midst.

Ben chuckled. Aunt Jerusalem had glowed with a special radiance these past few weeks, so Vernon's announcement came as no surprise. This marriage marked yet another turning point for his family . . . another new beginning for someone he loved dearly. No one was happier than he that his two *maidel* aunts had found such upstanding mates, even though he would miss his more outspoken aunt once she moved away from Willow Ridge.

"Rest assured that Jerusalem's not gonna be gone or forgotten," Bishop Tom added with a boyish grin. "She and my Nazareth have already declared that our visiting Sundays will be spent in Cedar Creek, while Vernon and Jerusalem will bless us with their presence on *their* visiting Sundays, when we have church. Seems like a *gut* solution for both our districts and our families."

Tom clasped his hands before him then, assuming a more serious expression. "As all those who've not yet joined the church leave the room, I'd suggest that the rest of us pray over which two men should become our new leaders. Preacher Gabe'll be sittin' in the kitchen while each of ya file by to whisper a name to him. We've got six fellas to consider: Micah Brenneman and his *dat*, Ezra, Henry Zook, Dan Kanagy, Atlee Glick, and Ben Hooley."

Ben closed his eyes, aware of the movement in the crowded room as the unbaptized young people stepped outside with the children in tow. *Grant me Your grace and strength, Lord, should Your hand find my shoulder, and should You deem me fit to lead Your people,* he prayed. *And bless the other fella who fulfills Your will, as well.*

"It is indeed a sacred morning," Vernon continued in his mellow voice, "when the Lord will show us His presence in a very physical yet mystical way, as He selects two new preachers for Willow Ridge. Let us recall how this process originated, as described in the book of Acts, the first chapter, verses twenty-one through twenty-six."

All sat silent as the visiting bishop began to read from the big Bible. "'. . . and they appointed two, Joseph called Barsabas, who was surnamed Justus, and Matthias,'" Vernon said in his resonant voice. "'. . . Thou Lord, which knowest the hearts of all men, shew us whether of these two Thou hast chosen that he may take part in this ministry and apostleship . . . And the lot fell upon Matthias; and he was numbered with the eleven apostles.'"

As Preacher Gabe shuffled toward the kitchen with a pad of paper and a pencil, it became more apparent why he deserved to retire. He looked stooped and slow . . . encumbered with age and the burden of caring for his bedridden wife, even though his granddaughter Millie was now staying with them. Meanwhile, Micah Brenneman and Matthias Wagler brought a small table to the center of the crowded room where the preachers stood. Everyone had become very somber, knowing what a huge responsibility they were about to cast upon two of their members—and upon their families.

Beginning with the eldest, the men filed into the kitchen to name their choices. As Ben reached the kitchen table, he murmured, "Micah," because he felt Rachel's husband would serve the Lord and their district with fresh, youthful energy. He noticed the tally marks on Gabe's paper, but he had no way of knowing which row denoted votes for which of the candidates.

As the women filed into the kitchen, the tension in the room tightened a couple of notches. Naomi Brenneman, Miriam's sister Leah, and Lydia Zook appeared particularly anxious, knowing—and fearing—that the lot might fall upon their husbands. Rachel's eyes looked wide as she awaited her turn to rise, but as Miriam passed her daughter on her way down the aisle, they clasped hands. As though her mother's faith and reassurance had passed into her, Rachel closed her eyes in prayer.

As his Miriam returned to her pew, however, not a glimmer of doubt or fear registered on her lovely face. Before she sat down, his wife gazed directly at him, and Ben knew she had named him despite the sacrifices she would make, and the loss of income and time they would have together.

Ben released the breath he'd been holding. The tension left his body as he returned Miriam's gaze and reveled in her unshakable faith. For several moments—or was it only a few?—the crowd around them disappeared. It was only he and Miriam, connected by invisible, invincible ties; a love far deeper than he could ever have imagined enveloped him. Had there ever been anyone who so completely believed in him? When Miriam smiled, Ben felt God's blessings and joy fill his soul.

Soon Preacher Gabe was shuffling down the aisle toward Tom and Vernon, to reveal the names of the men who'd been mentioned the most. The bishops nodded solemnly, took up four hymnals, and then each of them slipped a handwritten Bible verse into a book. They laid the four books on the table, shuffling and shifting them so no one could possibly know which ones held the verses.

Bishop Tom gazed at the men's side of the crowded room. "Will these fellas please come forward as I call your names: Micah Brenneman, Ben Hooley, Dan Kanagy, and Henry Zook."

Gasps went up from the women's side, but as Ben rose from his pew he fastened his gaze on Miriam once more. Bolstered by the sense of peace radiating from his wife's face, he took his place at the table and then reached for an *Ausbund*. The house was so quiet, he heard the wind whistling through a crack in the window behind them . . . *the Holy Spirit coming amongst us,* he mused.

The bishops walked solemnly to the ends of the table. "We'll begin on this side," Tom said. "Let the pages of your book hang freely, high enough that all can see."

To Ben's left, young Micah looked pale and wide-eyed as he raised his hymnal in shaking hands. The pages whispered as he ran his thumbs along their edges, but nothing fell out. He exhaled with relief and then looked at Ben.

Ben slowly lifted his hymnal, aware that every eye was focused on him. When he let the pages shimmy, out fluttered a white slip of paper, almost like a dove. As he caught it in one hand, a murmur of approval filled the room.

Serve the Lord with gladness, he read silently. Ben smiled at Bishop Tom, pleased that he'd chosen the hymnal containing the verse penned in his friend's script.

Then the suspense intensified. The next lot would fall to either Dan Kanagy, who raised sheep, or to Henry Zook, their local butcher and storekeeper. Dan's boys, Nate and Bram, would soon marry and move away to their new acreage, which would leave their *dat* shorthanded enough that taking on a preacher's extra duties would be a strain on him and Leah. But then, Henry was raising a raft of kids, so the burdens of running Zook's Market and managing their large family would fall to Lydia when her husband was studying to take on his new post, or out seeing to the needs of the Willow Ridge district.

Dan exhaled and closed his eyes. He thrust his hymnal up and shook it between his hands—

A wail went up from the women's side. All the wives seated around Lydia Zook wrapped their arms around her as they murmured their support. Henry, at the end of the table, didn't even bother to raise his *Ausbund*. His head fell forward and he squeezed his eyes shut.

"'Thy will be done on Earth as it is in Heaven,'" Bishop Vernon intoned as he placed his hand on Henry's shaking shoulders. "'This is the Lord's doing, and it is marvelous in our eyes.'"

"And He has blessed us with two fine new preachers," Bishop Tom went on in an excited voice. "It'll be an honor to work with Ben and Henry as they prepare to serve our district. It's a journey we'll make together, fellas, what with me still bein' green as your bishop."

"But no man walks this road alone," Vernon reassured them. "I'll be here often to assist you, as will

Jeremiah Shetler and Enos Mullet from your neighboring districts. Today marks a strong new beginning for the Willow Ridge district, and I'm honored that God has made me a part of it." He paused to gaze at the crowd as though every person there was a close, personal friend. "Let's proceed now with the ordination service, and then we'll celebrate during our common meal."

Once again Ben found Miriam's gaze . . . saw how her eyes glowed with devotion and unshed tears of joy. A few pews in front of her, however, Lydia Zook was crying openly, her shoulders hunched and shaking as her friends consoled her. Henry's stiff expression didn't hide his doubts . . . his abject *fear,* as he gripped the edge of the table so hard his knuckles turned white.

"We'll share a moment of silent prayer before we ordain these men," Tom said.

As all heads bowed, Ben closed his eyes. *Give me Your grace and strength, Lord. Show us how to help Henry past his resistance to Your will . . .*

As Annie Mae lingered in the doorway of the Brennemans' carpentry shop, she watched Nellie and Katie Zook chatting with Hannah Brenneman while the three younger Zook kids built a snow fort with Taylor and Brett Leitner. Inside the building, the Kanagy brothers and Jonah Zook were visiting with Seth and Aaron, who had opened their shop as a place to get in out of the wind until they were all called back into the house. Andy was in there, too, while Rhoda took part in the Members' Meeting.

But where did *she* belong?

Annie Mae's heart thudded sadly as she thought back over the Sundays when Josh, Joey, Timmy, and little Sara had frolicked outside with the Zook kids. She and Millie Glick had laughed and chatted while they'd watched the kids play, comparing notes on their dates with Luke and Ira Hooley . . . but now Millie was her grandparents' caretaker while Annie Mae worked six days a week at the Sweet Seasons.

She felt a growing separation . . . a chasm between where she had once fit in and where she found herself now. Because her *dat* had made such a muddle of things, Annie Mae no longer knew her place in the pecking order. And Dat might come back to torment her again . . . any day.

The wind made her shiver and pull her black coat closer around her. Why didn't she just step inside the carpentry shop to get warm? She'd known those fellows forever.

They'll think I'm scoutin' for a date. Or they'll make some remark about Adam, or . . .

Truth be told, she didn't know what to think about Adam. He still greeted her weekday mornings with the same open smile as he ordered his breakfast, yet he hadn't said one word about the motorcycle stashed in his barn—even though he'd had Rebecca over to look at it. Annie Mae was secretly intrigued that Adam owned such a shiny, sinful-looking vehicle . . . had even imagined herself riding on it, with her arms wrapped around him as the cycle's roar engulfed them and the wind whipped them on the open road.

But that was silly. He'd joined the church, and it was wrong for him to own a motorcycle, much less ride it.

Rebecca had read on her computer that such a bike might sell for more than twenty-five thousand dollars if it was in good condition. *Twenty-five thousand dollars!* Annie Mae couldn't fathom having so much money, much less understand how Adam had afforded such a cycle before he'd turned seventeen.

The honk of a horn brought her out of her musings. A low-slung car, bluer than a summer sky, was rolling slowly by out on the road. And then it stopped. Who around here would drive such a fast-looking set of wheels? And why would they be stopping where dozens of buggies were parked along Ezra Brenneman's long lane?

Suddenly, the doors on both sides of the car rose up—like wings! When they lowered again, the driver waved to her from behind the car.

Annie Mae's heart nearly leapt out of her chest. "Yonnie!" she hollered. And just that fast she was jogging toward the road, waving crazily. "Yonnie Stoltzfus, what're ya doin' in Willow Ridge? And in that fancy blue sports car, no less?"

His grin brought back a host of memories as he leaned nonchalantly on the roof, watching her. Yonnie Stoltzfus had been her ticket out of the house on more nights than she could count, before she'd even turned sixteen. He was the first boy who'd ever kissed her— and oh, could he kiss! *Better than Luke, even.*

Annie Mae halted at the road's edge, suddenly aware that her sister and the other girls were watching her. Yonnie remained on the other side of his car, resting on his elbows as he drank her in with his silvery-green eyes . . . *eyes like a cat,* she'd always thought. She swallowed hard, hoping not to sound silly—or worse yet, too eager to see him. "So what're ya doin' here?" she asked again.

"I came to see *you*, Annie Mae."

She sucked in her breath. Reminded herself that this reckless young man could come up with a line for every occasion, quicker than most folks could blink. "*Jah*, well, ya found me," she murmured.

"And you're lookin' gooood, too," he replied as his dimples came out to play.

Annie Mae clasped her hands together hard, as a way to keep in touch with reality. It had been so long since she'd gone out with anyone . . . but this wasn't a good time to think about leaving. "Um, ya must be doin' all right," she murmured, gesturing at the shiny blue car.

"Matter of fact, I am." His face took on the rakish glow she recalled from when he used to pull her close and pluck off her *kapp*, as they sat hidden away, kissing in somebody's cornfield. "I've got a really *gut* job now, and my own apartment. Not all that far from here."

Annie Mae heard the suggestion that slithered between his lines, like the serpent that had led Eve into temptation. She cleared her throat loudly. "Glad to hear it. Happy for ya—"

"You don't *look* happy, Annie Mae," he countered in a low voice. "I hear you're waiting tables, of all things."

Regret and shame stabbed at her heart as she glanced away. "A girl's gotta do what a girl's gotta do," she replied in a thin voice.

"Wanna ride?"

Oh, but she could hear the siren call of a fast car

roaring down the road with laughter spilling out its windows. Annie Mae also heard Levi and Cyrus Zook holler when someone called them back to the house for the midday meal. And she couldn't miss the way Nellie, Hannah, and Katie watched her to see what she'd do next. Yonnie was considered the wildest, fastest, *baddest* Mennonite boy around—which was exactly why she'd always adored him. "Better not," she replied after a too-long pause.

"Huh. You know you *want* to see what this Spyder'll do."

"Spider?" Annie Mae gazed longingly at the low, sleek car. In her heart, she sensed it was every bit as dangerous as a spider, too, but that didn't erase the memories of how her heart had pounded gleefully when Yonnie had tromped on the accelerator of his previous rattletrap car.

"C'mon, babycakes. Once around the block and I'll bring you right back."

Annie Mae pressed her lips into a tight line as she studied the way his blond hair shifted in the wind . . . how his eyes narrowed slightly and glimmered with the challenge she'd never been able to resist. "Sorry. Gotta go in now and—and see who the two new preachers are," she said, even as her body refused to move.

"And what's *that* supposed to mean?" he teased her. "They'll be exactly the same men when you get back from a ride. And since you're not a member of the church—still in your *rumspringa*—it's not like anybody can get after you for being a little late to eat your dinner—which is baloney sandwiches, most likely."

Annie Mae squeezed her interwoven fingers until they throbbed painfully. Never mind that the common meal in Willow Ridge was always hot and tasty, thanks to cooks like Miriam, Naomi, and the Hooley sisters. Hadn't she just been thinking she didn't fit in here anymore, when along came this fine-looking fellow in a classy car? Like the answer to her lonely prayer?

"Just got these wheels yesterday. Wanted *you* to be the first girl to ride with me."

Annie Mae watched Nellie, Katie, and Hannah as they headed across the Brennemans' yard toward the house, the backs of their black coats and bonnets all in a row against the snow. What would it hurt to go for a spin . . . just once around the block?

But when her sister turned to gaze at her again, Annie Mae exhaled the tempting thoughts that had almost eroded her resolve. "*Denki,* but I've gotta go," she said. "*Gut* to see ya, Yonnie."

Before he could change her mind, Annie Mae pivoted and resolutely started toward the house. Of *course,* the Brenneman boys, Jonah Zook, and the Kanagy brothers were just coming out of the shop with Andy, so they couldn't miss who was standing out in the road, tormenting her.

"Is that steam comin' out of Yonnie's ears?" Seth Brenneman teased. "Lookin' hot, hot, *hot!*"

"Boy howdy, ya wouldn't see *me* turnin' down a chance to ride in that car—or to drive it," his brother Aaron remarked.

Annie Mae glowered at their knowing grins. "Go right ahead with Yonnie, then! Who's to stop ya?" she retorted.

"Annie's got a boyfriend, Annie's got a boyfriend," Jonah Zook taunted her in an off-key singsong.

No danger of it ever bein' you, *either,* Annie Mae thought as she hurried past the clutch of fellows. Even though he was a year older than she was, he'd never been on a date or taken a girl home from a Singing, that she knew of.

As she reached the door to Naomi's kitchen, Annie Mae heard the squeal of tires and the whine of a revved-up engine racing away. She sighed loudly and tried to compose herself before going in to help set the tables for the common meal. Why did she feel as if she'd just missed her last chance to have any fun? And why did Yonnie Stoltzfus have to be so cute, and so well-off, besides? It just wasn't fair. . . .

Chapter Eleven

Adam surveyed Thursday's lunch offerings on the Sweet Seasons buffet table and then took a seat at Bishop Tom's customary corner table. The café's noonday crowd looked a little smaller today, maybe on account of the low gray clouds that promised a snowstorm. "Looks like there's a creamy chicken soup with lots of veggies, and a bean stew concoction, along with meat loaf and the usual fixings," he reported. "And it's my turn to buy."

"Nope, that's not happenin'," Tom insisted. "Long as you're workin' at my place, your meals're on me, Adam. It's the least I can do for the way you've made my ceilings and walls look like new again, and how the kitchen cabinets and drawers all open and close real smooth."

Adam shrugged. Because Tom's married daughters had taken a lot of the larger furnishings after their *mamm* had died, this job was relatively easy—and even though he was second-coating everything, the painting was going faster than he'd figured on. "Everything needs to be just right for when Nazareth moves in,"

Adam teased. "You'll have to get back into the habit of keeping the little woman happy, ain't so?"

"*Jah,* there's that," the bishop said with a chuckle. Then he nodded in the direction of the kitchen. "And here comes the other little woman we love, ready to take our orders. Get extra to take home for your supper, if ya want."

Adam glanced up as Annie Mae approached their table. She looked fresh today, well-rested and maybe wearing a new dress in a shade of blue that accentuated her eyes. His reading glasses were perched on the end of her nose, and as she poured their water, she nodded toward the laminated menus that were wedged between the sugar shaker and the ketchup bottle.

"Got a new menu today, fellas," she said. "Rebecca suggested we spruce them up to look more like the website—and Miriam's added a few new items, too. The double cheeseburger with bacon's been a big hit."

"Say no more," Adam replied with a laugh. "I'll take one of those, and I'm getting some soup and stuff from the buffet."

"Coke with that?" she asked as she scribbled on her order pad.

Adam paused. How had Annie Mae known he would prefer something different from his usual hot tea to go with that cheeseburger? "*Jah, gut* call. Doesn't hurt to change things around every now and again, ain't so?"

Annie Mae's mysterious smile made him think twice. "We've all gotta do that, *jah,*" she murmured.

"And I'll be loadin' up on the buffet today," Tom chimed in. "Miriam's beef and bean stew's one of my favorites."

"Help yourselves, then," she replied, "while I tell Naomi to get goin' on Adam's burger."

As he followed the bishop to the steam table, Adam waved at Miriam and Naomi in the kitchen, and gave a nod to Rebecca as she waited on a couple of English farmers who were regulars. He'd tried to convince Matthias to come here for lunch, but his brother preferred to snack on whatever they had in the fridge. *Would do him gut to get out more, and he'd be eating better—*

The low rumble of a powerful engine made Adam glance outside. He frowned. Last Sunday he'd seen that same fancy blue car pull up alongside the Brennemans' shop while they'd been selecting new preachers—and he'd watched as Annie Mae had scampered out to greet its driver, too.

When the engine revved before it shut off, Bishop Tom turned around, as well. "Here comes trouble," he murmured as Yonnie Stoltzfus unfolded his tall frame from the low-slung driver's seat. "But ya can't fault his eye for a fine-lookin' car."

"No doubt he's come back to visit with Annie Mae," Adam replied under his breath. He wanted to remark about the allure of fast cars and forbidden vehicles—but who was he to judge Yonnie, when he was still cleaning up the vintage motorcycle stashed in his barn? He'd wanted to confide in Bishop Tom about how he needed to get rid of the bike as well as the guilt trip it was still taking him on, but he hadn't found the right moment to discuss it this past week while he'd been painting.

When the bell above the door jingled, Yonnie paused to take in the dining room and its occupants. Adam studied Yonnie as he dipped up his chicken soup from the steam table. The infamous Mennonite

Romeo looked lean and mean in his dark leather jacket. His dramatic English haircut was really short on one side with a wing of blond hair dipping down over the other eyebrow.

A panther on the prowl, Adam thought as he picked up some packets of crackers. But he couldn't tell Stoltzfus to go back where he came from . . . and it wasn't like he could lay any claim to Annie Mae's affections, either. It was no concern of his if she took up with—

A loud crash made everyone look toward the doorway between the kitchen and the dining room. Annie Mae had dropped the two big haystack salads she'd been carrying, and her face was turning the color of the tomato wedges that waddled across the floor. Lettuce, ground beef, hash browns, and melted cheese were strewn over the broken plates at her feet.

She never reacts that way when she sees me, Adam thought. Yet he quickly set down his soup bowl and strode over to help her.

"Oh, but I've gone and made a big mess," Annie Mae wailed.

"Don't ya worry about it, dearie. I'll get ya two fresh salads made up in a jiffy," Naomi called from the kitchen.

"And I'm right behind ya with the broom," Miriam said as she bustled out. "Every one of us drops something now and again, honey-bug."

Adam extended his hand to a stricken Annie Mae. "Step away from that broken glass," he suggested quietly. "And maybe step away from what Yonnie's doing to you, too, before you get hurt."

What had possessed him to say that? When she gripped his fingers to step toward him, Adam suddenly wanted to pull her closer, into the protection of his arms. Anybody could see how Yonnie was pulling Annie Mae's strings to the point that she lost track of her better judgment.

Yet when she glared at him over the top of his reading glasses, she seemed anything but grateful. "I can handle it," she muttered as she stepped away from him.

By the time Miriam had mopped and Annie Mae had returned to the kitchen for two fresh salads, Yonnie had chosen a table on the far side of the café from where Adam and Bishop Tom were sitting. The Mennonite's smug smile didn't sit well with Adam, and neither did the way Annie Mae fluttered over to his table . . . *like a moth to a flame.*

"Much as ya don't like it, she's gotta figure things out for herself, son."

Tom's remark cut through Adam's dark thoughts and he exhaled loudly. "It's like watching two cars—or a truck and a horse-drawn rig—entering an intersection at the same time, and you can't stop the crash you know is coming," Adam muttered.

"Best thing to do is let go and let God handle it His way," the bishop reminded him gently. "He gave us free will, knowin' it would either keep us on the path to salvation . . . or lead us to perdition."

Adam nodded, but he didn't feel so good about that last option. As he ate his soup, which was loaded with chicken chunks and vegetables, he tried not to watch the way Annie Mae's face lit up as she took Yonnie's order . . . how she flirted back when he complimented her . . . how she all but *skipped* to fetch her next orders when Naomi called out that they were ready.

The double cheeseburger with bacon she brought him was the most awesome sandwich Adam had seen in a long while. He grabbed Annie Mae's hand as she turned to go. "Be careful," he pleaded quietly. "Yonnie and his cousins have been known to get girls in trouble, and you don't want to be another notch on his bedpost. You're better than that, Annie Mae."

Disdain clouded her face as she snatched away her hand. "I guess that's my beeswax—and none of yours," she retorted. "Can I get ya anything else?"

Jah, a zipper for my lips, Adam thought, but he shook his head.

"You can tell Miriam her beef and bean stew's the best ever today," Bishop Tom said with a smile. "And never forget that all of us are prayin' and wantin' the best for ya, now that you and Nellie are on your own."

Annie Mae's scowl could've curdled the cream in Tom's coffee. With a roll of her eyes, she tossed their bill on the table and stalked off to fetch more plates that awaited her on the pass-through counter.

Tom chuckled ruefully. "There's no figurin' women, Adam. They'll pretty much do what they're gonna do, and we men can either tromp down on them and pretend like we've got control, or we can—again—let the *gut* Lord handle it for us. I could tell ya all about losin' Lettie to that English fella, but I think ya see my point."

Adam nodded, wishing he hadn't lost his appetite for the fabulous double burger draped in cheese, which melted down over its three bacon slices. But he would eat every bite of it. Annie Mae Knepp would *not* ruin his lunch—or his life.

* * *

"Since when do you wear glasses, Annie Mae?" Yonnie teased. "Or do I drive you to such distraction that you can't see straight?"

Annie Mae laughed out loud. "You and your talk. Fulla hot air—and full of yourself, you are."

"So maybe I'd like some company. To keep from becoming totally self-centered." His light green eyes widened as he let his suggestion sink in. "C'mon, Annie Mae. When's your day off? We could go out riding. Like we used to."

Her heart fluttered like a wild bird trying to escape a cage. Months she'd gone without a date. It was wearing on her to work day in and day out, even if her savings account was growing steadily with each weekly deposit.

"All work and no play makes Annie a dull, dull girl," Yonnie hinted.

"Miss? More coffee, please?"

The English voice behind her brought Annie Mae out of her rose-colored fog. She pivoted, grabbed a carafe from the coffeemaker, and refilled all the cups around the dining room to give herself time to think. Rhoda was off this afternoon, helping Andy move boxes into their new apartment in the clinic building, and Rebecca was over there with them, setting up the Internet for her graphic design business.

See there? Those girls take time off, yet you haven't once asked Miriam for a break.

But she didn't want Yonnie to think she would drop her waitressing duties at his every whim, either. As Bishop Tom and Adam headed toward the checkout, Annie Mae stepped behind the counter to settle their tab. "Everything cooked to your likin' today, fellas?" she asked breezily. Then she pointed down into the glass pastry case. "Miriam just baked those chocolate chip brownies about an hour ago, and the monkey bread's fresh, too."

Bishop Tom laughed and waved her off. "Naz'll be over this evening with dinner for me—she's stayin' with Ira and Luke until we get hitched in a couple weeks," he added. "But why don't ya wrap up a loaf of that monkey bread. Looks like somethin' to get Adam and me through the afternoon while we're puttin' my downstairs rooms back together."

As she tucked a loaf of the cinnamon-scented confection into a cake box, Annie Mae could feel Adam gazing at her—ready to deliver another lecture, most likely—so she didn't look at him. "There ya be, Bishop. Let me get your change—"

"Nope, you keep the extra. Saves me walkin' back to lay it on the table." Tom's eyes crinkled as he smiled at her. "You've got a real gift for servin' folks, Annie Mae. Could be Miriam's business is boomin' partly because of the way ya take care of your customers."

"See ya tomorrow," Adam added as they went to put on their coats. "That bacon cheeseburger was the best I've ever had."

Annie Mae gawked at the bishop's generous tip. His compliment lingered like the aroma of Miriam's baking clung to her clothes when she left the café each day. And while Adam, too, sounded polite and encouraging . . . their good intentions drifted away like the steam rising from the coffee she poured for Yonnie a few moments later. "So what'll ya have?" she asked him. "The meat loaf special's awfully *gut,* and Miriam's sugar cream pie would be to your likin', as I recall."

"You remember all the right things about me, sweet

thing," he murmured as his eyes narrowed alluringly. "I didn't really come here to eat, but a slice of that pie would give me a chance to watch you *move*, wouldn't it? And lose the specs."

On her way to the fridge in the kitchen, Annie Mae slipped the reading glasses into her apron pocket. Naomi, Hannah, and Miriam were all filling orders, so she plated a piece of cream pie and hustled out of the kitchen before they could quiz her about Yonnie. Oh, but the smile on his face was a sight for her lonely eyes as she set his dessert on the table and then fetched the coffee carafe.

"So how long do you figure to be waiting tables?" he asked as she refilled his mug.

Her eyebrows rose. What could he mean by such a question? "Long as it takes," she replied breezily.

"Your *dat*'s really ticked off that you didn't go with him to start his new colony," Yonnie continued in a conversational tone. He cut the tip off his slice of pie. "Me, I was surprised you defied him that way, but impressed that you took your stand, too. I admire a girl who shows some backbone . . . not to mention such lovely body parts as—"

"Yonnie!" Annie Mae rasped. "Other folks can hear ya!"

He shrugged, forking up another bite of pie. "If you can't take the heat, get out of the kitchen . . . and into my car."

To keep her face from getting any redder, Annie Mae refilled water glasses around the dining room, relieved that the fellows from Willow Ridge had already left the café. Since when had Yonnie Stoltzfus ever spoken to her *dat*? He'd made a point of remaining invisible, all those nights he'd come to fetch her after dark. . . .

Yet even as she stood at the coffee machine to make a fresh batch, Annie Mae basked in Yonnie's comments . . . how he'd been impressed that she'd gone against her father's orders. Then she settled up with a table of four English gals who also bought pies to take home. By the time she'd boxed up their desserts and made change, only one other couple remained eating lunch, so she had no other reasons to stall. With all the nonchalance she could muster, Annie Mae returned to Yonnie's table.

"And how was that pie?" she asked as she again topped off his coffee.

"So when are we getting together?" he countered in a low voice. "I can't wait forever. And neither can you, girlie."

She nearly dropped her pencil and order pad. This chat would be so much easier if Yonnie didn't know so much about her, and yet . . . it was their shared experiences and secrets that fueled her longing. "I—I get off at two on Saturday," she stammered. "That'll just have to do ya."

"Oh, I *do* you, all right." Yonnie stood, towering above her as the scent of his spicy cologne tickled her senses. He placed his hands lightly on her shoulders, gazing down at her with a green-eyed triumph that made her shiver. "Somehow I'll make it through Friday and Saturday morning," he murmured. "Gives me more time to . . . rev up my engine. And it'll be Valentine's Day, too. Perfect."

He air-kissed her and then headed for the door, leaving his steaming coffee—and her—behind.

Oh, I'll do *you, all right.*

Annie Mae shook herself out of the spell Yonnie Stoltzfus was so very good at casting. Only after she picked up his pie plate did she find the fifty-dollar bill he'd folded underneath it.

Any fella who can drive a fancy car can afford to leave that kind of a tip, she reasoned as she stuffed the money in her pocket.

And yet, as she rang up Yonnie's bill—heard the loud roar of an engine, followed by the squeal of tires racing down the county blacktop—Annie Mae sensed that her Mennonite boyfriend might be paying it forward, for a lot more than pie. And for a lot more than he'd expected from her before.

Chapter Twelve

While Bishop Tom wrote out his check Saturday afternoon, Adam took a final look around the high-ceilinged yellow kitchen . . . walked to the door and gazed into the front room, with its fresh cream-colored walls. No two ways about it: he had accomplished minor miracles with his rollers, brushes, and fresh paint. And when Tom had shifted the contents of his pantry, closets, and the various nooks in this fine old home so Adam could paint them, he had also tossed out a lot of stuff.

"Can't thank ya enough for your *gut* work, Adam," the bishop said as he ripped the check from his checkbook. "This place hasn't looked so clean all at once since—well, maybe before the kids came along," he confessed. "And *denki* for cartin' off all those boxes of clothes and whatnot that still have some usefulness."

"Happy to help," Adam replied. "I'll haul them to the Mennonites' missionary center over past Morning Star after lunch. We Amish don't send people out to convert folks overseas, but I'm happy to donate stuff to that cause."

"I can't wait to see Nazareth's face tonight," Tom continued gleefully. "She and Jerusalem have been too polite to say so, but the place got cluttered after Lettie left. Even though my girls cleaned for me every now and again, they couldn't seem to pitch out their *mamm*'s stuff, or the odds and ends left from when they were kids."

"Matthias and I know all about that." Adam chuckled. "Maybe I could hire you to clean out *our* place, Bishop."

Tom's laughter rang around the fresh kitchen walls. "Not a chance. I'll have a new wife makin' me toe the line in just a week and a half," he replied. "I haven't been this excited since before I got hitched when I was your age, Adam."

As Adam climbed into his remodeling wagon, he had a lot to think about. Except for his gray-spangled hair and beard—and the crow's-feet around his eyes— Bishop Tom looked like a fit, well-situated young man ready to move forward . . . ready to be *happy* again. *Something to be said for that,* he thought as Jerry clip-clopped onto the pavement.

But what young woman in her right mind would marry into the Wagler household? And why did he think he could be any more responsible for a wife than he'd been for his *mamm*?

Adam sighed, urging his gelding closer to the shoulder so cars could get around his big wagon. While he'd been working at Tom's he'd looked for an opening—a lead-in to confessing about his motor-cycle and Mamm's death . . . the physical and emotional "clutter" he'd hung on to for too long. Yet when gaps in their conversation had come, Adam hadn't had the heart to ruin Tom's happiness about marrying

Nazareth by dredging up the past . . . the painful secret he couldn't seem to move beyond.

So here he was, still living in unresolved sorrow with Matthias, plodding down the same lonely road to nowhere, wondering where that road would lead him. . . .

When Annie Mae spotted the sky blue sports car humming toward her after her shift on Saturday, her heartbeat played hopscotch. Even as she realized how out of kilter it looked for a Plain girl to be riding in such a vehicle—and this while English and Amish farmers stood in line to have their horses shod at Ben's smithy—Annie Mae convinced herself she deserved this outing. High time she laughed and let go, after nearly two months of doing the right things, supporting Nellie and herself.

The car eased off the road and purred to a stop in the café parking lot, a few feet short of where Annie Mae stood. As the doors rose like wings, Yonnie's grin brought back old times. "Ready to ride, sweet thing?"

She gaped at the shiny car and its driver. Cautiously she slid into the low seat, holding her breath as the doors lowered around them. "My word, Yonnie," she whispered. "What sort of a wild contraption *is* this?"

"It's a BMW Spyder," he replied. "Big improvement over what I used to drive—but so what? It's good to see you, pretty girl."

"*Jah,* it's *gut* to see you, too, Yonnie." Annie Mae knew she looked pie-eyed, but she couldn't help it. Her heartbeat was galloping so fast and loud, she couldn't even hear the engine running.

"You're looking mighty fine, Annie Mae. And I'm

betting you'll taste even better than that pie you served up the other day, too," he said. "Here—be my Valentine." Yonnie reached behind her seat and then presented her with a bouquet of perfect, velvety red roses, in a sheath of lace and tied in a ribbon.

Annie Mae gasped. "Oh my word, I—" While she'd heard of other Plain girls getting Valentine flowers, it was a delight only to be enjoyed during *rumspringa*. She inhaled the roses' sweetness, searching for words. "*Denki*, Yonnie. Ya didn't have to do this. We've been runnin' around for a long time now, you and I."

"Maybe it's time I wised up and treated you like the special girl you are."

Annie Mae struggled to bring her thoughts back down to Earth. She reached into her coat pocket for the two twenty-dollar bills she'd stashed there. "Ya forgot your change Thursday," she said as she stuck the bills in his cup holder.

Yonnie's brow furrowed. "I intended for you to keep that so you could—"

"Not goin' down that road. That's too much tip for a slice of pie and we both know it."

His expression tightened. "My money's not good enough for you? Or are you too high and mighty to accept my help?"

He might as well have cut off the roses' blooms with his pocketknife. Annie Mae felt her hopes for a carefree afternoon plummet as he pulled over to the shoulder of the road. Was he going to put her out before they even left Willow Ridge?

"Tell me to my face you don't need that money," he whispered, crooking his finger in that teasing way she knew so well.

Still doubtful, Annie Mae leaned toward him—and

then gasped into the openmouthed kiss Yonnie claimed her with. His lips probed hers, insistent and sweet. As he tried to slip the money down the neck of her dress, she giggled, swatting at his hand.

"Humor me, sweet thing," he murmured against the sensitive skin behind her ear. "Let's not spoil a great day before it even gets started."

She couldn't argue with that. But then, when had she ever been able to anticipate what Yonnie might do or say, much less make him behave as he should? As Annie Mae pocketed the bills, she settled into the plush depth of her bucket seat again, cradling her bouquet in her arms. "All right, we'll do it your way," she murmured. "I'm all for keepin' it light and just havin' a *gut* time. Like we used to."

His lips quirked as he pulled out onto the road. "Maybe it's time to stop living in the past," he suggested. "It's not like you've signed on with the Old Order, so why not loosen up? You'd look really hot in tight jeans and a T-shirt with a hoodie—"

"Like I'm gonna buy English clothes!"

"So let me buy them for you. We both know Plain girls who've done that during their *rumspringa*," he coaxed. "You could keep them at my place."

Annie Mae gazed out the car window. This wasn't the first time they'd talked about her getting English clothes, because Yonnie wore them all the time. But he hadn't had an apartment before . . . hadn't sounded so insistent. "You've jumped the fence," she realized out loud. "You're never gonna join the church, are ya?"

"And why are we talking about *church?*" He plucked at her black bonnet, flashing his most engaging grin.

"C'mon, Annie Mae. Don't tell me you've turned into a stick-in-the-mud—especially now that your *dat*'s not breathing down your neck anymore."

It *was* getting awfully warm in his little car. As Annie Mae removed her bonnet and unbuttoned her black woolen coat, she noticed the glowing lights and numbers behind the steering wheel . . . so many gauges moving at once. She wondered how Yonnie could watch the road. Then she gaped, pointing to a small screen on the dashboard. "What on God's *gut* Earth—is that a picture of the road we're on?"

Yonnie grinned. "There's a built-in computerized navigation system. It shows you where to turn and—well, I could program this car to take me to the California coast, and I wouldn't need a map," he explained proudly. "Paper maps like we studied in school are obsolete now. And it'll also"—he tapped a button, which changed the picture—"show me what's behind the car when I'm backing up. So I don't hit anything."

Annie Mae shook her head, unable to grasp most of the things he'd just told her. The leather seat beneath her hand felt incredibly smooth and soft . . . rock music was pulsing softly from speakers behind her. For all she knew, this car might lift up off the road to soar above the snow-coated treetops if Yonnie were to push the right button. *And where did he come by the money for a car like this? And why does he even care about seeing a Plain girl like—*

"You all right, Annie Mae? You got awfully quiet." Yonnie's face lit up with a sly smile, as though he knew he'd rendered her speechless.

"Just feelin' like a fish outta water. Wonderin' where

ya found such a fine job around here, to be drivin'
such a car."

When Yonnie shrugged, the sleeve of his leather
coat whispered against his seat. "One of life's little
mysteries, eh? For once, I was in the right place at the
right time . . . with the right employer wanting me to
work for him."

"And what is it ya do now?" Annie Mae vividly
recalled the modest farmhouse where Yonnie's family
lived, where the paint was peeling in places . . . where
some of the boards in the barn's loft had nearly given
way when she and Yonnie had gone up there to horse
around.

*Horse? Why do I suspect Yonnie'll never drive a horse-
drawn rig again?*

"I'm a city commissioner. On the zoning committee
that decides about everything from new businesses to
promotional programs that'll attract residents, to—"
Once again he shrugged, as though his new job wasn't
all that unusual for a fellow who'd been raised Plain.
"Maybe you don't recall, but I took some business
classes at the junior college, and they've paid off.
Big-time."

Annie Mae fought a scowl. Why did Yonnie's answer
seem to sidestep her question? And then again, why
was she so skeptical? Miriam's daughter Rebecca had
learned her career in college, and Seth Brenneman
had taken plumbing classes at a trade school. . . .

But they're not driving cars that have doors like wings.

She put her doubts aside, however, as Yonnie wrapped
his strong, warm hand around hers. The important
things never really changed, did they? No matter how
much money you made, didn't family—the love folks

shared around their table each day—count for more
than what your bank account showed?

And it was nice to spend time with a man who made
her feel *special*. Even if his new gristmill became a huge
success, Luke Hooley would never invest in a fancier
rig or talk to her in this quiet, intimate way. And it was
a sure thing that Adam Wagler worked harder at his
remodeling than he ever would at winning a girl . . .
even if he secretly had a motorcycle stashed in his
barn, years after he'd committed to the Old Order.

Guys. There's just no figuring them out.

Annie Mae closed her eyes, willing herself to go with
the flow . . . to enjoy this outing with a fine-looking
young man who'd always taken her beyond the box of
her sheltered life. With Yonnie, she had experienced
wild abandon—had glimpsed possibilities that would
never have occurred to her with any other fellow she
knew. And wasn't that what *rumspringa* was all about?
Didn't the church teach that every experience, good
or bad, came about as a part of God's will?

"I love it when you close your eyes, Annie Mae,"
Yonnie murmured as he squeezed her hand. "I can see
how you look when you're kissing me . . . how your
long lashes brush your cheeks and your skin turns
pink like a rose."

Her face tingled with heat. She relaxed . . . sank
deeper into the seat, which cradled her backside in
warmth that surely must've come from a heater of
some sort. "Nobody's ever told me anything like that,"
she admitted.

"So let me be the first . . . to say all the things your
heart longs to hear," Yonnie responded softly. "You've

always been my best girl, Annie Mae. We can make that a full-time situation, if you say the word."

As her eyes fluttered open, Annie Mae's thoughts spun. Was he going to propose? Did he intend to marry her and—

"So where *are* we?" she blurted when he turned onto a road that looked newly paved. Up ahead she saw buildings . . . a bank, a grocery store, and other shops that were still under construction, with a white schoolhouse beyond them. On the snow-covered hillside above those places stood new homes, all freshly painted and shining in the afternoon sunshine. When Yonnie's car rolled slowly past a brick and stone marker, Annie Mae's mouth fell open.

"Higher Ground?" she demanded shrilly. "And why would ya be bringin' me *here*, when ya know *gut* and well—"

Yonnie cleared his throat. "It's where I live. My apartment's above the bank."

"I don't care where—turn around right this minute and take me home!" Annie Mae's temples pounded painfully as she stared out the car window. "How could ya think I'd want to come to where Dat's—well, he's up to no *gut*, for sure and for certain! He might've claimed that God spoke to him, leadin' him to start this new colony, but ya can't tell me he wasn't listenin' to the Devil instead."

Yonnie pulled into a parking space in front of Alma's Down-Home Café and leveled his gaze at her. "Is that the kind of claptrap you're hearing in Willow Ridge?" he asked calmly. "Maybe you should experience Higher Ground for yourself instead of believing the gossip of folks who've never been here. And besides . . . I thought you'd like to see the nice new home where your little brothers and Sara are living."

Annie Mae sucked in her breath. Hadn't she seen Joey and Josh, Timmy and Sara—their dear little faces—every night when she prayed for them? While she and Nellie and the others around Willow Ridge didn't speak of them as often these days, she missed her siblings fiercely . . . still worried about who was watching over them while Dat went about his business of setting up Higher Ground. And by the looks of all this *progress,* her father had been a very busy man, indeed.

"Can . . . can we drive past there?" she asked. "I—I don't wanna go in, understand. Just want to see the place."

For a few moments there was only the quiet hum of the car's engine as Yonnie gripped her hand, gazing into her eyes. "We can do that, sure. But let's stop by my place first . . . catch up on what I've been missing about you while I've been getting this beautiful new town on its feet."

How was she supposed to answer that? Yonnie had confessed that he worked for her father, and that he was partly responsible for the way Higher Ground had so quickly come together. Nothing had changed about him, really. Yonnie still wanted her kisses—and whatever other liberties she would allow him. And in exchange, she might get a glimpse of the siblings she yearned for.

"Promise me ya won't make me see Dat," she pleaded. "And promise me ya won't tell him I've been here— or you can take me right on back to Willow Ridge. I'll not have him thinkin' I intend to come back to him, *ever.*"

Yonnie's gaze didn't waver. "Not a problem. We've always had our secrets, you and I."

Could she believe him? Did she dare *not* go along with him, and miss the chance to see that her younger siblings were well situated? The steady *clip-clop! clip-clop!* of a horse's hooves rang out on the pavement and she swiveled in time to see a familiar blue wagon approaching.

"Adam!" She suddenly ducked down, barely shifting her roses from her lap before she crushed them. Why on Earth was *he* here—and at just the wrong moment? "Get me outta here, Yonnie. We can't have him—he'll be buttin' in and tryin' to take me—"

"We don't want that," Yonnie agreed with a chuckle. "Not to worry, Annie Mae. Once he gets past us, I'll pull around behind the bank so we can go upstairs the back way."

Was it her imagination, or did it take forever for Adam's horse to pull his rumbling wagon down the street? Desperately trying to sort out her scrambled thoughts, Annie Mae kept her head down. Even after Yonnie backed the car and then smoothly maneuvered it to a different parking spot, she remained folded in half, not daring to show herself.

Yonnie cut the engine. Ran his hand down her back to soothe her. "Hey. We're fine now, sweet thing," he said in a low, comforting voice. "Come on upstairs. There's no one else around, and the bank's closed. You'll be invisible, I promise."

Annie Mae longed to believe those words as she sat up . . . as the doors of the car glided skyward in a smooth, continuous motion that left her exposed. She needed to be tucked up out of sight, in case Adam decided to circle around town. After all, he'd

seen this flashy blue car when Yonnie had visited
Willow Ridge, and he'd expressed his opinions to her
in no uncertain terms.

*Step away from what Yonnie's doing to you, before you get
hurt . . . you don't want to be another notch on his bedpost.
You're better than that, Annie Mae.*

Why did Adam Wagler's words ring with so much
truth now, when she'd considered him extremely rude
for saying them the other day? And why had she
ducked out of sight when he'd driven past? At this
point, she didn't have much choice about going
upstairs with Yonnie if she wanted to see where the
kids were living. . . .

After she hurried up the stairs and entered the
rooms above the bank, Annie Mae realized what she'd
let herself in for. Yonnie's apartment wasn't much
bigger than the loft she and Nellie shared with Rhoda
Lantz. From the entry, she saw his kitchen . . . a bathroom off to the side of it . . . a front room with a TV
bolted to the wall . . . a bed with the sheets and cover-
let folded down, as if he'd brought her here for a very
specific purpose. . . .

*Lord, Ya gotta help me. I've gotten myself into a tight
spot and I don't know how to get out.*

"Come here, Annie Mae," Yonnie whispered. He
put her bouquet on the kitchen counter and then
stood behind her, slipping his arms around her waist.
"All those times we went out before? Making out in my
backseat or in the barn? Well, I can't get your kisses
out of my mind . . . want to feel your velvety skin and
finally see you . . ."

*Yonnie and his cousins have been known to get girls
in trouble . . .*

Too late Adam's warning echoed in her mind.

When Yonnie's tongue teased at the rim of her ear, Annie Mae squawked so suddenly that he jumped. She broke away, but she only got as far as his picture window before he caught her. He grabbed her hands and pinned them above her head, pressing her body against the cold glass . . .

Chapter Thirteen

Adam froze, his gaze fixed on the upstairs window of the bank. Out of curiosity he'd passed through Higher Ground on his way home from taking Bishop Tom's donations to the Mennonites' missionary center in Morning Star. When he'd seen Yonnie's sleek blue car idling in front of this new brick building—and then gliding around behind it—something had prompted him to circle the block and come back.

No two ways about it: that was a Plain girl's *kapp* and cape dress pressed against the window. The position of her hands left nothing to his imagination, either. Annie Mae had told him to butt out, but he quickly hitched his horse to the rail and then sprinted around to the staircase that ascended the back of the building. Up the steps he lunged, two at a time, as his heart beat a rapid tattoo that raced ahead of the worst-case scenarios in his mind.

"Stoltzfus!" he hollered as he pounded on the door. "Open up! I know what you're doing in there!"

Silence. Seconds went by.

Again Adam beat on the steel door. "Annie Mae? Are you all right?"

A cry rang out, but it was quickly muffled. Adam figured Yonnie for the type who would lock up, yet when he tried the door, it opened. He stepped inside, running toward the two figures on the far side of the small apartment. He had no idea what he'd do if Stoltzfus gave him any trouble, but he would *not* allow Yonnie to take advantage of a girl he knew to be innocent and naive, even if she gave the impression that she was wild and reckless on dates.

"What the—? Hold it right there!" Yonnie snapped as he dropped Annie Mae's hands and pivoted. "You've got no right—"

"I could say the same for you!" Adam retorted as he searched Annie Mae's face and clothing for signs that he'd arrived too late. "Let's get back home, Annie Mae. You've got no business being here."

Wrong thing to say. Though he'd heard her desperate cry and she'd seemed relieved to see him barging through the door, Annie Mae was now scowling at him. "What're ya doin' here, Adam?" she demanded defensively. "Don't tell me *you* work for Dat now, too."

So that was the way of it? Adam didn't waste time figuring out the ramifications of what she'd just revealed. He remained halfway across the apartment, sensing Yonnie would jump him if he came any closer.

"Annie Mae's eighteen," the tall blond taunted him. "Old enough to see who she wants—and that's not you, Wagler. Don't make me show you to the door."

"She's only seventeen," Adam countered, although he was clutching at straws, stalling for time. "I don't know what sort of stories you cooked up to get her here, but—"

"It's all right, Adam," Annie Mae interrupted in a strained voice. "He—he brought me here to see the kids. Really."

Adam bit back another remark. If that was Yonnie's ploy, to lure Annie Mae to Higher Ground on the pretext of visiting her little brothers and sister, this situation smelled even worse than he'd originally assumed. Was Yonnie actually planning to turn Annie Mae over to her father? Did Hiram *know* she was coming here? Adam had believed there was no love lost between this swaggering Mennonite and the former bishop of Willow Ridge . . . but who could have guessed that Yonnie Stoltzfus would be living in Hiram's new town? It seemed more than mere coincidence that the man who'd been driven out of Willow Ridge in a black Cadillac would be connected to that blue sports car parked behind the bank. . . .

"Please go," Annie Mae pleaded, clasping her hands in front of her apron. "It—it was *gut* of ya to check on me, but everything's fine here, Adam. I can handle it. Really, I can."

What was he to do? If Annie Mae insisted she didn't need him interfering with her social life, who was he to contradict her? Even though Adam's instinct told him Yonnie was up to no good, maybe he had misjudged Annie Mae. Maybe the girl who'd lived next door wasn't as innocent as he'd wanted to believe. Plain teenage girls had been known to try cigarettes and liquor and sex during their *rumspringa*. . . .

"All right then," he murmured. "I'll mind my own business and go home."

"Best idea I've heard all day," Yonnie agreed. Then

he sneered. "Man, but you could use a shower. No wonder Annie Mae wants nothing to do with you, Wagler."

Reluctantly Adam turned to go. It still didn't set right that Yonnie had brought Annie Mae to Higher Ground when he was apparently working for her *dat* now. And Annie Mae *had* appeared to be in a compromised position when he'd seen her in the window. . . .

What if you're wrong about her? What if she and Yonnie have been lovers for a long while and you're just slow to catch on?

Adam slammed the door behind him, more irritated—more wounded—by that idea than he cared to admit. As he descended the stairs, he shook his head about this whole situation. How could he have been passing through this fledgling town at just the right moment on this particular Saturday afternoon to catch Annie Mae with Stoltzfus?

God doesn't live in coincidences. He's working you into His plan. . . .

As Adam drove away, his big blue wagon rumbling loudly over the bumpy part of the road that wasn't yet paved, he figured he'd better get out of sight in case Stoltzfus was watching him. Yet something told him not to go too far.

"*Please* take me home," Annie Mae repeated. It annoyed her that Yonnie seemed even more determined to corner her after Adam had interrupted him—and it scared her, too, the way he'd pawed at her dress until she'd slapped his face. Did he think he could have anything he wanted because he was driving a fancy car? And working for her father? "Why'd ya think I'd want to come here to Dat's new town anyway?"

Yonnie stood before her with his arms crossed, looking far too tall and strong in a black shirt that tugged at his broad shoulders. That wing of blond hair was falling down over one cat-green eye, as though he knew just how hot he looked in his English haircut. "You haven't seen the kids yet."

"Then let's go!" Annie Mae stopped herself before she expressed her intense dislike—her distrust—of his motives. It was a long walk back to Willow Ridge, and Yonnie stood between her and the door, looking smugly predatory. She really, *really* should've gone with Adam. . . .

"What's your hurry, cupcake? Maybe I need to hear about your *thing* for Adam Wagler—because if he's stalking you, you must be giving him a reason," he continued in an edgy voice. "Now there's a loser if I ever saw one. What's he now, twenty-two? Still living with his brother and never goes out with girls? Makes me wonder if Adam even *likes* girls. Know what I mean?"

A gasp escaped her. "That's a bunch of baloney—"

"So why would you settle for baloney when you could be sharing steak with me?" Yonnie cut in smoothly. He walked over to his kitchen, opened the fridge, and held up a bundle wrapped in white butcher paper. "See this? Freshly cut rib eye, which I figured to be sharing with you, along with a bottle of really fine wine, to celebrate Valentine's Day and your visit. The first of many, I was hoping."

Annie Mae watched him closely, wondering what she could possibly say or do to get him off this one-track conversation. "So why is it ya started comin' around again, Yonnie?" she challenged. "As long as it's been, I figured ya had another girlfriend, or—"

He let the fridge door drift shut. "I wanted you to get Luke Hooley out of your system—see him for yet another loser who'll never be the man you need. What is it with all these single brothers living together in Willow Ridge, anyway?"

A worm of worry crawled in her stomach. Where was Yonnie getting his information about Luke and Adam? And did he figure his insinuations about them would make her want *him* more? The longer he talked, the farther away Adam would be . . . and Yonnie's over-confidence was wearing her thin.

"Look," she murmured, hoping she seemed reasonable rather than frightened, "it's real nice that ya got that steak and wine and those roses, and that ya gave me a ride in your car, and—" She shrugged in exasperation. "But ya should've known that once ya mentioned my sibs, I'd *have* to see where they're livin' . . . have to know they're okay before I could go along with whatever ya might want to do with me."

Yonnie's eyes flashed like green fire. He strode over and threw open the door. "Fine! Have it your way," he blurted as he tossed her coat at her. "Doesn't seem like much of a date to me, but your priorities have obviously changed."

Annie Mae slipped into her coat as she hurried down the stairs. She didn't like the way Yonnie had lashed out, but at least she was leaving his apartment, moving away from the alluring trap he'd set. When the doors of his car rose into the air, she ducked into the passenger seat before he could bring them down on her as payback for ruining his afternoon. She'd forgotten her roses, but maybe that was best.

Are ya still here, God? she prayed as Yonnie dropped angrily into the driver's seat. *This isn't goin' the way either of us wanted, so now it seems I've lit his fuse. . . .*

The car roared out of the bank's lot and spun gravel as Yonnie steered it up the hill, where several new houses perched on plots of land. Who was living here, so soon after Dat had started the colony? How had so many houses gone up so fast? Surely Plain folks around here would've heard why Hiram Knepp had left Willow Ridge—and wouldn't they want more acreage than what she was seeing along this road?

But that train of thought derailed as they approached the largest house in town. The lower half of the house was red brick and the upper story was painted a rich buttery gold, accentuated with gables and windows. The front porch spanned the entire width of the place and had a pillared railing . . . the double front doors were made of glossy wood, with oval glass insets. This home seemed anything but Plain, and nestled on the highest point of town, it seemed to be watching over its neighbors—*or lookin' down on them,* she thought. The large building still under construction behind it resembled the huge horse barn Dat had left behind, so Annie Mae had no doubt that this was where her father had transplanted the rest of her family. She held her breath. Yonnie slowed the car so she could stare through the low-slung windshield.

"Happy now?" he muttered. "As you can see, your sibs are living pretty high on the hog, and—"

"But who's takin' care of them while Dat's gettin' this town built?" she demanded. "It's been two months since any of us have seen them, and—"

One of the front doors burst open and out ran Joey and Josh, who were leading Sara and Timmy by the

hand. Even with the car windows closed, their loud
crying and distressed expressions made Annie Mae's
heart constrict. The kids were rushing down the front
steps as fast as their little legs would carry them.

"Stop the car!" she blurted. Instinctively she
grabbed for the handle, and then realized she had no
idea how to open these outrageous doors. "Yonnie, I
have to—"

Right behind the kids came a scowling young
woman who brandished a paddle Annie Mae recognized from the barn back home. Because she'd been
in charge of the kids' discipline after their *mamm*
passed, Dat had kept the paddle out there mostly as a
warning. But this young woman looked angry enough
to thrash them with it.

"You brats have gone and done it now!" she
screamed as the four children scattered on the snowy
lawn. "You are the stupidest, meanest little—"

Annie Mae grabbed Yonnie's arm and stuck her
face in his. "Let me *out* of this car. *Now!* That woman
will *not* hit my kids with that paddle."

Yonnie stared at her in disbelief, but he pushed a
button and the doors began their ascent. "Fine. If
that's how you want it—"

She ducked and propelled herself outside before
the doors had gone halfway up. "Joey! Josh!" she cried
as she dashed toward them. "Sara, it's me, punkin! You
and Timmy come over here to Annie Mae!"

Oh, but their tear-streaked faces looked pinched
and their clothes were hanging on their too-thin
bodies—and they were out here in the cold without
any coats. Her heart hammered frantically as she
called to them again, hurrying through the ankle-
deep snow.

"Annie Mae!" the twins hollered as one. Across the yard they sprinted, their arms stretched toward her, followed by her sister and Timmy. "Annie Mae, save us! Save us!"

Her soul lurched at their words. When Josh and Joey rushed against her, she nearly fell backward from the force of the impact. She hugged them hard, and for once they didn't fuss when she eagerly kissed their chilled faces.

"Annie Mae!" little Sara squealed as she led Timmy as fast as he could toddle. "It's weally you!"

"*Jah,* it is, angel." She instinctively caught Timmy when he launched himself at her, and then she grabbed Sara in her other arm. "*Ach,* but ya must be freezin'," she muttered. "Let's get ya outta here—"

"You there! What do you think you're doing?" the young woman demanded as she stopped several feet away from them. Her *kapp* was askew and her face was flushed as she struggled to catch her breath. She raised the paddle as though it were a club.

"And who're *you?*" Annie Mae challenged, stepping forward with a fierce scowl. "Obviously ya don't have a clue about keepin' kids—"

"I'm their new *mamm,* but they don't listen to a thing I—"

"*Nobody* paddles *my* sibs! And ya won't be usin' that thing on me, either," Annie Mae declared hotly. "Put it down!"

The young woman slowly lowered the paddle, staring at Annie Mae as she backed away. "So . . . who *are* you?"

"I'm their big sister. C'mon, kids—let's go home." Annie Mae gently bumped Joey with her backside to get him and Josh to let go of her legs.

"But you can't just take—Hiram never said anything about a—"

Annie Mae stopped dead still, clutching Timmy on one hip and Sara on the other. Josh and Joey were still clinging to her as though frightened for their lives while she processed what she'd just heard. The young woman in front of her was dressed in a bright flowery dress made from a Plain pattern, still gripping the handle of the paddle as she stared at Annie Mae. She didn't look any more than nineteen . . . so if she was calling herself the kids' new *mamm* . . .

"Dat didn't say a lot of things to a lot of people when he started up this town," Annie Mae muttered. "So I'll just take these kids off your hands, and we'll all of us be a whole lot happier. Come on, boys. Walk with me now."

She turned on her heel to start for the road and stopped.

The car was gone. The kids and this *girl* in the flowery dress had been caterwauling so loudly, Annie Mae hadn't heard Yonnie drive off.

And doesn't that just figure? she fretted as she looked up and down the street. Not another soul seemed to be around any of the new houses, and she saw no vehicles, either. *I've gotten myself into another pickle, Lord, and I don't know what I'm gonna do . . . so I guess we'll just keep walkin' 'til we figure it out. Sure wish I had a cell phone.*

"Hiram's not here to—you can't just take off with his kids!" the girl behind them cried.

"Watch me!" Annie Mae called over her shoulder. As she steered the five-year-old twins toward the road, she wished there was a feasible way to take along the kids' clothing, to fetch their coats—to get them back to Willow Ridge before everyone caught colds.

The snow had soaked through her shoes, and she felt Sara and Timmy shivering against her as they buried their faces against her shoulders.

But Annie Mae marched on down the street. She figured someone would call Dat if she used a phone in one of the stores to contact Miriam . . . if she could get the kids out to the county highway, surely a kind stranger would stop and give them a ride. . . .

Oh, but I'll give Yonnie a piece of my mind for drivin' off, leavin' us to fend for ourselves! she stewed as she hiked along.

Then she realized her visit to Higher Ground had just granted her fondest wish and answered her most fervent prayers: despite Yonnie's attempts to get her into bed, he'd made this long-awaited reunion a reality. Annie Mae sensed she'd pay for aggravating him this afternoon—just as Dat wouldn't let her get away with hauling off the wee ones. But what else could she do, after seeing how that young woman treated them?

"Annie Mae, I'm c-cold!" Josh piped up.

"*Jah*, how're we gettin' back home?" Joey chimed in. "Why'd that guy in the blue car drive away?"

Her heart throbbed painfully as she watched her little brothers hug themselves to keep warm. Maybe this wasn't such a good idea. What if they took sick because of her impetuous escape plan? If she went back to pack their clothes, surely that *girl* would have a phone she could use, and wouldn't fuss about getting rid of these kids she couldn't control. . . .

"Do ya wanna go back to the house, just long enough to fetch your things?" Annie Mae asked as they trudged on down the hill.

"*No!*" came the immediate reply, from all four kids.

Timmy began to wail and Sara grabbed her more tightly around the neck.

"Delilah's *mean* to us!" Josh declared.

"*Jah*, she is! And with Dat gone so much, she's always screechin' at us, too," Joey went on. "And when Dat's not around, she doesn't fix us dinner or let us get into the fridge for anything, neither."

"And we gotta eat cold cereal and store-bought bread coz she don't hardly know how to cook!"

Annie Mae's eyes widened as she trudged toward the county road. *Delilah's her name, is it? There's a biblical connection there,* she mused. But this wasn't the time to get caught up in Dat's love life. She would've concluded that young Delilah was merely his housekeeper, as Nazareth and Jerusalem Hooley had once been, except she'd called herself the kids' new *mamm* . . . which might explain why Dat had trimmed his beard and hair and dyed them black.

Oh what a tangled web we weave when first we practice to deceive. How often had she heard that adage as a child, from her own dear mother? Annie Mae set aside her memories and musings to focus on the road they were approaching. Her first priority was to find a ride back to Willow Ridge—

The *clip-clop! clip-clop!* of hooves behind them made Annie Mae turn and then gawk in disbelief at the big blue wagon rumbling toward them. "Adam!" she gasped. "Oh my God, ya must've—come on, kids! Stand to the side of the road while he pulls up for us."

"Adam Wagler!" Joey called out, while Josh waved both hands wildly above his head. "'Member *us?*"

Could this day get any crazier? Relief washed over Annie Mae as she stepped in front of the twins to keep them from rushing toward Adam's remodeling wagon.

As she gazed at Adam's intense expression, she couldn't recall the boy next door ever looking so powerful . . . so passionate about a purpose. And he was focused on *her*.

Forget that nonsense. He's only concerned about the kids, and gettin' us out of Higher Ground. Just doin' an old friend a big favor.

As Adam pulled his Belgian to a halt and hopped down to the road, Joey and Josh rushed at him. The stunned look on his face was priceless as he gripped their shoulders. "What's this all about?" he teased. "Do you miss me, or do you just want a ride in my big ole wagon?"

"*Jah,* it's real *gut* to see ya!" Joey gushed.

"So how come you're here?" his twin piped up. "Are you gonna live in Higher Ground, too?"

"Nope, that'll never happen," Adam replied as he glanced over their heads at Annie Mae. "Let's load you guys into the back where it's warmer. We can wrap you in some of my drop cloths."

"And how about you, Sara?" Annie Mae asked the little girl, who still clung to her shoulder. "Do you want to get in back with Joey and Josh? Or stay with me?"

"Joey and Josh!" Timmy blurted, reaching toward the brothers who were following Adam around to the back of his wagon.

Moments later the three boys were seated on the floor of the enclosed vehicle, delighting in the adventure of being wrapped in clean but paint-splotched lengths of heavy fabric. "You guys sit real still while we're moving, so you don't fall over my buckets and tools. No monkey business," Adam instructed as he pulled out a large towel. "I've got to shut the door, so it'll be kind of dark. But you're big brave boys, ain't so?"

"*Jah*, we're *gut*, Adam!" Josh declared.

"This'll be a really fun ride!" Joey said as he slung his arm around Timmy's shoulders.

"Okay, then. We'll see you when we get to Willow Ridge." Adam quickly fastened the latch that held the doors shut. Then he winked at Annie Mae, as though he had the boys and this situation effortlessly under control.

Annie Mae's heart rose into her throat. She sprang forward and hugged Adam hard with her free arm. He embraced her and Sara as though it were the most natural, common thing, and for a few moments they held each other with the toddler between them. Annie Mae closed her eyes, soaking up the strength and assurance she felt in Adam's strong arms, until they both exhaled self-consciously and stepped apart.

"Can't thank ya enough for hangin' around here," she admitted. "I should've left Yonnie's place with ya instead of—but we'll save all that for later," she said, glancing down at her little sister.

"Well, if you'd've left with me, we wouldn't have found the kids." Adam smiled ruefully as he tucked the towel around Sara. "I'm guessing that whole situation with the gal in the flowery dress is another story that can wait."

"You're not gonna believe—well, for now please take us to Miriam and Ben's so we can figure out what comes next," she said with a shake of her head. "I've learned more than I care to know today. I probably leaped when I should've looked, far as the kids are concerned, but—well, I just *couldn't* leave them here."

"Their faces are saying you did exactly the right

thing, Annie Mae," Adam replied as they walked to the front of the wagon. When he opened his arms, she handed Sara to him while she climbed inside.

When had she ever felt so grateful for someone being here when she needed him most? Yonnie's betrayal was already stinging, and once again Annie Mae had more questions than answers about her *dat* and what was going on in Higher Ground. Yet as Adam handed up her sister and then climbed into his wagon, Annie Mae sensed this day was finally headed in the right direction

She hugged Sara tight as the wagon lurched forward. "*Denki* again and again, Adam," she said in a tight voice. "Mighty nice of ya to watch out for me— for all of us."

Chapter Fourteen

What's going on here? Adam focused on the road, aware of the gently falling snow but far more aware of the shock waves radiating all over his body. Sure, Annie Mae was upset and she would've been grateful to *anybody* who could take her and the kids to safety. Yet in the moment they'd come together behind his wagon— even with her sister between them—something had flared. Something more than her gratitude and his relief.

Don't get tangled up in it, he reminded himself, as the litany of reasons for not dating any girl ran through his mind again.

But as Adam stole a glance across the seat, his heart thrummed steadily. With Sara cradled in her lap, half asleep and breathing deeply in total trust and comfort, Annie Mae suddenly seemed like the perfect woman to be sitting next to him, as his own beloved wife. He recalled watching Matthias and Sadie together and envying the closeness they shared—an inexplicable bond that made them so much more as a couple than the sum of their single selves. Which was why his brother was so very lost without her.

Back away slowly. Don't hurt her feelings, Adam's inner voice warned. *She's snatched Hiram's kids, so she's begging for trouble. And why do you think you could take on four little ones when you can't even fathom being responsible for their sister?*

Even so, as Annie Mae sat with her head resting on Sara's, her eyes closed and her long lashes curving down on her flawless cheek, she seemed like the antidote to all the doubts and fears that had plagued him since his *mamm*'s tragic death. Such *love* softened her face. Adam truly believed that God had sent him on the detour through Higher Ground, and had raised his eyes to the window of Yonnie's apartment, and had then told him to stick around after he'd confronted Stoltzfus. So why was it so far-fetched that God had an ulterior motive for bringing him to Annie Mae's rescue?

The preachers warn us against reading too much into situations that fall together so perfectly. While everything that happens is God's will, sometimes our interpretations stretch the truth in whatever direction we want it to go.

But when he stopped in the driveway of Ben and Miriam Hooley's house, and the boys scrambled through the couple's door without knocking, Adam couldn't deny that something was at work on a very high level.

"Oh my stars, would ya lookie here!" a familiar female voice cried.

"Joey and Josh and Timmy! You're a sight for these sore old eyes!" another gal in the house called out.

When Adam and Annie Mae stepped inside, it

seemed that quite a gathering was under way: Nazareth and Jerusalem Hooley were hugging the Knepp twins fiercely as Ben gleefully tossed Timmy into the air. Nellie, Rebecca, and Rhoda rushed away from the pots they'd been stirring at the stove, to take their turns at fussing over the Knepp boys. Miriam, too, was exclaiming over the kids, and when she saw Adam and Annie Mae, she hurried over.

"What's *this* about?" she asked as she gripped their hands excitedly. "When I saw Yonnie's car pullin' out this afternoon, I wasn't expectin' to see the whole rest of the Knepp family comin' back to visit!"

Annie Mae handed Sara over to Miriam so she could remove her coat. "It's quite a story, and I'm not sure just how it all came together." Her words tumbled out in a rush. "But at just the moment when Yonnie left me hangin' without so much as a clothespin, Adam came along, and—oh, Miriam, I don't know what to make of it!"

Annie Mae gripped Miriam's hand, as though to anchor herself for the waves she was about to make. "When we went past Dat's new house in Higher Ground, some girl named Delilah was chasin' the kids outside with a paddle! I just had to bring them back with me, and—and I have no idea what to do next."

Miriam's eyes widened like the plates on her table. The kitchen went totally silent. Ben and his aunts looked up from embracing the little boys, and then Adam realized that even Bishop Tom was here, his bearded face alight with wary surprise. All of them were gazing raptly at him and Annie Mae, as though frozen in a moment of utter amazement.

Adam wasn't sure whether to take off his coat or to

slip quietly out the door. With this many folks gathered
around, Annie Mae and her siblings would surely get
the care they needed—

"*I* think our next move will be washin' these faces
and hands," Nellie suggested as she took Sara from
Miriam's arms. "You boys come on back to the bathroom, to scrub up for supper."

"Fine idea," Rebecca chimed in as she steered the
twins and Timmy toward the hall.

As the kids were heading toward the other end of
the house, the adults gathered around Adam and
Annie Mae. "So what's this about ya bein' in Higher
Ground?" Jerusalem asked in a low voice. "I can't
think ya went to see your *dat.*"

When Annie Mae looked at Adam, he saw her hesitation . . . her fear and embarrassment about what had
happened in Yonnie's apartment. He returned her
gaze, silently assuring her that he'd support however
much of her tale she wanted to tell.

"That's a long story," Annie Mae hedged. "The
more important part is that Delilah said she was the
kids' new *mamm*—"

The Hooley sisters sucked in their breath, while
Ben and Bishop Tom's eyes narrowed.

"—yet she was chasin' them out of the house into
the snow, sayin' what stupid, mean little brats they
were. When they rushed at me, I just couldn't let them
go back to that—well, she's hardly any older than I
am!" Annie Mae continued in a strained voice. "And
the kids say she feeds them cold cereal and store-
bought bread, mostly—and they *refused* to go back into
that house. So I've been thankin' God that Adam was

drivin' by after Yonnie took off without us. And here we are."

Adam grasped her hand. Annie Mae looked so brave, yet so vulnerable. Her trembling prompted him to be strong for her—and for the kids who would return from the bathroom any minute now.

"So where was Hiram?" Bishop Tom asked. His brow furrowed as he read between the lines of Annie Mae's story.

"Delilah said he wasn't home," Annie Mae replied. "And she didn't put up the least bit of fight when I said I was takin' the kids—even though, when I said I was their sister, she . . . well, it seems Dat hasn't mentioned me or Nellie bein' part of his family."

Adam enveloped Annie Mae's trembling hand between both of his. The way Hiram had written off his two older daughters incensed him. She'd been dealing with much more than he'd suspected while he was driving her back to Willow Ridge.

"I'm so sorry ya had to go through that." Miriam slung an arm around Annie Mae and sighed. "Truth be told, we saw in *The Budget* that a Delilah Knepp was the scribe for Higher Ground—"

"But we figured she might be a Knepp cousin from over past Morning Star," Ben chimed in. He shook his head sadly as he looked at the others. "Sounds like Hiram didn't waste any time hitchin' up. But Joey and Josh have been known to stretch the truth now and again, so maybe—"

"Anybody can see they've lost weight, and they're none too clean, either," Nazareth put in. She glanced toward the hallway to be sure the kids weren't coming back. "Sounds like Hiram might've reeled in a new wife without tellin' her much about the kids until she'd said *jah* to marryin' him."

"No point in speculatin' about all of that," Bishop Tom pointed out. "We've got four children to look after—"

"And this is all my fault. Every bit of it." Annie Mae hung her head, closing her eyes against another wave of pain. "If I'd stayed with Dat—gone to Higher Ground with him like a *gut* daughter's supposed to—"

"Don't believe that for a minute," Adam stated firmly. He placed his hand on her back until she looked at him. "Your *dat* made his choices, and unfortunately they've not been *gut* ones."

"*Jah*," Miriam insisted as she gazed at the folks around them, "that's like sayin' it's all *my* fault the kids are in a bad way, because I didn't marry him. Don't go layin' this burden on yourself, child."

Ben, too, reached forward to gently grasp Annie Mae's arm. "None of the rest of us went with him, either, honey-girl," he reminded her. "The important thing is that ya saw the problem and got your sibs back amongst folks who'll take proper care of them. Ya did the right thing."

Everyone in their tight circle nodded emphatically, yet tears dribbled down Annie Mae's cheeks. "But when Dat gets back, he'll—and they don't have any clothes, or—"

As Bishop Tom stepped into their huddle, Adam could see the gears whirling in the bishop's mind. "I'm thinkin' the Zooks surely must have some pants, shirts, and dresses from when their youngest kids were this size."

"We could stop over there after supper and find out," Ben said.

"Fine idea," Tom agreed with an emphatic nod. "We can see how Henry's handlin' the fact that he's a preacher now—and this'll be his first call to become Christ's hands here on Earth."

Annie Mae followed the men's conversation as she swiped at her tears. "So . . . Miriam, this means I'd better quit waitin' tables to take care of the kids, what with Nellie goin' to school every day."

"*Ach,* but I'd be *so* happy to look after the boys and Sara again," Jerusalem cut in. "Leastaways, until I move to Cedar Creek with Vernon."

"Ya can't have any more time with them than *I* get, Sister!" Nazareth blurted. She smiled warmly at Annie Mae. "Seems to me you've been doin' real *gut* for yourself, workin' and settin' by some money—"

"So, what if the kids stay at *my* place?" Bishop Tom's face lit up as these new solutions took shape. "Adam's just finished paintin', and the rooms're all cleaned out, so that means you two Hooley sisters could move back to my farm, too—to look after the kids and me, as well. Sounds like a dream come true!"

Jerusalem clapped her hands while Nazareth beamed at the bishop. "That surely sounds cozier than bunkin' above Luke and Ira's mill," she replied. "Much as we love the nephews, comin' back to your place would be a big improvement—"

"And we'd be right there to tend our goats, too!" Jerusalem pointed out.

Bishop Tom looked like a fellow who'd just solved all the problems of the world as he smiled at Annie Mae. "We've got lots of cleared-out guest rooms now, if you and Nellie want to be there with the kids. I think it's real important for all you brothers and sisters to be together."

Adam let out the breath he'd been holding during this rapid-fire exchange of ideas. Just that fast, on the spur of an unexpected moment, this circle of friends had accommodated the six Knepps—had rearranged their lives to help a family in need. *This* was what Adam missed . . . the homey aromas of supper on the stove, along with the chorus of voices and the smiles that filled this home to the rafters with love and good-will. It seemed almost too good to be true—at least, considering the way things had worked out in his own life. "I should head home," he murmured. "Matthias will be wondering—"

"Get your brother and bring him back here for supper," Miriam insisted. "Always room here for you Waglers—and how could we not repay ya for takin' care of our Annie Mae and the kids today?"

"*Jah,*" Ben agreed, "you're the man who turned the page so the Knepps can start a whole new chapter."

"I was just passing through Higher Ground out of curiosity," Adam insisted, "after I'd delivered Tom's boxes to the Mennonites' missionary center—"

"Puh!" the bishop teased. "Humility's a *gut* thing, Adam, but—your *concern* for Annie Mae aside—there's no wrong in takin' credit for doin' what needed to be done."

Before Adam could protest that idea or Tom's hint about his feelings for Annie Mae, she stood square in front of him. She placed both of her hands on his shoulders, too, meeting his gaze head-on. "I was upset when ya barged into Yonnie's apartment," she murmured. "But ya had him figured right. And if ya hadn't stuck around Higher Ground until I got outta

there, the kids would still be walkin' in the snow with
no coats on, and I'd be a basket case tryin' to get
them home. *Denki* again for bein' way smarter and
more responsible than I was, Adam. You're a *gut* man,
ya know it?"

Adam couldn't breathe, much less find the words to
respond. Annie Mae's blue eyes were gazing straight
into his soul. But what did she see, really? She had *no
idea* how her words terrified him even as they made
him feel . . . respected. Cherished. *Loved*. And that
was the scary part—not to mention that the Hooleys
and Bishop Tom had witnessed her words. And
now they were watching for his reaction, awaiting his
response.

Adam cleared his throat. Annie Mae still had a grip
on his shoulders, and she would not be denied as she
kept gazing at him. He hoped whatever words came
out of his mouth wouldn't sound totally incoherent or
ridiculous. "I—I was watching out for myself, mostly,"
he admitted. "Couldn't have handled my conscience
if I'd driven away from Yonnie's place and then later
found out he'd—well—"

"I won't be seein' him ever again." Annie Mae's
smile wobbled, but her words rang with unwavering
commitment. "Even if he wasn't workin' for Dat, he's
gotten too big for his English britches and—well, he's
up to no *gut* in ways I don't even want to think about."

"Praise be to God," the bishop murmured. "If
you've seen the light about that Stoltzfus fella, Annie
Mae, my day's been made."

"Amen to that," Ben echoed.

Adam's heart was racing, but this was no time to
delve into what Annie Mae's words might mean for

him. From the hallway came the thundering of young feet.

"Let's *eat!*" one of the twins crowed.

"Rebecca says we're havin' creamed chicken and homemade rolls!" his look-alike chimed in. "And macaroni and goat cheese—with bacon!"

"And Naz'reth's lemon pudding cake!" Sara cried out ecstatically.

"Whoopie pies!" Timmy whooped. "Lotsa whoopie pies."

No wonder the house smelled sooo good. Adam's stomach rumbled at the kids' roll call of the supper menu, while everyone around him laughed and opened their arms to greet the cleaned-up Knepps. Everyone except Annie Mae, who was still smiling at *him.*

"Please stay," she whispered. "Get Matthias and come back, okay? It won't be the same celebration without you here . . . Short Stack."

Adam squelched the inner protest that had always protected him from getting too close when a girl appealed to him. After all, if he came back, he'd be in a roomful of people, and they'd be deciding the details of where the kids would stay. . . .

"All right, you talked me into it," he replied as he returned her smile. "See you in a few."

As he climbed into his wagon, Adam didn't notice the cold seat or frown about how the snow was starting to accumulate on the roadway. What had just happened in the Hooley house? While he'd figured the good folks of Willow Ridge would find a place for the Knepp kids, he hadn't anticipated being invited into this close-knit circle . . . sought after and commended. Annie Mae had reeled him in with her gentle insistence that she wanted nothing more to do with Yonnie, and that he, Adam Wagler, was a good man. She'd made it sound as though he *mattered* to her.

Hook, line, and sinker, his inner voice warned.

But—for this evening, anyway—he was okay with that.

Chapter Fifteen

What have I gone and done? Now Dat*'s sure to come after me!*

Annie Mae willed herself to lie still, because Nellie was fast asleep beside her in the bed they shared at Bishop Tom's. Across the room in a crib the Zooks had loaned them, Sara's deep, even breathing made her envy the little girl's comfort and trust. With Ben and the bishop's help, all six of them—plus the two Hooley sisters—had relocated to this home with surprising ease and lack of fuss after supper. In the next bedroom, the three little boys had fallen asleep nearly as soon as their heads had hit the pillows, delighted that Jerusalem and Nazareth were tucking them in again. From the bedroom on her other side came a duet of snoring that told her the Hooley sisters were sleeping peacefully, as well.

No one else seemed concerned about the consequences of her actions today, yet as the clock downstairs chimed midnight . . . one o'clock . . . two . . . Annie Mae wrestled with the decisions she'd made so impulsively. Although everyone at Miriam's had reassured her she'd done exactly the right things—and while she wouldn't have changed her behavior one iota, after the way Delilah had treated her siblings—her sense of doom felt like a fifty-pound bag of flour lying on her chest.

And because Tom Hostetler had taken them all in, Dat would wreak havoc on the new bishop, for certain. It wouldn't surprise her one bit if he barged in on Tom and Nazareth's wedding ceremony this coming Thursday, just as he'd made a scene when Ben and Miriam had married. And it would surely be *her*, his errant eldest daughter, whom he snatched up off the pew bench as he hurled his accusations and angry words.

And if Yonnie Stoltzfus told Dat about their visit to his apartment, and Adam's involvement with their escape from Higher Ground, poor Adam would suffer, as well.

Adam had been such a rock this afternoon. Was it her imagination, or had he let down his guard and warmed up to her? As she lay in the darkness, Annie Mae relived every touch of his sturdy, work-worn hands . . . every encouraging smile . . . the way he'd held her close after he'd wrapped the boys in a drop cloth to keep them warm.

Don't get caught up with Adam, her thoughts warned as she turned onto her other side yet again. *Why would he fall for ya now that four little kids and Nellie come as part of your package? Why would* any *fella court ya, now that you're responsible for so many lives?*

But she'd made her stand, as far as never seeing Yonnie again—with witnesses to hold her to it. Annie Mae sensed, however, that Yonnie wouldn't accept her rejection at face value—*because he'll walk away or come back whenever it suits him. So where does that leave you?*

Annie Mae frowned in the darkness. Why had she not seen this trait in Yonnie before? Years she'd known him, yet their times together had been carefree and adventurous and—

That's because ya didn't cross him. He said jump *and ya always said* how high?

Annie Mae rose from the bed to go to the window— anything to relieve the restlessness of her soul. Outside, the full moon shone with a lustrous beauty that made the fresh snow glimmer in the rolling pastures that stretched between here and the Kanagy place. The barns and silos stood peaceful watch over the countryside she knew so well, yet she felt she was seeing a different Willow Ridge.

Or was she seeing Willow Ridge with different eyes?

Lord, this is all so confusing and—and I don't suppose Ya have any reason to listen to me, after all the years I've spent runnin' the other way, not listenin' to You, Annie Mae prayed in silent desperation. *But so many gut folks could be hurt by my choices. So if Ya could steer me toward the right answers, I'll listen closer now. I'll pay attention, instead of lettin' Yonnie and my wayward inclinations get the best of me.*

Annie Mae stepped away from the window and then stopped. Her reflection in the dresser mirror across the room caught her by surprise: her white nightgown glowed in the moonlight, and with her black hair hanging to her waist, she resembled the angels Bishop Tom carved for his Nativity sets.

"For now we see in a mirror, dimly, but then face-to-face. Now I know in part, but then I shall know just as I also am known."

Annie Mae couldn't name the chapter and verse

that had just come to mind; at this breathtaking
moment, she felt painfully aware of how little attention she'd paid to the Scriptures. But the goose
bumps that prickled on her skin told her something
astounding was happening. While gazing into mirrors
was frowned upon because it fostered vanity, this
moment felt *holy* . . . like a sign from God Himself. An
answer to her prayer.

Her body relaxed and her pulse slowed. She gazed
without blinking, searching for meaning in this vision,
on this darkest night her soul had known since her
mamm had died. Indeed, it could well be her mother
gazing back at her from the glass, in the form of an
angel come to bear an important message.

Annie Mae held her breath, unable to look away. As
she recalled, folks in the Bible who'd been greeted by
angels had been terrified, yet she felt peaceful . . . as
serene as the snow-covered, rolling hills outside.

Is it you, Mamm? *Are ya tryin' to tell me something?*

Oh, but she wished she could speak aloud to this
vision and get the answers she'd yearned for since her
mother had passed. She'd been a girl of eleven, so un-
prepared to take on the responsibility of watching
over Nellie . . . and then for mothering the four wee
ones when her stepmother Linda had died in child-
birth, as well.

*But you did it. And you'll do what needs to be done again
and again, my child, for it's your purpose in life to care for
others—especially those who are defenseless and have no one
else to turn to. You are stronger than you know.*

Annie Mae turned to be sure no one else had
entered the room. She was the only one awake, yet

she'd heard a voice as clearly as if Bishop Tom had come to the bedroom door to speak to her.

It was all in your head. Don't go thinkin' it's real just because—

But the words *had* been real. She'd never been more certain of anything in her life. Annie Mae's hand fluttered to her heart as she considered what this little episode might mean. Why would she be seeing angels that looked like Mamm and hearing voices . . . unless she was going crazy?

Not crazy. Committed. Committed to moving forward on the right path, come what may.

Annie Mae's breath escaped slowly. She backed away, into the bedroom's shadows, but she'd seen what she was supposed to see. And she'd heard a voice intended for her ears alone.

At that moment, she knew exactly what she must do.

Annie Mae slipped back into bed, yet she was so awake—so *aware*—she had to force herself to lie very still and just *think*. In a couple of hours, Tom would be rising to milk his dairy herd, and it was he she needed to speak with . . . to share the new direction she had received. He would understand and help her, as he always had. The bishop would defend her and her siblings against Yonnie or Dat or whoever tried to dishonor her, for he was a beacon of the Old Order faith. Like a lantern in her father's darkness Tom would shine, and he would help her see the path she should take, too.

It was a Sunday when there was no church service in Willow Ridge, so Jerusalem and Nazareth would most likely devote their day to the children. The unhurried morning would be the perfect time to figure

out who would sew clothes for them and what would
happen if Dat came here to Tom's house. . . .

When she heard the bishop's footsteps on the
wooden stairs, Annie Mae rose and quickly dressed in
the darkness. As she braided her hair. wound it into a
bun, and then put on her *kapp,* Nellie slept on. And
that was just as well. Annie Mae hoped for some time
alone with the bishop . . . to be sure she hadn't misin-
terpreted her vision.

When she reached the kitchen, Tom was lavishing
apple butter on a slice of bread before he headed
through the snow to the barn. His eyes widened when
he saw she was up, but his smile was warm.

"Thought ya might sleep in, after yesterday bein'
so eventful," he mused. "If you're hungry, there's
plenty of—"

"I—I wanna talk to you," Annie Mae said breath-
lessly. "Can I go to the barn with ya while ya milk?"

"Now there's a request I don't often hear," he
replied with a quiet chuckle. "I'd be glad to have ya,
Annie Mae. Dress warm, now—there's boots in the
mudroom. Looks like we got several new inches of
snow in the night."

A few minutes later they were striding through
fresh, fluffy snow that came up over her feet, yet Annie
Mae felt warm . . . as calm as the blanketed countryside that surrounded them for as far as she could see
in every direction. Once again she was struck by the
beauty of Willow Ridge . . . rolling hills and tidy farmsteads where folks she'd known and loved all her life
would soon be lighting their lamps to start their day. It
was this unchanging sense of stability, this enduring
ritual, that reassured her as she and Tom entered the

earthy-smelling barn. For the past several years she'd
rebelled against the routine of her life—the ever-
necessary *rules*—as being dull and limiting. Yet now
Annie Mae took immense comfort in knowing that the
folks here stood firm in their beliefs and in the sense
that their lives had *meaning*.

The black-and-white Holsteins shifted in their
stalls, lowing and awaiting the bishop's tending—they
depended upon him as surely as the faithful all around
town looked to him for guidance and assurance.
When he'd turned on the generator, gotten the first
round of cows sanitized, and then hooked them up to
the milking machine, Tom turned to her. His face
glowed in the light of the lantern hanging on the wall
above them.

"What's on your mind, Annie Mae? You've had an
awful lot to deal with since your visit to Higher
Ground," he said in a low voice.

"I wanna join the church," Annie Mae blurted.
"Wanna start my instruction *now!* Or—or as soon as ya
can do that for me," she added in a less demanding
tone.

The bishop's smile was a sight to behold. "Praise be
to God!" he cried as he grasped her shoulders.
"Nobody's happier than I am to hear that, honey-girl."

Annie Mae had been holding her revelation inside
long enough that it spewed forth now. "I—I saw a
vision this morning," she rasped. "Well, it was my own
reflection in the mirror, really, yet it seemed like an
angel—maybe even Mamm—was tellin' me that I was
to take my vow and look after the kids as my purpose in life. And even if I have to remain a *maidel*—on
account of how fellas will most likely shy away from

latchin' on to all six of us—so be it. I'm ready to do that."

The bishop's swarthy face softened. His eyes glimmered as he gazed at her, contemplating what he'd say next. "That's quite a stand you're takin', but an admirable one," he murmured. "Truth be told, I believe the right fella will welcome ya into his heart and his home someday, no matter how many younger ones ya bring along. But meanwhile, can I ask ya what brought this on?" he said softly. "I don't doubt your intentions for a minute. But this *is* a mighty sudden turnaround for ya, Annie Mae."

Relieved that the bishop hadn't railed at her for saying she'd seen a vision, Annie Mae relaxed. "*Jah,* I understand why you're sayin' that," she murmured. "I think it's partly because I saw Yonnie Stoltzfus in a brighter light yesterday, considerin' some of the things he said and . . . wanted to do."

Tom nodded, remaining quiet so she would finish her thought. The cattle in the milking stanchions shifted their feet on the hard floor, yet he seemed in no hurry to turn his attention away from her.

Annie Mae cleared her throat. "It was like I could suddenly see how he was usin' that fancy car and his new apartment and a forty-dollar tip for pie—and even the roses he gave me for Valentine's Day—to coax me into jumpin' the fence with him," she admitted. "And I realized that he might just as quicklike *dump* me after I did that, and—and he was usin' the kids to lure me to Higher Ground, too. He's workin' for Dat now, ya know."

Tom's eyes widened. "Let me shift another bunch

of cows onto the milkers while I think about this, okay?"

She nodded, observing how he spoke softly to his Holsteins as he removed the milkers . . . how gently he welcomed the next cows, who took their turns without any need for coaxing. As Tom cleansed their udders and hooked up the milkers again, Annie Mae sensed she'd made the most important statement of her life to exactly the right man.

As he approached her again, Tom's expression waxed more serious. "So how was Higher Ground lookin'?" he asked her. "And how was it that ya made off with your brothers and sister, yet your *dat* hasn't called or come after them?"

"Delilah said he was gone," Annie Mae replied, thinking back to that fateful conversation. "Yonnie called himself the city commissioner. Said he was helpin' with the layout of the town and other stuff. I suppose a dozen or more houses are mostly finished, plus a bank and a café and a school—and of course, Dat's place sits on the highest hill and it's the fanciest amongst them."

"Hmm . . . could be Hiram's gone east to rustle up more folks to join his colony," Tom replied. "And from what I saw of his haircut, and of that car Yonnie's drivin', I can only guess your *dat*'s shifted over to bein' a really liberal Mennonite . . . maybe makin' up his own version of their beliefs—not that it matters," he added emphatically. "Right now, I'm just glad you've come to me this way, daughter. I'll do my best to keep ya out of harm's way."

"*Denki*, Bishop Tom," Annie Mae murmured. "I think, deep down, that angel I saw was tellin' me that the Old Order will be my refuge, my strength, for whatever comes at me. My father might've abandoned me, but the Heavenly Father will never, ever do that. So I'd best start payin' better attention to Him."

Tom's face took on a radiance that warmed Annie Mae all over. "Sounds to me like ya grew up—overnight," he replied in a prayerful voice. "And that's another way God works out His purpose. With some folks, it's a gradual path and they get to where they always knew they were goin'. And some folks, like Saul in the Bible, have to be struck down before they'll change their ways. But you, Annie Mae, came to a fork in the road and ya made your choice right there on the spot, believin' there was no turnin' back. I'm proud of ya."

Annie Mae bowed her head, feeling as though this servant of the Lord had just pronounced his benediction over her soul. For a moment, her eyes felt hot and her throat tightened, yet she wanted to whoop for joy at the same time. Then, an overwhelming sense of conviction cleared her mind and she simply basked in the goodness and compassion of the man standing before her. "*Denki* for listenin', Tom. I—I knew ya would."

He gently squeezed her shoulder. "This has been the finest moment I've known as a bishop. We started up a class a few weeks ago, for Rhoda's Andy and the Kanagy brothers—and Ben's joined us so he can learn more about bein' a preacher. You'll be in *gut* company, Annie Mae. Meanwhile, I can catch ya up on what we've already discussed, so you'll be up to speed by next Sunday."

Annie Mae lingered a few moments more, watching Tom tend his next batch of cows. It seemed the least she could do, to go in and start breakfast so good, solid food would await him and the others when they came to the table. When she stepped outside into the fresh snow, most of the world still slept in the serene darkness of a winter's night, yet she felt the hope of a bright new dawn. Annie Mae raised her face, sighing deeply with the rightness of it all as she gazed up at the glowing moon.

Denki to You, too, God, for listenin'. And for shinin' a light when I didn't know just how dark it was. . . .

Chapter Sixteen

When he and his brother opened the barn door early Sunday morning, Adam headed directly to the red blinking light on the wall phone. "Hope this isn't bad news," he remarked as Matthias lit a lantern. "Can't think who might've left us a message after we got back from the Hooleys' last night."

"I'm not keen on drivin' clear over to Ruth's on these snowy roads, but we don't have squat in the house for dinner, either," Matthias remarked. He stood in the glow of the lantern, waiting to listen to the message.

Adam pressed the PLAY button. *You fellas better stay right where you are today.* Their older sister's voice resounded in the barn. *The kids've all caught the flu, and I'm sure you don't want it. Have a blessed Sunday and we'll catch up to you later.*

"*Jah,* that makes me feel blessed all right," Matthias said sourly. "*One* of us should've stopped by Zook's Market yesterday."

"Well, *one* of us was delivering the bishop's boxes and got sidetracked with a passel of Knepp kids,"

Adam shot back. "And meanwhile that got us invited to Miriam's for a *gut* supper last night."

Matthias's eyebrows could've swept the cobwebs out of the rafters. "Are ya sayin' I should've laid aside that English fella's tack I was workin' on to—"

"Did you even think to get meat out of the freezer?" Even as he asked the question, Adam regretted the way their voices were rising along with their tempers.

"At least it wasn't *me* chasin' around Higher Ground, checkin' up on Yonnie Stoltzfus's girlfriend," his brother countered. "Now *there's* a useless pursuit, seein's how Annie Mae'll never quit runnin' around to give *you* a second look—and seein's how she's just askin' for her *dat* to come back and slap her around for snatchin' his kids."

Adam clenched his jaw against another comeback. He pivoted on his heel and went to fetch hay for the horses. "Somebody got up on the wrong side of the bed," he muttered to Jerry as he passed behind his gelding's stall. "Not that there seems to be a right side to it."

"*Jah,* well at least I'm not moony-eyed over a gal who looks right over the top of my head!" Matthias retorted.

Adam stopped. Turned around slowly. Consciously let out his breath as he counted to ten. "This is no way for us to be talking, Matthias. The Lord gave it a rest on the Sabbath and so should we."

"Fine." Matthias shrugged stiffly. "I'll not be doin' any work, so you're on your own, far as meals are concerned today."

"Fair enough."

Adam climbed into the loft and then tossed down three bales of hay to divide among the horses' stalls.

Already it felt like an endless, aimless day and the sun wasn't even up. Until Matthias had snapped about neither of them buying any groceries, Adam had been in a fairly decent mood, but now resentment hung around him like low-lying winter storm clouds. Why did Matthias talk as though it was such a terrible thing, helping Annie Mae and the Knepp kids? And why did his brother think he was getting interested in her, anyway? *Moony-eyed? Really?*

Adam took his time feeding Herbert and Jerry and their other horses, careful to stay out of his brother's way as Matthias filled the water troughs and then stomped out of the barn. He began to shovel out the stalls, taking his time. As this was a visiting Sunday, he entertained thoughts of driving over to Bishop Tom's—to see how the kids were doing, of course— but that would seem like an obvious play for a dinner invitation . . . and maybe Tom and the Hooley sisters would think he was there to see Annie Mae.

And maybe I would be.

Adam shook his head to rid himself of that thought. But if he didn't go somewhere, he'd either have to avoid Matthias all day or he'd be scrapping with him until they said things they would regret. The hungrier they both got, the nastier they'd feel, too. His gaze wandered to the back stall, then to the blue tarp. . . .

Anything involving a motorized vehicle was strictly forbidden on the Sabbath. Adam had purchased fresh oil and gasoline a while back, when Rebecca had told him to clean up the motorcycle before she ran an ad online for him. He hadn't had time to work on it these past weeks—and work was the wrong thing to be doing on a Sunday . . . *but who's to say I consider it work? Taking the cycle apart to clean it and then putting it together again isn't any different than assembling a jigsaw puzzle. It would be a labor of love, considering how keeping myself busy today would help Matthias and me love each other more. . . .*

Adam recognized the serpent's whisper when he heard it, yet as he headed toward the house, he knew he'd be spending his day in the barn after he'd found something to eat. No one would be out and around today—with the Knepp house sitting empty, nobody had any reason to come down their road—so no one would be the wiser about how he kept his idle hands from becoming the Devil's workshop. Cleaning the cycle would remind him how his mother had died because of his carelessness, and how he had no business daydreaming about Annie Mae embracing him behind the wagon yesterday . . . how they had gripped each other's hands last night . . .

In the kitchen, Adam spread peanut butter on stale graham crackers. His brother was stirring the last can of pork and beans into the can of tomato soup he'd hoped to snag for himself, but Adam said nothing. Clearly, if he didn't find any meat in the deep freeze that would thaw quickly, driving to New Haven for subs or pizza was their only alternative for hot food, as grocery shopping was another forbidden activity on Sunday.

Matthias sighed forlornly. "It was a lot easier when Sadie and Mamm cooked, and all we had to do was come to the table and eat it," he remarked.

Adam nodded, glancing at the table, which was cluttered with dirty dishes and mail. He scraped the last of the store-bought peach preserves from the jar onto half of his graham crackers, mentally shaking his head. He and Matthias made good money, yet they couldn't seem to get the cleaning or the laundry or the cooking routines down. And what kept both of them so all-fired busy that shopping had slipped their minds *again?*

Adam washed his unsatisfying breakfast down with the last of the milk. "Later," he said as he headed for the barn.

"*Jah,* see ya," Matthias muttered.

As he hurried toward the barn, Adam inhaled the cold morning air—so much fresher than what the house smelled like. He tingled with the anticipation of cleaning and restoring his motorcycle, even as he twitched because this was a sin on Sunday. But it seemed the lesser of two evils, keeping himself busy rather than sacrificing another day to the bitterness, grief, and despair Matthias preferred to wallow in. Later, Adam planned to treat Matthias to a large, steaming pizza covered in ham, sausage, and bacon with lots of olives and green peppers and sauce at the pizza place in New Haven. Just the thought of a meal that neither of them had to cook bolstered his mood.

Once inside the barn, Adam set to work. It was comforting to occupy himself here while the horses contentedly munched their hay and dozed, standing in their stalls. To get past staring at the sleek machine and the guilt it carried as an invisible passenger, he hooked up its battery to the solar panel—with which they recharged the car batteries that ran the lights and windshield wipers on their buggies. His hands knew what to do without much conscious thought, so Adam happily lost himself in the maintenance chores: changing the gas and oil . . . inflating the tires . . . cleaning the spark plugs . . .

In his mind, he recalled the forays he used to take on the back roads of Willow Ridge, way past Morning

Star and on toward Warrensburg. Driving and balancing on this cycle had come as second nature to him. With coaching from Allen Stoltzfus, he'd obtained his license shortly after he'd traded a horse to Allen for this vehicle . . . this wicked, forbidden machine that had carried him beyond Plain limitations. Adam could still feel the wind in his face and the inimitable thrill of revving the engine as his heartbeat accelerated with each change of gears.

For the first couple of months, when he'd spent all his spare moments on this cycle, he'd known the exhil-arating speed of freedom . . . halcyon hours when he'd been accountable to no one. Before his *mamm*'s death, he fully explored the lure of the open road and the English lifestyle that would make such a dream possible beyond his *rumspringa,* if he chose to leave the faith . . . and to leave his family.

But then, as now, reality butted in. Adam quickly dismissed the disturbing images of Mamm's buggy getting hit full-on by a truck in that intersection. It really was time to let go of those painful memories—or at least to release the crippling guilt they inspired. How could he do that?

When he opened the cycle's storage compartment to clean out any dead insects, he found his driver's license—complete with his photo on it, for he hadn't yet joined the Old Order when he'd earned it.

Adam stared. Had he really looked so reckless and young and daring a mere six years ago? By compari-son, he surely must be in his forties now, judging from the heaviness he felt some days.

That was then, this is now, he reminded himself. Every man he knew—including Bishop Tom—had indulged in a few daredevil activities when he was out of school and not yet married or committed to the church. The faith's founding fathers had understood the wisdom of letting young people—especially young men—sow their wild oats during *rumspringa* before settling down.

And while Adam didn't resent the settling-down part so much, he sure did miss the happiness he'd known in those days before Mamm had passed. But he had a successful, thriving business and a roof over his head. No room to complain.

Just room for improvement.

With a soft cloth, he lovingly cleaned the leather seat and the matching silver-studded saddlebags behind it. *Annie Mae would be just the sort of girl to climb on behind me and hang on for dear life as we shot down the straightaways.*

That pretty vision was a waste of mental energy. Yet it made Adam smile as he buffed the black fenders and the chrome pipes back to their original shine. His stomach rumbled, reminding him that several hours had passed since he'd eaten his peanut butter and graham crackers. Yet the contentment he felt compelled him to lavish a little extra elbow grease on the tires—

The barn door slid open on its track, letting in daylight and a rush of young voices.

"Adam Wagler! We came out to see ya—"

"*Jah,* and we've got presents!" two boys proclaimed in identical voices.

"We been colorin' perty cards!" a little girl chirped.

Before Adam could steer them away from his deepest, darkest secret, the four little Knepps charged around the corner of the stalls, their faces alight with smiles and sunshine.

Then Joey and Josh halted, their eyes wide. "Holy

cow!" one of them cried out, while the other one said, "That is one hot—*cool*—motorcycle ya got there!"

"Is it *yours,* Adam?"

How will you explain this? Adam's conscience taunted as he stood up, the polishing rag in his hand. "Well, look who's here!" he hedged, happy to see these little guys and Sara even if they'd surprised him at an awkward moment. "And how is it, living at Bishop Tom's with Nazareth and Jerusalem?"

The twins edged closer to gaze at the cycle, while Sara demurely approached him with several folded pieces of paper flapping in her tiny hand. "These are for you," she said as she held them up.

Adam's heart rose into his throat. Instead of taking her homemade cards, he swooped her up to rest against his shoulder. Her dark braids, which were wound and pinned to the back of her head, looked shiny and clean. She wore a dress that reminded him of the "pink pill" candies he'd loved as a kid. "*Denki,* Sara," he whispered around the lump in his throat. "Awfully nice of you to draw these—"

A movement behind the boys made him look up and his heart plummeted into his stomach. Annie Mae and Nellie had halted at the sight of the black motorcycle, their eyes wide as they looked from the bike to him.

"And *gut* afternoon to you ladies, as well," Adam croaked. "As you can see, I, um, wasn't expecting any company."

Was that a spark of admiration in Annie Mae's eyes—or was she gleefully planning to tell Bishop Tom what she'd walked in on? Just moments ago Adam had been thinking about her, and now she'd appeared, as though summoned by his wayward thoughts.

"Well, now," she murmured as she slowly approached, never taking her eyes from the black vehicle. "This must be the motorcycle Rebecca was talkin' about a while back. I can see why she was so excited about it."

Adam exhaled, aware that Sara was fiddling with her papers on top of his head. Why hadn't he figured Rebecca would tell Annie Mae or Rhoda about the transaction she was setting up for him? For that matter, Ben and Miriam probably knew about it . . . *and even so, no lightning bolts have shot through the ceiling, calling God's wrath down on you.*

"*Jah,* I figure it's been stashed in here plenty long enough, considering how I'm not to be riding it anymore," Adam said quietly. And that's *all* he intended to say, too. No need to delve into why he'd stopped riding it, or why he'd had such trouble getting rid of it.

Nellie's hand went to her mouth as she giggled. "Adam, ya gotta hold real still now," she said as her focus settled above his face. "Sara's makin' a hat for ya."

"*Jah,* a dunce cap!" one of the twins crowed.

"Oh, don't anybody tell Jerusalem," his brother chimed in, "or she'll be makin' *us* wear one when she starts playin' school with us again!"

A chuckle bubbled up from deep within Adam, and with the effort of standing absolutely still for Sara's hat-making, his laughter came out in strained spurts. The pixie in his arms was giggling, too, and Timmy was pointing up at his head, stomping his small feet as he laughed. Despite Adam's best efforts to hold still, the papers fluttered to the floor.

Annie Mae quickly retrieved them. How was it that the gloom of his morning had suddenly disappeared, along with some of the anxiety about this dark, shining secret he'd been keeping in the barn all these years?

When Annie Mae gave him the folded papers, the simple crayon drawings tugged at his heartstrings—but not as much as the expression on her flawless face as she gazed down at him. "There's a story here, Short Stack, and I can't wait to hear it when it's just you and me," she said in a low voice. "I'd ask for a ride, but I've told Bishop Tom I'm takin' my vows as soon as possible. And what with you already belongin' to the church, that wouldn't look so *gut.*"

"And then there's the snow," Adam pointed out, although the intensity of her gaze seemed to be driving all rational thought from his mind. "Not so *gut,* far as the traction on these old tires goes."

"*Jah,* the snow," she echoed softly. "A reminder of how white and pure and clean we come when we're washed in the blood of the Lamb, our Jesus."

Adam blinked. It wasn't like Annie Mae Knepp, the previous bishop's rebellious daughter, to go calling up religion. Nor had he figured she'd take her instruction immediately on the heels of yesterday's events.

But hadn't he done the same? Hadn't he seen the church as his refuge after he'd endured more than his soul could handle, the day he was to blame for his mother's death? It didn't feel one bit safe to him, knowing Annie Mae would insist on hearing the story behind this vintage motorcycle . . . but that wouldn't happen today, what with the kids being here. "Some of us could use a cleaning up with the help of Jesus," he agreed. "But for right now—"

"Right now, I'm thinkin' we should clean up that kitchen of yours, Adam," Nellie remarked wryly. "While we talked with Matthias, it was easy to see that you bachelor brothers could use a little help."

Adam cringed. It was embarrassing enough that

these visitors had caught him with his motorcycle, but it was downright humiliating that they'd seen the kitchen in such filthy disarray. "Matthias and I need to clean, all right, but it's the Sabbath," he pointed out.

Nellie shared a purposeful look with her sister, shrugging. "Cleanin' can be *fun*—like playin' instead of work—when you're doin' it at somebody else's place," she said. "And even on Sundays, we girls wash the dishes and redd up the kitchen after meals, just like the fellas tend the livestock chores."

"And by the way, we're supposed to bring you Waglers back to Tom's for some of Jerusalem's soup at suppertime," Annie Mae chimed in. "Meanwhile, she and the bishop and Nazareth are knee-deep in plans for the wedding on Thursday, so we're keepin' the kids out of their way. It's all *gut*."

Adam's mouth dropped open. Just that fast, the Knepp sisters had volunteered to brighten his home and supply his supper. *It is all gut—if you don't mess up their kindness. Accept it without a fuss.*

He smiled again at Sara, who'd made herself quite at home in his arms. "I can't argue with anything you've said," he admitted. "And I'm grateful you'd want to help us out of a fix we're in, on account of how *one* of us brothers didn't think to do any grocery shopping. You Knepps have come to our rescue—like an answer to a prayer."

Was it his imagination, or did Annie Mae's blue eyes twinkle? "Let's call it payback," she murmured. "How about if we girls get started on that kitchen and we'll see ya when you're ready to come in?"

Adam nodded, relinquishing Sara when Annie Mae opened her arms. He was still uncomfortable that the kids would most probably blab to the bishop about his cycle when they got back to Tom's place. But he'd caused this problem himself, by keeping the vehicle—and its secret—for so long. And Annie Mae would demand the full story. She was too curious to let him explain the cycle away as merely a memento of his *rumspringa*.

This was a fine fix he'd gotten himself into. But then, *fixing* was exactly what he'd needed for a long, long time now.

Chapter Seventeen

Annie Mae drove the buggy into Bishop Tom's lane and stopped outside the barn. Her heart was thumping like an excited puppy's tail as she glanced back to watch Matthias and Adam pull in behind them. Her little brothers had ridden with the Waglers, and that tickled her, but she wanted to make an important point to them before everyone went inside . . . because she suspected Adam could use a favor.

"How about if ya unhitch us, Nellie, while I grab the boys?" she said. "They don't need to carry on about how we, um, *worked* to get that kitchen clean again. Among other things."

"I'm with ya there," Nellie replied. "We toyed with the truth of the Sabbath a bit—not that we weren't doin' the Lord's work, helpin' Matthias and Adam. Never seen a fridge that looked so empty and pathetic."

Annie Mae stepped briskly to the Waglers' rig. When the buggy door opened, she extended her arms to catch the twins and Timmy before they could hop out. Joey and Josh looked like overfilled balloons, ready to burst with their discovery of Adam's motorcycle.

"We need to talk, boys." Annie Mae gazed intently at them until they returned her attention. "I want ya to think about how itchy ya feel when you've done somethin' naughty and ya don't want anybody else to find out. Do ya know what I'm talkin' about?"

Their young faces tightened as they thought about it. "Like when the Zook boys came over before Christmas and helped us hitch up Dat's sleigh?" Joey ventured.

"And we knew we wasn't s'posed to ride by ourselves, but we sneaked out to race with them anyway?" Josh chimed in.

"I'm glad ya remember that—and how bad it all turned out when that English fella's car hit the sleigh." When Annie Mae glanced at Adam, his quizzical expression threatened to make her laugh and ruin the mood she'd set. "And ya recall how ya didn't get rid of all the itchy feelin's about it until ya told Jerusalem and Nazareth how sorry ya were, ain't so? They'd figured out what you'd done, but until ya confessed the details yourself, ya didn't really come clean."

Joey and Josh looked at each other in that way twins had of communicating silently.

Annie Mae leaned closer, hoping to drive her point home with a minimum of fuss . . . hoping her brothers really listened. "It's the same way with Adam," she continued in a purposeful voice. "So that's why I don't want ya runnin' inside blurtin' out to Bishop Tom—or to *anybody*—about that motorcycle. Adam's feelin' that same itch, and it's not our place to tattle on him—"

"Jerusalem gets after us for tellin' tales," Joey interrupted with a decisive nod.

"'Specially when we're tryin' to pass off the trouble onto somebody else," Josh finished.

"Ya got it just right," Annie Mae said as she squeezed the twins' shoulders. "So it's best for all of us to let Adam have those itches—"

"Itches in his britches!" Timmy piped up.

Once again Annie Mae nearly laughed and ruined the serious mood—and Adam was biting back a chuckle, as well. "Right," she replied. "Which means we'll let Adam do the confessin' in his own *gut* time. He's doin' the right thing, gettin' the cycle ready to sell because he knows he's not supposed to ride it. And he knows God's watchin' every move he makes, too— just like God knows every little thing you boys're doin'. And He heard ya say you'd keep your lips zipped."

From the corner of her eye, she saw Nellie and Sara heading for the house. Annie Mae gazed one more time at each of her three brothers. "*So*—what's gonna happen as soon as ya get into the house?" she quizzed them.

"I'm gonna pee!" Joey announced.

"Me, too—and wash up for supper," Josh joined in. "I'm so hungry I just might eat all of Jerusalem's alphabet soup myself."

"Supper!" Timmy echoed. "Grilled cheese sammitches."

"All right then," Annie Mae drew her finger across her lips, as though closing a zipper. Then she stepped out of the buggy's doorway. "We're countin' on you guys to be as *gut* as your word."

When the three boys had scurried halfway across the yard, they threw themselves down in the fresh snow to make angels. Annie Mae started toward the house. The Wagler buggy rolled toward the barn but Adam caught up to her and grabbed her hand while his brother parked.

"Whose side are you on?" he teased, although his deep brown eyes seemed serious. "Nice job, covering my butt, Annie Mae. But you forced my hand about telling Bishop Tom about my motorcycle."

Annie Mae shrugged, although she didn't feel nearly as nonchalant as she was trying to appear. Adam was gazing at her, gripping her hand, making tingles dance up her arm. "Did I? Confessin' is a private matter, between you and Tom—and God—the way I see it."

"You said right out that *you* wanted to hear the story behind that cycle."

"And I do." Annie Mae let the grin she'd been suppressing bloom all over her face. "Who knew the boy next door had a fast black bike like they ride in motorcycle gangs? I suppose you've got the black jacket and bandanna with the skulls on it, too?"

"What if I do?" Adam challenged. He widened his eyes and stood taller, so his nose nearly touched hers.

Annie Mae felt strangely, dangerously happy about how this day had turned out. "I'm joinin' the church soon, but that doesn't mean I'm turnin' into a saint, ya know. If ya want to practice on your confession, I'm all ears—and your secret's safe with me, even if ya sell the cycle without sayin' a word to Bishop Tom."

Adam smiled, even though wariness—or something else she couldn't define—flickered briefly in his eyes. "We'll have to wait and see how it all comes out, won't we?"

Over the next few days, Adam observed Annie Mae as she took orders and poured coffee at the Sweet Seasons, wondering how she stood the suspense about when her father would get his revenge. While they were all riding high about rescuing the four youngest Knepp kids, it was only a matter of time before Hiram would swoop in and chastise his eldest daughter for presuming she knew what was best for his children. From there, it was an easy assumption that her *dat* would strike at *him*. . . .

"Here ya go, Short Stack," Annie Mae said as she set his plate of pancakes and eggs in front of him on Wednesday morning. "Don't forget—we'll be closed tomorrow for Tom and Nazareth's wedding."

"I'll take home something from the bakery case for tomorrow's breakfast, then. Why don't you box up whatever you think Matthias and I will like? You can't miss."

Adam saw that his brother and the Kanagy boys were chatting at the steam table as they loaded their plates, so he took a moment to really look at Annie Mae. Shadows underlined her eyes and an anxious expression tightened her pretty face this morning. Was he imagining it, or did she glance toward the door a lot? "From that aroma of roasting chickens, I'm guessing Miriam's started cooking for the wedding feast. A man could spend his whole day in here, inhaling that heavenly scent," he said.

As he'd hoped, this happy subject brought Annie Mae's smile out. "Oh, *jah*, we're busy bees," she replied. "A bunch of us will be havin' a pie frolic here after we close the café at two. The Brenneman boys are settin' up tables in their shop today, for the meals."

"It's handy that Miriam and Naomi can do the baking here—and that the wedding guests just have a short walk to the shop from the bishop's house to eat their dinner," Adam remarked as he poured syrup on his cakes. "How're Tom and Nazareth holding up?"

"Oh, Naz is giddier than a girl! Jerusalem finished her new blue wedding dress last night, and got her white apron and *kapp* all pressed," Annie Mae replied wistfully. "It's such a wonderful-*gut* thing that those sisters have found fine men to love at this time in their lives."

Adam couldn't miss Annie Mae's poignant tone. "That'll happen for you someday," he murmured. "To everything comes a season, after all."

And where had *that* idea come from? Adam quickly cut into his cakes, hoping Annie Mae didn't take it as a hint that *he* intended to make that dream come true for her.

"When I told Bishop Tom I intended to join the church, I also vowed I'd remain a *maidel,* to support my sibs," she replied quietly. "I believe that's why the Lord led me to find them, and also brought me to the Sweet Seasons, so I can make the money to do that."

Adam wanted to kick himself. "I—I didn't mean to let on about—"

"Oh, no, what ya said didn't bother me a bit, Adam." Annie Mae gazed directly at him, all the way into his soul. "I know now that those kids are my most important responsibility—gettin' them through school and into their own lives—because who else is gonna do it? Certainly not Delilah. Or Dat."

When the bell above the door jingled, she smiled at the English folks coming in for their breakfast. "I'll be right with ya," she called over to them. "Sit wherever ya want." Then she focused on Adam again. "Enjoy your food, Short Stack. I'll be back in a few to see if ya need anything."

As Annie Mae bustled to the serving window to pick up the steaming plates that awaited her, Adam considered their conversation. What young woman of seventeen vowed to remain single so she could support her brothers and sisters? Annie Mae sounded absolutely positive that God had intended this burden to be hers alone . . . as though she were to sacrifice her own future. Her happiness.

What with Timmy being about three, it would take another dozen years before he'd finish school. It might be awhile before he found an occupation . . . which would make Annie Mae thirty before she considered herself eligible to wed. *By then, she'll already have raised a family . . . might not want to marry a man who'll expect a brood of his own. . . .*

"You're a million miles away, Brother," Matthias remarked as he sat down with his plate. "Mooning over Annie Mae, no doubt."

"She's vowed not to marry until she's raised her sibs," Adam murmured. "I've never known a girl her age to—"

"So that gets ya off the hook!" Matthias interrupted with a chuckle. "Annie Mae's smart enough to know nobody'll be in a hurry to hitch up with her—although it *was* nice to see how quick she and Nellie whipped our kitchen into shape."

Adam scowled. He had a notion to pick up his plate and move to another table, because his brother's attitude was getting old. While most Amish men did indeed believe women were the keepers of home and hearth, Adam hoped there was a place for some love and respect . . . even romance, between a husband and his wife. Annie Mae deserved to be more than some fellow's slave.

Rather than keep this negative banter going, Adam took a big bite of his ham steak. It wasn't as though he planned to relieve Annie Mae's burden by marrying her, after all. But her statement of purpose—the way she faced her mission square in the face instead of whining about how she couldn't handle it—certainly gave him something to think about.

Makes you look pretty pathetic, too. All these years you've stayed away from relationships to avoid such responsibilities. . . .

Adam's fork stopped halfway to his mouth. Sometimes that voice in his head irked him, but it was usually right. He could do a better job of manning up, in the responsibility department—but for now he would finish eating and move on. He had a job in New Haven today, installing fancy organizing systems in three closets for a woman who said her husband was all thumbs, when it came to handling a hammer and nails.

"Later," he said to Matthias as he slipped a few bills under his plate.

"Bring something home for supper. Shoppin's not on my honey-do list today," his brother replied.

Shaking his head, Adam proceeded to the checkout. Annie Mae rang up his tab and then handed him two white bakery boxes, a small one stacked on a larger one. "Have a *gut* day, Adam, and I'll see ya at the wedding tomorrow."

"*Jah,* we'll be there. Nobody in Willow Ridge wants to miss that," he replied. "*Denki* for the takeout. I'm not going to look at what ya boxed up until I get it home, or Matthias might not get any."

"Hold these boxes by the bottom," she said. Was that a twinkle in her eyes?

As Adam stepped outside, noting how the bigger box felt awfully warm, the cold air accentuated the aromas of sugar, cinnamon and . . . something that reminded him of lasagne. He was barely inside his remodeling wagon before he popped off the boxes' lids, his resolve eroded by the mouthwatering smells that filled his vehicle. His jaw dropped. Annie Mae had wrapped up a loaf of raisin bread that was still warm, along with four fruit-filled pastries. The second, heavier box held a foil pan of casserole that oozed cheese and tomato sauce and—

How did she know Matthias has refused to shop for supper? Adam quickly closed the box, knowing he'd burn his finger taking a taste. Upside-down pizza casserole had been listed as the lunch special on the café's white board, and he was eager to dig into it even though he was full to bursting with pancakes, eggs, and ham. Annie Mae had him and his brother all figured out. It was her thoughtfulness that touched him, though—

And her strength. And her faith. I could take lessons from that girl. . . .

For single fellows with no intention of tying the knot, weddings were mostly an opportunity to load up on a really good dinner. Yet Adam suddenly looked forward to attending Tom and Nazareth's service tomorrow. He didn't read too much into this change of attitude as he directed Jerry to turn left on the blacktop, toward New Haven. He just savored the sense of being *happy*.

Chapter Eighteen

Annie Mae sat between Nellie and Millie Glick on the pew bench, with Sara in her lap. Peering between the bearded and clean-shaven faces on the men's side of the room, she focused on Josh, Joey, and Timmy. Jerusalem was Nazareth's side-sitter, so she couldn't help with the kids during the church and wedding services—and when her little brothers had clamored to sit with Adam, he'd seemed pleased that they wanted to. And wasn't *that* a fine surprise? It was almost as gratifying as the way the boys had been behaving like perfect little gentlemen all morning instead of wiggling and punching at each other, as they often did.

The church service, almost three hours long, had just ended, so Annie Mae took advantage of these few moments to catch up. "It's so *gut* to see ya!" she whispered as she grasped Millie's hand. "Been way too long!"

The freckles on Millie's nose shifted when she grinned. "Oh, the *long* part is watchin' after the grandparents. It's like livin' in a funeral parlor," she murmured as she rolled her eyes. "Told Mamm I *had* to get outta there today. Hopin' to catch Ira for a while . . . maybe even skip out on the dinner."

Millie scanned the men's side then, probably trying to catch Ira's eye. Annie Mae noted how her red-headed friend, once so carefree, seemed a lot older than her sixteen years now. *Maybe I've put on some age, too,* she reflected. But this was no time to think about it. Nazareth and Tom were taking their places before Bishop Vernon Gingerich—Jerusalem's fiancé, from Cedar Creek—and Bishop Jeremiah Shetler from Morning Star, who'd been so helpful when her *dat* had fallen from grace.

"We gather now for a joyous, momentous occasion," Vernon began in a resonant voice. "It's my honor—truly a high point in my life—to join my longtime friend, Tom Hostetler, with Nazareth Hooley, who so beautifully complements his strengths and compensates for his few weaknesses. How sweet it is to behold God's plan and purpose blossoming into love for these, His two devoted servants."

Annie Mae sighed languidly. Vernon Gingerich spoke in such a rich, melodic voice that everyone in the huge room—which had been expanded by taking down the wall partitions to accommodate more than two hundred guests—settled in to listen to this familiar wedding ceremony. How wonderful it felt to be seated here with Nellie and Millie, alongside Rebecca—who had dressed in Plain attire, as she did for weddings. Rhoda and Rachel, Miriam and Naomi, sat a few pews closer to the front, among other women she'd known all her life. Tom's four married kids and their families had come, as well as dozens of other Hostetlers and Hooleys from other districts and states. Literally everyone from around Willow Ridge was here, too, except for Preacher Gabe, who was home with his bedridden wife, Wilma.

These are my people . . . my family now, Annie Mae realized with a deep sense of satisfaction. She felt surprised yet pleased that Nellie had recently decided to join the church, as well—forfeiting her *rumspringa* to commit herself to the Old Order at a very young age. Annie Mae smiled at her sister, feeling a deeper kinship . . . feeling safe in the belief that they and their younger siblings would be well cared for, as one of the benefits of coming into the fold.

"'. . . charity suffereth long and is kind; charity envieth not,'" their deacon, Reuben Riehl, was reading from the big German Bible. "'Charity vaunteth not itself, is not puffed up; does not behave itself unseemly . . . is not easily provoked—'"

The loud *wham!* of a door made everyone suck in their breath and look toward the kitchen.

Annie Mae, however, remained facing forward, hugging little Sara closer as fear jangled her nerves. The tattoo of a man's boots crossed the kitchen floor in a familiar beat as she exchanged a concerned glance with Nellie. The hair at her nape prickled.

"It's Dat," her sister whispered, gripping Annie Mae's wrist.

The men seated across the room confirmed the identity of their intruder with expressions of disbelief. Ben Hooley stood up, and Bishop Tom took a step back so he, too, could see what was happening.

"Hiram, you know full well that you're disrupting a sacred ceremony," Bishop Shetler said sternly. "You're not welcome here."

"I've come for my children." Her *dat*'s terse reply

came from a few yards behind Annie Mae's pew bench. "*No one* has the right to stand between a man and his family—nor should you be harboring my eldest daughter, who kidnapped them."

Annie Mae prayed for God's protection, or for a hole to open in the floor and swallow her. Across the crowded room she saw Josh and Joey craning for a look at their father, while Timmy burrowed into Adam's lap the same way Sara was clinging to her.

"And why has it taken ya five days to come lookin' for them?" Bishop Tom queried. "With the passin' of so much time this week, I figured ya were willin' for Annie Mae to take on the—"

"I just returned from Ohio," her father shot back. "I was gathering souls for—"

"You've got electricity in Higher Ground," Bishop Tom countered as he stepped toward the aisle. While his voice remained low and controlled, he appeared every bit as adamant as the man he opposed. "So ya can't tell me you've not got a phone in your home, as well—and ya probably carry a cell nowadays. Are ya sayin' Delilah didn't call ya when Annie Mae reclaimed her siblings?"

Annie Mae slumped lower on the bench, cradling Sara's head to her shoulder to muffle her crying. Her little sister was shaking all over—and what did it say about conditions in the new Knepp household if this toddler was so terrified of her own father?

"That's neither here nor there," her *dat* answered in a rising voice. "I've come for *my children*—"

"Is Delilah your wife, Hiram?" Ben Hooley demanded. "We hear she's young enough to be your daughter."

Annie Mae cringed as she recalled her confrontation with Delilah . . . how the kids were screaming and scattering across the snow to escape the paddle in her hand. Nellie looked too scared to breathe, for fear she'd draw Dat's attention. From the sound of it, he was now standing at the end of the bench behind theirs. Annie Mae was grateful to be sitting in the center of the pew with Millie, Rebecca, and Hannah Brenneman between her and her father.

"Delilah and I are one in the eyes of the Lord," Dat stated firmly.

"*That's* your answer? Marriage as *you* see it now? Well, for us, it's not *gut* enough," Bishop Tom blurted. "I can't allow these innocent children to return to a household founded upon sin and filled with such depravity."

The women seated in front of Annie Mae were whispering behind their hands, glancing toward Hiram in dismay. A few more of the men from Willow Ridge rose, taking their stand.

"Don't go spouting off about *morality* to me, Tom Hostetler, considering how you were sneaking around with Nazareth before your first wife died," Dat retorted. "I am their father—"

"There's a difference between begettin' kids and bein' their *dat*," Ben cut in stiffly. "You've no more integrity than a tomcat, feedin' an unsuspectin' young woman pretty promises so she'd be your live-in babysitter—"

"And what of the welts on Sara's and Timmy's legs?"

As "ohhs" and more whispering hissed around the room, Jerusalem Hooley rose from her bench in the front. Annie Mae squeezed her eyes shut, recalling the sick feeling she'd gotten when she'd helped with the children's baths that first night. Delilah had indeed left the marks of her incompetent wrath on the two littlest ones . . . Joey and Josh were harder to catch.

Jerusalem turned to face Hiram, her face tight with disgust. "I was *appalled* to see that their little behinds had been whipped with some sort of switch until blood was drawn," she continued in a horrified rush. "And I know that *you,* Hiram, would rather be anywhere than near your children when they're misbehavin'—"

"And *you* of all people should know that children need discipline!" he countered to drown her out. "Spare the rod and—"

"But they're only two and three years old!" Miriam cried out as she, too, stood and turned around. "What could those children have possibly done to deserve such a beating?"

"Sounds to me like this Delilah's no more than a child herself," Nazareth chimed in from the front. "*She's* the one who needs the switch taken to her!"

"Bishop Tom did the right thing, takin' in your family," Ben declared loudly. "And after what-all we've learned, Hiram, had Tom not done it, I would've made a home for your kids myself rather than let *you* take them."

"*Jah,* we've got a place for them, as well," Dan Kanagy said as he rose to join the other men. "I believe God has clearly been workin' out His will, after He saw how you used your twins' sleigh accident to wrangle land from that English fella. The Lord's moved you out of Willow Ridge to do your dirty work elsewhere, and I say *gut* riddance."

"Your kids are home now." Ezra Brenneman spoke out from his wheelchair. "Right where they're supposed to be."

As Nellie's arm went around her shoulders, Annie

Mae huddled with her two sisters. How humiliating, to have the details of their family's separation coming to light in such a public way. But she was grateful that Dat had shown up *here,* where so many others would stand up for her and the kids, rather than confronting her when she was alone.

As Vernon Gingerich encouraged the crowd to stop chattering, Bishop Tom stepped down the side aisle until he was only a few feet in front of her father. "Despite the example you've set with your questionable behavior, Annie Mae is joinin' the Old Order church," he announced. "All of us admire the way she's supportin' the kids herself, remainin' a *maidel* to—"

Her father's derisive laughter rang around the room. "Annie Mae's been sneaking out with boys since she was thirteen—not to mention seeing Luke Hooley at *his* age. So do you really believe she's sincere?" he taunted. "My city commissioner tells me she's no more honorable than—"

Something inside Annie Mae exploded, like a pie blowing up in the oven. Gripping Sara, she shot up off the pew bench. It was time to speak her piece instead of hiding from this conversation, which was being carried on as though she and the kids weren't present. "I don't believe a thing Yonnie Stoltzfus says," she blurted. "I want nothin' more to do with him, after he tricked me into goin' to Higher Ground. And especially now that he's workin' for *you!*"

The crowd sucked in its breath, leaving the room hot and airless as Annie Mae held her father's daunting gaze. He hadn't taken off his long black coat and broad-brimmed hat, as though he'd figured it would be a quick in-and-out to reclaim his children. His scowl deepened, and with his short, pointed beard and his coal-black hair he resembled the Devil. "Your insolence and lies will send you straight to hell, Annie Mae," he stated. "I *cannot* allow my children to stay here—"

Suddenly her *dat* stepped into the row, heedless of Hannah's and Rebecca's shrieks as he grabbed for Sara. The little girl screamed and struggled to escape him, which made Timmy start wailing on the other side of the room. Annie Mae backed farther down the row, as Tom, Ben, Dan, and some of the other men rushed over to restrain her father. The women scrambled over the benches, crying out for God's mercy, while Millie and the other girls around Annie Mae scattered as though afraid for their lives.

Annie Mae's heart was pounding so hard she couldn't breathe, but she held tight to her little sister. Oh, what a mess this was . . . a scene like she'd never dared to imagine as four men surrounded her *dat*.

"Hiram, this is wrong and ya know it!" Tom beseeched him as he pinned one of Dat's arms behind his back.

"Think what you're doin' to your family, carryin' on this way," Ben chimed in as he grabbed his other arm. Dan Kanagy and Micah Brenneman had planted themselves between Annie Mae and her father, looking ready to pummel Dat if he advanced any farther.

Seeing a cleared path between the pew benches, Annie Mae scrambled over to where some of the women stood. Rushing into Miriam's arms with Sara, she pressed her face against the stalwart woman's shoulder. She was so thankful that Nellie had gotten over here, too . . . grateful that Matthias Wagler and other fellows had gathered around Adam and her little brothers to form a shield. Yet who would've dreamed they would need to?

Finally her *dat* relented. He stepped back into the aisle, shaking off the grips of those who held him. His face was still contorted with anger, but he didn't seem inclined to come after Sara again. "Fine," he spat. He brushed off his coat as though to rid it of any vermin the men might have left on its sleeves. "I'll return to Willow Ridge with the police," he threatened. "We'll let the authorities handle this situation."

"The only authority here is God, Hiram," Vernon intoned as he, too, came to stand before Annie Mae's father. "It appalls me that you've forgotten that on so many levels."

Dat glowered. "Ah, so it's fine for you folks to call the cops on *me* for a parking violation, but when I—"

"Not a one of us will allow you to take your children back under these circumstances," Jeremiah Shetler stated. "I'm sorry they've witnessed this interruption of a sacred ceremony and further evidence of your arrogance, Hiram. You've been excommunicated from Willow Ridge for several reasons, and you're not welcome here for several more."

"As though any of you can stop me from coming!" Dat countered, looking ready to spit on the fellows who'd confronted him. "You've not seen the last of me. Mark my words."

With swift strides he crossed the room to glare at Adam, who held Timmy to his shoulder while Josh and Joey clung to him from either side. "And don't think you're man enough to protect my children from me, Wagler—not after the way you broke into my home and helped Annie Mae steal things from it.

You're a den of vipers, all of you!" he declared to the crowd.

With that, her father stalked from the crowded room, pausing to glower one more time at Annie Mae. Silence rang for several moments after his loud, rapid footsteps and the slam of the kitchen door died away.

"Praise be to God for His grace and protection," Vernon declared in a reverent voice. "I believe a few moments of silent prayer are in order, to restore a proper sense of dignity and respect before we resume Tom and Nazareth's ceremony."

Annie Mae exhaled . . . wiped the tears from little Sara's face . . . rejoined Nellie in the pew bench alongside Millie and Rebecca and the other girls. She rested her head on her sister's tiny shoulder, inhaling Sara's innocent sweetness, ever so grateful that this lamb hadn't been snatched from her.

What would I do without You and these gut *friends you've surrounded us with, Lord?* she prayed. *I don't deserve the gift of Your love, but I promise I'll do my very best for my brothers and sisters . . . and I thank Ya that Adam was spared* Dat*'s wrath, as well. Be with us in the coming days, for who can tell what* Dat *might do next?*

As the women around her raised their heads, Annie Mae opened her eyes. Order and rightness had been restored, both within Bishop Tom's home and in her soul. She still felt jittery from the way her father had charged between the pews . . . would recall his threatening expression for a long while. But as Vernon Gingerich began the exchange of Tom and Nazareth's vows, she relaxed. What a joy it was to behold the love on their faces as they solemnly repeated the words that would bind them as man and wife.

And what a surprise to see that Adam was gazing right at her.

Annie Mae blinked, yet she didn't look away. How handsome he looked in his black vest and white shirt—and how manly, with Timmy in his lap. Her little brother closed his eyes to suck his thumb, comforted and comfortable. She'd rarely seen Adam hold a child this way, and her heartbeat eased into a steady thrum. While she still burned with curiosity about the motorcycle parked in his barn, Annie Mae treasured the gift of this moment when Adam was reaching out to her in an eloquent silence that said so much, as the ceremony continued.

She smiled. And so did he.

Chapter Nineteen

Adam spent the rest of the morning getting up his courage.

After Hiram Knepp's intrusion, when Adam had watched so many from Willow Ridge stand up to their former bishop—and had then beheld Annie Mae's fierce bravery as she faced her father—the rest of the ceremony went right by him. He was aware of Vernon and Jeremiah preaching and leading Tom and Nazareth in their vows, yet all he heard, again and again, was Annie Mae's vehement denouncement of Yonnie and his connection to Hiram. All he saw was the expression of a lioness as she clutched Sara in the face of her father's declaration that she was going to hell. Only when Hiram had grabbed for her sister did Annie Mae back away and seek safety.

Here was a woman he looked up to . . . in more ways than one.

Yet the idea of asking Annie Mae for a date made him falter. What if she said no?

But what if she says yes? he fretted. *What if you take her for a ride this afternoon and your tongue ties into knots? After knowing her all your life, what'll you find to talk about? What'll impress a young woman who's raising her brothers and sisters? She's way out of your league. . . .*

And yet, Adam felt amazed that he was even considering a date, after years of denying himself the company of young women he believed he could never take care of.

So don't think of it as a date. Who says it has to be forever—or even more than this one time?

Later in the afternoon, he watched Annie Mae scrape plates and clear tables after folks had finished the main course of a wedding feast that had filled him in so many ways. Miriam, Naomi, and the other women had outdone themselves with the "roast," made of succulent chicken and savory stuffing . . . mashed potatoes and sweet, creamed celery, as well as glazed carrots, an array of fruit salads . . . warm, fresh bread upon which butter made from Bishop Tom's cream had melted like liquid gold. It was time for pie and other sweets now, yet Adam's stomach seemed so full of butterflies he didn't think he would taste his dessert—even if he got a slice of the same spicy apple pie like Annie Mae had left on his wagon seat awhile back.

Suddenly she stood before him, clearing his place. "And how was your dinner, Short Stack?" she murmured, as though the Kanagy brothers and their fiancées weren't seated on either side of him.

"Wonderful-*gut*," he murmured. Without his mind's permission, his hand closed around hers.

Her blue eyes widened, yet her smile made his heart thump like a drum. He *had* to say something now, or forever lose the moment—and all credibility. "What . . . what would you think about a ride this afternoon?" he asked in a voice she probably couldn't hear. "Or—well, I suppose you have to keep track of the twins and—"

Annie Mae's face lit up like a spring daisy. "It's Nellie's turn for that," she replied pertly. "I spent most of yesterday bakin' and helpin' Miriam with this meal, so I'm ready to be off my feet."

Adam's eyes widened. "Have you had a chance to eat your dinner? I don't mean to rush you, or—" *She said yes, oh my Lord, she wants to—*

Annie Mae winked at him and leaned closer. "Truth be told," she confided, "we cooks and servers grabbed a quick bite while everybody was congratulatin' Tom and Nazareth, before folks walked over from the house. I haven't had my pie yet, but—"

"So what would be our chances of taking our dessert along?" Adam asked, wondering where such bravado had come from. "And if there's any of that fabulous apple pie with the brown sugar and lemon—"

"I think I know where to find us a couple slices of that," she teased. Annie Mae looked around the Brennemans' crowded cabinet shop, which had been transformed by white-draped tables for the wedding feast. "Why not go hitch up your rig? I'll be out as soon as I can snatch us some pie and tell Nellie and Rhoda I'm leavin'. I'm an extra helper, anyway—not one of the gals with an assigned job."

In for a dime, in for a dollar, Adam realized as she bustled away with her bin of dirty dishes. He scooted his chair back, giving a little wave to Nate, Bram, and their ladies. "You folks enjoy the rest of the day—and it was really nice meeting you Coblentz girls," he added as Mary and Martha grinned knowingly at him.

"No doubt what *you're* up to, Wagler," Bram teased.

"*Jah*, enjoy your *pie*," Nate chimed in.

Adam made his way between the crowded tables, fighting a huge grin. When he'd arrived at the wedding this morning, he'd had no idea he would leave the celebration early—and with Annie Mae, no less! It felt good to step outside and whistle for Jerry . . . to hitch up his rig with occasional glances back toward the shop, even if he still felt a few butterflies. His best strategy would be to show his support, to focus on Annie Mae's feelings after the way her father had barged in and tried to grab the kids. No matter how strong she'd appeared during that confrontation, she was bound to have lingering doubts about Hiram showing up again—

"Short Stack! Are ya ready?" she called out to him.

Now *there* was a loaded question. Adam glanced up to see Annie Mae jogging toward him with her black coat flapping open and her bonnet flying by its tie string behind the pie plate she carried. Her radiant face gave him pause. Her exuberance suggested she was really glad to be going out with him—

It's only a ride. Doesn't have to be a date, his thoughts reminded him.

So what if it does *lead to something?* his heart countered. *After all, Nate Kanagy swore off women after his first fiancée stiffed him, and look how happy he is now.*

When Adam opened the door to his rig, Annie Mae stepped up inside it before he could offer her a hand. But wasn't it just like this resilient young woman to look after herself? When he got in on the other side and closed his door, he gazed at her for a moment. "Better scenery than I had driving over here this morning," he remarked.

"*Jah,* this *is* a perty pie," she quipped. "And I guess Matthias'll have to find his own way home, ain't so?"

Actually, Adam hadn't even thought about his brother. "He'll manage. Let's get on down the road before the kids try to follow us. I mean—" He gripped the reins, immediately regretting that remark. "If you think the twins and the two wee ones'll worry about you leavin' them, we can—"

Annie Mae pressed her finger against his lips. "Nellie's got us covered," she whispered. "And Jerusalem's spendin' time with the kids—gettin' them acquainted with Vernon Gingerich—knowing how she'll miss them once she moves to Cedar Creek. So it's just you and me . . . Adam."

The way his name floated from Annie Mae's lips set him adrift like a red-and-white bobber on a summertime pond. The snowy hillsides and his waiting horse and the hundreds of people finishing their dinner disappeared, and it *was* just him and Annie Mae, alone together with a pie that smelled of cinnamon and brown sugar and lemon. He glanced at the dessert that sat between them on the seat. "Wow, you brought us four big pieces," he murmured. "Didn't think there'd be so much to spare, what with all those other folks waiting for their dessert."

Her smile tickled him deep down. "As many of these pies as I baked, I didn't *ask*. I consider it a gift to a fine fella who looked after my family today," she murmured. "Can't thank ya enough for standin' firm when Dat came at ya this morning. He . . . he had no call to do that."

Annie Mae's gratitude moved him, especially considering how *she* had been the strong one during Hiram's intrusion. "While I can see where it's a man's right to collect his own kids," Adam replied as he took her hand, "I couldn't miss the way Timmy and the twins were so afraid of him. And when Jerusalem mentioned the welts on the little ones' bottoms, that was the last straw. They belong with you, Annie Mae," he insisted. "With folks who know what's best for them, better than Delilah ever will."

Her smile got stronger as she placed the pie plate on her lap. "The boys were so excited to be sittin' with ya, Adam. And when Dat stormed in, I couldn't miss how they stuck with ya, trustin' ya to look after them. I . . . I hope that doesn't scare ya off."

Adam nipped his lip. Without apology or hesitation, Annie Mae had just nailed the issue that any man who got interested in her would face. The least he could do was give her a straight answer. "I've known those kids since they were born," he pointed out. Holding the reins in one hand, he gently clapped them on Jerry's broad back. "I've known *you* since you were born, Annie Mae. So I'm not scared . . . exactly."

She looked suddenly vulnerable, even as she tried not to. "Like I told ya, Adam, I've decided to stay a *maidel* until the kids—"

"That's no life for a girl like you," Adam blurted, gripping her fingers. "I'd really hate to see you saddled with all that responsibility yourself, working in the café while you tended the kids in the evenings, but— but—"

Well, he'd stepped in it with one foot, so he might as well stand full-on in his crappy predicament. No sense in Annie Mae getting her hopes up, setting her sights on a man who wouldn't measure up when it came to family responsibilities. "Maybe I ought to talk about that motorcycle," he hedged. His voice remained steadier than he'd thought it would, so he went on. "That sounds like I'm leapfrogging over your situation and into mine, but you asked for that story. So maybe it's time I told it to somebody."

Annie Mae's hesitant expression gave way to the curiosity he'd sensed earlier, when she'd been surprised that *he* would own such a mean machine. "I'm listenin'," she said softly. She looked ready to scoot closer to him, but she seemed to sense he needed some space while he bared his soul. She was smart that way.

Adam let his Belgian set the pace as they rolled down the road past the bishop's house. He could feel the waves of patience and understanding that radiated from the young woman beside him. Was this the same rebellious Annie Mae who rode the roads with the likes of Yonnie and Luke?

Not anymore, she doesn't, his little voice reminded him. And he believed it. He believed *her.*

"I traded my best horse for that cycle, right after I turned sixteen," he began in a faraway voice. "Allen Stoltzfus—Yonnie's cousin—needed to get married right quick, and a dependable horse suited him better than a vintage Indian Chief motorcycle."

"How did a kid his age come to have a bike like that?" Annie Mae interrupted. "I mean—it's not my business, but Rebecca says that cycle's worth a *lot* of money."

"*Jah,* I was shocked when she told me how much a similar bike had sold for," he confirmed, keeping his eyes on the road. "Truth be told, I don't know how Allen came by it—except it wasn't in very *gut* condition then. But the moment I laid eyes on it, with that red trim and those silver studs along the edge of the seat, I had to have it." He let out a rueful laugh. "Allen let me keep it at his place, so the folks and Matthias never saw it . . . never realized how quick I learned to handle it while I was cleaning it up, and then got my license to drive it."

Annie Mae's lips quirked. "Plenty of Plain boys learn to drive, ya know. No sin in that when you're in your *rumspringa*."

Ah, she had to mention *sin*. Adam smiled wistfully as he thought back over that time of his life. "I spent every possible moment joyriding on that bike," he continued, "to the point that I neglected my chores. Wasn't always home when I was supposed to be, either. I . . . I had promised Mamm I'd pick up Ruth from her house cleaning job one afternoon, because the two of them and Etta were going to a quilting frolic. We were having an early supper so they could leave on time."

Adam allowed the steady clip-clop of Jerry's hooves to settle his accelerating heartbeat. He wanted to loosen his shirt collar but he didn't dare release Annie Mae's hand. Her steady grasp might be the only thing that kept him connected to present-day reality, rather than getting swallowed up by a past that had haunted him for so long. She waited patiently for him to continue, looking wise beyond her seventeen years.

"Suffice it to say I forgot all about fetching Ruth," he said with a sigh. "And since Dat and Matthias weren't yet home from their field work, Mamm hitched up a rig and went to pick up my sister. She had no idea where I was or what I was doing . . . even when I roared past her on the motorcycle. I was wearing a helmet and jeans, so I could've been any English kid out tearing up the back roads on a summer afternoon. And a thousand times I've wished I *was* somebody else's kid that day, believe me."

Adam waited for Annie Mae to show some sign of

disapproval, because he certainly deserved it. Instead, she nodded, probably thinking back to what she recalled about his mother's death while also jumping ahead to the conclusion . . . the damning details that nobody else had ever heard. Adam closed his eyes, trying to clear the lump that was thickening in his throat.

"Next thing I knew, her horse was screaming behind me, spooked by my motorcycle. And . . . and when I turned my head, I saw it racing into the intersection, out of control." Adam paused, recalling the fatal accident so clearly that he still shook all over. "Tires squealed on the highway, but the truck driver didn't have any chance of stopping in time—"

"Oh, Adam. Oh, dear God, I had no idea," Annie Mae whimpered. She scooted next to him, set the pie on the other side of the seat, and slung her arm around his slumped shoulders.

"Ah, but see, that's not the worst of it," he confessed wretchedly. "Stupid and scared as I was, I didn't dare see to Mamm or ride the cycle home to tell Dat what had happened. I—I went back to Allen's to park it, and then waited for the sirens to clear out before I started back." He let out a bitter laugh. "Truth was, I was too shook up to pedal my bicycle, and I couldn't have seen the road for crying my eyes out. Gave some thought to not going home ever again."

Annie Mae let out a shuddery breath and swiped at her eyes. "*Jah,* I can understand why you'd feel that way. That was a horrible-bad thing to watch."

Adam's eyes widened. "You don't get it, Annie Mae. I *killed* _my mamm_, and then I was too much the coward to admit it," he rasped. "Didn't show my face at home until I figured the sheriff had been by to let the rest of the family know about her. And I never once let on to them about why Mamm's horse had spooked, or what I'd been doing when I was supposed to be fetching Ruth."

Annie Mae's mouth opened and then closed as tears streamed down her face. She held his gaze, sorting out the details of his story, yet not once did he see signs of disgust or hatred or blame. "Adam, that's the saddest thing I've ever heard," she whispered. "Brings to mind the day my *mamm* passed . . . she was feelin' poorly, about ready to have a baby, so Dat and little Nellie went on to church that morning while I stayed home with her. The baby was . . . stillborn," she recalled in a forlorn voice. "And then when Mamm kept bleedin' and bleedin', I wanted to run and get the midwife but . . . but she begged me not to leave her. I was only eleven. Didn't know what else to do."

Adam pulled over to the side of the road and halted the horse. He leaned into Annie Mae's misery, wrapping his arms around her as she tightened her hold on him . . . as they both sighed and shuddered together. "*Jah,*" he whispered when he could speak again. "But you did what your *mamm* told you to. I did *not.*"

"Same difference," she blurted. "She was gone and there was nothin' I could do to save her or bring her back." Annie Mae sniffled loudly and then sat up straighter. "Of course, when Dat got home and found me bawlin' and holdin' her hand, with her blood all over the place, he railed at me—even though the doctor had warned *mamm* that another baby might well do her in. I was too young to understand all the details about baby-makin', so . . . so I believed Dat when he said her passin' was my fault."

Adam bit back a retort. He recalled how the gossip

had flown about the bishop's disregarding the doctor's orders and how his second wife, Linda—mother of the four little ones—had passed in the same way. Hiram Knepp was hard on his women.

Yet through the years, Annie Mae had risen to the challenges of her difficult youth. Maybe some of her wilder nighttime adventures with guys had been her way of compensating for having to grow up too soon.

Or maybe she'd figured out something he'd missed.

Adam raised his head from her shoulder to engage her gaze again. "So how did you get past losing your *mamm* and then having Linda die the same way?" he asked quietly.

Annie Mae thought for a moment. "Back when I first started seein' Yonnie, I went to one of his Mennonite church services—partly to impress him but mostly because it would irritate Dat," she admitted with a soft laugh. "The preacher spoke about how God's love is bigger than all our sins put together—and how, if ya ask His forgiveness, He'll give it to ya. No matter who still condemns ya for what you've done."

Adam considered this. "I can't think your *dat,* or Gabe—or even Tom—would say such a thing on a Sunday morning," he murmured. "The *Ordnung* says you have to go on your knees before the bishop and the preachers and the members. To be forgiven for my *mamm*'s death, I have to confess. And then accept my punishment."

"I think ya just *did* that, Adam."

Adam frowned. Was he missing something? Or losing his concentration because he and Annie Mae still sat in each other's arms?

"*I* heard every word ya confessed," she clarified.

"And if ya tell Bishop Tom about this, that doesn't mean he'll order ya to do a kneelin' confession like Dat would have. Besides, you're still punishin' yourself for the mistakes ya made all those years ago," she insisted as she held his gaze. "Ya think God didn't hear ya? Ya think He doesn't know how you've suffered?"

Adam blinked. Annie Mae made it sound so simple—but then, she was young and hadn't yet joined the church. "But, see, my whole point of telling you this story was so you'd know why I can't be trusted— can't risk taking on a wife or having a family, because I know that when push comes to shove, I'll let them down."

As comprehension dawned on her face, Adam braced himself. Surely Annie Mae would scoot away from him now, so as not to be contaminated by his guilt . . . his weakness. His cowardice. Yet she brought her hand to his face and stroked his hair back from his temple with a tenderness he hadn't known since— well, since he'd been a child, sitting in Mamm's lap. He saw himself mirrored in Annie Mae's unblinking blue eyes, and he felt his fear drifting away. . . .

"Comin' from me, this is gonna sound a little odd, maybe," Annie Mae murmured. "But I think we should pray on this and see what comes of it."

She bowed her head before he could reply, so Adam did the same. It wasn't how he'd seen their spur-of-the-moment date unfolding, yet Annie Mae seemed to know what she was talking about. Listening to her, he could grasp the *possibility* of releasing his unshakable beliefs about his mother's death—

"God, Ya just heard Adam lay out the guilt and the burdens he's been carryin' for so many years," she said in a reverent voice. "I hope You'll forgive him when he asks Ya to—especially on account of how young he was when he made these mistakes. And then I hope You'll show him how to forgive himself, too."

Adam sat motionless, his eyes still closed. He and Annie Mae had addressed God with their arms still around each other—not the most churchlike position for petitioning the Lord. Her prayer had touched him deeply, however. The sweetness of her voice and the simple sincerity of her words made him see what he'd been blind to for so many years: he'd believed his burden was his alone, too onerous to reveal even to God.

And how foolish was that? Adam mused. *You saw* Mamm*'s wreck, and knew what I was thinking all along, God, for all these years . . . yet I never once figured You'd believe I was sorry enough unless I followed all the Old Order rules. Will . . . will You forgive me?*

Adam slowly let out the breath he'd been holding. He opened his eyes. Annie Mae had laid her head on his shoulder . . . no lightning bolts had cut through the roof of the rig to show God's anger with him. Matter of fact, he felt relaxed and comfortable—with Annie Mae, and with letting go of his deepest secret. "You know," he murmured, "my real reason for joining the church so soon after Mamm passed was to keep myself from finding any more trouble. It wasn't because I had any strong religious convictions."

Annie Mae chuckled softly. "Protectin' yourself. Same as I am." She widened her eyes at him, getting back to her earlier happy mood. "Now that Dat's left town, these folks in Willow Ridge will look after the kids and help me with them. They'll do their best to see that Dat's meanness doesn't take us down. That's why I know I belong here, as a full member of the church."

"You've got that right," Adam replied. He loosened his hold on her, but kept his arm around her shoulders as she, too, eased out of the intense embrace they had shared. It felt better than he'd figured on, sitting this close to Annie Mae, and he hated to break the mood.

"With Tom bein' the new bishop, there's a whole different feel to Willow Ridge nowadays," she continued in a thoughtful tone. "If ya talk to him about your *mamm* and that motorcycle, he might consider that you've done all the confessin' ya need to. I can't see him lordin' that mistake over ya, like Dat would've. Tom's gonna be so *gut* for this district."

"He's a breath of spring, for sure," Adam replied. *And so are you, Annie Mae Knepp.*

What a startling thought. To keep from plunging too deep too fast, Adam steered the conversation down another trail. "Tom's a man with an eye for a fine vehicle, too. So maybe he'll have ideas about how I can test drive that cycle without breaking my church vows," he mused aloud. "It's ready to sell, but I wouldn't feel right about saying it'll run the way it's supposed to, unless I take it out on the road."

"Oh, but I'd like to come along when ya did that," Annie Mae admitted with a mischievous grin. Then she got serious again. "Could be that ridin' your cycle will be another step toward facin' down your guilt about your *mamm,* too. Kind of like gettin' back on a horse that's thrown ya . . . so ya won't be afraid of that horse nor too scared to ride at all anymore."

How did she come up with such ideas? Adam gazed at Annie Mae, amazed at her wisdom and compassion. Even though the cycle's saddlebags weren't designed to be a passenger seat, he had a sudden mental image of her riding behind him, her arms wrapped tightly around his waist, as they flew down the road . . . with her long black hair flowing loose, out of the confinements of her bun and *kapp* . . .

He exhaled to get that alluring image out of his mind. It wasn't proper for a man to see a woman's hair unfurled unless she was his wife.

"You hit the nail on the head, Annie Mae, about me not riding that cycle—not being able to turn loose of it, either, because of the guilt thing." Adam sighed, releasing some more of his pent-up anxiety. "It'd probably be best to wait for warmer weather. If I'm going to sin to test ride it, I might as well make it a really *gut* sin, ain't so?"

Annie Mae's laughter filled his rig and was so contagious, he joined her . . . let go like he hadn't in way too long, far as expressing any sort of happiness.

No, this is what joy feels like. Don't let it slip away. . . .

"Is it time for pie?" she asked pertly. "All this serious talk has gobbled up that quick dinner I ate."

For a moment, Adam could only watch her lips move. He took in the slender beauty of her face and the way it lit up when she laughed. "Pie," he mumbled. "Comes a time I'm not ready for pie, you might as well put me six feet under. But let's set all that funeral talk behind us, shall we?"

"Fine idea, Short Stack." Annie Mae turned to grasp the pie plate that was behind her on the seat, but then she playfully held it beyond his reach. "I'm glad we could talk this way, though. When folks go too long with heavy stuff on their chest, it really holds them down. And I'm *tired* of bein' held down."

Adam quickly dismissed the suggestive image her

remark brought to mind . . . suddenly had *ideas* about how he wanted to hold Annie Mae, and none of them were sanctioned by the church.

But two could play this game—so he reached in front of her to grab for the glass pie plate. "If you're gonna tease me with that thing—"

"Ya love it when I tease ya, Adam. Ya know ya do."

With just the slightest angling, his lips found hers. Adam moaned, knowing this was *not* the way to keep his feelings for Annie Mae in check as he sorted out his secret sin and his cycle and his guilt and . . . but why was it, again, that he'd been so set against falling for her? He kissed her fervently, tenderly, with all the wonder he'd missed out on by swearing off girls when he was only sixteen.

And bless her, if Annie Mae felt that other guys were better kissers, she wasn't letting on. She set down the pie plate without breaking off the kiss, and when both of her arms twined around his neck, Adam didn't have the will . . . the strength to disappoint her by pulling away.

Who are you kidding? You don't want to let her go . . . maybe not ever.

When Annie Mae finally slipped her lips from his to gasp for air, Adam scooted away from her, trying to clear his fogged thoughts. "Don't go thinking this means I want to get married, or—"

"How many times do I have to tell ya I'm gonna stay a *maidel*?" she countered softly. But her whispery voice gave away the same emotions he was denying. "Besides, if I was to marry every guy I've kissed, I'd have way too many husbands, Adam," she added breezily.

Well, *that* put things back into perspective. Adam sat back against the seat, where he belonged.

"That came out all wrong," Annie Mae whimpered. "I've only kissed two other fellas, and you ... well, you're the only one who's worth his salt, Adam. Just sayin'. Not expectin' it to go any farther than this. Really."

Adam glanced over at her. Thumbed away a fat tear before it fell. "Hey. It's all right, Annie Mae. *Really*," he murmured.

After a moment she busied herself unwrapping the two silverware bundles she'd dropped into the glass plate with the remaining slices of pie. She handed him a napkin, smiling wryly. "Brought these along in case things got . . . messy."

"*Jah.* Who knew?" Adam smiled at her, because it seemed Annie Mae had a way of lifting his spirits, no matter what sort of mess he'd gotten himself into. "It's all *gut*—the talking, the kissing—and for sure, you bringing this pie," he added. "So let's enjoy it for what it is, without getting in too deep. We've both got enough heavy stuff going on right now."

She nodded. Then she cut the tip off one slice of pie and held it in front of his mouth.

Adam's heart stopped. Just when he thought he'd gotten his emotions under control, Annie Mae was offering him the first bite with the look of a girl whose heart might as well have been on that fork. But he opened his mouth . . . and then closed his eyes over the sheer, sweet goodness of soft apples bathed in brown sugar with a hint of lemon and a hefty helping of cinnamon.

Why is it, again, that you could never marry Annie Mae?

Chapter Twenty

"We'll bow for prayer, askin' God to bless this session as we teach and learn about membership in His church," Bishop Tom said as he met the gazes of everyone present on Sunday morning.

Ben bowed his head. As he sat in one of the upstairs bedrooms with Bishops Tom and Vernon, Preacher Henry Zook, and the five who were receiving their instruction to join the church, he knew a true sense of fulfillment. From downstairs, the voices singing a familiar hymn provided accompaniment for this meeting, which would take about half an hour before the main part of the service began. Now that he was a preacher, Ben was adjusting to a slightly different rhythm in his Sunday morning worship. He found it gratifying to be here with such a venerated leader as Vernon Gingerich—just as he was thrilled at the size and makeup of the group seeking to join the Old Order. And he was happy to be hosting church in his new home, as well.

"It's a blessing to see you among us now, Annie Mae and Nellie," Vernon said after a few moments of their silent prayer. "Nate and Bram Kanagy, while you watch the construction of your new sale barn and home, it's a wonderful thing to witness your commitment to the Old Order as you anticipate your marriages to Martha and Mary Coblentz. And it's a special joy to assist you, Andy Leitner, as you seek to become Amish and a vital part of the Willow Ridge community with your nursing skills."

Ben smiled at their earnest expressions, recalling his own time of instruction—back before the gal he'd proposed to in his youth had married another fellow, who'd come into a large farm. "It's my pleasure to be helpin' with these sessions, as well," he said, "because it makes me review the *Ordnung* and the Dordrecht Confession of Faith we're studyin', from the viewpoint of a new preacher. So I'm learnin' right along with ya."

Beside Ben, Henry Zook grunted. The store-keeper seemed resigned to his new post as preacher, but he would be no bright, shining beacon of faith for these seekers. So Ben had decided that this group was to be his first, special mission. He would dedicate himself to being a positive influence to these five as they made the most important decision of their lives, because every one of them could have chosen a different road. Andy might have decided to forgo his love for Rhoda Lantz, considering how difficult— how nearly *impossible*—it was for an English fellow to be accepted into the Amish faith. Bram and Nate were successful in their auction and horse-training businesses and could have jumped the fence to take up worldly ways. Annie Mae and Nellie had endured countless confrontations with their father, to the point Ben was amazed that these girls would take on the same faith that Hiram had twisted like a pretzel to fit his own arrogant purposes.

The session flew by, and then they went downstairs to join the others for church. It gave Ben a whole new perspective, sitting up front with the bishops . . . made him pay closer attention, too—with even greater respect for the way Tom and Vernon delivered their sermons of nearly thirty minutes and then an hour, respectively, without notes. He had no idea how he would pull so many words from thin air with Tom's down-to-earth applications of the Bible to their everyday lives, or with Vernon's soul-searching eloquence, come time for him to begin preaching.

But then, these men are so attuned to You, Lord, they simply believe . . . and their messages come forth. Give me their faith. . . .

Partway through Vernon's sermon, the door at the far end of the front room slammed. Ben sat straight up and the rest of the men turned around—prepared to meet Hiram head-on. But it was Gabe Glick, looking sheepish for the way the wind had snatched the door from his unsteady hand.

Vernon paused, his face radiating his gladness—and relief, as well. "It's a fine thing to have you join us, Gabe," he said in his rolling voice. "I take this to mean your Wilma is resting comfortably this morning."

Gabe removed his broad-brimmed hat, nodding slowly. "Millie's helpin' with her, and she let me oversleep," he explained. "I hope you'll all pardon me for bein' so late—and for interruptin' your message, Bishop."

Heads nodded and folks relaxed as Vernon began speaking again. Ben was pleased that Gabe was able to join them on this cold February morning—glad he'd been able to get away from home for some fellowship with his friends.

From the women's side, Ben saw Miriam gazing at him. How sweet it was to be a part of this wonderfully close-knit community because she had loved him from the moment he'd blown into town. Rootless he'd been, traveling the Midwest in his farrier wagon, until this fine woman had given him a reason to stay and make something of himself. Without her, he wouldn't be enjoying marriage in this beautiful new home. . . .

The singing of the slow, traditional hymns, punctuated by kneeling in prayer, brought them to Bishop Tom's benediction at the close of the service. The women headed to the kitchen while the men began rearranging the pew benches and setting up the long tables for their common meal. It wasn't proper to be prideful, but Ben felt particularly pleased that the home he'd built for Miriam could accommodate these church services more comfortably than most of the other families' houses did. When he caught sight of Adam and Matthias Wagler across the extended front room, which bustled with men and boys, he made his way over to help them.

Ben grabbed the corner of the table they were setting up and then leaned close to Adam's ear. "So how's it goin' with Annie Mae?" he asked quietly. "I was glad to see the two of ya takin' off together after Tom's wedding."

"It was just a ride," Adam hedged, "with apple pie being the main reason for it. She likes to bake it, and I like to eat it."

"That's all the reason most of us need." The glimmer in Adam's eyes said more than his words, so Ben didn't press for details. He'd always wondered why the younger Wagler brother wasn't courting someone, and it was easy to see that Annie Mae had more spring in her step whenever Adam was eating in the Sweet Seasons.

But time would tell. Any man would be wise to take things slowly with Annie Mae, considering the fellows she'd been dating—although Ben admired her greatly for denouncing Yonnie Stoltzfus, who'd become a cog in the wheel of her father's ever-circling deceptions. He wasn't upset that Annie Mae had quit seeing his brother Luke, either, as Luke wasn't known for committing to relationships any more than he was to the faith. As the women carried out platters of sandwiches and filled the water glasses, Andy Leitner held up his hand to get everyone's attention.

"My new clinic wagon's here!" he announced jubilantly. "Rebecca has printed up cards with the new number, for everyone to post alongside their phones."

A collective *oh!* filled the room, and folks surged toward Andy for one of his cards.

"And in case you're concerned about your call going to my message machine, unanswered," Andy went on, "Bishop Tom has allowed me to use the call forwarding feature. So if Rebecca, my office assistant, doesn't answer you right away, your call will ring on the mobile phone in my wagon. Or, after hours, it'll ring in my family's apartment above the clinic."

"This is *not* to say everybody in Willow Ridge gets cell phones!" Bishop Tom clarified. "We're allowin' this on a trial basis for the clinic, on account of how Andy wants to respond to emergencies as quick as he can. If I hear folks're callin' him at all hours of the night for situations that can wait 'til the next day, we'll put a stop to it. Every man has to have his rest."

"And what if somebody's sick on a Sunday? Is Andy allowed to work then?"

Everyone got quiet, looking toward Lydia Zook, who'd asked the question, and then toward their new bishop for his answer.

Tom stroked his silver-spangled beard, unruffled. "Vernon and I have been discussin' this very subject, about how when ya allow one new convenience—like Andy's phone system—a dozen new questions arise from it. And workin' on the Sabbath is a debatable situation."

"We're all aware of how our Lord Jesus defied the religious leaders of his day by healing on the Sabbath"—Vernon continued the discussion—"and it could be said that we bishops and preachers do the bulk of *our* work on Sundays—no matter what you might think about the quality of our sermons."

Folks laughed, their faces alight with interest.

"So for now," Bishop Tom went on, "we've told Andy to answer all his calls, but to keep us informed of how many patients he tends on Sunday. We're pleased to have him amongst us with his healin' skills. I believe we Old Order folks should welcome new opportunities, if we handle them properly."

"Hear, hear," one of the fellows remarked.

"So when can we quit shavin' and let our mustaches grow?" another man asked in a half-teasing voice.

Vernon laughed, as this topic came up every now and again. While U-shaped beards were the mark of married Amish men, with the longer beards symbolizing Christ-like maturity and experience, forefathers of the faith had considered mustaches a reminder of European military officers—too militant a look for men who practiced pacifism. "I don't see that change coming anytime soon," the bishop from Cedar Creek replied.

"So when can my *dat* marry Rhoda?" a little boy piped up.

"So she can be our new *mamm*?" his sister added.

Again Ben smiled. Brett and Taylor Leitner were so eager to complete their family and so willing to make the sweeping changes their new Plain life required. Bishop Tom extended his hands to the youngsters, who grasped his fingers and beamed up at him. "We're all waitin' for that day, kids," he said kindly. "I see it as God's will that your house has sold and you're movin' to your new place next week. And your *dat*'s takin' his church instruction classes. And you'll start your homeschoolin' with Nellie Knepp as soon as ya finish out your school year in New Haven, ain't so?"

Brett and Taylor nodded eagerly. The boy was dressed in a black vest and broadfall pants while his sister wore a solid purple dress with a white pinafore—clothes Rhoda had sewn for them—and her hair was pulled back into a bun beneath a *kapp*. What a precious sight they made. Ben considered it another positive step for Willow Ridge that this fine family was being considered for inclusion in the Amish church.

"Your *dat*'ll become a member in God's *gut* time, and when the other folks here decide he's ready," Tom continued. "Can ya be patient a while longer?"

"No!" Brett blurted, but Taylor elbowed him.

"*Jah,* he can," she insisted in her little-girl voice. "We're workin' on that part."

Rhoda then murmured something to them, already looking and acting so much like their *mamm,* that Ben got a thrill from watching her. The Lantz triplets had all matured so differently, yet each of them radiated their mother's finest qualities. Their frequent visits to this home were such a blessing to him and Miriam.

After they said a silent grace, the common meal went more quickly than usual, because several folks wanted to look at Andy's new clinic wagon. And what a marvel it was! Ben noted that its basic, boxy structure didn't differ much from his farrier wagon, on the outside—except two solar panels on top allowed Andy to plug in some basic pieces of medical equipment. Inside, there was an examination table, a sink, and cabinets along the walls that provided storage for his supplies.

Posters of the inner systems of the human body covered the walls, and the diagram of a baby inside its mother held Ben's attention. Wouldn't it be *something* if Miriam would someday carry his child? What a blessing—what a miracle—if she could conceive all these years after giving up hope of having more children.

As Ben walked up the road toward home, he felt filled with love and joy and hope. This had been quite a Sunday! Truly a time when God had revealed His presence among those receiving their instruction, and when Preacher Gabe had walked in, and in the wonder of Andy Leitner's wagon.

More blessings than I can count, Lord, he mused as he stepped up onto his wide front porch. *And for that, I'm truly grateful.*

Chapter Twenty-One

As February gave way to March, Annie Mae focused on her waitressing by day and on her siblings in the evenings. When she wasn't waiting tables, she was at Miriam's sewing shirts, pants, and dresses for the four little ones . . . riding herd on Josh and Joey so they didn't disrupt Tom and Nazareth's life as newlyweds . . . cooking supper with Jerusalem . . . doing a mountain of laundry with Nellie . . . watching over her shoulder, knowing Dat might return at any time. And during these activities she kept her thoughts about Adam in a tight, straight line.

Oh, but she had dreams about riding that wicked-sleek motorcycle with him, even as she kept herself so busy. But such ideas would only get them both in trouble. Hadn't she already led Adam astray while they sat in his rig after Tom's wedding, with her remark about how he loved it when she teased him? Such behavior wasn't so very different from Eve's tempting the original Adam, after all. If she were to become a responsible, sincere member of the church, she needed to stop saying such suggestive things because they only got her into the same sort of predicaments she'd fallen into with Yonnie Stoltzfus. Even so, Adam's kiss lingered on her lips. . . .

And of course she saw Adam nearly every morning at the Sweet Seasons. His smile betrayed his own secret thoughts as he accepted the plate that held his silver pot of tea, letting his fingers linger on hers just a moment too long. Once in a while, when Matthias and the other fellows were at the buffet table, Adam held her gaze as though he, too, recalled that long, sweet kiss in his rig.

"How are you, Annie Mae?"

"I'm *gut.* You?"

"Crazy-busy with remodeling work. The kids doing all right?"

"Growin' like weeds."

"How about boxing me up something to take home? And some of your special apple pie, if you've got it. . . ."

Memories glimmered in Adam's eyes as they reached the end of their typical conversations, but he didn't ask her out again. Annie Mae figured it was just as well. She and Adam had shared important feelings in his buggy—had helped each other over some bumps in their private roads—and they had reached an *understanding* about not going any further . . . not letting that kiss lead to another. And another.

Because if Adam ever kissed her again, Annie Mae knew she'd never keep her end of the bargain. She'd be chasing after him the way she used to pursue Yonnie and Luke. Even if she had the time for flirting with Adam Wagler, he was keeping enough of a distance to send an undeniable message: *We've both got plenty of stuff going on right now.*

And yet, as the snow melted to reveal greening grass and the spring sunshine brought buds out on the trees, Annie Mae felt restless. Was life passing her by? While she believed she'd chosen the path God intended for her, raising her younger siblings, she wasn't yet eighteen. A difficult, lonely road stretched before her. And how long could she expect Bishop Tom and Nazareth to share their home? They didn't say as much—and they seemed devoted to the kids— but Annie Mae suspected they yearned for time to themselves. She also wondered if Jerusalem wasn't postponing her marriage to Vernon Gingerich so Nazareth didn't have to deal with the kids by herself all day while Annie Mae worked at the Sweet Seasons. And that wasn't what she'd intended at all.

Things would be so much simpler if Adam would just wake up! she mused one afternoon while walking home after her shift at the café. *He said right out that saddlin' myself with so much responsibility was no life for me, yet he might as well be hidin' under that tarp with his motorcycle. Can't he see how perfectly the pieces would fit together . . . how the kids are crazy about him, and how much easier his life would be with me keepin' his house clean and cookin' for him and Matthias . . . ?*

But those ideas implied marriage, and Annie Mae didn't see that happening. She got so caught up in her glum thoughts, walking along the road with her head down, that she had no idea about the car trailing slowly behind her—until the horn honked.

Annie Mae gasped, turning. Yonnie Stoltzfus lounged in the driver's seat of his shiny blue car, his arm draped over the passenger seat. The convertible top was down and he was watching her with hooded eyes that told her exactly what was on his mind. She walked faster, saying nothing.

"You've got no call to be stuck-up, Annie Mae."

Her pulse raced. She lengthened her strides, wishing Bishop Tom's house wasn't another quarter of a mile down the road. Out here, between the Brenneman place and the Hostetler lane, Tom's Holsteins munched on the lush grass, watching her with their placid brown eyes . . . which was no help at all, if Yonnie kept badgering her.

"It's a great day for a ride, sweet thing," he called out as he rolled slowly alongside her. "Thought you'd enjoy some fresh air and sunshine after slaving in the restaurant all day."

Annie Mae hugged herself, almost jogging now. She wasn't good at climbing pasture fences. Didn't want to contend with the top row of barbed wire to get away from the road. . . .

"Hey!" Yonnie said more insistently. "Cat got your tongue? Or has Wagler been Frenching you so much that—"

"Stop it!" Annie Mae blurted. "Shut up and leave me alone!"

The car screeched to a halt. Yonnie raced around in front of her, scowling as he blocked her path. "That's no way to talk to me when I'm trying to be friendly."

"If you're my friend, you've got a funny way of showin' it," Annie Mae blurted. She tried to get around him, but Yonnie grabbed her by the shoulders so hard she yelped.

"Get in the car. We need to talk."

"Let *go* of me! You're hurting—"

"Oh, this is *nothing*." Yonnie gripped her forearms and brought her face within inches of his. His pale green eyes narrowed and his ragged breathing fanned her face. "You can either get in my car, or I'll *put* you there."

"No! Leave me—" Annie Mae shrieked when Yonnie quickly slipped his arm beneath her bottom and lifted her effortlessly. She kicked and flailed at him, slapping his face. "Put me down! You've got no call to—"

"Stupid move, slapping me," he grunted as he dropped her into the passenger seat. "I was gonna go easy on you, but now I'm mad."

Before Annie Mae knew what else to do, Yonnie hopped into his idling car, lowered the doors, and then took off with a squeal of his tires. Bishop Tom's cows raised their heads at the loud noise. Annie Mae desperately wanted to wave her arms at Nazareth and Jerusalem, who were planting vegetables in the garden, but Yonnie would surely do something even meaner to her if she tried that. The familiar countryside passed in a blur and soon they were turning off the pavement, down the gravel road out by the Kanagy farm.

Clinging to the door, Annie Mae muffled her sobs as the wind whipped her face. Even if she had nerve enough to hurl herself out of the fast-moving car, she would surely break some bones—and Yonnie would either leave her to suffer, or he'd toss her back into the car without regard for her injuries. Neither option was good.

What can I do, Lord? she prayed desperately. *Ya gotta help me—please!*

Yonnie turned a corner so fast, she screamed as gravel went flying. Then she squinted through her tears. Was that a big blue wagon up ahead?

Yonnie cursed and wheeled around in the road,

nearly going into the ditch to complete the turn. As he roared off in a different direction, Annie Mae began to cry harder. That wagon had to belong to Adam, and if he'd seen her in Yonnie's fancy car he would surely believe she was out joyriding.

She closed her eyes and faced forward. Doubled over in the seat to stifle her sobs in her apron. She had a feeling Yonnie was taking her to Higher Ground for whatever *talking* he'd had in mind. Was Dat in on this conversation, too, having his employee do the legwork?

"No need to hide from Wagler, like last time," her driver derided her. "Where we're going, he won't follow, if he's smart. And even if he does, he'll not want anything more to do with you."

Annie Mae's heart sank into her churning stomach. What on Earth did Yonnie mean by *that?* Maybe he was just scaring her into submission. . . .

When he pulled the car to a sharp halt a few minutes later, Annie Mae sat up warily. They were indeed in Higher Ground. Yonnie had driven up the hill and pulled in beside the biggest house in town. Annie Mae's heart hammered and she felt like throwing up, but vomiting in Yonnie's car would only make him angrier.

When her *dat* stepped out the side door of the house, his mocking expression told her that he and Yonnie had plotted this all out . . . that they'd cooked up a nasty plan, knowing when she would be walking between the Sweet Seasons and Bishop Tom's house. Delilah came out behind him, her arms folded smugly across her chest. It looked as though Judgment Day had arrived.

"We have some issues to discuss, young lady," her

father said in an ominous tone. His dark eyes glittered in the afternoon sunlight. "Since you haven't seen fit to return your brothers and Sara to their rightful home—and you haven't begged my forgiveness for the way you defied me in Willow Ridge—your reckoning is at hand. I hope you're prepared to do penance."

Adam lumbered down the road toward home as fast as Jerry could haul his wagon. There was no mistaking whom he'd seen riding in Yonnie's distinctive blue sports car, yet even as he urged his horse faster, he tried to sort out his thoughts. He'd believed Annie Mae when she'd sworn she wanted nothing more to do with that Mennonite troublemaker—not only to him, but in front of everyone at church. Was she in trouble, being driven away from Willow Ridge against her will? Or was she playing him for a fool?

If something happens to Annie Mae because you tried to second-guess what's going on, you'll never forgive yourself. But his Belgian wasn't built for speed, and as his cumbersome wagon clattered down the road, Adam felt keenly aware of the minutes ticking away. The fact that Stoltzfus had spun in a complete circle and raced off in the opposite direction told the tale, didn't it? If Yonnie would've been showing off his passenger, for pride and spite, he would've raced past Adam's wagon, throwing gravel while trying to spook Jerry.

But Yonnie had turned tail. So he was surely up to no good . . . and this, coupled with the way everyone still wondered when Hiram would wreak his revenge and reclaim his kids, agitated Adam all the more. Even if he got to the barn and saddled a faster horse, he could only assume that flashy blue car was heading toward Higher Ground . . . and by the time he arrived wherever Yonnie had taken Annie Mae, she could be in bad trouble.

But he had to try. If all things worked out as a part of God's will, it was no mistake that he'd caught sight of Annie Mae in Yonnie's car . . . and he was the only other person out on those back roads at that particular moment.

As his house and the outbuildings came into sight, Adam wavered. It only made sense, timewise, to hop on the motorcycle—but would it get him to Higher Ground? He'd started the engine a couple of times but still hadn't taken it for a test run . . . had pondered if it was the right thing to do, going against the *Ordnung*, which forbade him to operate a motor vehicle.

What if this is an emergency? It's only a sin to ride that cycle—you could confess and be forgiven. But if Annie Mae's life is on the line, no amount of confessing will bring her back . . . you'll be just as much to blame for whatever befalls her as you were for Mamm*'s death.*

Was he overreacting? Surely Yonnie wasn't fool enough to endanger Annie Mae's life . . . but what if something went wrong? What if Hiram was also involved, and his quest for vengeance got out of hand? Hiram wasn't known for moderation, and now that Yonnie was on his payroll, Annie Mae was outnumbered and outmanned.

Adam pulled Jerry to a halt in front of his brother's harness shop, which sat out by the road. "Matthias!" he hollered as he hurried inside the white frame structure. "Call Officer McClatchey—or the sheriff—or Ben—or Bishop Tom. Or all of them."

Matthias looked up from the length of black leather

harness he was cutting on his worktable. "And what's got the bee up *your* butt?"

"Stoltzfus is taking Annie Mae to Higher Ground—"

"Didn't I warn ya that she'd—"

"Don't mess with me!" Adam countered vehemently. "For once, just do as I've asked, all right? If I'm riding off into some sort of disaster, I'd like to think you've got my back. Unhitch Jerry, too, okay?"

Adam didn't wait for an answer. Once outside, he slapped his Belgian's tawny rump and urged him up the drive, jogging alongside the huge horse as it hauled his wagon off the road. "You wait here for Matthias, fella," he murmured when they reached the shady side of the barn. Then he sprinted inside it, past the troughs and stalls.

As he yanked the tarp away from the motorcycle, his pulse thundered. Once again he heard the shriek of Mamm's horse . . . saw the extended cab pickup plow into her buggy as she flew out of the seat and onto the road.

Adam grabbed the black helmet and put it on . . . straddled the black leather seat with its silver studs, and rammed his foot down on the kickstarter lever. *Ride with me, Lord, and then I promise I'll sell this thing and follow the rules,* he prayed. *Just this once . . . because it's Annie Mae. . . .*

Out of the barn he rolled, restraining his urge to gun the engine until he was well past Jerry and Herbert and the other horses. The cycle rumbled beneath him, a sleek black panther bunching its muscles to spring out of the driveway. Adam sucked in a deep breath. It was one thing to get past his memories of Mamm's accident, and another thing altogether to ride this machine after nearly six years of keeping it under wraps. Would he remember how to balance as he went around the corners? Or would he spin out on the loose gravel and fling himself off the bike before he even approached Higher Ground?

When Adam reached the bottom of the lane, he accelerated. He concentrated on Annie Mae, yet tried not to let his vivid imagination outrun his confidence, far as what might be happening to her. Increasing his speed as he wheeled onto the highway, Adam smiled in spite of this serious mission. His body remembered how to relax and move with the bike . . . and riding again felt better than it should. At least Higher Ground took him away from Willow Ridge rather than through it, but he couldn't worry about the reactions if his friends spotted him. They wouldn't see his face for the helmet, after all—even if his broadfall pants, suspenders, and green shirt marked him as a Plain man.

Adam had forgotten how much faster a cycle traveled than a rig, and he was soon within sight of the brick shops, fresh houses, and the monument that marked the entrance to Hiram's colony. He didn't have a clue what he'd do when he found Annie Mae . . . or how he'd convince Yonnie or Hiram to let her go.

But what if he had it all wrong? Maybe Yonnie had *not* taken her to Higher Ground, and maybe Annie Mae's father had no connection to this situation. Adam downshifted to a slower speed. He circled behind the bank, checking for the blue car, and then cruised the main street of the business district. A few gals in Plain-style print dresses gawked at him as they strolled along the sidewalk, as did the men in their straw hats and tri-blend broadfalls with suspenders.

Adam wished he had special vision that allowed him

to see inside the stores and Alma's Down-Home Café, although he doubted Yonnie had taken Annie Mae shopping, or to dinner. He decided to start at the top of the highest hill and work his way down. It didn't take long to find what he was looking for. . . .

Yonnie had apparently been in such a rush, he hadn't concealed his whereabouts: the bright blue sports car parked beside Hiram's house confirmed Adam's worst-case suspicions. While he hated to alert the folks inside that fancy house of his presence with the motorcycle's rumbling, he didn't want to park too far away, either. He was Annie Mae's ride home, and he might have to take out of here pretty fast, once he found her.

Adam rode slowly up the circle drive and parked at the opposite end of the porch from Yonnie's car. Placing his helmet on the seat, he prayed he'd do the right thing . . . prayed his appearance wouldn't make things worse for Annie Mae. It would be proper to knock on the double doors, yet Adam suspected the folks inside weren't having a family chat in the front room. The kitchen was often the setting for serious discussions.

As Adam went around Hiram's new house, he noticed right off that the butterscotch paint didn't cover the white primer . . . an uncaulked crack gaped at him where the board and batten siding met the red brick foundation. Such shoddy workmanship told him no Plain carpenter from hereabouts had constructed this house. He listened closely for voices, but even though the March day was warm and pleasant, the windows were closed.

The quiet rumbling of gravel made Adam pivot. Never had he been so glad to see the county sheriff's SUV. Officer McClatchey got out of the passenger side as Clyde Banks slid out from behind the wheel. Their eyebrows rose, as though they wondered why he was standing in the shadow of the Knepp house.

"Glad to see you guys," Adam said. "I got worried when I saw Yonnie Stoltzfus driving Annie Mae Knepp out of Willow Ridge in that blue car—especially after the way Hiram railed at her when he barged in on Bishop Tom's wedding a few weeks ago."

The sheriff was a middle-aged fellow, heavy-set but with an air of stern efficiency about him. "Receiving two calls from Willow Ridge—"

"One from your brother, and the other from your bishop," Officer McClatchey clarified.

"—gave me the idea we'd better check it out," Banks confirmed as he studied the house. "Domestic disturbance, is it?"

Adam wasn't sure about the lawman's lingo, but as he began to tell what he knew, glass tinkled behind him. A saltshaker flew out the window, and the shriek that followed it could only be Annie Mae's.

"*No!*" she cried out. "Don't you cut my hair! Anything but—"

The horrified heartbreak in her voice was more than Adam could stand. Amish girls were taught from birth that tampering with their hair was a sacrilege of the unholiest sort. Ignoring Officer McClatchey's suggestion to wait—to let the two of them go in first—Adam bolted toward the side door and then into the house.

The scene in the kitchen turned his stomach. Annie Mae was struggling and kicking, mewling like a terrified kitten, as Yonnie stood in front of her, pinning her arms to her sides. Delilah stood behind her, holding Annie Mae's waist-length ebony braid away from her neck. Adam's first impulse was to rush over and pry Annie Mae out of her captor's grip, but her father's stance and expression stopped him in his tracks.

Hiram stood poised with a straight razor. He looked over at Adam, laughed, and then—with one horrible whack—he lopped off his daughter's hair. Annie Mae's screams had risen to fever pitch, but at the vicious *hiss* of the razor she stopped struggling . . . hung her head to sob dejectedly.

"This is what happens to those who disobey the *Ordnung* and defy me," Knepp said coldly. "Annie Mae no longer deserves to be my daughter—or a child of God. So the Lord told me to—"

"That's wrong, and you know it!" Adam protested.

"Hold it right there, Mr. Knepp," the sheriff asserted in a no-nonsense voice. He and Officer McClatchey had stepped inside during the commotion, stopping on either side of Adam. "You've done enough damage here. We don't want anybody getting cut with that razor."

"Get out of my house," Hiram snapped. He scowled at Adam. "You had no right to bring them here, Wagler. We discipline our own rather than allowing English law enforcement to—"

"It was Tom Hostetler who called me," Officer McClatchey countered. Both lawmen were slowly approaching the four folks who stood in the middle of the kitchen. "He suspected that Annie Mae had been abducted in the blue convertible that's parked outside. What would you know about that, Mr. Stoltzfus?"

The fact that these uniformed officers knew his name took some of the starch out of Yonnie's smug expression. He let go of Annie Mae and glanced nervously at Hiram.

Clyde Banks stopped a few feet away from them. "Doesn't matter whether you answer that, young man. We've heard from three witnesses who saw and heard you burning rubber to get out of Willow Ridge, with Annie Mae in your car," he said as he extended his beefy hand. "Now, if you'll close that razor and hand it over, Mr. Knepp, we'll talk about this in a rational manner."

But the foul deed had been done. Adam regretted looking at Annie Mae in her shame and torment, without a *kapp* covering her head, yet he didn't dare take his eyes off the scene. Her ragged-edged hair stopped just below her ears now—not much longer than his own. Delilah was backing toward the wastebasket with Annie Mae's long black braid.

"Don't even *think* about throwing that away!" Adam cried as he glanced around the cluttered kitchen. He grabbed a plastic shopping bag from the counter. "If you think what you've done to Annie Mae is fair, or decent, or Christian—well, let's cut off *your* hair now! 'Do unto others'—like the Golden Rule."

"Get away from me," Delilah jeered. "No one wants you here, so *get out.*"

When she threw the braid at Adam, as though it were a menacing black snake, he stuffed it in the sack. What he'd do with Annie Mae's hair, he had no idea, but his pulse was pounding so furiously he could only act on impulse. Meanwhile, the sheriff had taken the razor—without Hiram slashing at him, thank goodness—and Yonnie was stepping away from Annie Mae as though she had a contagious disease.

"Come on, honey-girl, I'll take you home," Adam murmured, extending his hand to her.

"Do you want to press charges, Annie Mae?" Officer

McClatchey asked quietly. "From what we've heard, you were abducted—brought here against your will—"

"To her father's home," Hiram interjected hotly. "Annie Mae is a disgrace to her faith and her family— but again, this is no concern of yours, McClatchey. I've had enough of your fines and interference and—"

"And I've had my fill of calls about *you*," the policeman retorted. Then he resumed his usual calm demeanor, used a gentler tone as he addressed Annie Mae again. "If you press charges, we can take these three to the station and—"

Annie Mae's red-rimmed eyes widened fearfully. She covered her face and then shook her head, whimpering.

"There's your answer for now," Adam murmured as he slipped an arm around her shaking shoulders. "Let's get you back to—"

"I—I can't go anywhere lookin' like this," Annie Mae rasped. She began to cry again as she clung to him. "What will Miriam and the rest of them say? What will the *kids* think if I tell them Dat—"

"You brought this on yourself, when you walked out on me at Christmas," Hiram reminded her coldly. "The children witnessed your defiance—your disobedience—then, so they will now see the consequences of your poor choices. You can tell them you're no longer my daughter because—"

"Enough out of you!" Adam cried. He badly wanted to get Annie Mae out of this house before she endured any more degradation. Leaning closer to her, he wished he knew how to make her feel better . . . knowing such magical phrases didn't exist for an Amish girl who'd been defiled by her own father. "We'll figure it out," Adam reassured her. "If anybody knows an answer to this, Miriam will, ain't so? Shall we go to her place?"

"I—I can't let folks see me—"

"You can wear my helmet. Nobody'll know it's you."

Her eyes widened when she realized which vehicle she'd be riding back to Willow Ridge.

"Or, if it would make you feel safer, these fellows will take you home," Adam said, nodding toward the two lawmen.

Annie Mae shuddered and then she sniffled loudly. "Let's go, Adam. We'll let the officers finish up here."

Gripping the plastic bag, Adam steered her gently toward the door. Annie Mae felt so fragile, and her expression held such anguish as they stepped outside into the early spring sunshine. Gingerly, she reached behind her head to feel the blunt edges of her hair, and then burst into fresh tears. "I didn't think Dat would really do it," she whimpered. "He snatched away my *kapp* and then Delilah unpinned my bun, and— I'm so embarrassed for ya to see me this way—"

"Shhh," Adam murmured. "I know you for who you really are."

"And—and here ya stuck out your neck, riskin' a ride on your motorcycle to come after me," she continued in a hiccuppy voice, "and I can't even have the fun I've been daydreamin' of, ridin' the roads with ya. I'm a real bad mess, Adam. Not makin' any sense, and I'm sorry—so sorry—"

Adam hugged Annie Mae's shoulders. "You've done absolutely nothing wrong," he insisted. "Everybody in Willow Ridge will side with you when they see—"

"But I can't *stand* for anybody to see me this way! Especially the kids!"

Adam sighed as they walked toward his cycle. This

wasn't her vanity talking, it was her lifelong upbringing in the Old Order. There were no right answers, and if they lingered while Annie Mae kept spinning in this doleful conversational circle, she ran the risk of hearing more of Hiram's abusive remarks. Adam gently placed the black helmet over her head. "You look like one tough biker babe, you know it?" he teased as he fastened the chin strap. "I wish the ride was going to be easier on your backside, but hang on tight and I'll get you back to town in a few. All right?"

Adam straddled the motorcycle to hold it steady, facing forward while Annie Mae gathered her dress up and then swung her leg over the cycle to settle behind his seat. He put the white bag into the compartment in front of him, so her braid would remain safe while they rode. As she slipped her arms around his waist, he, too, wished they could be riding the roads together under more carefree circumstances. Adam kicked the starter lever, let the engine idle for a moment, and then eased the cycle away from Hiram's front porch.

When they'd reached the road, Annie Mae leaned closer to talk near his ear. "So—what'll ya tell Miriam and Preacher Ben when we pull up and you're drivin' this cycle?"

This change of topic—the hint of playfulness in her voice—sent shivers through him. Adam wished he could pivot in Annie Mae's embrace to kiss her, but this wasn't the right time—even if she hadn't been wearing his helmet. She had asked a legitimate question, though.

"Guess I'll start by telling the truth," he replied. "Between your story and mine, the Hooleys are in for quite an earful."

Chapter Twenty-Two

When the motorcycle stopped alongside Ben and Miriam's house and the engine went quiet, Annie Mae kept her arms around Adam. He had been her rock, someone solid to cling to after she'd been abducted. Defiled. *Shattered.* As her breathing kept time with his, she wished she could stay right here, soaking up Adam's strength and warmth, beneath the camouflage of his helmet. She wasn't sure she'd be able to stand up. Her joints felt like melting gelatin and her heart . . . her heart cried out for God's mercy even as she wondered where God had gone after Yonnie had tossed her into his car.

Adam wove his fingers between hers, wrapping her arms more tightly around his sturdy midsection. "Are you all right, Annie Mae?"

She winced. He meant well—had no idea how that question would haunt her, just as she couldn't imagine when she'd have a positive answer to it. She sighed forlornly, hanging on to him for as long as she could.

"Dumb question. Sorry."

"It's all right. *Denki* for gettin' me here . . . away

from Dat." After several more seconds passed, Annie Mae raised her head. "Might as well go inside," she mumbled. "The sooner we break the news, the sooner I can deal with it."

Adam toed the kickstand down and then eased out of her arms, standing alongside the cycle to help her off. Sensing her need to remain covered, he kept the helmet in place but lifted the dark shield in front of her eyes. "If there's anything I can do—anybody I can fetch so you can talk to them—"

Oh, how I miss you, Mamma. Annie Mae remained upright somehow, yet inside she was caving in, wishing Adam didn't have to endure more of her tears and anguish.

"—just say the word," he continued in a voice that caressed her scarred soul. "I had no idea your *dat* would do such a spiteful, hateful thing to you."

Annie Mae clenched her eyes against a stream of fresh tears. "Well, since I'm not his daughter anymore, I guess that's the finish of it," she muttered. "He won't be comin' back ever again to torment me, ain't so?"

Even as the words rushed from her mouth she didn't believe them—and she regretted the anguished expression she'd put on Adam's face. Viewing him from the narrow opening of the helmet limited her vision . . . this must be how a horse felt while wearing blinders. And maybe, far as Adam was concerned, she *had* only seen a small part of him even though she'd known him all her life.

"Not if *I* can help it, your *dat* won't be coming at ya again," Adam blurted. "Oh, honey-girl, when he raised that razor to—"

Adam crushed her in a hug, burying his face against her shoulder. Once again Annie Mae wished he were taller, for times like these when she needed to feel protected by a man's height and size, and yet . . . hadn't Adam Wagler rushed to her rescue again and again these past months? Hadn't he proven that his fortitude came not from physical superiority but from a well of compassion that seemed to be bottomless? When Adam looked up into her eyes again, Annie Mae saw a fierce determination—a steadfast devotion—like no other man had ever shown her.

*So why am I figurin' this out now, after I've been ruined? When I'm so untouchable—*unclean—*that no decent fella would have me?*

Annie Mae swallowed these bitter sentiments about how blind she'd been. Plenty of other bridges had to be crossed today, without throwing romance into the mix, making the situation stickier.

"Sorry," he mumbled again. "I'm supposed to be the man here, taking charge, instead of knuckling under to my own—"

"Adam Wagler, you're the strongest, most reliable—most *decent*—fella I know," Annie Mae blurted. "There's not a sorry thing about ya, far as bein' weak or fallin' . . . short."

His lips quirked. He took a moment to soak up what she'd just said as he smiled at her reference to his size. "Well, then," he said in a bolder voice, "shall we see what Miriam and Ben and Tom have to say? That's the bishop's rig parked by the corral."

Annie Mae blinked. She'd been so focused on her own aching heart that she hadn't noticed the un-hitched buggy by the pasture gate. It made perfect sense that if Tom had called the sheriff, he had also come here to confer with the district's strongest new preacher. "What if Tom brought the kids? What'll I—"

"Whatever comes along, we'll handle it," Adam murmured as he got the plastic bag out of his front compartment. He grasped her hand. "Your brothers and sisters will always love ya, Annie Mae. It's your hair ya lost, not your heart. Not your self, nor your soul."

Oh, but she wanted to kiss him for saying that, but it would only complicate her life further. Nodding, she started for the door, savoring the warmth of his sturdy hand wrapped around hers. "*Denki*, Adam," she murmured. "Can't thank ya enough."

"You already have, honey-girl."

Once they had knocked and Miriam answered the door—and then welcomed her with a fierce embrace—Annie Mae wondered why she'd been so afraid to come to these folks. Ben and Tom rushed over to them, too, and Rebecca came out of her room, but Miriam wasn't letting go of her.

"Annie Mae! When we heard about Yonnie—oh my stars, but it's *gut* to see ya back here safe and—" Miriam stepped back then, gazing at the helmet that covered her entire head. "Why on God's *gut* Earth are ya wearin' a black helmet, honey-bug?"

Adam cleared his throat. "Well, there's *my* story about that, and there's Annie Mae's," he replied in a low voice. "You'll hear them both, but I think we'd better show you . . . what her father's done to her."

"So Yonnie took her to Hiram's place?" Bishop Tom asked. "Naz and Jerusalem heard that blue car takin' off like a screamin' demon, and we figured there'd be trouble."

"*Jah*, well . . . here it is." Annie Mae held her breath, grateful for the way Adam helped her with the unfamiliar chin strap and then assisted with the lifting of his bulky headgear. As the helmet cleared her neck and then the top of her uncovered head, everyone in the room sucked in their breath.

"Let me get ya a *kapp*, child," Miriam said as she rushed toward the stairway. "Who could've believed Hiram would—"

Rebecca's hand flew to her mouth, while Ben and Tom stared and then looked away, out of respect for her appearance . . . her shame. Annie Mae hung her head, wondering how many times she'd have to relive today's humiliation . . . how many folks she would have to repeat her story for. . . .

"Your *dat* did this to ya?" Ben asked in a raw whisper.

"It's a sacrilege," Bishop Tom muttered. "An abomination, and a sign of the evil that's infected every part of him now."

Evil. It was the word she'd not dared to use in reference to her father, yet Annie Mae felt somewhat comforted . . . vindicated, because Bishop Tom had called a spade a spade. "The sheriff asked if I wanted to press charges, but—"

Annie Mae pivoted on her heel, overcome once again by shame and a pain that refused to be relieved. "I couldn't do it," she continued in a tiny voice. "I was too scared of him comin' back to snatch the kids—to hurt *you*, Tom, because I'm stayin' with ya. He—he says I'm no longer his daughter and not a child of God, either—"

"Well *that*'s a lie!" Ben blurted.

"Don't ya believe anything that man says," Bishop Tom said vehemently.

"Those are words no child should ever hear—and a question from the police that no child should ever have to answer." Rebecca strode forward, engulfing

Annie Mae in her embrace. "I am so sorry, Annie Mae. I can't imagine the hurt you've endured."

Adam held up the white plastic sack. "I—I'm not sure why I grabbed it, but after Hiram lopped off her hair with a straight razor, I just had to save it."

"A *razor?*" Miriam exclaimed as she hurried back with a fresh pleated *kapp*. "My stars, what was that man thinkin'? The Lord be praised that he didn't use it on *you*, Adam."

Rebecca peered sadly into the sack, shaking her head. Then she looked up as Miriam was unsuccessfully trying to fit the prayer covering over the blunt ends of Annie Mae's hair. "When I wear a *kapp*, I comb my hair back and wind the ends into curls, held in place by a couple of bobby pins. It keeps the hair flat against my head."

Annie Mae had seen Rebecca in her Plain clothing when she'd celebrated her birthday with Rhoda and Rachel, and at Miriam and Ben's wedding—and just last month at Tom and Naz's ceremony. "I was wonderin' how ya got your short hair to stay put."

Rebecca took Annie Mae's hand. "Come on back to my room, and I'll show you how I do it. And let's take your braid, too. I have an idea."

After a quick glance at Adam, Annie Mae went along with Rebecca and her mother, back to the *dawdi haus* wing where this triplet who'd been raised English was now living. Rebecca had no intentions of ever becoming Amish, but there was no doubt in anyone's mind that her computer, her fresh ideas, and her kind heart were doing a lot of good for people and their businesses in Willow Ridge.

"This'll probably work better if you wash your hair,"

Rebecca mused as she pointed toward the bathroom in her apartment. "Meanwhile, I'm going to check something online. Towels are right there in the cabinet by the sink."

Annie Mae entered the sunny yellow bathroom with Miriam behind her, noting how Rebecca had kept it looking Plain rather than cluttering the room with makeup and hair gadgets. The sink was fairly deep and had a hand-held sprayer, so when the water was warm, Annie Mae leaned over it.

Oh, but it felt *horrible* and unnatural, to run her fingers through such chopped-off hair. Annie Mae squeezed her eyes shut against tears, wishing her anguish would go away. Would she ever feel safe again, or . . . socially acceptable? It would be *years* before her hair grew back.

"Let me help ya with that," Miriam said softly. Her hands worked water and then shampoo through Annie Mae's hair, gently kneading her scalp . . . rubbing away the tension that had bunched in her neck muscles. "No matter how bleak and desperate our lives look, the Lord's standin' with us through every storm," she murmured. "He doesn't promise we'll always see a bright, shiny rainbow when it's over, but He does give us the grace and courage to start a new day . . . if we'll accept those gifts."

Annie Mae stood up, allowing Miriam to massage her wet hair with a towel. "*Jah,* I knew I'd be stirrin' up a storm when I brought the kids back with me," she murmured. "I'll get by. Might take a while, but I've got a lot of mighty fine folks watchin' out for me."

"For sure and for certain ya do. And I'm pleased to be one of them."

When Annie Mae sat down in the bedroom chair a few moments later, Rebecca reached into her dresser drawer for a box of bobby pins. "My English grandma used to pin up her hair this way every night for the hairdo she always wore, or I would never have thought of trying it," she remarked. "It takes a little practice, but I've gotten to where I can keep the curls nice and tight even though I can't see what I'm doing back there."

"Nellie—or Nazareth—could help ya with that, too," Miriam said.

Annie Mae watched in the dresser mirror while Rebecca parted her hair in the center and then combed it back above her ears. She began winding a section at a time around one finger, holding each curl with two crossed bobby pins . . . winding and pinning . . . winding and pinning.

"Let me try that," Annie Mae murmured.

It felt awkward at first, and it took a while to get the winding motion just right, but after a few attempts she got the coils to stay in place against her head. When Annie Mae finished, Miriam placed the fresh *kapp* on her and Annie Mae tied the strings under her chin. "If I keep it fastened, I'll stay covered when I step outside into the breeze," she said, looking this way and that in the glass.

She had a center part, as she'd always had . . . her hair looked as though it were tucked back into a bun beneath the *kapp*, except there was no rounded bump at her crown. From the front, she looked . . .

I look just like myself, except my strings are tied instead of hangin' loose. I can live with that. Dat *might've scared the livin' daylights out of me, but he won't keep me down— and my hair* will *grow.*

Annie Mae sprang up from the stool and grabbed Rebecca in a hug. "*Denki* ever so much," she rasped. "I think I'm gonna make it now."

"That sounds like the Annie Mae we all know and love," Miriam joined in as she slipped her arm around Annie Mae's shoulders. For a long, lovely moment the three of them stood in this huddle, savoring the warmth and affection that thrummed with every beat of their connected hearts and souls.

"And look what I found online," Rebecca said, pointing toward the laptop she'd opened on her dresser. "It's Locks of Love, where they make wigs for kids who've lost their hair to cancer or other diseases. What if we donated *your* hair, Annie Mae? Lucky for us, it's in a braid so they can accept it."

"*Jah,* my hair's so thick, braidin' it makes the bun easier to coil," she remarked. As the three of them looked at the gallery of recipients . . . before and after photos of young girls who were bald, and then smiling brightly in their wigs, a lump rose in Annie Mae's throat. "Oh my," she whispered as she read the text. "It says these girls might *never* have hair again, so . . . so what am I bawlin' about? I say we do it!"

"Makes my heart sing just thinkin' about what a gift your perty black hair'll be," Miriam said as she swiped at her eyes. "You're a fine girl, Annie Mae. So much stronger and wiser than your *dat.*"

"I'll be glad to send in the donation form and your hair for you," Rebecca offered. "You'll change some-body's life, you know it?"

Annie Mae's heart welled up. Wasn't it just like Miriam—and now Rebecca—to make everything right again? She took one last peek in the mirror. "Maybe, since the kids never see me before I'm dressed of a morning, I won't have to tell them right away what Dat did to me," she murmured. "They're too little to understand what-all's goin' on with him and Delilah—or why he took the razor to my hair—and . . . well, I just hate to let on like he's a monster. He's their *dat*, so even though they're scared of him and Delilah lately, they still think he hung the moon and stars."

Miriam hugged her close again before they left the *dawdi* apartment. "Tom and Naz and Jerusalem can help ya talk about that, when the kids get curious. The right words'll come, in God's *gut* time," she said firmly. "It'll all work out, honey-bug."

And for now, at least, Annie Mae could believe that.

Chapter Twenty-Three

"That's quite the helmet you've got there, Adam."

As the ladies went to the other end of the house, Bishop Tom and Ben stood patiently, with expectant expressions on their bearded faces. Adam knew it was time to come clean . . . not just to admit he'd sinned by riding a motorcycle today, but to clear the slate, far as why he hadn't been able to move past his mother's death.

"*Jah,* it *is* a fine helmet," he replied as he gestured toward the front door. "Ya might as well see the rest of the evidence, so the both of you can decide what sort of punishment I deserve."

Ben and Tom glanced at each other but followed him outside without further comment—until they caught sight of the black motorcycle parked beside the porch, glimmering in the afternoon sun.

"Holey socks, now *that's* a road machine!" the bishop declared as he approached it. Then he studied Adam, raising one eyebrow. "And where'd ya come up with this, son? Unless I miss my guess, this old Indian

Chief's worth a perty penny . . . but it's costin' your soul a lot more than that, ain't so?"

Ben was walking all around the cycle, taking in its shiny black fenders, silver chrome, and the studs outlining the seat and the saddlebags. "I've not lived in Willow Ridge all that long, Adam," he said in a pensive voice, "but you're the last fella I'd expect to see on such a cycle. Always steady and dependable, you've been. Not just talkin' the talk, but walkin' the walk, far as our faith is concerned."

Adam inhaled deeply. After the way Annie Mae had listened to his story with such acceptance—and after what he'd witnessed at Hiram Knepp's house—getting this story off his chest didn't seem so difficult. Confessing to these two friends was small potatoes, compared to what Annie Mae had endured today.

"I was mighty glad I still had this bike, when I saw Yonnie racing off with Annie Mae this afternoon— *not* that I'm any less guilty for keeping it so long after I joined the church," he added. "But . . . well, I stashed it in the back stall of the barn as a reminder of how I was to blame for my *mamm*'s death. And how I couldn't trust myself to be responsible for anyone ever again. Including a wife and kids."

It had taken everything he had in him to admit his guilt out loud. Again. Yet now that his words were free-floating on the spring breeze, no more substantial than the aroma of Miriam's dinner coming through the kitchen window, Adam wondered why he'd allowed this story to hold him captive for so long. During all the years he'd kept his secret inside him, the memories of that fateful day had controlled the most important years of his life . . . making him an emotional cripple. A mere shell of the man he was intended to be.

Bishop Tom's brow wrinkled. "As I recall, your mother's rig was broadsided by a pickup truck, out on the highway," he said quietly.

"*Jah*, because when I roared past her on this motorcycle and spooked her horse, it went crazy out of control, running through the intersection," Adam replied in a tight voice. "If I'd gone to fetch my sister, instead of joyriding all afternoon, Mamm wouldn't have been out on the road. And to make matters worse, I was too scared to circle back to the accident and help her . . . too *yellow* to let on to Dat or any of my family that I was to blame for her death."

After a few moments of silence, Ben cleared his throat. "So, I'm guessin' this happened during your *rumspringa*? A lot of us fellas had our adventures in those days, some of them not so honorable or—"

"But your *mamm* didn't die because of a noisy motorcycle you'd been hiding from your family," Adam protested.

"No, but I had a driver's license, and an old beater of a car stashed behind an English friend's garage," Ben replied. "And I had more close calls in it than I ever admitted to."

"*Jah*, me, too," Tom chimed in. "Matter of fact, I drove Vernon Gingerich out to the English cattle ranch we worked on when we were young bucks. Got pulled over by the cops a few times . . . could've gotten the both of us killed once, when I was stupid enough to drive drunk. But more to the point," he continued in a soft, intense tone, "you're tellin' us you've been livin' with this guilt and fear for years—"

"Since I was sixteen, *jah*," Adam rasped, closing his eyes.

"—instead of askin' the Lord's forgiveness, and

instead of acceptin' His wisdom and His will for what happened that day," the bishop went on. He shook his head, resembling a kindly father reprimanding his young son. "I know it's been hard on ya, thinkin' you were to blame, Adam, but where's your faith? All this time you've been sittin' through church, but not hearin' a thing we've said about takin' your troubles to God." Tom paused to smile wryly. "So much for the power of my sermons."

Adam looked up, enthralled by the beatific expression on Bishop Tom's face. "I didn't want to confess in front of everybody, because they'd know how . . . hideous I really was. Totally irresponsible. A killer and a coward."

"But see, that's where ya didn't think it through," Ben remarked as he placed a warm hand on Adam's shoulder. "Who says you'd've had to confess at a Members' Meeting? Ya could've told Preacher Gabe, or Tom—"

"Not Hiram," Adam blurted. "He would've made a spectacle of me. Or . . . at least I think he would've. Maybe I've been assuming a lot of things all wrong."

Bishop Tom considered this. "Hiram aside, ya came to Ben and me of your own free will, confessin' what ya did. Far as I'm concerned, your sin—your story— stays amongst the three of us, right here, right now, unless ya care to tell it to other folks yourself," he said quietly. "So you've done the first part, by admittin' to your sin. Now you've gotta believe that God'll forgive ya. And ya have to forgive yourself."

Adam's lips twitched. "You sound like Annie Mae, when I told her about this."

Bishop Tom shook his head, chuckling. "Well, then, believe who ya will—but *believe*," he insisted. "Annie

Mae's a *gut* girl and ya could do a lot worse than keepin' company with her. Just sayin'."

"*Jah, jah,* I hear you." Adam looked away, suddenly wanting to laugh and whoop and express this new sense of relief—of freedom—that filled him. There would be no Members' Meeting called for the purpose of grilling him like a pig on a spit. He could finally *let go* of the guilt. And because God had witnessed the accident, He had known Adam's circumstances all along . . . just as his parents, now looking down from Heaven—where all was known with a deeper understanding than folks on Earth could possibly comprehend—probably realized what he'd done on that horrible day, as well.

It was a wonderful thing to think about, this forgiveness. This grace from God.

These soul-opening revelations did not, however, change the fact that Sheriff Banks and Officer McClatchey were pulling into Ben's driveway. When the SUV stopped and the lawmen got out, Tom and Ben greeted them with hearty handshakes. "Mighty glad ya got to the Knepp place when ya did," the bishop said. "Sounds like the situation with Hiram and Annie Mae got edgy."

"Knepp's a piece of work," Clyde Banks agreed. "A lot like that rogue bishop out in Ohio—Sam Mullet—who got himself and some members of his church convicted for hair and beard cuttings awhile back. Wish we could've taken Hiram and that Stoltzfus kid to the station to put a little fear in them, but I'm not surprised Annie Mae wouldn't press charges." The sheriff smiled at Adam then. "That was an admirable thing you did, facing up to Hiram and defending

Annie Mae. But we need to talk about you being on the road with this motorcycle."

The sheriff's tone warned Adam to keep his mouth shut—not that he was afraid of either uniformed fellow, because they were both circling his motorcycle with obvious appreciation.

Officer McClatchey ran his hand over the silver-studded saddlebag. "I've got a collector friend who'd give his eye teeth to own this vintage bike," he remarked. "But it seems your license plate has expired . . . and I'm wondering if you've got a valid driver's license."

Adam's stomach bottomed out. He'd been so concerned about the spiritual ramifications of driving his cycle that he'd forgotten about the legalities. He opened the compartment on the front console and handed over his Missouri license. "I was legal when I was sixteen," he said sheepishly, "but this cycle's been stashed in my barn for so many years, I forgot about that part when I took off on it this afternoon. And truth be told, I drove over here without wearing my helmet, too, because Annie Mae had it on."

"You had more pressing issues on your mind," the sheriff said with a nod. He glanced over Officer McClatchey's shoulder, looking at the license.

"I suppose you're going to write me a ticket," Adam said with a sigh. "Don't have a lot of cash on me, but my place is just down the road. I can fetch however much money you need and settle it, right here and now, I hope. I'm selling this cycle, see. I don't ever intend to ride it again."

"For what it's worth, Adam's just confessed to ridin' this bike, which goes against our Old Order faith." Bishop Tom spoke up. He laid a reassuring hand on Adam's shoulder. "Might not be your way to mix church and legal matters, but for my part, I'm convinced he's sincere about not takin' it out anymore . . . even if it *is* one fine-lookin' ride."

Officer McClatchey exchanged a glance with Clyde Banks and then focused on Adam. "All things considered, I think we can waive the ticket—if you agree to leave the bike here, so you don't ride it home and break the law again."

Adam's eyebrows shot up. Could any more unexpected events and reprieves possibly occur in one day? "I could do that, *jah*. Thanks for—"

"And if you'll give me your phone number, I'll see that my friend gets ahold of you," the policeman continued. Then he winked. "Don't be afraid to make him pay full value for this beauty, either. Haggling's a game to him. Aim high—and don't back off."

Adam blinked. While he understood the strategies folks used at auctions and mud sales, bidding high or low, it seemed odd for one friend to insist that another friend pay full price for something. "Chances are *gut* that the money'll end up in the Amish Aid fund, anyway," he said as he scribbled his phone number on the slip of paper the sheriff offered him. "Or it'll help Annie Mae support her sibs."

Preacher Ben clapped him on the back. "I like your way of thinkin', Adam. The trick'll be gettin' her to accept your help."

"I think we've settled it then," the sheriff declared. "You fellows have a good evening, and we'll hope we don't have to deal with Hiram Knepp again."

As the SUV pulled onto the county blacktop, Adam felt greatly relieved by the officers' goodwill and generosity. "How about if I roll this motorcycle into your barn, Ben?" he asked. "There's no telling when I might hear from that friend of Officer—"

Adam's mouth closed and then opened again. Annie Mae was coming down the Hooleys' front porch steps, looking directly at him. Looking . . . settled and strong again. From this angle, there was no way to tell that she'd lost her hair. While most girls wore their *kapp* strings dangling loose, Adam thought the bow tied beneath Annie Mae's chin gave her an air of determination . . . a sense that she knew who she was and where her boundaries were set.

"So how're you doing?" Adam asked her. "You . . . you look real *gut*."

Her eyes sparkled, even as she clasped her hands in front of her a little nervously. "I'll make it," she said softly. "Might need some help with the kids' questions—"

"And I'll be there for ya," Bishop Tom assured her. He looked at Ben and Adam then. "It'd be a *gut* idea for somebody to escort Annie Mae to and from work, and to see that Nellie gets to school, and that the wee ones are always with adults from here on out."

Preacher Ben nodded. "*Jah*, we don't want a repeat of what happened today. All of us want you and your sibs to be safe and happy, Annie Mae."

"Count on me to help, too," Adam chimed in. "And just for the record . . . you had it right. I just talked to these guys about riding my cycle the day Mamm died."

Her blue eyes widened. "And how'd that go?"

Adam felt another wave of welcome relief flowing over him. "It's all *gut* now. I'm squared away, far as confessing goes. And Officer McClatchey knows a fellow who might buy my bike."

Annie Mae's tremulous smile did funny things to

Adam's insides. "Seems to me the Lord's been busy makin' a lot of things right this afternoon, even after some things went wrong in Higher Ground," she remarked.

Bishop Tom nodded in agreement. "Ready to go home now, Annie Mae? The cows'll be wonderin' where I am."

"*Jah.* Jerusalem and Nazareth'll be makin' supper and I should be helpin' with that. It'll keep me busy. Focused." She smiled at Adam, almost shyly. "*Denki* again for comin' after me today. You're a lifesaver, ya know it?"

A lifesaver. Now didn't that put a different twist on his opinion of himself for these last several years? As Adam watched the bishop escort Annie Mae to his rig, he couldn't help smiling. His heart felt ten sizes bigger, filled with hope—even as he realized she wasn't going to be over her father's abuse anytime soon.

But it seemed worth his while to wait . . . to work on forgiving himself while he encouraged Annie Mae to move forward, as well.

Chapter Twenty-Four

"It might be best if we talk to the kids about your hair tonight," Bishop Tom said as the rig rolled down the road toward his farm. "While ya look real *gut*, all things considered, they're gonna ask about why you're tyin' your *kapp* strings. It's better to tell them straight-out while I'm around, rather than you gettin' caught short by their curious questions, ain't so?"

Annie Mae sighed. She had *so* hoped to give this matter a rest for a while. "All right. I suppose that might be best," she murmured. "Josh and Joey aren't ones to miss my *kapp* fittin' different than it used to, now that ya mention it."

"They've been helpin' me fetch the cows' water and feed, so I'll steer them out to the barn first thing," he agreed. "That'll give ya time to answer Jerusalem and Naz's questions, too. Those two were fit to be tied when they heard the squeal of Yonnie's tires and saw him takin' out down the road with ya."

Annie Mae felt like a target that everybody in Willow Ridge would be aiming at over the next few days . . . but at least they would all rally behind her, too. Wasn't that why she'd insisted on joining the church, after all?

The bishop's rig wasn't but halfway to the barn before the back door of his house flew open. Nellie and the kids raced outside, clamoring her name, while Jerusalem and Nazareth hurried toward her at a more sedate pace. Their concern for her had etched their wrinkles deeper this afternoon, it seemed, and as the kids threw open the buggy door, their little voices told the tale.

"Annie Mae! Annie Mae!" little Timmy and Sara cried as they clambered into her lap.

"Did ya go to Dat's house?" Joey asked as he stepped up beside her.

"Was that nasty Delilah there?" his twin demanded as he stood on her other side.

Nellie hung back a few feet, her eyes riveted to the bow beneath Annie Mae's chin. "We um, prayed real long and hard for ya," she murmured.

"Oh, but it's *gut* to see your sweet face!" Nazareth gushed, while Jerusalem studied her closely. "We surely did wonder what might be happenin'—"

While everyone was talking at once, Bishop Tom came around to the passenger side of the buggy and held up his hand for silence. "Your sister's had a rough afternoon, kids," he began. "But thanks to Adam and the sheriff—and that nice Officer McClatchey who came when you twins had your sleigh wreck—and thanks to your prayers," he added with a smile for Nellie and the two older women, "Annie Mae came through her time of trial. But your *dat* and Delilah cut off her hair, so we need to be extra nice to—"

"He *what?*" Nazareth and Jerusalem chorused. Nellie's hand flew to her mouth. The boys and little Sara got very quiet. Their faces grew somber.

Annie Mae closed her eyes to keep from crying again. But wasn't it better that everyone heard this story at once, so they could work it through their systems—and so she, too, could move beyond today's traumatic events?

"Lemme see!" Timmy blurted as he grabbed for her *kapp* strings.

"Timmy, you leave your sister's *kapp* alone!" Nazareth said as she rushed forward to grab him. "Boys are *not* to meddle with girls' prayer coverings—"

"It's all right," Annie Mae murmured as she closed her hands around her little brother's inquisitive fingers. "Let me out of the rig, so this'll be easier."

Nellie steered the twins backward while Nazareth took Sara and Bishop Tom hoisted Timmy to his shoulder. Annie Mae stepped to the ground, turned her back to everyone, and then slowly removed her *kapp*. "Rebecca showed me how to pin my hair," she explained in the strongest voice she could muster. "And—and she found a place to donate my braid, so a kid with cancer can have a wig made from it, so I—"

Nazareth clutched her shoulder. "My stars, I never dreamed I'd see the day when your *dat* got so out of hand that he—"

"Do ya want to say what-all happened?" Jerusalem asked quietly. "Or would ya rather let sleepin' dogs lie?"

Everyone behind her got quiet—gawking at the pin curls clinging to her head, no doubt. Annie Mae couldn't help but notice how subdued Jerusalem sounded . . . and as she heard Nellie quietly crying, it seemed best to reveal all the details. Much as she hated to consider it, her *dat* might make these women his next victims because they were taking care of *her*. They should know exactly how low Hiram Knepp would stoop . . . how reprehensible he had become.

Annie Mae gazed into Bishop Tom's eyes for strength. "Yonnie knew all along how Dat intended to . . . humiliate me," she recounted. "Soon as he shoved me into the kitchen, Dat started in with his list of ways I'd sinned against him. I started hollerin' when Dat said he'd take me down a peg or two by cuttin' off my hair—broke away from Yonnie and then grabbed a saltshaker and threw it at him, hopin' to run off—but he ducked. So it crashed through the window. And he grabbed me again."

Annie Mae took a deep breath to still her racing heartbeat. While that window glass had broken, just as her heart and soul had shattered at that terrifying moment . . . she had endured and survived. She had been spared. And she now stood among the folks she loved best, safe again. This realization gave her the strength to go on.

"While Yonnie held my arms down, Dat snatched off my *kapp* so Delilah could unpin my braid. I . . . I fought them as best I could—"

"Ya didn't stand a chance with all *those* heathens workin' against ya," Jerusalem muttered.

"—but Dat flipped open a straight razor—"

Nellie's whimper made Annie Mae wonder if she should stop, but Tom nodded his encouragement. "When did Adam come in? And the police?" he asked gently. "You're doin' fine, Annie Mae. We're all in this with ya."

She recalled the fierce outrage on Adam's face when he'd burst through the door. "Adam, bless his soul, came rushin' in with the sheriff and Officer McClatchey behind him, or . . . well, we can't worry about what might've happened if you folks hadn't called them—and if ya hadn't been prayin' so hard for me," Annie Mae added quickly. "When Delilah held up my braid, Dat whacked it off before the police or Adam could stop him. It was Adam who saved my braid, though . . . and who got me out of there and took me to Ben and Miriam's."

She left out the motorcycle, as that was Adam's story to tell. And she didn't want to repeat the part where Dat had disowned her and said she was no longer a child of God, either. Not in front of Nellie and the kids.

Tom squeezed her shoulder. "While I'm supposed to say God's will is bein' carried out, and that we're to forgive your *dat* for what he's done," the bishop addressed them quietly, "I've never seen the likes of such dangerous hatred. The best we can do is pray on it now, askin' God to keep us all safe and to shine His light on our darkness—and to shine on Hiram's darkness, as well." Tom bowed his head, leading the rest of them.

After a few moments, with only the breeze riffling the trees and the shuffling of the cows in the milking barn to break their silence, everyone opened their eyes. Annie Mae tied her *kapp* on again and turned to face the others. "It's *gut* to be here—"

"I don't *never* want to go to Dat's house again!" Joey blurted as he grabbed her around the waist.

"Didn't I tell ya how mean Delilah was?" Josh bleated as he clutched Annie Mae from the other side.

Their remarks cut her deeply. Five-year-olds shouldn't say such things about their father or the . . . young woman he had chosen to be their keeper. But it was a reminder to Annie Mae that she wasn't the only Knepp child who had suffered. Didn't Sara and Timmy still have faded scars from the switchings Delilah had given them? Didn't Nellie still cry herself to sleep now and again?

"We six kids have each other," Annie Mae murmured as she hugged the boys close. "And we're blessed to be livin' with Naz and Jerusalem and Bishop Tom, here in Willow Ridge where folks consider us *family*. So don't you worry about a thing, because God's brought us this far and He's not gonna leave us in the lurch. Do ya believe that?"

As each of her siblings met her gaze and nodded solemnly, Annie Mae drank in their earnest expressions . . . their dear, sweet innocence . . . their love and trust. And because she knew how they depended upon her to be strong, she would find a way to protect them. To nurture them. To set aside her own anguish and put these kids first in her life.

There was simply no other way for her to go on.

Saturday morning, Adam stood in Ben Hooley's barn trying not to grin like an idiot. Trent Searcy, the English fellow Officer McClatchey had mentioned, kept circling the motorcycle, saying what fabulous condition it was in as he ran his fingers over the leather and chrome and studded saddlebags. "This Indian Chief dates back to the early forties!" he exclaimed as he shook his head incredulously. "Do you have *any idea* what this bike's worth?"

Adam knew a loaded question when he heard one, from a man who probably assumed Amish folks were clueless about real-world matters. Searcy was dressed in jeans and a Led Zeppelin T-shirt, with a silver-spangled beard and shoulder-length ponytail. "*Jah*, I do," he replied. "I could sell it on eBay for about thirty thousand. Since all the money's going as a charitable donation, though, I'm hoping for more than that."

When Searcy stopped circling to look at him straight-on, Adam wondered if he'd inflated the price too much, trying to help Annie Mae. He hadn't told anything but the truth, however: thanks to Rebecca's research, he had stated a fair market value—his bottom line—and had left this fellow some wiggle room. He really, really didn't want to bother Rebecca with an eBay transaction, but—

"What sort of a charity are we talking about?"

Again Adam hoped not to overstate his case. "We've got a young, single girl in town who's been left to raise her five brothers and sisters," he explained. "The bike's been sitting under a tarp in my barn, not doing me one bit of *gut*, but this sort of cash will help keep her family fed and together. She's not one to accept handouts, but working full-time at the Sweet Seasons across the road won't pay their bills, either. Especially if any of them gets sick."

"Ate an awesome breakfast over there this morning,"

Searcy remarked as he rubbed his stomach. "Randy McClatchey told me not to miss it."

"Chances are this gal was your waitress. But I want to keep this between you and me, and keep her name out of it, understand," Adam insisted. "If she knew what I was doing, she'd refuse my help. She's stubborn that way."

Searcy's laughter made Ben's horses look up from the hay they were munching. "I like her already! Will you take a check? Or shall I go to the bank in New Haven and get you the cash?"

Somehow Adam kept from whooping and jumping up and down, even though no amount had been mentioned. Trent Searcy had the air of being well-off, but a check for thirty thousand dollars—*thirty thousand dollars!*—could bounce mighty high if it wasn't any good. He wanted to be cautious without seeming not to trust this English guy. "I have my accounts there, too, so why don't we both go?" Adam reasoned aloud. "It'll save me the trip to make the deposit. And if I put the money directly into her account, she can't argue with me, can she?"

Trent extended his hand. "I like the way you operate, Adam. Let's go to the bank, and then swing by home for my trailer."

During the short ride, Adam answered Trent's questions about Willow Ridge and his remodeling business. When they got to the bank, he remained in the lobby while Trent handled the transaction with the teller. She was a lady he often made his remodeling deposits with, and after a few moments she called him over to the window. "Is this money being deposited into your business account, Adam?" she asked. "We can transfer it electronically, if you'd like."

"Not my account, no. I don't have a number with me, but . . ." Adam paused. He hadn't mentioned Annie Mae's name previously, thinking to protect her privacy if Officer McClatchey had told his friend about Hiram Knepp's misdeeds. But then . . . if Trent's check was good, surely his intentions were, too. "Move it into Annie Mae Knepp's account."

"Certainly. What a sweet, hardworking girl," she remarked as she tapped on her keyboard. Then she slid a form across the counter. "If you'll sign here, beneath Mr. Searcy's signature, we'll be all set. I'll have your deposit slip momentarily."

Adam picked up a pen on the counter. He skimmed the document, saw the amount—and then stared at Trent. "That . . . that's *very* generous of you, sir," he rasped. "Thanks a *lot*."

Searcy winked. "That addition to your donation helps me justify my vintage motorcycle hobby," he said. "I admire the way you Amish watch out for each other. And if you've got any business cards, Adam, I'd like to throw some work your way when the opportunities arise. Family-owned businesses are the backbone of this region, and it's in everyone's best interest to keep them profitable."

Adam couldn't argue with that. And when all was said and done, and Trent Searcy was rolling down the county blacktop with the black motorcycle on the trailer behind his Navigator, Adam couldn't dispute the deposit slip in his hand, either.

Thirty-five thousand dollars!

It would be a challenge not to share this news with Rebecca or Ben or Miriam or Bishop Tom—but Adam didn't want to take the slightest chance that Annie Mae would hear about his deposit secondhand. And now that the deed was done, the biggest challenge was getting her to accept his gift in the spirit with which he'd given it.

He needed to find the perfect time and place to tell her. . . .

Chapter Twenty-Five

At the end of the church service, Ben watched their deacon, Reuben Riehl, stand to give some announcements. On this springtime Sunday, with the windows open and a gentle cross breeze keeping the crowd comfortable, he was again pleased to be hosting church in the home he'd built for Miriam . . . happy about how the placement of the windows and the house's position on a ridge provided welcome circulation of fresh air in their home as the weather got warmer.

"It's my pleasure to announce the upcoming wedding of Bishop Vernon Gingerich to Jerusalem Hooley," Reuben said in a voice that carried over the large crowd. "They've set Thursday, April seventeenth, as their date."

Ben elbowed Vernon, who sat beside him with a boyish grin on his face. "Marryin' on her birthday, eh?" he whispered.

"I'll never forget our anniversary that way," the white-bearded bishop admitted as they rose for Bishop Tom's benediction. "Two celebrations, two gifts—and a day I've vowed to devote to my wife each year when it rolls around. Life's meant to be celebrated."

After Tom had pronounced his final words of the church service, he called for a brief Members' Meeting. "While this isn't something that requires a vote, I feel it's a matter all of us need to be aware of," he said. His serious tone immediately had folks focusing more intently on him.

Tom glanced toward the women's side. "There's no easy way to say this and spare Annie Mae's feelings," he began, "but she's agreed to let me tell ya that Yonnie Stoltzfus abducted her last Thursday. And when he took her to Higher Ground, Hiram . . . her father cut off her hair."

The women sucked in their breath and turned to gaze at Annie Mae, seated in their midst. The men sat taller, outrage evident on their faces.

"She's handlin' it real well," Tom went on, "but this incident should make us all more aware of the trouble that might come to her and Nellie and the kids—or to any of us here in Willow Ridge. I'm askin' ya to be more vigilant," he continued in a more insistent voice. "We called the local law officers, but that didn't keep this sacrilege from happenin'—and it only made Hiram that much madder. Your prayers and consideration'll be greatly appreciated. Enough said. Let's enjoy our common meal."

Everyone rose then, and chatter about Hiram's latest affront filled the large room. As the women clustered around Annie Mae, Nellie, and little Sara, their expressions bespoke their dismay—and their support. Ben strolled toward Adam Wagler, who'd spent the morning with Joey and Josh Knepp on either side of him, while Timmy had been perched in his lap. "And how're you fellas on this fine day?" Ben asked the boys.

"We're *gut*," came the unanimous, if subdued, reply.

"Ready for dinner and some runnin' around outside, most likely," Ben remarked as he winked at Adam.

"I wanna play *now*," Timmy crowed as Adam set him on the floor.

"Take some of the bigger boys, then," Ben advised. "Maybe Levi and Cyrus Zook—"

"And Brett!" one of the twins piped up. Gazing between the men who were setting up tables, he beckoned eagerly to Andy Leitner's boy.

"But we've gotta stay out of the mud and the poop," his look-alike declared, "or Annie Mae'll have our hides. She just made us these new church clothes."

"And ya look mighty fine in them, too," Ben replied as he noted their black pants and the vests they wore over crisp white shirts. "Go out and have your fun for about fifteen minutes—but if somebody pulls into the lane, I want ya to skedaddle back in here, all right?"

The boys nodded and shot out the door.

Ben sighed, glancing at Adam. "Never thought I'd see the day when I had to warn our youngsters about folks who might snatch them while they're playin'," he said. "Especially when it's a parent we're talkin' about."

"I hate scaring them about their *dat,* too," Adam replied as he looked across the room. "Annie Mae seems to be holding up pretty well. Doesn't want to upset the younger ones by showing her own fear, most likely."

A movement caught his eye, and Ben turned to see Miriam scurrying along the edge of the crowded room toward the *dawdi haus* wing. And why would she be going into Rebecca's rooms while the rest of the women were in the kitchen unwrapping the food they'd brought? Ben smiled . . . saw an opportunity to spend a few moments alone with his beautiful bride. "Excuse me a minute," he murmured as he slipped away from Adam.

When he passed through the door Miriam had closed, Ben had *not* expected to hear a miserable gurgling coming from the bathroom—nor was he prepared to see his wife doubled over the toilet. He joined her, steadying her as she finished vomiting. "Honey-girl, I had no idea ya were feelin' poorly—"

"Me neither," Miriam rasped as she righted herself. "Sure hope I've not caught a flu bug. Or maybe those eggs in the breakfast casserole were bad."

Ben considered this as she rinsed her mouth and splashed cool water on her flushed face. He'd devoured a second serving of that same casserole, and *his* stomach was rumbling because it was time for dinner. . . .

His heart skipped into a quicker rhythm as he handed her a towel. "Is there somethin' you'd like to tell me, perty girl?"

Miriam blotted her face. "What're *you* thinkin'?"

Barely able to control his grin, Ben gently grasped her shoulders. "Well, we *have* been havin' our share of fun before we go to sleep at night," he hinted.

Miriam's jaw dropped even as she shook her head. "Oh, I don't think I could possibly be—not after all those years when Jesse and I couldn't—"

"I'm not Jesse." Ben pulled her close, so excited he could barely breathe. "Could it be that *you* weren't the reason no more Lantz kids came along?"

Her grip tightened as an "ooohhhh" escaped her. When Miriam gazed up at him, her dear face was turning three shades of pink. She was trying not to cry—or was she laughing? It was one of the sweetest things Ben had ever seen, and he knew he'd remember this moment forever.

"You keep this under your hat, Mister Benjamin Hooley!" she insisted. "We don't know for sure what's goin' on, and I don't want a false alarm gettin' everybody all stirred up for nothin'."

Ben hugged her close again. "Whatever you say, Missus Benjamin Hooley," he teased. Then he kissed her temple . . . kissed her slowly on the lips. "I love ya more than life itself," he whispered. "And every day I spend with ya, Miriam, I can't wait to see what happens next. Now you've *really* got me wonderin'. But your secret's safe with me."

Miriam swatted his backside and turned him toward the door. "Get back out there before folks think we're foolin' around in here. A gal's gotta use the bathroom once in a while, after all. That's my story and I'm stickin' to it."

Ben did as he was told, valiantly trying to keep a telltale grin from his face. This being the end of March, some quick nine-finger math suggested they might be having a blessed event in the Hooley household right around Christmastime. Now *there* was a gift that would keep on giving—and after the unfortunate incident with Annie Mae this week, it put him in a much happier frame of mind, too.

"Everything all right?" Matthias Wagler asked as Ben helped him and Adam scoot a long table into place.

"Never better," Ben replied breezily. "Sometimes,

just the look on a woman's face can change *everything*, ain't so?"

Annie Mae ate her cold sliced ham and salads even though she wasn't hungry, for if she appeared upset, the women would only cluck over her more. While it was a blessing that everyone had expressed their regrets about what Dat had done, she'd *had* it with folks patting the back of her *kapp* where her bun used to be.

But that's the worst of it—and the pity and the head-shakin' are behind ya now. It was such a lovely day, Annie Mae was ready to step outside with the kids while the other women cleared the tables and put away the left-over food—until a warm hand on her shoulder made her turn around.

"Adam! How are ya?" she asked. Even if his Sunday clothes needed pressing, his smile seemed especially . . . meaningful today. "*Denki* for lettin' the boys sit with ya again this morning. The twins think they're too big to be over on the girls' side with Nellie and me now."

"Happy to have them. While they're perfectly quiet," he said with a chuckle, "they wiggle around enough to keep me awake during the sermons. Not a bad thing, that."

"If they get too antsy, be sure to tell me—"

"I'm not a bit concerned about that," Adam said as he stepped closer. "What I *am* interested in is a walk on this fine spring day. Join me?"

Annie Mae sensed something was on Adam's mind, but she didn't want to anticipate too much. The pity party folks had thrown this morning had taken its toll and she was hoping to relax this afternoon. "I was thinkin' to watch the kids—"

"Rhoda and Katie Zook are already out there," he replied smoothly. "Shall we stroll?"

"You go along now, Annie Mae," Miriam said with a flick of her dish towel. "All work and no play, well— it's not a *gut* way to let our lives go by. The other young people are already out by the barn, settin' up the volleyball net."

Annie Mae blinked. She didn't feel so much like "young people" now that she'd taken in her siblings— and at twenty-two, Adam was beyond joining their games, as well.

"Shall we head across the road, down the lane at the Lantz place?" Adam asked as they stepped outside. "What with the apple trees blooming, the orchard might be a pretty place for a stroll."

"I suppose now that Rachel and her Micah live there, it's really the Brenneman place," Annie Mae remarked, "even if it goes past Ben Hooley's smithy. Lots of changes in this town these past few months, if ya think about it."

Yet when Adam wove his fingers between hers, Annie Mae wasn't sure *what* to think. She was contented to look down the long rows of Rachel's garden, where the peas, lettuce, radishes, and onions were off to a fine start. Bright red and yellow tulips swayed in the breeze on either side of the front steps, and the white porch swing moved as though an invisible someone might be sitting in it, enjoying this fine day.

"I'm thinking to make a few changes myself," Adam said.

Annie Mae's eyes widened. His tone seemed a bit

mysterious, although he also sounded confident that whatever new path he was considering was the right one—and wasn't *that* interesting? As they started across the orchard between the blooming apple trees, she decided to explore his statement a bit. "And what sort of changes are we talkin' about? Are ya ready to sell your motorcycle? Or are ya—"

"Sold it Saturday," Adam replied. "Officer McClatchey told a friend of his about it, and . . . and he didn't bat an eye about payin' the price I asked for."

As she thought back to Rebecca's research on what his cycle was worth, Annie Mae let out a low whistle. "Glad to hear that. But mostly I'm happy ya found a way to move forward, instead of clingin' to those bad memories about your *mamm*'s wreck."

"I've got *you* to thank for that, Annie Mae." Adam's pitch had risen a bit, as though he might be nervous. "The way you listened when I was talking about Mamm's death helped a lot, come time to tell Preacher Ben and Bishop Tom about it. Both of them understood what I'd been going through at sixteen. Said the whole matter was behind me now, and that I'd made the only confession I needed to—especially since I was sellin' the bike."

"See?" she chirped. "Didn't I tell ya it was mostly *fear* keepin' ya from that little chat?"

They were passing across the back of Dan and Leah Kanagy's property, where Leah's stacked, white hives buzzed with her bees. Adam stopped just inside the windbreak of spruce trees that flanked the next road. When he turned to face her, Annie Mae sensed he had planned this route to give them some privacy. She—and a lot of other girls—had been known to linger behind these dense evergreens with a boy after Singings, before going home.

"I'm changing the way I think about my future," Adam went on. He held her gaze as he grasped both of her hands. "And I was wondering—"

The loud rumble of a muffler drowned out his next words. Even though Annie Mae understood that Adam was preparing to say something very important, the commotion across the road had her looking over his shoulder instead of into his eyes.

Then Annie Mae frowned. "Now why's that big truck pullin' up into our lane?" she muttered. Still clasping one of Adam's hands, she shifted so she could see between the tall evergreens. "And this bein' Sunday, why would anybody . . . that's a *ramp* the driver and another fella just lowered out of the back."

Adam turned to gaze between the trees with her. Now that the truck's engine was shut down, the clank and clatter of the metal ramp sent an ominous chill up her spine.

"Something tells me this is your *dat*'s doing," he said in a low voice.

As they stepped between the trees for a better look, Annie Mae wished she hadn't. "Is that big wooden sign at the road a—"

"FOR SALE sign," Adam confirmed as he gripped her hand harder.

A little cry escaped her. "Why didn't ya tell me about this before we walked—"

"I had no idea, honey-girl," he rasped. "This must've happened while we were in church. The sign's from that Hammond fellow's real estate company."

"So . . . so Dat's sellin' the home place." Annie Mae struggled to draw a breath. "Emptyin' out all the—"

She pivoted, unable to watch as the two men wheeled her *mamm*'s china hutch into the truck. Had they even taken out the dishes? Were they going to remove every piece of furniture she'd grown up with? A truck that size would hold a lot of—

Annie Mae heard a keening sound before she realized it was coming from her own throat. When Adam took her in his arms, she was too stunned—too numb—to protest. She curled herself around him so her head found his sturdy shoulder, unable to suppress the tears that now spotted his black vest. "I suppose it's wrong to think any of Mamm's pieces would've come to Nellie or me, after the way we walked out," she whimpered. "After all, we've been livin' without that furniture for months now, and—and it's only *stuff*—"

"*Jah,* but it's *your* stuff," Adam whispered. "I'm sorry we happened over here when we did. Do you want to head back to Ben's?"

Annie Mae sniffled loudly. Where could she possibly go to forget what she'd just witnessed? Was there to be no end to this crying, this upheaval? It was almost as though Dat had known she and Adam would be walking past here after church. Every time her father thought of some other way to make his presence known, she would be dragged across the emotional coals, scorched again. Dat knew just how and when to pull her strings, so his actions would have the nastiest impact on her.

"Annie Mae, I—maybe this isn't the best time to talk about what's on my mind." Adam gazed up into her face, gently thumbing away her tears. "But I want you to know that even when it seems like your world's getting loaded up and hauled away—like you'll have nothing to fall back on—I . . . I deposited the money from sellin' my bike into your account, honey-girl. So even if you keep thinking you won't marry—or you won't marry *me*—you'll not have to work so hard to support your sibs."

Annie Mae felt her mouth drop open and then close again. "What are ya sayin', Adam? That makes no sense, that you'd put the money from sellin' your cycle—"

"But *you* were the one who got me to the point I could get rid of it, along with all the guilt I was hanging on to," he said earnestly. "That bike's been in the barn for years, so it's not like I'll miss the money—not like I *need* the money. But if . . . if you change your mind about getting married, I want to be first in line to—"

"Adam Wagler!" As the full impact of his words sank in, Annie Mae backed out of his embrace. "You are *not* tellin' me ya put thirty thousand dollars into my—"

"No, it was um . . . thirty-five thousand," he murmured as he pulled a slip of paper from inside his vest. "The fella who bought it wanted to chip in on—when he heard you were keeping the kids and—"

"So ya made me out to be a charity case? To a total stranger?" Annie Mae cried. "This ranks right up there with gettin' my hair whacked off! How am I supposed to—I feel like I've been bought and paid for, Adam. It's like I'll owe ya for the rest of my life, because I can't possibly—"

"Annie Mae, it's not like that," Adam pleaded.

But when he gently grasped her arms, Annie Mae yanked away as though his hands were burning her through the sleeves of her dress. "I thought we had an agreement! I thought we weren't gonna think about— and now you've gone and turned the tables on me, knowin' I can never repay—"

"I don't *want* to be repaid—"

"Leave! Just leave me alone," she blurted as she walked backward, away from him. Then she turned, so she could jog out of range, out of sight of such a conniving, scheming man whom she'd believed was her friend.

This was no time to return to Ben and Miriam's where everyone in town would quiz her about why she was upset—again. Annie Mae headed toward Bishop Tom's house, on the other side of the Kanagy place. She just wanted to walk and walk, maybe until she walked off her legs. Eventually she had to return to the kids, to her reality, but right now she was wound too tight to be around anybody.

Annie Mae strode back through the orchard, oblivious to the apple blossoms this time, to cut through Rachel and Micah's yard and then across the Brenneman place . . . along Bishop Tom's back lot and past his dairy barn to the road. She turned left toward the county highway, on the far side of the Sweet Seasons where no one still at the Hooleys' place would see her.

Up ahead stood the clinic that would soon open, with Andy Leitner's medical wagon parked alongside it. For years the building had stood vacant, after housing a flower shop and then a hair salon. With the Brennemans' and Adam's remodeling work, it was now transformed for a new purpose that would truly serve their community. Not only would Andy see patients there, but his family now lived in half of the building. Rebecca had an office for her graphic design business upstairs, too, so she could work there when she wasn't serving as Andy's receptionist on the main floor.

Annie Mae stopped to admire the white window boxes, a homey touch Rhoda had requested. Cheerful purple and yellow pansies caught the afternoon sunshine . . . pansies that could withstand the chill of early spring yet bloom well into summer.

Didn't everything about this clinic speak to *change*? To the possibilities that became reality when people allowed God's love to transform them, the way this building had taken on a whole new purpose? Andy Leitner had risked *everything*—had sold his home and his car, and was shifting his kids out of public school. And he was taking instruction to join a church that had the power to veto his membership . . . all because he and his kids loved Rhoda so much.

Andy had also graciously, gratefully accepted the thousands of dollars folks at Ben and Miriam's wedding had donated toward his new clinic—not to mention the money that had poured in from Plain folks across the country who'd seen Miriam's note about his new venture in *The Budget*. The Amish helped their own. . . .

Thirty-five thousand dollars.

Annie Mae let her shoulders relax. She unwadded the deposit slip she'd been clutching, gazing at the numbers in disbelief. Adam had not only received the full amount his motorcycle was worth, but the fellow who'd bought it had chipped in five thousand more . . .

and the bank teller had been their accomplice, authorizing the deposit into her account.

They did it because they want you and the kids to be secure. Isn't this the same sort of love—a gift from God through folks here on Earth—that Rhoda and Andy have accepted?

Annie Mae let out a ragged sigh. She'd been upset about the FOR SALE sign at the house . . . and seeing those men loading Mamm's china hutch had ripped yet another hole in her heart. It wasn't Adam's fault she'd witnessed these unfortunate events when he was pouring his heart out to her . . . *even if you keep thinking you won't marry—or you won't marry me—you'll not have to work so hard to support your sibs.*

She sighed again. Had she been listening to Adam, she would have heard these words plainly . . . would have heard his no-strings-attached intentions. And while everyone in Willow Ridge had shown her extraordinary compassion, who else had made such a generous commitment to her future? He had risked giving all his cycle money to her, not knowing if she would ever marry him. The money was hers even if she eventually wed another man. Now *that* had taken some kind of faith! And something else neither of them was quite ready to name yet . . .

If you change your mind about getting married, I want to be first in line.

A little thrill went up Annie Mae's spine. Here was a fellow who'd vowed never to marry—never to commit to such responsibility—yet now he was considering *her,* knowing five siblings came as part of the package. *That* took courage, and a sincere change of heart.

What'll it take to change your *heart?*

With a last glance at the pansies shimmering in the breeze, Annie Mae began the walk back to Bishop Tom's place . . . back to her reality, yes, but didn't she now have the resources to remodel her reality any way she chose to? Adam had left her options with him open, while he'd opened up a whole realm of new possibilities. The very least she owed him was an apology and her thanks.

Chapter Twenty-Six

Adam was hunting up a good excuse not to eat breakfast at the Sweet Seasons Monday morning, except—as usual—the pickings were slim at home. And Matthias would show him no mercy when it came to badgering him about avoiding Annie Mae. When his brother had returned from the Hooleys' yesterday and found him home alone, there had been plenty of questions about the walk he'd taken with her. Saturday afternoon Matthias had quizzed him about selling his motorcycle . . . to whom and for how much, and what did he plan to do with the money? Maybe start a nest egg for when he got hitched?

Adam had hedged on most of those questions . . . hadn't told his brother—or anyone else—about depositing his cycle money into Annie Mae's account. Had that been a foolish thing to do? As he went downstairs in the soft shadows before dawn, he could see several ways to spend a chunk of that money on the poor old house that had been neglected since Mamm, Dat, and Sadie had passed.

What had he been thinking, to tell Annie Mae he
was interested in marrying her? Why would she move
into this sad bachelor home? Why would she want to
look out the kitchen sink window and see the house
where she'd spent several years of her life, where a
stranger would soon be living? Far as he knew, no one
from around Willow Ridge was hunting for a new
home—not that any of them could afford it. When
their former bishop had built that place for his new
wife Linda, along with the huge barn for the Belgians
he bred and sold, everyone had raised their eyebrows
at what such a palatial place as Bishop's Ridge must
have cost him.

But what did that matter? Annie Mae had all but
spat in his face yesterday. So now his most urgent decision was where to eat breakfast. Then maybe he could
reconcile himself to giving thirty-five thousand dollars
to a young woman who clearly didn't want it. Or him.

After he and Matthias had done the horse chores,
Adam climbed into his wagon and headed on down to
the Sweet Seasons. Maybe he could engage the Kanagy
boys or the Brenneman brothers in conversation so he
wouldn't have to deal with Annie Mae, other than or-
dering his breakfast.

*What sort of attitude is that? What's done is done, so man
up, even if a fool and his money . . .*

When he stepped inside the café, Adam saw that a
vanload of folks from the Morning Star senior center
were taking up several tables. Annie Mae was patiently
writing down their orders, so she didn't look up when
the bell above the door jingled. It was Rebecca who
breezed over to wait on him, so Adam relaxed . . .
ordered the number four with hot tea, and then

chatted with Bishop Tom when he returned from the buffet table.

"So, how's married life treating you by now?" Adam asked. It seemed like a safe topic. Tom Hostetler was the happiest man on the planet, given the grin he wore these days.

"I highly recommend it." The bishop cut into his ham steak. "Nazareth's spendin' every possible minute with Jerusalem before the wedding—she and Vernon are gettin' hitched at our house, ya see—so there's lots of plannin' goin' on. Oh!" he added as he leaned closer to Adam. "They're also gettin' up a surprise birthday party for Annie Mae this comin' Thursday afternoon. Hope you and Matthias can join us. It's not every day she'll turn eighteen."

Adam glanced over toward the tables of folks from the senior center, but instead found Annie Mae in the kitchen, conferring with Naomi at the big black cookstove. How many eighteen-year-olds had thirty-five thousand dollars in the bank?

Enough of the sour grapes. Time to man up, remember?

"And Nazareth believes that while I'm eatin' breakfast here," Bishop Tom continued blithely, "I'm tendin' some of my church duties, keepin' up with fellas in the district. So who am I to argue with that?"

Adam found a smile as Rebecca set a plate of pancakes and bacon in front of him. "Glad it's working out so well for you, Bishop. Nobody nicer than Nazareth."

"It could be the same for you, son." Tom glanced over to where Annie Mae was bending over an English lady's shoulder, describing the items on the menu. "I was real glad to see the two of ya go strollin' yesterday."

"*Jah*, well, don't get your hopes up," Adam muttered. "*I* did, and all I got for my trouble was a piece of her mind—and an eyeful of her walking away."

"Ah." Bishop Tom forked up a big bite of hash browns that dripped with melted cheese. "Maybe she was still upset from folks carryin' on about her hair gettin' cut off. Annie Mae's not one who likes attention."

Adam doused his cakes with syrup. "Didn't help that she saw a moving van in the driveway at Bishop's Ridge, either. Did you know Hiram's got the place up for sale now?"

"No!"

Tom began firing questions at him, and Adam gave what details he knew, as well as speculating about the situation in general. By the time he'd finished his breakfast, he'd managed to pass the entire time without so much as making eye contact with Annie Mae. Even as Rebecca rang up his tab, it seemed Miss Knepp was busy in the kitchen, loading a tray with filled plates . . . perhaps evading him as much as he'd been avoiding her.

But when Adam got into his wagon, he found a warm lattice-top rhubarb pie on the seat. There was a note written on the inside of the bakery box lid: THANK YOU, ADAM. I'M SO SORRY. PLEASE FORGIVE ME.

Adam sucked in his breath. The heavenly scent of the pie wasn't the only thing that seemed enticingly sweet right now.

He hopped down from the wagon, rushed through the café's door, and spotted Annie Mae in the far corner, clearing away his dishes. Adam quickly made his way between the tables to where she stood chatting with Bishop Tom. Without a word he slipped his arm around her, stood on tiptoe, and loudly kissed her cheek.

Then he was off again, with the memory of Annie Mae's very pink face and startled blue eyes to chuckle about for the rest of the day.

Chapter Twenty-Seven

"*Gut* mornin', Annie Mae!" Miriam called out from the counter of the Sweet Seasons kitchen. "And happy birthday to ya, too."

Annie Mae closed the back door and leaned against it, her thoughts swirling. Bishop Tom now drove her to work at five, when he finished his milking, and this morning his secretive smile had suggested something was brewing at the Hostetler house.

"*Denki*, Miriam," she replied. "I suppose it is a big day. When I was a kid, I couldn't wait to turn eighteen, and yet . . . here it is. Another Thursday at the Sweet Seasons—but I *so* appreciate ya hirin' me on," she added quickly.

It seemed Miriam knew some secrets, too, judging from her kitty-cat grin. She'd already baked pastries and was now rolling out crusts for pie. "Some days start out normal and then, in the blink of an eye, they get a lot more interesting, ain't so?"

"Like Monday, when Adam smooched me in front of God and everybody?" Annie Mae put on a clean white apron and joined Miriam at the counter, where fragrant steam rose from three pans of sticky buns. She got out the bin of frosting and thinned some of it with milk.

Miriam chuckled. "Ya could've knocked me over with a feather when he reached up to kiss ya. It was just so *cute.*"

"Um, there's more to the story. When . . . when Adam sold his motorcycle?"

"Ben said Officer McClatchey's friend was like a bee flyin' to a red flower."

"Adam put all that money in my bank account. Every dime of it." Annie Mae's fingers trembled as she drizzled frosting over a pan of rolls. "He—he wanted to be sure I could support the kids. Said it didn't mean I had to marry him, or marry *anybody,* but—"

Miriam stopped rolling out piecrusts to gaze directly at Annie Mae. "I've thought Adam was sweet on ya for a while now, but this frosts the cake. Actions speak louder than words."

"But I feel funny about takin' it. Told him I felt bought and paid for," she went on in a rising voice. "I apologized with a pie—which, the *pie* was the real reason he kissed me. But when I think about what Adam could be usin' that thirty-five thousand dollars for—"

Miriam let out a little cry and dropped her rolling pin.

"—I wonder if his gesture was a little *too* generous. Ya know?"

Miriam considered this for a moment. "It takes me a *gut* long while to clear thirty-five thousand dollars," she agreed quietly. "But other than givin' ya the money and smoochin' ya—right in front of the bishop, so it's not like he was sneakin' around—has Adam done anything ya felt was . . . improper?"

Annie Mae shook her head. "He's been on a job out of town this week, puttin' in longer days. He forgave me for spoutin' off at him Sunday when I was upset about the FOR SALE sign and the movin' van."

"And how would ya feel about Adam if it was just you and him?" Miriam queried softly. "No kids to consider. No money involved."

That was the *real* question, wasn't it? Annie Mae drizzled frosting over the second pan of rolls. "We've been friends all our lives, but kinda blind to each other, ya know?" she murmured. "After my runnin' around with Yonnie and Luke, and some of the things I've said to Adam—and then gettin' my hair whacked off—why would he want a girl like *me*? I'm a magnet for trouble from Dat, and—"

Miriam gently grabbed her by the shoulders. "Silly goose," she whispered. "You've *grown up*, and so has Adam. No need to feel unworthy, or not perty enough, or—well, any fella would be blessed to win your ever-lovin' heart, Annie Mae. If I had sons, I'd want one of them to marry ya. Ya weren't born my daughter, but I'm claimin' ya right now."

Annie Mae's mouth dropped open. Miriam Hooley wasn't a woman to mince words or to stretch the truth. The expression on her face left no room for doubt, either. "Oh my," she murmured. She set down her bowl of frosting to keep from spilling it.

When Miriam hugged her close, Annie Mae wrapped her arms around the woman who'd become so much more than an employer and a lifelong friend. How many times had she longed to confide in her own mother these last few months? Whenever she'd felt low, Miriam had stepped in to listen, and to encourage her.

"I want ya to start right now, on your eighteenth birthday, believin' that you're one of God's special rays of sunshine sent to Earth to bless us all with your light," Miriam said firmly. "Will ya do that for me?"

How could she refuse such a heartfelt request? Annie Mae managed to nod as she remained in Miriam's embrace. "*Jah.* I'll try."

"Work on it. That's all I'm askin', on account of how God's not finished with any of us yet." Miriam giggled softly. "He's not finished with me, either. Can ya keep somethin' under your *kapp?*"

Annie Mae's eyes widened. What could Miriam possibly want to share with her alone?

"I'm gonna have a baby! *Me,* who for years thought that could never happen again!"

The two of them squealed and hugged again, laughing and crying at the same time. Annie Mae's heart was thumping in her chest and suddenly her own concerns seemed so minor, in light of Miriam's joy. "I'm so happy for you and Ben!"

"*Jah,* well, you and Ben are the only ones who know," Miriam quipped. "I—I was about ready to *pop* for not tellin' somebody. But now that Andy Leitner's confirmed it, I'll be wearin' everybody out with progress reports, and—"

"As well ya should!" Annie Mae chuckled. "It's even sweeter, what with you and Rachel carryin' at the same time."

Miriam glanced through the back window and then straightened her apron. "Here come Naomi and Hannah, so let's be workin' at rolls and pies like nothin' else is goin' on. When I see my three girls together, they'll hear the news before I let the cat out of the bag for everybody else."

"My lips are zipped." Annie Mae took up her bowl of frosting again. She greeted the two Brennemans as she always did of a morning, but it was difficult to act as though nothing exciting had just been revealed.

To me, she mused as she fought a grin. *Miriam shared her miracle with* me . . . *and gave me a miracle, too. I see things much more clearly now.* . . .

After Ben gave her a ride home from a busy shift at the Sweet Seasons, Annie Mae stepped through the back door of Bishop Tom's house. The kitchen was mysteriously quiet and deserted, all scrubbed and tidied up. Why did she smell food, yet Jerusalem and Nazareth were nowhere to be seen? And where were the kids? As she walked cautiously past the big kitchen table and the cleared sideboard, did she dare to hope that someone had decided to throw her a—

"Surprise!"

"Happy Birthday!"

"Surprise, Annie Mae! Did we fool ya?"

The front room suddenly came alive. Joey and Josh leaped out from behind the upholstered armchairs, while Sara and Timmy rushed from behind the sofa, laughing. Bishop Tom, Nazareth, Jerusalem, and Nellie stepped out from the pantry, behind her.

"Happy birthday, Annie Mae!" they chorused.

"And it's *gut* ya got here when ya did," Jerusalem added. "We thought the kids might bust wide open with keepin' quiet, once we saw Bennie's buggy pullin' in."

Annie Mae's heart swelled at the sight of the front room: the partitions were down as though they were preparing to host church. On the long table where Bishop Tom usually carved his Nativity sets, a big birthday cake with her name on it sat beside a glass bowl filled with rosy pink punch—and too many other goodies to count. "Ohhh," was all she could manage as she saw the presents on a smaller table and clusters of balloons arranged around the room.

Then everyone she knew started arriving! Miriam and Naomi came straight over from the café, carrying platters of sandwiches, while Seth and Aaron Brenneman, joined by Micah and Rachel, also streamed in, with Ezra rolling behind them in his wheelchair. And here came Rhoda, with Brett and Taylor rushing in to greet the other kids, followed by Andy and Ben. As Annie Mae greeted her guests, the room rang with chatter. Folks began filling plates with food—for meanwhile, Nazareth, Jerusalem, and Nellie had been carrying out big bowls of fruit, her favorite macaroni salad, and coleslaw.

Leah and Dan Kanagy joined them, too, along with Nate and Bram and twin redheads, whom they introduced as their fiancées, Mary and Martha. Ira Hooley came in with Millie Glick, who hugged Annie Mae as they handed her birthday cards—and even Luke had a smile for her. Then Cyrus and Levi Zook burst in, followed by Katie and Jonah and even their parents, who must've closed the market so the whole family could celebrate with her. Mary, Priscilla, and Eva Schrock from the quilt shop congratulated her, too.

And wasn't *that* something? It was like a wedding day, when the Willow Ridge storekeepers closed up to observe a big celebration. Annie Mae gazed around the crowded room, amazed that everyone had come here for *her* . . . despite the troubles her *dat* had caused among them. When someone behind her put a hand on her shoulder, Annie Mae turned to see Adam with a bouquet of sweet-smelling lilacs.

"Happy birthday, honey-girl," he murmured as he gazed into her eyes.

For a moment, there was no one in the room but the two of them. Annie Mae accepted the Mason jar of lavender flowers and inhaled deeply. "Oh, but these are a breath of spring," she whispered. "Those bushes out back of your house always did grow the sweetest-smellin' lilacs, Adam. *Denki* for thinkin' of me today."

Adam's lips quirked. "Oh, it's gotten to be more than just today," he admitted. Then he gestured toward two young women coming in through the kitchen. "Rebecca's brought somebody I think you'll want to meet. I'll put your posies on the table."

Annie Mae returned Rebecca's sunny smile and wave, making her way through the crowd. The young woman at Rebecca's side was a Plain girl who looked to be Nellie's age, and seemed understandably shy in this roomful of strangers.

"Annie Mae, this is Louisa Kuhns," Rebecca began. "I'm so glad she could come to your birthday party because, well"—she gently put her arm around the girl's shoulders—"Louisa's just gotten her new wig. And it was made from your hair, Annie Mae."

Was it her imagination, or did the whole room go quiet? Annie Mae gaped, taking in Louisa's pleated white *kapp*, which covered her ears but revealed a section of black hair on either side of her face, pulled down from a center part. On closer inspection, she realized the girl had no eyebrows or lashes, but when Louisa's smile came out, like the sun from behind a cloud, Annie Mae couldn't help but love her. "I don't mean to stare—don't know what to say," she whispered around the lump in her throat.

Louisa grabbed her hands. "Well, I'm here to say *denki*, Annie Mae," she replied in a soft, sweet voice. "My cancer's in remission now, and it means so much to have hair again. Even though donors aren't supposed to find out who received their hair, I just had to meet you when I found out how you . . . lost your braid," she continued as she glanced ruefully at Annie Mae's tied *kapp* strings. "Knowing another Plain girl provided it is truly a touch of grace. I'm really sorry about the circumstances, though."

Annie Mae gripped Louisa's thin fingers. "Puh!" she murmured. "My hair'll grow back, and I'm healthy as a horse. That's two blessings ya just reminded me of, and—and now ya need to meet all the folks here in Willow Ridge who've been lookin' after me and my sibs."

As word got around the crowded room about who Louisa was, the women came over to meet her, the kids brought her a plate of goodies, and happy chatter filled the big room again. Then Sara called out, "Annie Mae! Come and blow out your candles! I'm ready for cake and ice cream!"

When her little sister and Timmy grabbed her hands, Annie Mae had no choice but to make her way to where Nazareth was lighting all eighteen candles spaced around her large, rectangular cake. Miriam was behind the table stacking plates and arranging forks, while Bishop Tom was coming from the kitchen with big bins of his homemade ice cream.

"Hope ya like strawberry *and* chocolate *and* cherry vanilla," he teased. "We didn't know which flavor was your favorite, so I made some of each!"

Overwhelmed by so many wonderful surprises, Annie Mae threw her arms around the bishop. "How am I supposed to thank ya for all you've done for me?" she asked. "My word, this is the biggest, best birthday party—"

"And hearin' ya say that is all the thanks I need," Tom said as he returned her hug. "You've come a long, long way, and I'm proud of ya, Annie Mae. I wish ya all the happiness your heart can hold."

"Took me awhile, but all eighteen candles are lit, honey-girl," Nazareth crowed.

"Say, folks!" Jerusalem clapped her hands as she spoke above the noise of the crowd. "It's time to sing to our Annie Mae while she blows out *all these candles in one breath!*"

As lighthearted laughter rang around her, Annie Mae positioned herself before the glowing cake, smiling at the deep pink lettering on the white frosting . . . the strawberry punch . . . *three* kinds of ice cream. What a celebration! How could she possibly deserve so much fuss?

Miriam caught her eye and winked. "When ya make your wish, aim high," she advised quietly. "God's listenin'. And you're only eighteen once."

As the room filled with voices singing "Happy Birthday," Annie Mae leaned down, took a deep breath—and then saw Adam gazing at her with the look of a lovestruck puppy. His clear baritone rose above the other voices, as though he were singing straight from his heart to hers.

I wish . . . I wish to accept all the love in this room—and to live up to Your expectations, Lord, she prayed. Then she blew as hard as she could. About half the candles went out, and before anyone could tease her, Annie Mae inhaled again.

I want to marry Adam and live happily ever after.

As she blew out the rest of the flames, applause and cheers erupted around her.

"I figured ya were windy enough to hit all the candles at once," Nellie remarked beside her. "Even if they *are* spread all the way around that big cake."

Annie Mae smiled slyly. "Maybe I had more than one wish."

As the kids crowded around the table for cake, calling out their ice cream preferences to Bishop Tom, Annie Mae slipped over to be with Adam. She wanted to wrap her arm around his sturdy shoulders, but this wasn't the proper place to display such affection—or to seem too pushy. Sure, Adam had brought her a fresh bouquet and was smiling up at her as though she were the only girl in the room, but she shouldn't make any assumptions.

"After the way I blew up in your face, last time we took a walk," she murmured, "I'm hopin' you'll want to walk again, later today . . . maybe after all these folks have gone home?"

Oh, but Adam's grin tickled her! His dark hair was glossy and clean, combed back over his ears at enough of an angle to look almost English . . . just a little bit bold. His clean-shaven face set off deep brown eyes that glimmered at her. Had he always been such a striking fellow, or was he a new man now that he'd sold his cycle and released his guilt? "Best idea I've heard today. A party for just you and me."

"*Jah,* I'd like that . . . Short Stack."

Adam chortled at the nickname. "Shall I come by for ya, then? What time?"

Seeing that the folks crowding around the cake table seemed in no hurry to leave, Annie Mae murmured, "I'll be there soon as I can, okay?"

"I'll be ready for ya, too—soon as I've had my cake and ice cream, of course."

Chapter Twenty-Eight

Adam sat on the front porch swing as the pearl gray of early dusk settled around him. Folks had stayed at Bishop Tom's through the supper hour to enjoy the sandwiches, salads, and desserts—which was a good thing. He'd scrambled to wash the piled-up dishes and to redd up the front room before Annie Mae came over. He couldn't do anything about the FOR SALE sign that still hung at Bishop's Ridge, but he'd planned his strategy . . . gathered his courage and prepared himself for her visit. A walk *she* had requested.

And here she came, strolling alongside the fenced pasture where Dan Kanagy's sheep grazed. She looked prim yet queenly in her cape dress of deep rose, her white apron, and her *kapp* with its strings tied in a bow beneath her chin. Adam stilled his swinging . . . felt the exact moment when Annie Mae's eyes found his. He stood, his whole body thrumming as he crossed the yard and the road.

When she ducked behind the windbreak of evergreens, Adam chuckled. "You're looking mighty pretty— and happy, Annie Mae," he said as he followed her.

"That's a fine thing now that you've turned eighteen, and maybe turned a few corners, too."

"If a girl can't be happy after a birthday party like that one, she needs a swift kick and a talkin'-to."

Adam held out his hand, feeling a jolt when their fingers linked. "I'm in the mood for some talking . . . among other things."

When her blue eyes glimmered, he couldn't resist kissing her cheek—even though he wished he were standing on the higher side of the slope. And yet, when Annie Mae's arms encircled his shoulders and she kissed him full on the lips, Adam found absolutely nothing wrong with the way they fit together. Their kiss lengthened, lingering in the shelter of the whispering evergreens.

"I've been wishin' for that," she murmured after she eased away. "Hopin' I haven't blown my chances—and your patience."

"That'll never happen," Adam replied. "Let's stroll over home, to the swing out back. The lilac bushes are tall enough that Matthias can't spy on us there."

"Matthias needs a new woman—something better to do than spyin' on *you*."

"You've got that right," Adam replied. "And now that I've thought about things from a different angle . . . you've got *everything* right, Annie Mae."

As they strolled across the road, Annie Mae's gaze did funny things to his insides. Adam prayed he wouldn't say something totally stupid tonight. The breeze was gentle and warm as the evening settled over them with a serenity only longtime friends could feel. Adam couldn't recall ever *yearning* for a new future, a fresh start, the way he was at this moment. Yet he yearned with a confidence he'd not felt before.

Annie Mae glanced toward the large white house on Bishop's Ridge. "I'm sorry for the way I blew up when we saw that fella haulin' out Mamm's stuff," she murmured. "I hope you'll forgive—"

"You were forgiven even before you put that pie in my wagon." Adam led her up the wooden porch stairs that creaked with their ascending weight. "Anybody would've been upset. And we can't help but wonder who'll move in."

"I can't do a thing about that, so I've quit worryin' about it. Right now, I just want to be with you."

Adam inhaled to corral his runaway thoughts. As they entered the front room, he was glad he'd cleared away the clutter . . . grateful that in the deepening shadows and the glow of the lamps, his house took on a homey warmth that camouflaged its faults.

Annie Mae looked around with a smile. "I remember so many rainy afternoons when you boys and Nellie and I played Monopoly in here—"

"*Jah,* because you always won!"

"—and that time we set up the croquet set, usin' chairs for wickets," she continued with a giggle. "Oh, but your *mamm* was fumin' when Matthias hit a ball so hard it bounced up and broke a lamp!"

It seemed like a lead-in he shouldn't ignore, so Adam took a leap of faith. "Truth be told, it's time to fix things up around this place. I could use a female perspective on wall colors and what furniture to replace and—"

"And I've always loved this embroidered plaque," Annie Mae said as she led him to the kitchen doorway. "What a perfect Bible verse—'behold, I make all things new.' Don't change *this,* all right?"

Adam looked at the framed picture his mother had made, probably before he was born. "From the book of Revelation," he murmured. "We've had a few of those lately."

"And it's about *you*, Adam," Annie Mae insisted in a rising voice. "Not only does it fit with your remodelin' business, but it's—well, it's workin' on *me*, too."

She fished something from her apron pocket . . . the reading glasses he'd put on her way back in January, before he could've guessed where such an impulsive gesture would lead. "I'm seein' things more clearly now, because these bring the details into focus, just like ya said," Annie Mae murmured. "Not a day goes by that I don't have these specs in my pocket, and— and I think of ya every time I dress in the morning, or pull them out to read a recipe or—"

When Annie Mae shrugged, her recent worries seemed to fall away. "You've made all the difference in my life, Adam. I'm just . . . sayin'."

For a moment he got lost in her crystal blue eyes. Here was another golden moment he shouldn't allow to pass by. "Annie Mae, would you let me court you and—"

"Only if ya won't stop there. And . . . well, there's one more thing."

Adam held his breath. After such pleasant talk that had all been going his way, something about the lift of Annie Mae's brow warned him not to rush into a proposal. "*Jah?*" he asked after several moments ticked by.

"When I go to the bank with Miriam tomorrow, I'm havin' the teller put that bike money back in your account."

And what did *that* mean? Adam held her gaze, even as his heart started sliding into his stomach. "Now, why would you want to—I thought we talked about that, and—"

"I can't let ya give me that much money, Adam," she stated somberly. Then her lip twitched. "But I could let ya *spend* it on me—and on all the things ya want to fix in this house."

He let out an exasperated sigh. "But I'll be doing the work myself! I don't *need* that money to—"

Annie Mae placed her hands firmly on his shoulders. "The six of us Knepps aren't a destructive bunch, but we make for some wear and tear," she explained. "Ask Bishop Tom about the chalk drawings in the upstairs hallway ya just painted for him—and about how much we *eat*," she went on. "It takes a chunk of change to pay our way, Short Stack. Just fillin' up the fridge and the pantry's gonna make your eyes bug out, considerin' what you and Matthias are used to shoppin' for."

As her words sank in, Adam blinked. "Are you saying you'd want to—"

"Marry ya?" Annie Mae's eyes got shiny. But instead of crying, she smiled almost shyly. "I've decided you're right about how stayin' a *maidel* would make for a lonely life. Are *you* sayin' you're brave enough to take me on? Along with the rest of us?"

Above them, footsteps made the upstairs hallway creak. Adam gestured toward the back door. "Let's go out to the swing. No reason for Matthias to eavesdrop on this conversation."

"*Jah,* because then he would *envy* us. And envy's a sin," she teased.

Adam's pulse thrummed steadily as, hand in hand, they stepped out into the cool evening air. Birds chirped as they found their nests for the night, and the lilac bushes sweetened the breeze with their heady perfume. He couldn't recall a prettier spring in Willow Ridge. And the pieces of his future seemed to be falling effortlessly into place, as long as he agreed with Annie Mae's way of financing it.

And she hadn't *refused* his gift, after all. She was merely redirecting it—*repurposing* it, folks said nowadays. As a man who rebuilt and transformed everything from ductwork to plumbing to hard-wood floors, Adam could appreciate that concept.

So all it would take to complete this new vision of his hearth and home was one little word. . . .

Annie Mae stepped between the tall lilac bushes and smiled. The swing out here hung from a wooden A-frame and was completely surrounded by green, leafy branches and their fragrant blooms. She slid onto the slatted wooden swing, running her hand over smooth white enamel that seemed to glow in the twilight. "Oh, but I can recall how we kids used to kick up our heels, pumpin' as hard as we could, to see if we could swing all the way over the top of the frame."

"*Jah*, it's *gut* that Mamm stopped us before we fell out on our heads, too." Adam slipped his arm along the top of the swing. "But I've gotta say . . . my heart's thumping with the same sort of thrill right now as when we were playing our daredevil games here."

Annie Mae let herself slide down slightly, so her head rested on Adam's arm and she was looking *up* at him. And he looked *good* from that angle. "Mine, too," she admitted. "But it's not a scary thumpin', like cows stampedin'. It's because I feel happy and safe and . . . like I'm right where I'm supposed to be. I think I could sit here amongst these lilacs forever."

"We could arrange that," Adam whispered. He brushed his lips so tenderly across her cheek, she closed her eyes with the sweetness of it. "I want to fix up the house for you while we court, and then I *do* want to marry you, Annie Mae. If you'll have me."

It was the most serious moment of her life, yet Annie Mae began to giggle. She slipped her fingers into Adam's soft hair and guided him toward another long, slow kiss like she'd been wanting so much lately . . . like she looked forward to sharing for a long, long time.

"If I'll *have* ya?" she teased softly. She smiled into his dark eyes, where she saw herself reflected in their depths. "I think I already do."

What's Cookin' at the Sweet Seasons Bakery Café?

Because I love to cook as much as Miriam and Naomi do, here are recipes for some of the dishes they've served up in BREATH OF SPRING. The weather is warming up in Willow Ridge but the gardens aren't yet producing, so these dishes reflect that time of year when Plain folks empty out their freezers and use up the quart jars of last summer's harvest, preparing for the fresh food to come. I constantly read Amish cookbooks, *The Budget*, and Lovina Eicher's weekly newspaper column, *The Amish Cook*, so I can say yes, the convenience foods you see as ingredients are authentic!

I'll also post these on my website, www.Charlotte Hubbard.com. If you don't see the recipe you want, please e-mail me via my website to request it, plus bookmarks, etc.—and let me know how you like them! I hope you enjoy making these dishes as much as I do! Yum!

~Charlotte

Sausage and Rice Casserole

Here's an easy dish that feeds 6 to 8 people and makes the house smell wonderful while it's baking. You can use any kind of sausage, cheese, and rice your family enjoys most.

    1 lb. sausage
    2 C. grated cheese
    3 C. hot cooked rice
    1 can cream of mushroom soup
    1 tsp. each onion powder, garlic powder
    Salt and pepper to taste
    3 eggs, beaten
    1 4 oz. can of mushroom pieces
    ½ C. milk

Cook the sausage, crumble, and drain. Combine cooked rice and 1½ cups of the cheese. Spread into a buttered/sprayed 2-quart casserole dish. Sprinkle sausage over rice. Combine rest of the ingredients except for ½ C. of the cheese. Pour over the sausage. Sprinkle remaining ½ C. cheese over on top of everything. Cover loosely with foil and bake at 350° for 40 to 45 minutes.

Macaroni and Goat Cheese

Homemade mac and cheese surely must be the ultimate comfort food, and the goat cheese in this recipe adds creaminess and just enough zing to set this recipe apart from others. I use whole wheat macaroni, which adds extra nutrition. For seasonings, I like some garlic powder, ground dill weed, and parsley.

    2 C. dry elbow or shell macaroni
    2 T. butter
    2 T. flour
    2 C. milk
    1–2 T. of dried herbs/seasonings
    Salt and pepper to taste
    4 oz. goat cheese
    8 oz. shredded sharp Cheddar cheese
    4 oz. shredded Parmesan cheese
    1 C. soft bread crumbs
    1 T. melted butter

Cook macaroni according to package directions; drain, rinse, and set aside.

In a large saucepan, melt butter over medium-low heat. Stir in flour until well blended and bubbly. Gradually add milk, stirring constantly; continue cooking and stirring until slightly thickened. Add the herbs, salt, and pepper, then stir in the goat cheese and Cheddar. Stir in about 3 ounces of the Parmesan cheese. Continue cooking and stirring until cheeses have melted. Stir in the drained macaroni and turn into the prepared baking dish.

Combine bread crumbs with melted butter and toss with the remaining Parmesan cheese. Sprinkle over the casserole. Bake for 25 to 30 minutes, until bubbly and nicely browned.

<u>Kitchen Hint:</u> Do heels of bread loaves go uneaten at your house? I keep them in the freezer and chop them

in the food processor to make bread crumbs for recipes like this one.

Hot Fudge Cake

This fabulous dessert has to be one of the best choco- late concoctions I've ever made—and by using so much cocoa powder (Hershey's Special Dark is my favorite), you can almost convince yourself that those antioxidants make this a healthy fix for your chocolate cravings! The sauce remains syrupy and makes enough to spoon over your ice cream, as well.

> 1 C. all-purpose flour
> 2 tsp. baking powder
> 1 tsp. salt
> 1 C. unsweetened cocoa powder
> 1 C. sugar
> ½ C. milk
> 2 T. shortening or coconut oil, melted
> 1 tsp. vanilla

Preheat oven to 350° and butter/spray an 8" or 9" square pan. Mix together flour, baking powder, salt, cocoa powder, and sugar. Stir in milk, melted shorten- ing and vanilla. Spread mixture in the prepared pan (it will be very stiff).

Sauce:

> 1½ C. brown sugar
> 5 T. cocoa powder
> 1¾ C. hot water

Mix brown sugar and cocoa powder and sprinkle over the cake batter. Pour hot water over all. Bake at 350° for 45 minutes, or until cake feels firm beneath the sauce. Serve warm with ice cream. Refrigerate leftovers.

<u>Kitchen Hint:</u> You can rewarm leftover cake in the microwave. Separate into pieces with sauce over each piece, cover, and heat in 30-second intervals until it's as warm as you want it.

Ham Loaf

Here's a nice alternative to meat loaf, and it picks up a tangy sweet-sour taste from the glaze as it bakes. You can ask someone at the meat counter in the grocery store to grind your ham—or use a hand-cranked grinder, as Amish women do, or use a food processor blade, as I do. When cold, this loaf slices well for sandwiches!

    1 lb. ground ham
    1 lb. ground pork
    1 large onion, finely chopped
    2 eggs
    ⅔ C. cracker crumbs
    ⅓ C. Minute tapioca
    ¼ C. milk

<u>Glaze:</u>

    ¼ C. cider vinegar
    ½ C. water

½ C. brown sugar
1 T. mustard

Preheat oven to 350°. In a large bowl, combine the ground ham, ground pork, onion, eggs, cracker crumbs, tapioca, and milk. Mix thoroughly and form into two loaves. Place in a sprayed/greased roaster or baking pan. Mix the glaze ingredients in a small pan and boil for a few minutes, then pour the glaze over the ham loaves. Cover and bake about an hour and a half, basting occasionally. Glaze will thicken as it cooks down. Allow to cool about 15 minutes before slicing, and serve with glaze.

<u>Kitchen Hint:</u> Minute tapioca isn't just for pudding or thickening fruit pies! In this recipe, it gives the ham loaf a firmer texture so it won't break apart when you slice it.

<u>Another Hint:</u> You can also bake your loaves in a large crockery cooker for about 6 hours, but the glaze won't thicken as much.

Lime Bars

Here's a twist on traditional lemon bars—same soft-gooey-sweet-tart filling, but made with lime instead of lemon!

2 C. flour
½ C. powdered sugar
1 C. butter or margarine, softened
4 eggs

2 C. sugar
4 T. fresh lime juice
Zest from one lime
4 T. flour
1 tsp. baking powder
2 drops green food coloring
Powdered sugar for topping

Preheat oven to 350°. Grease/spray a 9" x 13" pan. Combine the flour, powdered sugar, and butter or margarine until well blended. Press dough into the bottom of the pan, and bake for 20 minutes. Meanwhile, beat the eggs, sugar, lime juice and zest, 4 T. flour, baking powder, and food coloring. Pour over the crust and bake 20 to 25 minutes more. Sprinkle with powdered sugar and cool. These will freeze well with wax paper between layers of bars.

Creamy Chicken Vegetable Soup

Here's a potful of comfort food for a chilly day, and the tomatoes give this version of chicken soup a little something out of the ordinary. Serve with warm, crusty bread for a satisfying meal.

1–1½ lb. of chicken legs and breasts
4 bouillon cubes (chicken or vegetable)
3 large carrots, halved lengthwise and sliced
3 large stalks of celery, sliced thin
2 large potatoes, cubed
1 large onion, coarsely chopped
1 14 oz. can of diced tomatoes
Basil, salt, garlic, and lemon pepper

3 bay leaves
1 can cream of chicken soup

In a large pot or Dutch oven, cover the chicken pieces with water and boil them about half an hour or until the meat's cooked through. Reserve the broth. Cut the meat from the bones and into small pieces. Meanwhile, add the carrots, celery, potatoes, onion, and tomatoes to the broth with the bouillon cubes and seasonings, to taste, and the bay leaves. Add in the cooked chicken pieces. Simmer, covered, for about an hour, adding more water or purchased chicken broth as needed.

Remove the bay leaves. Add the cream of chicken soup last, stirring until it's blended into the broth. Taste and adjust seasonings.

<u>Kitchen Hint:</u> If you like a more filling soup, add a cup of uncooked rice or macaroni after the vegetables are soft. You'll need to add another cup or two of broth (or of water and bouillon cubes) to accommodate the way the starch will absorb the liquid as it cooks.

Beef and Bean Stew

Here's a great filler-upper supper for a cool evening, and since it's made from canned ingredients, it goes together quickly. Serve in bowls, or over split biscuits or corn bread.

1 lb. ground beef
1 large onion, diced
1 20-oz. can of diced tomatoes, undrained

1 can chili beans, undrained
1 can hominy, drained
1 can corn, drained
1 T. cornstarch
¼ C. water
Dash of Worcestershire sauce
Salt, pepper, garlic powder, dill weed, basil, or other
    seasonings

In a large skillet, brown beef and onion until cooked through; drain the grease and return this mixture to the skillet. Stir in tomatoes, beans, hominy, and corn and bring to a low boil. Mix the cornstarch and water, then add to stew as a thickener. Add Worcestershire sauce and other seasonings to taste, and simmer over low heat for about 15 more minutes. Serves 4–6.

<u>Kitchen Hint:</u> Like beans? You can add another can or two of any sort of drained beans (pintos, kidneys, blacks, etc.) You can also serve this fragrant stew over rice or mashed potatoes.

Easy Warm Peaches

I came up with this idea one morning "on the fly," when I wanted a warm fruit to serve over baked oatmeal. Warm peaches also taste good with granola sprinkled over them.

1 small bag frozen sliced peaches OR
1 large can of sliced peaches
Cinnamon

Place sliced peaches, still frozen, in a skillet over low heat. As they thaw and cook, stir to distribute moisture (add a spoonful of water, if needed) and sprinkle with cinnamon to taste. When peaches are heated through and liquid becomes syrupy, remove from heat and serve. If using canned peaches, pour just enough of the syrup into the skillet with the fruit to keep it moist, and stir over low heat, adding the cinnamon.

<u>Kitchen Hint:</u> You can also prepare warm peaches in the microwave. With frozen fruit, heat for two-minute intervals until all the slices are warmed through and the cinnamon is evenly mixed in. With canned fruit, use one-minute intervals.

Annie Mae's Apple Pie

Looking for a way to perk up an old standby? What a difference it makes to use brown sugar and fresh lemon rind along with your favorite firm apple—my choice is usually Jonagold, Honey Crisp, Braeburn—or a mixture of them.

    6 C. tart, firm apples, cored, peeled and sliced
    ¾ C. brown sugar
    2 T. cinnamon
    Dash of salt
    4 T. all-purpose flour
    Grated rind of one lemon
    1 T. fresh lemon juice
    3 T. butter
    Pastry for a 10" double-crust pie

Preheat oven to 375°. Place apple slices in a large bowl, add brown sugar, spices, flour, the lemon rind and the juice, and mix until apples are coated. Place filling in the bottom crust and dot with butter. Slice the other crust into strips and weave for a lattice top; flute the edges. Cover the edge with foil and bake for 25 minutes, then remove the foil and bake for an additional 25 minutes. Makes 8 large slices.

<u>Kitchen Hint:</u> I can never get the foil to stay around my crust edge, so I use a nifty adjustable silicone pie shield instead. You can find them in kitchen gadget shops or online.

Sugar Cream Pie

Here's a something-from-nothing dessert made from simple ingredients already on your shelves. The filling is very much like a classic blancmange, except the Amish add butter, pour it into a crust, and call it pie!

    2¼ C. milk
    ¾ C. sugar
    ¼ C. cornstarch
    ½ C. butter or margarine
    2 tsp. vanilla
    1 baked 9" pie shell
    Cinnamon to taste—2 tsp. at least

Pour the milk into a medium pan and stir in the sugar and cornstarch. Cook over low heat, stirring constantly until the mixture is blended smoothly and starting to thicken. Add the butter/margarine, still stirring, until the mixture resembles a soft pudding. Remove from heat and add the vanilla. Pour the filling into the pie shell and sprinkle the cinnamon over the top. Chill.

<u>Kitchen Hint:</u> This is also tasty in a graham cracker crust. You can't freeze this pie, so gee, you'll just have to eat it all while it's fresh!

Upside-Down Pizza

Plain folks are eating more Italian-style food these days, and one-pan meals like this one are popular with cooks who must feed large families on a limited budget.

    1 lb. hamburger or sausage
    Salt and pepper to taste
    1 small onion, diced
    1 medium green pepper, diced
    2 C. pizza or spaghetti sauce
    1 T. Italian spices
    2 C. shredded cheese (mozzarella or Colby are
       good)
    1 C. flour
    2 eggs
    1 C. milk
    1 tsp. vegetable oil
    ½ tsp. salt

Brown the meat with the salt, pepper, onion, and green pepper. Drain off excess grease and add the pizza sauce. Grease/spray a 9" x 13" pan and preheat the oven to 425°. Spread the meat mixture in the pan.

Sprinkle the cheese on top. Mix the flour, eggs, milk, oil, and salt. Pour over the meat and bake uncovered for 25–30 minutes until browned. Cool for 10 minutes to set before serving.

Annie Mae's Favorite Macaroni Salad

This is a fabulous salad that serves a crowd. The difference is in the dressing. Amish cooks tend to add sugar to their dressings. If you're watching your calories, you can omit the sugar and still have a tasty dish that'll be a hit at potlucks and picnics.

> 3 C. uncooked elbow macaroni, shells, etc.
> 3 hard-cooked eggs, chopped
> 3 stalks celery, chopped
> 1 medium onion, chopped
> 1 small red bell pepper, seeded and chopped
> 3 T. dill pickle relish
> 2 C. creamy salad dressing (e.g., Miracle Whip)
> 3 T. yellow mustard
> ¾ C. white sugar
> 3 tsp. white vinegar
> 2 tsp. celery seed
> Salt and pepper to taste

Bring a pot of water to boil, add macaroni, and cook according to package directions. Drain and set aside. In a large bowl, combine the chopped eggs and vegetables. In a smaller bowl, blend the rest of the ingredients, then combine this dressing with the macaroni, eggs, and vegetables. Cover and chill at least

2 hours (or overnight) before serving. Serves 10–12. Keeps about 3 days in the refrigerator.

<u>Kitchen Hint:</u> I make this salad with whole wheat macaroni, which adds fiber and doesn't change the taste a bit. I also like to mix pasta shapes, using a cup of each!

Look for the fifth Seasons of the Heart novel,

HARVEST OF BLESSINGS,

next February.

"Welcome back to Willow Ridge, Nora. It's a pleasure doing business with you."

How weird is this? Sixteen years ago, Nora Landwehr had never imagined herself returning, much less accepting the keys to a prime property from the man who'd been the bishop when her father had sent her away. But this little Amish spot in the road had changed a lot. And so had she.

"Thanks, Hiram," Nora murmured. "I hope I've done the right thing."

"At least you've arrived while your parents are still alive—if you can call it that." His gaze followed the road toward where the Glick house stood a ways back from the county blacktop. "Mending fences in your situation will be much like opening Pandora's box. Once you raise the lid, all your secrets will swarm out like hornets, whether you're ready or not."

His choice of words made her wonder if she'd been wise to confide in Hiram Knepp . . . to even go through with this transaction. But it was too late for second-guessing. As her gaze swept the panorama of Willow Ridge farmsteads, Nora was amazed at what she saw. From this hilltop perspective, Willow Ridge looked like an idyllic little town where nothing hostile or cruel could ever happen—like Mayberry, or Walton's Mountain. But appearances could be very deceiving. "So, does Tom Hostetler still live there where all those buggies are parked?"

"He does. He's the bishop now."

"This being Thursday . . . is that a wedding or a funeral?"

Beneath Hiram's short laugh, Nora imagined the *bwah-hah-hah-hah* of a melodrama villain. "As you probably realize," he replied wryly, "a wedding, in retrospect, might indeed be a funeral of sorts, depending upon how it all works out. Annie Mae's marrying Adam Wagler today."

Nora thought back . . . waaay back, to when Adam must've been about school-age and Annie Mae Knepp had been a toddler—

And you're not there to see your daughter marry, Hiram? She bit back her retort. Her Realtor had hinted that Hiram had committed even more heinous sins than she had . . . and after all, her father hadn't attended *her* wedding, either. If Hiram had been run out of Willow Ridge, she and this man with the devilish black goatee had a lot in common.

Nora didn't want to go there.

She was looking for a way to move Hiram along, so she could figure out where her major pieces of furniture would fit before the moving van got here. And yet, if everyone in town was at the wedding, this would be a fine time to look around. . . .

"I'll have my crew remove the Bishop's Ridge

entryway sign tomorrow." Hiram's voice sliced through her thoughts. "That way you won't be living in my shadow."

Nora didn't miss the irony there. Every Amish colony lived in its bishop's shadow—and she sensed the cloud over Willow Ridge had gotten a whole lot darker of late, even if Hiram no longer resided here. "That'll be fine. Thanks again."

"What will you do with that big barn? I miss that more than the house."

Nora smiled. No need to tell this renegade everything, for who knew what he'd do with the information? "I have some ideas," she hedged. "Figured I'd live here a while before I committed to any of them."

Finally, Hiram was headed down the road in his classic, perfectly preserved black Cadillac. Nora closed her eyes as the summer breeze caressed her face. She'd really done it . . . spent her divorce settlement on this house and acreage with the huge barn, in the town where she'd probably be greeted with hatred and hostility as she stirred up old grudges like muck from the bottom of a farm pond.

But blood is thicker than water . . . isn't it?

Once the shock and accusations ran their course, Nora sincerely hoped to reconnect with her family. To ask forgiveness and make her peace while creating a purposeful, productive new life. Was she acting even more naive and fanciful than when she'd believed Englischer Tanner Landwehr was her ticket to a storybook ending?

Nora glanced at her watch. Still an hour before the van was to arrive. She slid into her red Mercedes convertible to cruise town while she could still pass as an English tourist—not that anyone would see her.

Everyone from Willow Ridge and the nearby Plain settlements would be at Adam and Annie Mae's wedding.

Once on the county blacktop she turned left, away from town, and drove past a timbered mill with a picturesque water wheel. With its backdrop of river rocks, wildflowers, and majestic old trees shimmering in the breeze, the mill at Willow Ridge was a scene straight out of a Thomas Kinkade painting.

Nora turned back toward town. Henry and Lydia Zook's home looked added-onto yet again, and Zook's Market had expanded, as well. The white wooden structure sported a new blue metal roof that glimmered in the afternoon sunlight. A handwritten sign on the door proclaimed the store closed today for the Knepp-Wagler wedding.

Purposely not looking at her childhood home yet, Nora focused on the fine new house built on what had been the northeast corner of her father's farm. Across the road sat a building that housed the Sweet Seasons Bakery Café and a quilt shop—more new additions, although she recalled the blacksmith shop behind them, and the large white home down the lane, which had belonged to Jesse Lantz. From what she could tell on the Internet, Jesse had passed on and Miriam had opened a bustling business. Who could've guessed an Amish woman would have a website with delectable pictures of her meals and bakery specialties?

A little way down the road stood the Willow Ridge Clinic, with what appeared to be a horse-drawn medical wagon parked beside it. Yet more startling changes . . . but as Nora headed down the gravel road on the left, the Brenneman Cabinet Shop looked the same as always. So did Reuben Riehl's place, and

Tom Hostetler's dairy farm, where black-and-white cows grazed placidly in the pasture with the red barn in back of the tall white farmhouse. Dozens of black buggies were parked along the lane and around the side of the barn, yet the place looked as manicured as her former lawn in Ladue. Not so much as a scrap of paper or a missing shingle marred the Plain perfection of this scene.

The sound of an ancient hymn drifting out Tom's windows compelled Nora to stop. She'd all but forgotten the German words, yet the power of hundreds of voices singing in one accord made her suck in her breath. She swallowed hard as the melody seeped into her soul, its slow, steady cadence stilling the beat of her heart.

Quickly swiping at tears, she drove on. Could she *really* go back to three-hour church services, hard wooden pew benches, and endless, droning sermons? She couldn't recall the last time she'd attended a worship service. You couldn't consider a quickie ceremony in a Vegas wedding chapel *worship*, after all.

Maybe you won't have to worry about sitting through church. You haven't been allowed back into the fellowship yet. Haven't been forgiven.

Nora drove around the large loop that passed the Kanagy place and then a few homes where the Schrocks and other Mennonite families lived. She rolled past the fork that led to Atlee and Lizzie Glick's place—she wasn't ready to go down *that* road yet—and followed the curve that meandered in front of the Waglers' house and then past her own new residence. Definitely the finest house in town.

But what shall it profit a man, if he shall gain the whole world and lose his own soul?

Nora let out a humorless laugh. Her father, ever the sanctimonious Preacher Gabe even among his immediate family, had often quoted that verse to chastise her for wanting new dresses or some doodad she'd seen at Zook's. The mere memory of his harsh discipline tightened her chest even after sixteen years of living in the English world. If that was her visceral reaction without even seeing him, how did she think she could face him in person? So much water had gone under that proverbial bridge that Gabriel Glick would never, *ever* cross it to see his errant, banished daughter.

Nora brought herself back into the present. The moving van hadn't yet arrived, so she pulled back onto the county highway where she'd begun her trip down memory lane. While everyone in town was at the wedding, she had the perfect chance to revisit her childhood home. To prepare herself for the ordeal she would soon face.

She pulled into the lane and parked behind the house . . . slipped into the back door, knowing it wouldn't be locked. Stood in the kitchen, which appeared smaller and shabbier than she recalled, as though it hadn't seen fresh paint since she'd left. How odd—and how sad—to stand in this hub of the house and not detect even a whiff of breakfast.

Nora moved on before she lost her nerve. She felt like an intruder—and she wanted to be long gone before anyone came home from the wedding. She peeked into the small downstairs room where she and her mother had sewn the family's clothes on an ancient treadle machine—

Nora gaped. On a twin bed lay a motionless female form, like a corpse laid out in a casket. Was this what

Hiram had meant by implying her parents were barely alive? Did she dare approach, or would this woman pop up like a zombie from an old horror movie and leer at her with hollowed eyes and a toothless grin? Nora wanted to bolt, yet she felt compelled to at least look this woman—surely her mother—in the face. If Mamm was so far gone, why wasn't someone sitting with her? Or was she merely napping, too tired to attend the wedding?

Holding her breath, Nora slipped silently to the bedside. Even though the room felt stuffy in the July heat, a faded quilt covered her mother's shriveled form up to her chin. A *kapp* concealed all but the front of her white hair, so all Nora saw was a pallid face etched with wrinkles. The eyes were closed, and again Nora felt as though she was observing a stranger in a casket rather than looking at her own mother. Last time she'd seen Mamm, her face had been contorted with indignation as disgust hardened her piercing hazel eyes—

And suddenly those eyes were focused on her.

Nora froze, unable to look away. Not a muscle moved in her mother's face yet Mamm's gaze didn't waver—until her eyes widened with recognition. Or was it disbelief, or fear? Or an emotion Nora couldn't interpret without other facial cues?

She didn't stick around to figure that out. Hurrying from the airless room and back through the kitchen, Nora burst through the back door. She couldn't gulp air fast enough as she climbed into her car and sped down the lane. She felt as though she'd stared Death in the face and Death had stared right back. If she looked in the rearview mirror, would a skeleton in a cape dress and *kapp* be chasing after her?

Her tires squealed as she turned onto the hot blacktop and sped toward her new home. What a relief to see the moving van lumbering across the bridge by the mill! Nora made the turn onto Bishop's Ridge Road too fast and fishtailed in the gravel, righting herself just in time to steer up the driveway toward the house. She pulled around behind the huge barn—to be out of the movers' way, but also because she felt compelled to conceal her car.

Better get over that, she chided herself as she got out. *You live here now, whether the neighbors like it or not.*

She was approaching the house when a tall, broad-shouldered figure stepped out of the shade behind it. His straw hat, broadfall pants, and suspenders announced him as Plain, and there was no mistaking the fascination on his handsome face. Yet Nora hesitated. Had this stranger been roaming around in her house? *Note to self: call a locksmith.*

"Something I can help you with?" she asked breezily. Better to believe in basic Amish honesty than to accuse him of something he might not have done. It wasn't as if he could take anything from her empty house.

"Just coming over to meet my new neighbor," he replied in a resonant voice. "I'm Luke Hooley. That's my gristmill on the river."

Books by Bestselling Author
Fern Michaels